ROUGH SEAS

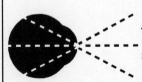

This Large Print Book carries the
Seal of Approval of N.A.V.H.

ROUGH SEAS

SHERRYL WOODS

THORNDIKE PRESS

A part of Gale, a Cengage Company

Farmington Hills, Mich • San Francisco • New York • Waterville, Maine
Meriden, Conn • Mason, Ohio • Chicago

Copyright © 2018 by Harlequin Books S.A.
Molly Dewitt Mysteries.
First published as Hot Money and Hot Schemes by Dell Publishing, 1992.
Hot Money © 1993 by Sherryl Woods.
Hot Schemes © 1994 by Sherryl Woods.
Thorndike Press, a part of Gale, a Cengage Company.

**LIBRARY OF CONGRESS CIP DATA ON FILE.
CATALOGUING IN PUBLICATION FOR THIS BOOK
IS AVAILABLE FROM THE LIBRARY OF CONGRESS**

ISBN-13: 978-1-4328-6674-7 (hardcover alk. paper)

Published in 2019 by arrangement with Harlequin Books S.A.

Printed in Mexico
1 2 3 4 5 6 7 23 22 21 20 19

CONTENTS

Dear Friends,

Welcome back to tropical Miami, where murder and mayhem compete for attention with the romantic banter of single mom Molly DeWitt and sexy detective Michael O'Hara.

In *Rough Seas,* the two will be solving the murder of a prominent socialite in *Hot Money,* then following up in *Hot Schemes* with a crime that's very personal to Michael and much of the Cuban exile community in South Florida.

Over the course of the four books I've tried to give you a peek into various parts of the fascinating South Florida cultural mix right along with light mysteries and a bit of romance. If you missed the first volume, be sure to head right back to the bookstore for *Tropical Blues,* which contains the first two books in the series.

Meantime, happy crime-solving!

All best,
Sherryl Woods

■ ■ ■ ■

Hot Money

■ ■ ■ ■

Hot Money

1

Miami, Florida
1993

As Molly DeWitt listened to two elegantly clad women scheme to take a Miami philanthropist to the monetary cleaners, she tried to recall exactly how her neighbor and best friend, Liza Hastings, had managed to talk her into showing up for this black tie charity affair. The last thing she remembered clearly was saying an emphatic no.

That had been a month ago. The next day the fancy, embossed invitation had appeared in her mailbox. A week after that, Liza had begun dropping pointed hints about her failure to reply, especially when the cause was so worthwhile — saving the spotted owls in Oregon and Washington, among other endangered creatures.

"I replied. I said no," Molly recalled saying quite clearly.

The ensuing discussion about the responsibilities of friendship had lasted no more than one or two weighty moments. Then Liza had left her to wage a battle with her conscience.

It wasn't that Molly had no conscience. It was simply that she'd grown up attending lavish affairs like this and had sworn on the day of her debut that she never would again. It had always seemed to her that if the women in the room had donated an amount equivalent to the cost of their gowns, there would have been no need for a fund-raiser at all. She could recall mentioning that to Liza on a number of occasions. Liza, unfortunately, had very selective hearing and a skill at arm-twisting unrivaled on the professional wrestling circuit.

The clincher, of course, had been Liza's persuasive appeal to Michael O'Hara. For a hard-nosed, macho homicide detective, the man had the resistance of mush when it came to saying no to a woman as committed to a cause as Liza was. He'd looked shell-shocked as he'd written out his sizable check.

"What are we doing here?" he asked now as he nabbed another glass of champagne from a passing waiter.

Molly thought he sounded rather plaintive. She scowled at him. "We wouldn't be here if you hadn't succumbed to Liza's pressure. You had your checkbook out and those tickets in your hands before she even finished saying *please.*"

"You could have stopped me."

"How was I to know you intended to drag me along with you? For all I knew you planned to ask that charming go-go dancer who was all over you at Tío Pedro's a few weeks ago."

He grinned. No, actually, he smirked.

"Go-go dancer? Your claws are showing, Molly. Marielena is in the chorus of a Tony Award–winning musical on Broadway."

"Whatever."

"Besides, I was hardly likely to ask her when this is your friend's event. I'm almost certain Liza indicated this was a package deal — you and the tickets, all for a paltry five-hundred-dollar contribution." He groaned. "Do you know how many tickets to Miami Heat games I could buy with that?"

"Don't tell me. Tell Liza. I'm wearing a dress that cost nearly double that."

"I thought a former debutante would have an entire collection of ball gowns."

"I do. In size four. I'm an eight now," she said, giving him a warning glare, "and if you make one single snide remark about how I could have starved myself back into those fours, I will personally dump the next tray of champagne I see over your head."

He regarded her curiously. "Are you always this charming at galas?"

Molly felt a momentary pang of guilt. She squashed it. "I get testy when I spend more than a week's pay on a dress that with any luck I will not wear again in this lifetime."

"At least you can save it for the Academy Awards or the Emmys, even the Miami Film Festival. Surely, in your position with the film office, sooner or later you'll have to drag it out again. Where is a cop supposed to wear a tux?"

"Save it for your wedding," she shot back. Considering Michael's avowed status as an eligible bachelor, it was as close to a curse as Molly could come. The alarm in his eyes improved her mood considerably. She linked her arm through his. "Toss down the last of that champagne and let's go mingle."

Actually, now that she was beginning to resign herself to an endless, tedious evening of polite chitchat and lavish praise of the canapés, Molly discovered that she could appreciate the setting, if not the reason for her presence.

For the event Liza had commandeered Vizcaya, the closest thing Miami had to a palace. Built on a grand Italian Renaissance scale between 1914 and 1916, the former winter home of industrialist James Deering faced Biscayne Bay, which dutifully shimmered like a sea of diamonds under the full moon. A soft breeze, laced with the tang of salt air, swept over the estate. Most of the crowd was milling around under a striped refreshment tent on the south lawn or walking through the surrounding gardens, as formal and lavish as any in Europe, no matter that the gatehouse across the road now served as Molly's own office.

The romantic setting was perfect for stealing kisses or seducing the high rollers into parting with their money. Molly caught sight of Liza amid a cluster of Miami's well-to-do socialites, including the event's chairwoman, Tessa Lafferty. They were all preening for the photographer from the morning paper. Liza's dramatic, off-beat dress in a shade referred to as tangerine — at least in the produce section, if not on the fashion pages — looked as out of place in the midst of all those pastel beaded gowns and stiff hairdos as a bold bird of paradise would among sweet and fragile magnolia blossoms.

As she and Michael got close enough to identify the women with Tessa, Molly guessed they would ante up a good thou-

15

sand dollars apiece before Liza let them escape. Most would consider it a small price to pay to have their friends see them on the society page a few days from now.

Molly watched in amusement as Liza went into her hard sell.

"How does she do that?" Michael asked in wonder as checks and promises changed hands.

"Liza has no shame when it comes to protecting the environment and any critter living in it. She will grovel if she has to."

"How much do you figure an event like this will net?"

"Fifty to seventy-five thousand, maybe more," she said as Michael's eyes widened. "If Liza had actually chaired the event, she would have tried to lure a couple of celebrities into town. With a little star power and maybe one of those fancy silent auctions, she could have doubled the profits. A shindig like this in Los Angeles could pull in a cool million."

"The soccer team raised seventy-five dollars at a bake sale last month and considered it a coup," he said. "Why didn't Liza go for the big bucks?"

"Because, as I understand it, the chairwoman did not take kindly to suggestions from her committee."

"The chairwoman is an egotistical idiot," Liza muttered under her breath as she joined them just in time to catch the gist of their conversation.

"She did manage to get all the upper-crust scions of the oldest Miami families to turn out," Molly reminded her, pointing to the women who still surrounded the chairwoman.

"Sure, but she ignored the rest of the community," Liza countered. "If a few of us hadn't set out to corral people like you and Michael, we would have had to have a nurse on duty to hand out vitamins at the door or the whole crowd would have fallen asleep by nine."

"Don't you think you might be exaggerating just a little bit?" Molly asked. "You're just miffed because you wanted Julio Iglesias to sing and she'd never heard of him."

"Forget Julio Iglesias. I doubt I could have talked her into inviting Wayne Newton. When I mentioned holding an auction, she practically choked. She claimed it had no class." Liza stood on tiptoe to kiss Michael's cheek. "Thanks for coming, you two. Mingle. Have fun. I've got to go see if I can get old man Jeffries to cough up a few thousand bucks before he dies. I've heard he's willing to save the manatees. Maybe I can get him

17

together with Jimmy Buffet and put together a benefit concert."

Liza disappeared around a hedge, leaving the two of them staring after her.

"Where does she find the energy?" Michael marveled.

"I think it takes about twenty minutes and the mention of a cause to recharge her batteries." Molly glanced up. "Are you interested in checking out the food?"

He shook his head. A wicked gleam lit his dark brown eyes. "Not right now. I'm more in the mood to shock this stuffy crowd."

"Oh?" Molly replied cautiously. The last time Michael had that look in his eyes he'd kissed her senseless. It had played havoc with her already wavering resolve to keep this man at arm's length.

"Follow me."

He held out his hand, and after a momentary hesitation, Molly took it. "Exactly what do you have in mind?"

"I intend to start by removing selective pieces of clothing."

She stopped in her tracks. "You what?" It wouldn't do to get too elated under the circumstances. She had a discouraging feeling he wasn't about to lure her into one of the mansion's many bedrooms and have his way with her, thereby settling the matter of her resolve once and for all.

He grinned. Those wicked sparks intensified. "Scared, Molly?"

"Of you? Never!" she declared staunchly.

"Then let's go."

As they crossed the lawn, stopping several times along the way to chat, Molly's pulse reached an anticipatory rate that would have her in the hospital down the block if it continued unchecked. The music drifted on the night breeze, swirling around them. The slow, romantic beat was counterpointed by laughter that grew more distant as they reached the shadowy fringes of the estate. Michael's hand curved reassuringly around hers.

"Put your hand on my shoulder," he instructed, standing before her. "Lift your foot."

"Is this anything like that game where you put different body parts on different circles until everyone ends up on the ground in a tangle?"

"Sounds fascinating," he said, "but no." He removed her shoe and tucked it in his pocket. "Other foot."

"Michael, I do not intend to romp around this place barefooted."

"Careful, *amiga.* Your stuffy social graces are showing."

In return for that remark, she nearly planted her remaining spiked heel atop his foot. Unfortunately, as a volunteer soccer coach, to say nothing of being witness to a fair amount of gunplay, Michael possessed reflexes that tended to be lightning-quick. He stepped nimbly aside. Molly's heel dug into the dry, sandy soil, which effectively removed her shoe just as he'd intended in the first place.

He glanced at her stocking-clad feet. "How about those?" he inquired of the sheer, iridescent hose that shimmered against her legs.

"Is this one of those kinky things I've read about?"

"Last I heard there wasn't anything kinky about sitting on a dock by the bay, but I'm game if you want to show me."

"You would be," she muttered darkly, trying not to let her disappointment show. Kinky with Michael O'Hara might have had its good points. She wasn't about to be the one to initiate it, though. She glanced at the limestone ledge, worn smooth by time, then at the water lapping gently against it. "You don't actually expect me to sit on that, do you?"

"Of course not," he said, sweeping off his jacket and spreading it before her.

20

Molly had a hunch the gesture wasn't entirely due to gallantry. In fact, she was almost certain she heard him sigh with relief as he shed the hated, restrictive attire. She glanced from Michael to his quite probably ruined jacket, then to the water that seemed ominously dark in this shadowed corner.

"What do you suppose is in there?"

"A little seaweed. A few fish. Nothing to worry about."

"Maybe you don't consider having barracuda nibbling at your toes to be risky, but I'm not all that enchanted with the idea."

"I doubt there are any barracuda lurking down there."

"Not good enough," she said. "I want conviction in your voice or my toes stay on land."

"Ah, Molly. Where's the romance in your soul?" he murmured, just close enough to her ear to give her goose bumps. His finger trailed along her neck, then over her bare shoulder.

Molly shivered and halfheartedly wished she'd selected a gown with more fabric. She was entirely too responsive and Michael was entirely too skilled at this seduction stuff. Another five minutes and the society grandes dames truly would have something to shock the daylights out of them. As an

21

alternative, Molly practically dived for the ledge. She stuck her feet, outrageously expensive stockings and all, into the bathwater-warm bay.

Michael's amused chuckle was entirely too predictable. As he sat down next to her, she considered — for no more than an instant — tumbling him into the bay so he could cool off his . . . libido.

As if he guessed her thoughts, he grinned at her. "Don't even think about it," he said.

"What?" she inquired innocently.

Suddenly, something brushed past her foot, ending all thoughts of retaliation. As it made contact again, it became clear that it was something considerably larger than a guppy or even a damned barracuda, she thought as a scream rose up in her throat and snagged.

"What —" she asked in a choked voice. "What is that?"

"What is what?" Michael said, instantly alert to the change in her voice.

She was already standing, water pooling at her feet as she pointed at the murky depths. "There's something in there."

"Probably just some seaweed."

"I don't think so. It felt . . ." She was at a loss for an accurate description. "Slimy."

"That's how seaweed feels," he said,

sounding so damned calm and rational she wanted to slug him.

"Does it also feel big?" she snapped.

"Big like a manatee?" he said, obviously refusing to share her alarm. "Maybe one is tangled in the mangroves."

Molly wasn't sure exactly how she knew that Michael was wrong, but she was certain of it. "Maybe we should go get a flashlight."

"By the time we do, I'm sure whatever it is will be gone."

"Michael, humor me. If it is a trapped manatee, we ought to free it or Liza will never forgive us. If it's . . ." She swallowed hard. "If it's something else, we ought to do, hell, I don't know. Just get the flashlight. I'll wait here," she said before she realized that she'd be left alone with something that every instinct told her was very human and very dead.

Michael had taken two steps back toward the house, when she grabbed his arm. "Never mind. I'll go for the flashlight. Give me the car keys. You stay here."

His expression suddenly serious, he handed over the keys without argument, either to humor her or because his own highly developed instincts for trouble had finally kicked in. "Don't say a word to anyone, Molly. There's no point in alarming everyone unnecessarily."

She nodded, then took off across the lawn, oblivious of the stares she drew as she raced barefooted through the guests, across the central courtyard of the house and down the driveway to the parking lot. It could have taken no more than ten minutes, fifteen at the outside, but it felt like an eternity before she made it back to where Michael was waiting. She'd grabbed a glass of champagne and chugged it down on the way. She had a hunch she was going to need it.

Michael took the flashlight from her trembling grasp and shone it onto the water in front of where they'd been sitting. At first it seemed she must have been mistaken as the glare picked up no more than a few strands of seaweed, a tangle of mangrove roots, a curved arm of driftwood. As the light skimmed across the surface and back again, Molly's heart suddenly began to thud.

"There," she whispered. "Move it back a little. See?"

What at first seemed to be no more than seaweed moved sensuously on the water's surface. It was a distinctive three-carat diamond that finally caught the light, broke it into a hundred shimmering rays and removed any lingering doubts about the exact nature of Molly's discovery.

"Oh, my God," Molly whispered, her gaze fixed on the glittering ring that she herself had once coveted at a charity auction. Though her stomach was pitching acid, she forced herself to look again, just to be sure.

Michael's arm circled her waist. The flashlight wavered in his grasp and the light pooled at her feet, instead of on the water. "Are you okay?" he asked.

"As well as anyone would be after discovering another body," she said in an aggrieved tone. "For someone not even remotely interested in signing on for homicide investigations, I have a nasty suspicion I've seen almost as many murder victims as you have in the past few months."

"Don't you think you're jumping to conclusions? We have no way of knowing whether the woman was murdered until we get the body out of there."

"Trust me," Molly said. "Tessa Lafferty would never willingly ruin her hairdo, to say nothing of her designer gown. If she felt ill, she would go home, send the dress to the secondhand store on consignment and then climb between her two-hundred-dollar sheets and die. If she's in that water, it's because someone heaved her into the bay."

"I know that name. Wasn't it on the invitation to this shindig?" Recognition spread across his face, then dismay. "Isn't Tessa Lafferty the woman Liza described as an idiot?"

She glared at him. "What are you suggesting?"

"Nothing. I'm just asking, purely for purposes of clarification, if it's the same woman."

"It is," Molly conceded, then jumped to her friend's defense. "But Liza would never kill her just because she didn't want some Latin singer that Liza has the hots for to sing at this bash."

"Did I say she would?"

"No, but I know how you think."

"Do you really? How is that?"

"Like a cop."

"Then I suppose you won't mind obeying an official police request."

She regarded him warily. "Which is?"

"Go into the house and call the police."

"You are the police."

"Not here. Will you just go make that call?"

"Only if you promise that Liza will not be on the list of suspects you turn over to the Miami police."

"Sweetheart, you and I are on that list of

suspects. Now move it."

Molly didn't waste time arguing that they provided tidy alibis for each other. She was more concerned with warning Liza that inviting a homicide detective to a charity function was just about the same as inviting trouble.

2

With Michael's hand clamped firmly around her wrist, Molly was more or less obligated to leave the murder investigation in the hands of the proper authorities, members of the Miami Police Department who arrived with sirens blaring. Damn the man, beyond insisting that everyone remain on the grounds and seeing to it that the security guards enforced the rule by barricading the routes to the parking lot, he didn't ask a single question of anyone himself.

"It's not my jurisdiction," he said for the tenth time when Molly mentioned that a few casual inquiries surely wouldn't offend the Miami police.

What she didn't say was that asking a few questions would help to keep her mind off the image of Tessa's body being untangled from the mangroves, then placed rather indelicately on the bank awaiting further examination by the medical examiner before its removal from the grounds. Tessa hadn't been in the water long enough for her body to be distorted or ravaged by fish as it might have been had she remained undiscovered, but that didn't make it any less distressing to see her poor, bedraggled, lifeless form lying there. Because she needed a distraction, Molly pressed Michael for some sort of action.

"But what about Liza? Don't you feel any obligation at all where she's concerned? I don't even know where she is. Shouldn't we at least find her?"

"Any obligation I feel toward your friend was pretty well wiped out when I forked over the money for the tickets to tonight's affair."

Molly scowled at him. "That was not the sort of obligation I was talking about."

"I know," he said succinctly.

Refusing to admit aloud that she was worried by Liza's inexplicable absence ever since the discovery of the body, Molly pleaded, "At least let me find her and talk to her. She's bound to be distraught. Who'll want to donate more money to all these environmental causes after this?"

"From what I hear, any publicity is good publicity when it comes to raising public awareness of a cause."

"Spoken like someone who's taken PR one-oh-one. I know there are those who believe that as long as the name is spelled correctly, public relations benefits will be reaped, but I'm not sure that applies to a murder investigation. If this gets ugly, the coalition that sponsored tonight's event is bound to be tainted by it. Besides, Liza is my friend. I want to be supportive."

She also wanted very much to be reassured that Liza had spent the past hour or so in the midst of this throng and not off on one of her solitary nature hikes around the grounds. She left that thought unspoken. Michael was sharp enough to figure it out anyway, just as he'd noticed the handful of yachts docked at the boat landing and notified the guards to block that route of escape as well. Now, unless someone dived into Biscayne Bay and swam away, the suspects were pretty well contained on the grounds. She didn't want to think about how far away the killer might have gotten in that time before the body was discovered.

"Molly, just let the police solve this case as quickly as possible without any of your amateur interference. That's the best thing you can do for Liza," he said.

"I thought you said my instincts about these things were good."

30

"Did I say that?"

"Just a few short weeks ago, as a matter of fact."

"I must have been in a state of shock after seeing you heading straight into the clutches of that film director's killer. Close calls always muddle my thinking."

"Michael!"

"Molly!"

"Oh, never mind," she grumbled. "I'll wait right over there."

He grinned. "No. You'll wait right here, with me."

If she'd been five years old, she would have sulked. As it was, she stuck with what she hoped would appear to be nothing more than mild disappointment.

"I'll make it worth your while," Michael added.

She regarded him doubtfully. "How?"

He touched one finger to her chin, tilted it up and covered her mouth with his. The kiss — or maybe it was simply shock — took her breath away. Michael was not prone to public displays of affection, unless she counted the one time she'd seen him patting his ex-lover's fanny in parting. As a result, she wasn't wild about the intent behind the kiss. She had a feeling it had less to do with seduction than it did with distraction. Whatever the dubious intention, however, it momentarily wiped the murder out of her mind. Right at the moment, she couldn't ask for more than that.

"Isn't this a conflict of interest or something?" she murmured eventually, her back pressed against wallpaper that the guidebook she'd picked up indicated was some nineteenth-century French woodblock pattern.

"Not that I know of," he said. "For once we're both on the same side and operating in the same official, or should I say unofficial, capacity."

"But you are a policeman, despite the fact that you aren't on duty, and you did discover the body."

"You discovered the body," he corrected. "I just happened to be around at the time."

"A technicality. Michael, aren't you the least bit curious about what's happened here tonight?"

"Curious, yes. Anxious to get involved, no. You seem to forget I have a caseload as tall as the Sears Tower as it is. I don't need to chase ambulances, like some starving attorney. You also seem to forget that every time *you* stick *your* nose into one of these incidents, your ex-husband and your boss go through the roof. Do you enjoy taunting them?"

"Hal DeWitt and Vincent Gates have absolutely nothing to do with this. Liza is my friend and I want to help her solve this thing quickly so she can minimize the damage to the cause. It's rare to get a coalition of environmentalists all working together this way and I want it to be successful for Liza's sake. Maybe I even owe it to Tessa Lafferty, too," she said, warming to the noble sound of that.

"Why? Because you didn't contradict Liza when she described the woman as an idiot, a statement, I might add, that could put your friend on the short list of suspects? I read all the time about the nasty, vicious competitiveness that fund-raising spawns. Vizcaya itself got its share of headlines just a year or so ago because two groups of supporters couldn't agree on anything. You're not on this committee. You're not responsible for your friend's actions. Therefore, as far as I can see, Tessa Lafferty's death has nothing to do with you. Play it smart for once and keep it that way."

Molly realized she couldn't very well tell him she was feeling guilty because she herself had coveted that diamond ring Tessa was wearing. She vaguely recalled from long ago Sunday school lessons that coveting what your neighbor had was a significant sin. It was probably not one that a man who dealt in homicides could relate to very easily. Admittedly, it was also a pretty flimsy excuse for involvement in a murder investigation. Protecting Liza was another matter altogether. Liza had stood by her when she'd been under suspicion in the murder of their condo president. Molly owed it to Liza to do the same for her now.

Momentarily thwarted from doing any significant, obvious sleuthing, however, she gazed around the central courtyard where the police had gathered everyone who fit into the open space. Others were crammed into the surrounding rooms, much to the distress of the museum's curator. A few guests had been allowed onto the terrace under the watchful eye of two policemen.

With Michael looking on, Molly moved through the crowd, conducting what she hoped was a casual search for Liza. When she finally spotted her across the terrace race going over the guest list with a uniformed officer, Molly sighed. "Thank God," she murmured.

"You didn't really think she'd skipped, did you?" Michael asked, clearly surprised by her apparent lack of faith.

"No, of course not," she said loyally.

He regarded her intently. "Molly, was something going on between Liza and the Lafferty woman that the police should know about?"

"Absolutely not."

"Molly?"

"You already know Liza detested her. Isn't that enough?"

"I suppose," he said skeptically.

Desperate to change the subject, Molly pointed out Tessa's husband to Michael. "See. He's right over there. Isn't the husband always the prime suspect in a case like this?"

Sixty-year-old Roger Lafferty didn't look like a man who'd just committed a murder. He looked stunned. He was sitting on a stone bench, surrounded by friends. His normally jovial, round face looked suddenly tired and crumpled, as if all of the air had been squeezed out of him.

"How was the marriage?" Michael asked.

"Okay as far as I know, though how he managed to stay married to her is beyond me. From what I've heard, Tessa was not easy to live with even before she turned menopausal. Since then, she's been a holy terror."

"What about the other guests? Was she

35

feuding with any of them?"

Molly was thrilled with the question, not because of the content but because it was proof that he was getting hooked, after all. It was possible to take the cop out of his uniform, but obviously he couldn't shut off his analytical mind.

"Jason Jeffries," she said at once, seizing the first name that popped into her mind. She wondered why. She barely knew the philanthropist, though she certainly knew his reputation for largess. Lines from needy organizations practically formed outside his office, like starving ants parading toward a bowl of sugar.

"The man Liza expects to hand over big bucks to save the manatees?" Michael said.

"That's the one."

"He's here tonight?"

"Right over there," she said.

Jason Jeffries had pinned the detective in charge of the investigation against a pillar. That was no mean feat, given Detective Larry Abrams's impressive stature and the fierce gleam in his eyes. Jeffries had him cornered all the same and was demanding that everyone there be released immediately.

"Not bloody damn likely," one policeman just behind Molly muttered wearily when he overheard the demand. "We'll be lucky if we get out of here by dawn."

Thank God she'd had the foresight to arrange for Brian to stay overnight with a friend, Molly thought. There would be no need for her son to know about the murder before morning when she could tell him herself. Relieved on that point, and before Michael could stop her, she turned to the officer.

"So," she began as casually as if she were merely inquiring about the weather. "What's the cause of death? Has the medical examiner determined that yet?"

"You'll have to wait for that information, just like everyone else," he said stiffly.

Molly interpreted that to mean he didn't know.

"I heard she was strangled," a woman standing just behind Molly said in a conspiratorial whisper. Though she was a tiny, bird-like woman, she cast a defiant look at her scowling husband, a man Molly recognized as the chief financial officer for one of the remaining solvent banks in town.

"Shut up, Jane," Harley Newcombe snapped. "I doubt whatever you overheard in the ladies' room came from the medical examiner.

"Women are nothing but a damn bunch of gossips," he added, looking to Michael for sympathetic support. He glared at the hapless Jane again. "I told you we had no business coming tonight. These people all hate each other. There was bound to be trouble of one sort or another."

Michael's gaze narrowed. "What do you mean, they all hate each other?"

"The infighting in this crowd, especially among the wives, makes one of those high-profile family feuds over money look like sandbox bickering. I never saw anything like it before in my life. You think men play down and dirty in business? That's nothing compared to the way these women go at it."

He shook his head in obvious male bemusement at women's ways. Molly was tempted to point out that at least half of the people at this affair and on the board of the charitable organizations involved were men, but Michael had latched on to a skimpy clue and clearly intended to shake it until it yielded real evidence. She was so grateful for that she kept her mouth clamped firmly shut.

"Was Tessa Lafferty involved in the feuding?" he asked.

"Hell, she's the one who started it from what I've heard," Newcombe said, his disgust evident. "Typical catfighting when you get a bunch of women together."

"Harley Newcombe, that is not so," his wife retorted with unexpected spunk, saving Molly the trouble. "It's the men who stuck their noses into things and made everything complicated. That horrible, overbearing Jason Jeffries has to control everything he's involved with. He treated Tessa like she didn't have a brain in her head."

"Why shouldn't he treat her any way he damned well pleases? He's coughing up most of the money."

"He gave a single donation —" she began.

"For a hundred thousand."

"And that entitles him to run things? This coalition had raised three times that before he ever got involved. If you ask me, that awful man is trying to buy his way to sainthood. It's probably penance for some horrible sin he's committed in the name of the almighty dollar."

"Just drop it, Jane. You don't know what the hell you're talking about. If you could manage money, I wouldn't be covering all those bounced checks of yours every month."

Since it was clear that the conversation was rapidly disintegrating into a familiar family squabble, Molly again turned her attention to the generous, if difficult, Jason Jeffries. She spotted him lurking in the shadows near the buffet table, apparently consoling himself with food after his failure to get his way with the detective.

Obviously a man who'd ignored physicians' warnings about obesity, cholesterol, and smoking, he stood with a cigar in one hand and a croissant mounded with rare roast beef in the other. His expression couldn't have been described as content, but it was darned close to it.

Molly slipped away from Michael's side while he continued to cross-examine Harley Newcombe. She approached the robust philanthropist, whose old family money came from paper goods or adhesive bandages or a combination of all those indispensable items that survived economic blips, recessions, and even the occasional full-blown depression. His bushy black brows, which almost met in the middle above dark, piercing eyes, rose slightly at her intrusion.

"You after my money, too?" he groused.

A puff of tobacco smoke hit Molly square in the face. She barely resisted the urge to snatch the offending cigar out of his hand and stomp on it. She settled for saying, "You don't have enough to make me put up with your smoking."

A chuckle rumbled through him. He

tapped off the embers and put the cigar aside. "You're a sassy little thing. I like that. Half the people in this place are scared to death of me."

"That's because they want something from you and I don't."

"You sure about that?"

"Absolutely."

"Not even a hint about the way Tessa and I have been fussing and feuding for the past couple of years?"

Molly caught the unexpectedly mischievous twinkle in his eyes and grinned. She had a hunch she could get to like Jason Jeffries. She hoped like hell he wasn't the murderer. "Okay. You caught me," she admitted. "I would like to know more about that."

"You interested just for the sake of gossip or you have a better reason?"

"I'm interested because my friend cares about every single environmental cause that stands to benefit from tonight's event and this murder could put her and her causes in jeopardy."

"Loyalty, huh? Can't remember the last time I saw much evidence of that in this crowd," he said, echoing Harley Newcombe's opinion. "Most of 'em would sooner stab each other in the back than lend

41

a helping hand."

Even though she'd heard the complaint before and seen evidence of it herself, she didn't want to believe it. She wanted to believe that everyone was like Liza, who was totally committed and honestly believed it was her obligation to make the world a better place. Surely others who signed up for one of these charitable boards or committees felt the same way.

"Don't you think you're just a little bit cynical?" she said hopefully.

"A little bit? Hell, girl, I've lived a long time and I'm damned cynical. I have cause to be. Human beings have a tremendous capacity for hurting their fellow man, to say nothing of God's creatures. What they'll do to them is a crying shame."

"Didn't you and Tessa agree on that much at least?"

"Sure we did."

"Then what was the problem between you?"

"To understand the answer to that you'd have to go back thirty years or so, before your time, I suspect."

"Barely," Molly admitted with great reluctance. Her thirtieth birthday was less than two weeks away. She was not looking forward to it. Too much of her life was not the way she'd planned for it to be. "So what happened between you and Tessa thirty years ago?"

Jason Jeffries knew how to draw out suspense. He ate the last bite of his sandwich, wiped his pudgy fingers delicately on a pristine white handkerchief he drew from an inner pocket, folded it neatly, and put it away. Then, with an air of nonchalance that had Molly gnashing her teeth, he took her arm and led her deep into the shadows on the terrace.

Considering that Jason Jeffries might very well be a suspect in Tessa's murder, Molly knew she should have been terrified at being lured farther away from the crowd. A distant rumble of thunder and the dimming of the outdoor lights emphasized the warning. Instead of being frightened, however, her anticipation soared the way it always did when she knew some major clue was about to be revealed.

Only when they were alone and the bay was spread before them did he speak.

With his unflinching gaze pinned directly on her, he said quietly, "It all started when I married the damned woman."

3

Discovering that Tessa Lafferty and Jason Jeffries had been married was like discovering that a tiger and a bumblebee were distant cousins. Molly spent a full two minutes processing the image of the unlikely relationship before she managed a coherent word.

"What?" Okay, it was weak, but it was the best she could do given the astonishing nature of his revelation.

Jason Jeffries grinned. "Hadn't heard that one, had you? Not many people have. Tessa liked to keep it a deep, dark secret. She hated failure, and believe me, our marriage was a doozy of a disaster from the first day."

"Do the police know?"

"They do. Why would I try to hide a thing like that? Folks may not recall much about it, but there are records down at the courthouse." He waggled a finger under her nose. "Let this be a lesson to you. There's no use

44

denying the truth. It'll just backfire on you, when you least expect it."

"But revealing it might move your name to the top of the list of suspects and distract the police from the real killer."

He beamed at her. "Thank you for assuming that I'm innocent. You're a good judge of character. I didn't do it. If I was planning to murder Tessa, I would have done it years ago when I discovered she loved money, hated sex, and used men the way folks with a cold use tissues. Took me less than a month to catch on. We were divorced six miserable months later. Can't for the life of me figure out how a man as smart as Roger Lafferty got himself married to her."

"You did."

"But I was young and naive at the time and I didn't stay married to her the way Roger has."

"You must have been . . ."

He scowled at her with feigned ferocity. "Don't waste your energy trying to count backward, young lady. I was forty-two. Should have known better, but Tessa was a decade or more younger and she was a beauty. That blond hair of hers was natural then, and just like silk. She had a figure that would stop men dead in their tracks. She had a way of making a man do things that were downright foolish."

"Then don't you suppose that's the same effect she had on Roger?"

"By the time they met, she'd been around the block a few times. The word was out, especially in our crowd. He ignored it all. His wife had just died. He was lonely. And Tessa took advantage."

"But you said yourself, men in love do foolish things."

"They do indeed," he agreed. "That's why I avoided another folly like that one. After Tessa, I steered clear of women with marriage on their minds. Can't trust 'em to behave the same way, once they have their hooks in you."

"You never married again?"

"No."

She regarded him speculatively, searching for signs of regret, some hint of sorrow over his ex-wife's death. "Some might think that indicates you never got over Tessa. Were you still in love with her?"

"Good Lord, no!" he said with genuine horror at the notion.

"Then why the fights?"

"She was a vain, silly woman. Lately she actually latched on to a little power, thanks to Roger's standing in the community. Power and stupidity are a dangerous combi-

46

nation. I warned her again and again that she didn't know what the hell she was doing. I'm on a lot of boards in this town. I know a thing or two about fund-raising and a lot about business. I got my hands on the books after a couple of these fund-raisers and threw a holy tantrum over the waste. I threatened to expose her as a fraud if she didn't start bringing the profit margin in line before we had the IRS staring over our shoulders, eyeballing every little thing, questioning our nonprofit status."

That might have been reason for Tessa to fear Jason, perhaps even a motive for her to murder him, but Jason wasn't the one who'd been found floating in the bay.

"Did you two quarrel tonight?" Molly asked, wondering if perhaps Tessa had lured Jason to that secluded spot intending to clobber him with something, only to have the tables turned on her in a struggle. Not that there was any indication from Jason Jeffries's perfectly tailored, unmussed tuxedo that he'd struggled with anything more taxing than that oversize roast beef sandwich. Of course, to a man of his girth and height, a woman of Tessa's fragile frame would be little more than a pesky nuisance. He could probably have nabbed her by the nape of her neck and tossed her aside without even breathing hard, even if he was in lousy shape.

"Nope. No quarrel," he said.

The flat denial shattered the volatile scenario Molly was envisioning.

He elaborated. "Never said a word to her. I spent most of the evening talking to that perky young gal who's after my money to help save the manatees."

"Liza Hastings," Molly said, wondering how Liza would take to being described as either "perky" or a "gal." She was close to ten years older than Molly. Thanks to incredible genes and an exercise regimen that would do in Jane Fonda, she didn't look her age. However, she did not suffer sexist little euphemisms kindly. Of course, chances were good that Jason Jeffries knew that and simply refused to mend his ways to suit her.

"Liza," he said. "That's the one. Girl's got a head on her shoulders. If she'd been running this thing tonight, they'd have made a bundle."

"I suspect she'd agree with you about that."

He regarded her with renewed interest. "Is she your friend, the one you mentioned earlier?"

"Yes."

He nodded approvingly. "I like that. A couple of tough cookies. You keep in touch. Tell your friend to make her plans. Don't schedule anything before the height of the winter season, though. Might as well take all those snowbirds for all they're worth. She can send me the bills. I'll underwrite whatever she wants to put together to save the manatees. Sign up that Buffett person to help. We'll teach this town a thing or two about fund-raising."

He turned and strolled away with astonishing grace for a man of his age and size. Judging from the direction in which he went, Molly had the distinct impression Jason Jeffries intended to try to slip away from the murder scene. She warred with her conscience over whether she ought to try to prevent him from going, then decided that this would be the perfect time to turn over a new leaf. She would leave his capture in the hands of the police.

As she made her way back to the central courtyard, enclosed in recent years to protect it against the ravages of salt air and humidity, Molly toted up the suspects so far. It was an incredibly short list, and two people she happened to like were on it — Jason Jeffries and Liza. Before the evening

49

was out she had to see to it that they were cleared or, at the very least, that the suspects list grew to a sufficient number to assure reasonable doubt.

Based on what Jeffries had told her, she wondered if Roger Lafferty was still as enamored of his wife as he had been. Perhaps his patience had been wearing thin and some incident tonight had sent him over the edge. The only way to find out would be to talk to him. Since that seemed unlikely given the cadre of protectors surrounding him, she decided a little chat with the Laffertys' closest friends would be in order. Surely Carl and Mary Ann Willoughby were around here someplace. Hopefully, not right at Roger's side.

Molly eased around the fringes of the courtyard, hoping to spot the couple who usually co-chaired every event involving the Laffertys. Instead, she ran smack into Michael.

"Where the devil have you been?" he demanded.

She regarded the tense set of his jaw with some surprise. "You sound upset."

He muttered a curse in Spanish, one Molly had made it a point to look up since he used it so often. If her son had used the English version, she would have grounded him for a month. She had less say over Michael's choice of vernacular.

"Upset?" he said finally in English. "Why would I be upset, *amiga*? A woman was killed less than two hours ago. Someone in this crowd likely did it. And given your foolish penchant for snooping —"

"Sleuthing," she corrected. It was a fine distinction, and an important one to her way of thinking.

Eyes black with anger glared back at her as Michael ran through his entire repertoire of colorful curses, at least one of which Molly suspected implored the gods to lend divine assistance. He looked as if he were just itching to shake some sense into her. Molly's chin went up.

"Don't use that sort of language around me," she said huffily, and turned on her heel.

"You don't speak Spanish," he shot back, though he looked somewhat chagrined when she peeked at him over her shoulder.

"I speak enough," she informed him.

His gaze narrowed. "Enough to carry on a conversation? Or just enough to get yourself into trouble on the street?"

"Tío Pedro says I order dinner in perfect Spanish."

"Tío Pedro would tell you that if you

mangled every word. He's a gentleman."

"A gentleman who would be appalled by the language you just used around a lady."

"Okay, yes," he conceded. "I apologize. But that does not negate the stupidity of your going off alone in the dark in the midst of a murder investigation."

"I wasn't alone," she said, and recounted her conversation with Jason Jeffries. As she'd expected, the information she'd gleaned took Michael's mind off what he'd viewed as her foolish disappearance.

"By the way, I'm sorry if you were worried," she added at the end. It had been a long time since anyone had genuinely cared what happened to her.

"I was worried," he said emphatically. "You tend to think you're indomitable. It's a dangerous state of mind when you're messing with a murderer."

Molly conceded the logic in his warning. "I know you're right. I just assume everyone will dismiss me as some naive, slightly nosy single mother and spill their guts to me without thinking anything of it."

"They might have done that six months ago, but I suspect most of these people know all about your involvement in solving those other murder cases. They'll be on guard with you, or worse, they'll consider you an enemy who's getting too close to the truth. The good Lord may protect fools, but even He can do only so much. For your sake and the sake of your son, stay out of the investigation, Molly. I can't put it any plainer than that."

"But Liza could need my help."

"I still wish you'd tell me why you're so convinced she needs help."

"I've explained that," she said stubbornly.

"She's openly stated that she detested the woman," he repeated. "Okay, then, the best way you can help Liza is by being supportive and staying alive. Meddling in the case won't do it." He watched closely as if to assure himself that she'd gotten the message. Finally, he nodded in satisfaction. "I want to go fill the police in on what Jason Jeffries told you."

"He said he'd already told them."

"And you believed him?"

"Yes."

"Molly, a man who just committed a murder might not be above a little lying."

"He didn't do it," she said staunchly. "Not any more than Liza did."

"I'm glad you're convinced, but I think I'll share the information with the police just the same. Stay put," he said when she started to wander off in the opposite direction.

She stayed where she was until he was out of sight, then set out to mingle some more. Inside. In plain view of lots of witnesses. There was no telling what she might overhear. Listening wouldn't be breaking her vow to Michael. Not exactly anyway.

Besides, she really wanted to get a better sense of what Tessa Lafferty had been like. Clearly Liza and Jason Jeffries had pretty jaded views of the woman. Her own contact with her had been limited. Surely there were others who held more kindly memories.

Then again, if all the rumors she'd heard over the years were true, maybe not.

4

Tessa Lafferty was a bitch. Everyone said so, according to Liza's frequent, biased reports over the months of planning for this gala. Everyone had a story to tell about how Tessa had slighted them, run roughshod over them, offended them, or, in some instances, even betrayed them. They discussed her lousy behavior as if tolerating it were some kind of badge of honor. Molly was surprised half the women on the committee hadn't gone out and purchased buttons declaring I SURVIVED TESSA LAFFERTY.

And yet, to Molly's amazement, they worked with her. When she'd asked why, Liza had pointed to her powerful name, her sizable bank account, and her formidable determination to get the job done. Mary Ann Willoughby had also run interference.

Despite the enjoyment her committee had once taken in ripping her to shreds, apparently things had changed now that the discovery of her body indicated some discretion was called for. As Molly circled through the rooms surrounding the courtyard on Vizcaya's lower floor — the Adam Library, the Renaissance Hall, the East Loggia, the Music Room, the Banquet Hall, and then finally the Tea Room — she was astounded at how many of these previously declared enemies suddenly adored the woman.

"So generous," said one aging dowager, who only a few weeks ago had cut Tessa dead in a Bal Harbour boutique favored by the society matrons. Word of the slight by Patrice MacDonald had spread like wildfire. Even Molly, who was not normally plugged into that particular rumor mill, had heard about the incident by nightfall. Liza's report had been especially gleeful.

"Such an organizer," commented another, who'd battled to have Tessa removed as chairwoman for one of her own pet charity functions.

"A class act. Truly a class act," noted yet another, whom Molly recognized as the wife of a man who'd just recently had a widely known, passionate fling with the ever-so-classy Tessa.

The three women managed to deliver their praise with straight faces, a feat that Molly felt was deserving of some mention. She joined them against the backdrop of a stained-glass wall, beyond which the lit gardens were on display. Since all that glass reminded her of a church, perhaps it would be enough to inspire a few confessions.

"I'm sure you all must be distraught," she said, lacing the observation with a heavy dose of somber sympathy that she hoped would cover her inexplicable nosiness. "I know you all traveled in the same social circle. How long have you known Tessa?"

She glanced first at Patrice MacDonald, whose platinum blond hair had been lacquered into place with sufficient spray to withstand a hurricane. Her beaded gown dipped low in front to reveal an impressive amount of cleavage. It was a daring display for someone of her age. Not even the diamond and pearl necklace at her throat could draw attention upward.

"Years," the dowager said with a frosty smile. "I recall when Tessa moved to Miami."

There was every indication from her tone that Patrice still considered Tessa to have been an interloper, even though Molly knew for a fact that Tessa's family had settled in Miami at least fifty years earlier. The two women had grown up within blocks of each other in Coral Gables, had attended the same private schools and the same coming-out parties. Their fathers had both served on the prestigious and very exclusive Orange Bowl Committee, which only in recent years had reluctantly begun to add women and minorities to its membership.

"And you?" Molly asked Helen Whorton, who championed half a dozen causes, though she focused most of her attention on the needs of the area's major teaching hospital. "I seem to recall that you were both trying to raise money for diabetes research."

"Alzheimer's," Helen corrected tersely, her arthritic hands nervously twisting the pale mauve chiffon scarf that the designer no doubt had intended as a wrap to cover saggy older arms. Her eyebrows, which had risen after several face-lifts, gave her a perpetual air of surprise. The skin under her chin was smooth, however. She probably considered it a fair exchange.

"Wasn't there some argument?" Molly inquired with the innocence of a newborn.

"A minor disagreement," Helen murmured, glancing around with a look that a suspicious mind might have interpreted as desperate. "I really must find George. I can't imagine where he's disappeared to."

"Don't fret, dear," Patrice told her. "I'm sure he and Clark are somewhere together, probably trying to tell the police how to do their jobs."

Molly wondered if George Whorton and Patrice's escort, attorney Clark Dupree, were having any better luck at that than she usually had. Before she could become too distracted by that speculation, she took one last stab at eliciting an honest reaction from the women before one of them wised up and told her to take a hike. She turned to Caroline Viera, the youngest of the three and the wife of a major banking figure. Her acceptance in this particular set of old Miami society was silent testimony to her husband's commanding position.

"Were Tessa and Roger close friends with you and Hernando?"

"Roger and Hernando are business associates," the petite, elegant woman, who'd recently made an annual best-dressed list for the second time in a row, said coolly. "I knew Tessa only by reputation."

"You've never served on any committees with her?" Molly asked, surprised. She'd thought committee work was a way of life in this crowd.

Caroline arched one carefully sculpted brow disdainfully. "I have little time for

59

committees. I have a business of my own to run."

"Of course," Molly said at once, surprised that she'd forgotten that Caroline Davis-Whitcomb had built an impressive list of professional credentials before marrying Hernando. A few decades ago, she would have given all that up after the wedding, using her skills when called upon on a slew of committees. Obviously, however, Davis-Whitcomb Inc. had continued to thrive after the marriage and Caroline was proud of the fact.

"Public relations, isn't it?" Molly added.

"*Advertising* and public relations."

"Isn't tonight's event one of those you handled on a *pro-bono* basis?" Molly asked. It was all beginning to come back to her now. Liza actually had described the elaborate arrangements necessary to keep Caroline and Tessa apart yet focused on the same goal.

Caroline hadn't built a million-dollar PR business by not knowing her stuff. In her best public relations manner, she shrugged indifferently. "At my husband's request, I believe I did have someone assigned to help out. The firm often does that for worthy causes."

Before Molly could even formulate another question, Patrice linked her arm through Helen's. "Darlings, I believe I see George and Clark going into the courtyard. Surely Hernando cannot be far away. Shall we go see what they've learned?"

The three brushed past Molly in a whisper of chiffon without so much as a farewell. She could understand their rush. What puzzled her more was why none of the three had asked a single question about her discovery of the body, a fact that had surely made the rounds by now. Unless, of course, one or all of them knew everything there was to know about exactly how Tessa Lafferty had ended up in Biscayne Bay and didn't much care about Molly's own role in tonight's sad events.

Molly walked outside where it was quieter. She was still toying with the concept of one of the three being a murderer, bringing her list of suspects up to a more respectable five, when Liza found her. She looked absolutely spent, as if every ounce of her normal vivaciousness had drained away.

"This could very well be the worst night of my life," she announced wearily, rather than with her more typical dramatic flourish. Without regard for propriety, she hiked her narrow skirt up well above her knees to permit more freedom of movement and paced in an agitated circle.

"Liza, you'll have to pay extra to replace the lawn, if you keep that up," Molly said finally, regarding her friend closely for some hint that it was guilt, not simply distress, that had her in such a state.

Liza gave her a rueful smile, stopped in place, and allowed her skirt to slither back down over slender hips to where it belonged. She ran her fingers through her cropped hair, currently darkened to a shade of auburn that wouldn't clash with her dress. The gesture left the modified flattop in erratic spikes. "How could this happen, tonight of all nights?" she demanded, as if she expected Molly to have an answer.

"If a woman's going to be murdered, it might as well be someplace with a whole houseful of suspects," Molly retorted.

Liza glared at her. "Are you implying that this was premeditated?" she said sharply.

"I'm not implying anything," Molly soothed, her concern growing over Liza's oddly defensive behavior and that unexplained absence. "I'm just saying that there are five hundred people here, any one of whom had the opportunity to kill Tessa. It sure as hell beats shooting her in her own living room with that private security guard you told me they have on duty standing at the front gate. Why did Roger hire that guard anyway? You'd think the Dobermans would be message enough for any burglar contemplating a break-in."

"The neighborhood's changing."

"Are we talking about Coral Gables, that bastion of the rich?"

"There are old-money rich and then there are the other kind," Liza pointed out. The tension in her voice seemed to be easing, as if she felt she were on safer turf. "Tessa was convinced that half the houses in their neighborhood belong to big-time drug dealers now. Roger wanted to make sure some disgruntled vagabond didn't come barging into their house by mistake."

"Are you sure there hadn't been threats against him or Tessa?"

Liza looked startled by the implication. "I'm not sure of it, no," she said slowly. "But why would either of them be in any kind of danger?"

"Obviously one of them was."

"Unless Tessa's death was an accident," Liza said hopefully. "Maybe she stumbled, hit her head, fell into the bay, and drowned. You know how high her heels were. I'm surprised she didn't fall flat on her face every time she tried to take a step on this grass."

"She was found in the water next to one of the most deserted sections of the estate," Molly reminded her. "Why would she have gone all the way over there alone? Surely you don't suppose she needed a respite from all of the adulation being heaped on her as a result of tonight's success?"

"I have no idea, but that brings up something else," Liza said, a speculative gleam in her eyes that should have made Molly instantly suspicious. "What were you and the hunk doing over there?"

Molly refused to feed Liza's insatiable need to meddle in her love life, or lack thereof. "Having a quiet glass of champagne."

"Right," Liza said skeptically.

"That's all," Molly insisted, though there was no mistaking the defensive note in her own voice now. She would not admit, even to her very best friend, that she had followed Michael to that isolated spot in the wild hope of sharing a steamy romantic interlude.

Perhaps, she thought suddenly, Tessa had indulged in a similar fantasy. Not with Michael, of course, but some other guest?

"Liza, was Tessa still having an affair with Hernando?"

"Hernando? Surely by now he had wised up."

"Then someone else?"

Liza regarded her as if the very idea of Tessa as a femme fatale were ludicrous. "I'm surprised her own husband shared a house with her. I can't imagine some other man finding her passionately exciting. That thing with Hernando must have been a fluke."

"You're prejudiced," Molly pointed out, not quite ready to divulge what Jason Jeffries had told her about Tessa's penchant for using and discarding men. "Think about some of the men involved with this particular fund-raising project. How did she get along with them? Did she flirt, bat those false eyelashes of hers? Did they come on to her?"

Liza's expression turned thoughtful. "I suppose there was a certain chemistry between her and old man Jeffries. I always thought it was because they were highly competitive, but maybe there was an edge of passion to the outward expressions of hatred and distrust."

"Maybe once upon a time," Molly confided. "He just told me he and Tessa used to be married."

"Now there's a picture," Liza said, her expression far less astonished than Molly might have liked. "I thought he had better sense."

"I believe he views it as a youthful indiscretion. You weren't surprised about their marriage, were you?"

Liza actually paused to consider the question. "Now that you mention it, no. I think I'd heard it before."

"Who told you? He said Tessa liked to keep it a secret."

"Unless they were married in a wedding chapel in Vegas, divorced in the Dominican Republic, and never passed through Miami in between, it wasn't a secret," Liza said flatly. "Have the police questioned you yet?"

"Not really. I gave a statement about discovering the body to Detective Abrams when they first got here, but that may be it for me. I think Michael would prefer it if I never got within a hundred yards of the police. He suspects it will only whet my appetite for investigating the murder myself."

"Which, of course, it will," Liza observed.

Molly scowled at her. "What about you? Liza, I have to ask. Where were you earlier?"

The question seemed to take her friend by surprise. "You mean when Tessa was killed, don't you?"

Molly winced at the look of betrayal in Liza's eyes. "Yes."

Liza sighed heavily. "I can't tell you that."

"But . . ."

"I can't."

"What if the police ask?"

"They did. I was the first one they questioned. After Roger, of course."

Molly didn't like the sound of that. "Why?"

"They didn't say, but obviously you weren't the only one wondering about where I'd been. And I suspect Roger told them that Tessa and I were at odds over the way this fund-raiser was being run."

"At odds? Isn't that a little like suggesting the troops in Vietnam were a mere military presence?"

"Whose side are you on?"

"Yours, but everyone knows you and Tessa couldn't stand each other. Roger's testimony won't be the last they hear along those lines. You said you blew up at her at the last committee meeting. I assume there were others present."

"A whole roomful," Liza admitted. "Okay, so there is a block of time I can't account for. I suppose that means I had opportunity and a possible motive, but you have to admit that makes a pretty weak case. When was the last time someone killed someone just because they were terminally dim-witted?"

Molly moaned. "Liza, you have to stop

saying stuff like that."

"Why? It's the truth. Do you know how much money that woman wasted on invitations because she just had to have one that was die-cut and embossed so it would make a statement? Four thousand dollars, that's how much. She didn't even use recycled paper, for heaven's sake. When I heard that, I hit the roof." She took to pacing again, her temper heating up all over again. "And I'll tell you what statement it made. It said she was more concerned with her own ridiculous image than she was about the environment. She should have been shot."

"Liza!"

Molly's protest apparently penetrated. Liza sighed heavily. "Jesus! I know I shouldn't say stuff like that, but it makes me so furious . . ."

"How furious?" Michael inquired lightly as he joined them.

Molly and Liza both swallowed hard, then tried to explain at once.

"Hold it! Stop!" he said when he could finally get a word in. "You don't have to convince me that the remark was entirely innocent, but you'd better be careful where else you say things like that. The detective in charge of this case is a by-the-book kind of guy. There will be a lot of pressure, given the status of those attending tonight. He is going to be very anxious to see that it's solved in a hurry."

"I tried to tell her," Molly said.

"I know. I'll shut up," Liza promised. "I just had to get that off my chest."

"In the future vent your anger in the privacy of your own home," Michael suggested mildly.

Hoping to distract him from a full-blown lecture, Molly inquired, "What's happening in there? Have the police narrowed the list of suspects down yet?"

"That's not something they're sharing with me."

"What about the cause of death?"

"I'm not on the need-to-know list for that either."

Molly glared at him. "What good is being at a murder with a policeman if he won't tell you anything?"

"Maybe next time you'd prefer to be escorted by your ex-husband. I understand he loves this sort of thing."

The dig struck home. Hal DeWitt loved being around money and power. It gave him the perfect opportunity to suck up. Molly was sure the only reason he was absent tonight was because Liza's name had been on the invitation and he'd guessed Molly would be in attendance.

"If you're going to ruin a reasonably pleasant conversation by bringing up my ex, I think I'll take another walk around the grounds until the police want me."

To her chagrin no one tried to stop her when she strolled off in the direction of the catering tent. It was too bad, too, because she was just in time to see society caterer Neville Foster launch into a shouting match with one of the hapless servers who'd been in charge of shaving off wafer-thin slices of rare roast beef earlier in the evening.

"What do you mean, it is missing?" he screamed, hands on narrow hips. "How could you be so careless, so inept?"

"It was there earlier," the man insisted stubbornly, refusing to be intimidated by Neville's outrage. "I recall lighting the candles myself."

"So you are saying that one of the guests just happened to walk off with an antique silver candlestick tucked in her purse?" the caterer inquired so sarcastically that Molly winced. "What would anyone at this affair need with such a candlestick? No doubt they own pieces three times as valuable."

Molly glanced at the other end of the buffet table where a heavy, ornate candlestick still held a softly glowing candle. She could

think of one distinct reason someone might
need such an object. It would make a dandy
murder weapon.

murder weapon.

5

The expression on Michael's face was not
particularly welcoming when Molly came
tearing back around to the terrace where
she'd left him and Liza comparing notes on
the murder.

"Where did you run off to this time?" he
inquired testily.

"You won't be quite so cranky when I tell
you what I discovered," Molly retorted.

"Try me."

"I've found the murder weapon. Well, I
haven't found it exactly, but I know what it
was."

He refused to look impressed. "Considering that no one has established that Tessa
Lafferty was murdered, that's quite a feat,"
he said.

She decided to ignore his stubborn denial
of something everyone else on the grounds
accepted as true. The police were certainly
treating the death as if it were a homicide,

even if the word hadn't been used yet. That was enough for Molly.

"A silver candlestick is missing from the buffet table," she said, deciding no embellishment was needed. Michael would get the implication. She noted the reluctant spark of interest in his eyes with satisfaction.

"Are you trying to suggest that Tessa Lafferty went for a stroll with someone toting along a heavy candlestick?" he inquired doubtfully. "Wouldn't she have noticed?"

It was a reasonable question. Molly had already thought of it. She had an answer. "If the murderer was a woman, it could have been in her purse."

Michael cast a significant look at the tiny evening bag in her hand, then glanced at Liza. She carried no purse at all.

"Okay, yes, mine's too small," Molly conceded. "But we won't know about the others until we look."

"You're wasting your time. There's not a woman in the place carrying a purse large enough to conceal more than a tube of lipstick and maybe a solid gold compact," Liza chimed in.

"Have the two of you spent the evening checking out every woman's purse?" Molly shot back irritably. If she couldn't find a logical means for the killer to have gotten that candlestick from the buffet table to the murder site, she saw her discovery's importance diminishing.

"No. I have a thing for observing likely places to conceal a murder weapon," Michael countered. "It's just one of those things cops do instinctively."

Molly caught the slip and beamed. "Then you do agree, albeit somewhat belatedly, that it was murder?"

"I agree that's one possibility," he conceded with obvious reluctance.

"That's a start," Molly said, gleefully determined to pursue what was clearly the best lead they had. "If the candlestick was the murder weapon, then maybe somebody arranged a rendezvous with Tessa, sneaked up behind her, and knocked her out. Anyone could have slipped through the shadows with that candlestick without anyone noticing. I'll bet it's at the bottom of the bay even as we speak."

"I'll mention the possibility to the investigating officer," Michael said dutifully. "Then I suggest we get out of here."

"Now? But what about the investigation?"

"It's under control without your help."

"I just meant it seems early to be releasing suspects."

"You consider yourself a suspect? I'll admit I found your reluctance to dip your toes in the water a bit suspicious, but I never really considered the possibility that you might know Tessa Lafferty's body was in there."

Molly scowled at his good-natured sarcasm. "There are times, Michael O'Hara, when I find you incredibly irritating."

"I know the feeling. Liza, do you want to ride home with us?"

"Shouldn't I stay?"

"If the police are through questioning you, I don't see why. They'll want a formal statement tomorrow, but tonight I think, for all intents and purposes, the party's over."

"I suppose," Liza said dismally. "Can you imagine what the coverage will be like in tomorrow's paper once the reporters get wind of this? I'm surprised the place isn't overrun already."

"It is," Michael told them. "The police are keeping them at bay. I'll see if we can't slip out to the parking lot via the south access road, rather than going through the front door. We should be able to evade the bulk of them that way."

While he went off to have one last conversation with Detective Abrams and the other investigating officers, Molly regarded Liza with concern. "I'm sorry I gave you such a rough time earlier, but I'm worried about you. Are you really okay?"

"Okay?" Liza said, a hysterical note in her voice that Molly had never heard before from a woman who climbed mountains and trekked through rain forests without a qualm. "Of course I'm not okay. I might have hated Tessa but I didn't want to see her murdered and I especially didn't want her to die in the middle of a party that meant a lot to all these environmental projects she championed. Do you know what it'll be like to get someone to chair the next event after this?"

"That reminds me," Molly said, hoping to put things into perspective for Liza. The evening might have turned bleak, but the future held brighter potential. "You obviously made quite an impression on Jason Jeffries. He said he would underwrite the next fundraiser, if you'll chair it. He suggested next winter, when Miami is packed with wealthy snowbirds. He doesn't seem worried that you'll have any problem surpassing the success of this event."

"What success?" Liza moaned. "Our profits are probably nil. The guests are all being detained as murder suspects. My best friend thinks I could be a killer. And the caterer will probably sue because his antique silver candlestick is missing. Neville charges for every damned napkin. God knows what price tag he'll put on that candlestick."

"Liza, I do not think you're a killer," Molly said indignantly, though she had to admit she could see where Liza might have gotten that idea.

"You may not *want* to think that, but you've definitely considered the possibility. You've gone into that same mother-hen mode you adopt when your son has done something wrong, but you're determined to present the best possible side of things to anyone who might attack him for it."

"I know you did not kill Tessa Lafferty," Molly said with more conviction. "But I do think that you're high on the list of suspects, especially if you refuse to explain where you disappeared to in the middle of the party. Let me help."

"I'm not worried for myself, dammit. I'm worried about what will happen to the environmental coalition I worked so damned hard to form. Now everyone will want to go back to their own narrow interests and that's no way to impact legislation."

"I don't think you need to worry about that. Not really," Molly insisted. Michael's earlier assessment had come to the same conclusion. At the time she had vehemently disagreed, but now she could see how all the attention could be turned into a public relations coup if it were managed properly. "This party will be the talk of the town tomorrow," she promised.

Liza regarded her with a wry expression. "You're certainly right about that, but it won't be the sort of talk likely to advance our cause. If the killer's goal was to divide us all, he couldn't have picked a better way to do it. No one will want to be affiliated with a coalition when its board members are being killed off."

"Not necessarily. Why don't we find Caroline Viera and get some advice on how to handle this with the press? We'll need a plan if we run into any stray reporters on the way out."

They found a stoic, somber Caroline Viera at her husband's side. Normally charming and outgoing, Hernando looked wan and troubled, either because he feared his affair with Tessa was about to become public knowledge or because he'd been the one who'd clobbered her. Molly gazed into his bleak eyes and reassessed the possibilities. Perhaps it wasn't remorse or guilt that had turned his olive complexion pasty, but sorrow. It was entirely possible that he had truly cared for Tessa more deeply than his usual quick conquests.

Since it was hardly fitting to console the bereaved married lover of the also married dead woman, especially with his wife present, Molly was at a loss. She gratefully turned her full attention to Caroline. "Could we speak to you a minute? We need your advice on something."

"Now?" Caroline asked, casting a worried look at her husband.

"Yes," Liza said, linking her arm through the woman's and drawing her away. "You're the public relations expert. How should we handle the media? Can we salvage anything from tonight's disaster?"

There was a spark of interest in Caroline's eyes as she considered the challenge. "Here's what I'd do," she said after several thoughtful moments. "I'd tell the media that Tessa's death has put the fate of all of these environmental causes in jeopardy. As tragic as her death is, we cannot allow it to signal the end to her commitment."

Molly could practically hear the closing quotation marks at the end of the statement. Caroline paused.

"One other thing," she said finally. "Try to get to Roger. See if you can convince him that in lieu of flowers a memorial fund be established for these causes in Tessa's honor. I suspect donations will pour in, out of guilt if not out of respect."

Liza looked a bit more hopeful. "Caroline, you're a genius."

"I'll bill you accordingly," she said with a faint smile that warmed her cool, classic elegance. "Liza, you're the one who ought to take over the reins of this now. I know you prefer to work behind the scenes, but you're good with people and you genuinely care. You wouldn't be in it for the glory."

"I've been trying to convince her of the same thing. She has Jason Jeffries's backing, too," Molly said.

"Good for you. He might be an old curmudgeon, but he's well connected. If you have his blessing, you can set this town on its ear. I'll do anything I can to help," Caroline said with obvious sincerity. "I don't say that lightly either. When I commit to a project, I follow through."

Liza's worried expression had slowly begun to brighten. "Thank you. I'll think about it. And thanks for the advice about the media," she said just as Michael joined them.

He pulled Molly aside. "We can get out of here. Are you two ready?"

She glanced at Liza, who was looking

more exhausted and frazzled than she ever had in all the time Molly had known her. Crusades usually charged her batteries. Until the last few minutes the prospect of this one had seemed merely to drain her. Right now she was beginning to look wilted and forlorn again.

"Liza, are you ready to go?" Molly asked gently.

"I'm as ready as I'll ever be," she said.

"Just remember Caroline's advice and we'll have it made."

The three of them slipped through the doors onto the south lawn, then set out along the access road that was currently occupied by the caterer's truck and several police cars. The narrow road wound through the dense cover of banyan trees and other tropical foliage before emerging in the parking lot.

Molly was just about to celebrate their clean escape when she spotted Ted Ryan, the earnest, wily reporter from the morning paper, perched atop the hood of her convertible. Despite the formal nature of tonight's party, he was dressed as usual in faded jeans, a rumpled short-sleeved shirt, and boat shoes. No socks. Either it was his usual attire or Molly had only run into him when he'd been dragged out of bed late at

81

night to cover a breaking story.

"I knew you'd be along sooner or later," he said cheerfully. "Hi, Molly. Hey, O'Hara. What's happening inside? My butt was getting damp from sitting alongside that fountain at the end of the walkway. They wouldn't even bring us any hors d'oeuvres out there, much less any information. I've got an hour until deadline. I'm a desperate man."

"So what else is new?" Molly said drily.

"If you want a statement, you'll have to talk to the police, Ryan," Michael said.

"No, wait," Liza interrupted. "I'll make a statement on behalf of the committee." She proceeded to deliver Caroline's suggested comments verbatim, earning Molly's admiration and a startled look from Michael.

Ted Ryan didn't look nearly as impressed. "So what?" he said bluntly. "I need suspects. I need details. What did the body look like when it was discovered? My photographer's out there in a boat right now, trying to get close enough to the scene of the crime to get pictures. They've already carted the Lafferty broad away by now, haven't they?"

His evident disappointment grated on Molly's nerves. "Your interest in the gory details shouldn't surprise me," Molly said. "That is what you get off on, isn't it?"

82

"Hey, come on," he said, clearly hurt by her assessment. "I'm just trying to do a job here. You're the best sources I've got."

"In that case, you are in serious trouble, my friend," Michael informed him. "We're not feeling very talkative."

"Molly?" Ted pleaded.

"Sorry. I can't tell you any more than I have already," she said, grateful that he wasn't aware that she had actually discovered the body. If he knew that, he'd never let her alone and she was in no mood to recall the sensation of brushing up against Tessa's submerged form.

"You've told me precisely nothing," he said glumly. Then his expression brightened. "How about we trade information?"

Michael shook his head. "As innocent bystanders we don't need your information."

"Not even the fact that the Laffertys were headed for an ugly divorce?"

"That's gossip," Michael said, his expression blank. If the announcement had stirred his interest, he'd determined to keep it hidden.

Molly was less inclined to dismiss the news so readily. "Who's your source?" she asked.

"Can't reveal it," Ted said smugly.

83

"How nice," Michael commented drily. "A reporter with ethics." He opened the car door for Molly and Liza. When they didn't climb in, he shrugged and walked around to the driver's side and got in himself. Just to emphasize his impatience, he started the engine.

Molly scowled at him and tried to figure out how she could wheedle more information out of Ted Ryan, while giving nothing away herself. If Tessa and Roger had been about to split up, that could have a definite bearing on the case. Since Roger was reportedly wildly in love with Tessa, it must have been her decision to walk away from the marriage.

"Who was filing for the divorce?" she asked.

"The old man."

"Roger?" Liza said, her astonished tone matching Molly's reaction. "Why? I'd always heard he was nuts about her."

"He was until he found her in bed with one of his best friends."

"Hernando Viera," Molly guessed.

"Who?" the reporter said blankly. "That's not the name I was given."

"Who then?"

"Dupree. You know him?"

"Clark Dupree, one of the city's most

prominent development attorneys," Molly said, barely hiding her astonishment. Aside from being Roger Lafferty's best friend, he was also Patrice MacDonald's regular escort. That could certainly explain why she'd cut Tessa dead in that Bal Harbour boutique. It might also explain why she might want to murder her.

6

Clark Dupree and Tessa Lafferty. Now,
there truly was a picture, Molly thought,
exchanging a startled glance with Liza. The
dapper, slick, courtroom savior of more
than one major South Florida development
and the woman who professed to be dedicated to saving the environment from the
encroachment of just such developers.

Admittedly Tessa was no Marjorie Stoneman Douglas, the well-known, feisty environmentalist, who had been an outspoken
proponent of preserving the Everglades well
past her hundredth birthday. But Tessa had
been widely regarded as antidevelopment.
Obviously her ethics, such as they were, had
never carried over into her bedroom, something that probably should have been clear
from the first indication that she had affairs
the way some women changed hairstyles.

"No comment?" Ted prodded, obviously
pleased that his revelation had rendered

them speechless.

"What's to say?" Molly said discreetly. "Do you think that has some bearing on the case?"

"Roger Lafferty was here tonight, right?" the reporter said. "With his wife?"

"Yes. What's your point?" she responded, being deliberately blank in the hope that Ted Ryan would spill more valuable information.

"So was Clark Dupree."

"With Patrice MacDonald," Liza reminded them.

"If you ask me, that raises all sorts of possibilities," the reporter said. Then, as if he were expounding on a Ph.D. dissertation thesis, he added, "Jealousy always tops the list of motives in cases like this. We've got triangles all over the place."

"Then I suggest you share your insights about the geometric arrangement of the suspects with the investigating officers," Michael said stiffly. He glared at Molly and Liza. "Are you two coming or not?"

"We're coming," Molly said, defeated. Michael wasn't about to let them trek back inside for more sleuthing. They might as well go on home and compare notes. Maybe one of them had noticed something that would yield a clue when added to what the others had seen.

Ted Ryan sidled closer to Molly and edged her away from the car. "I'll call you later, okay?" he said in an undertone not meant to be overheard.

Something in his voice set off warning bells inside her. "What for?"

"So we can talk without the cop listening to every little word." He gave her a conspiratorial little smile that she belatedly realized was meant to make her heart flip over. Instead, her stomach turned. Surely he wasn't flirting with her.

"Mr. Ryan . . ."

"Ted."

"*Mr. Ryan,* I really don't have anything more to say," Molly said dutifully.

It was one thing to snoop around herself. It was quite another to share her observations with the media. Michael had been right about that much at least. That really would be asking for trouble with her boss and her ex-husband. The fewer times her name was mentioned by the media, the better they both liked it. It had appeared all too often in recent months and usually in connection with messy murder cases just like this one. It was past time for her to start maintaining a very low profile. Vince had already been pressed to fire her; twice, in fact. He'd held out so far, but she couldn't count on that happening again.

Engaging in some fast-talking, she did her best to discourage Ted Ryan from calling. Unfortunately, judging from his expression and his persistent nature, it was unlikely to do any good.

"What time is he calling?" Michael inquired when they were finally on their way home.

"Who?"

"The young stud."

Molly regarded him in astonishment. "Ted Ryan? A stud?"

"The man has the hots for you."

She laughed aloud at the mere idea of that, then wondered if that hadn't explained the way he'd made her feel, that hint of flirtatiousness she'd caught in his voice. "Please," she protested, though not as vehemently as she might have moments earlier. "He's barely into his twenties."

"And you aren't out of your twenties. I'm telling you he's got a thing for you. I could see that last time we bumped into him during the Miami Beach investigation."

"The only thing Ted Ryan has the hots for is a good story. He's very ambitious and he figures I might know something that will enhance his position at the paper."

"Oh, I don't doubt he's after your mind, but believe me, he hasn't missed an opportunity to survey your body as well. Thoroughly, I might add." His scowl grew more ferocious. "Top to bottom. And back again."

"I get the picture," Molly mumbled.

"You sound miffed, Detective," Liza observed from the backseat. She sounded downright delighted by it, too.

Molly regarded the pair of them as if they'd both gone around the bend. The possibility that Michael O'Hara might be jealous was almost as ludicrous as the thought of Ted Ryan being genuinely infatuated with her.

She was so caught up in that particular scenario, she completely missed the opportunity to spend a couple of hours comparing notes with Liza and Michael. He parked her car, walked them to the doors of their neighboring apartments, then departed with barely a good night, still clearly disgruntled by the whole episode with Ted Ryan. Molly stood staring after him in astonishment.

Liza slipped inside her own condo, muttered something about exhaustion, and shut the door. Molly was left standing in the hall, wide awake, with not a single soul to talk to.

"It would serve you both right if I did call Ted Ryan," she grumbled as she slammed her door behind her.

"Brian, why don't we go to Vizcaya today," Molly suggested the next morning the minute her son walked in the door after his overnight visit with his friend Kevin. She winced at his choice of attire, a clashing combination of red and hot pink with some turquoise thrown in. She probably should have been grateful that his socks at least matched. Hell, she thought, she ought to be thankful he'd even remembered socks. She wondered if she dared to hope that he'd taken his toothbrush.

"How come you want to go there?" he asked.

"I'm a mother. Do I have to have a reason?" she responded, because to be perfectly honest, she didn't have one.

Though she'd thought about it all night, she couldn't explain rationally exactly why she felt this compulsion to follow through on Tessa's murder. Part of it had to do with friendship and protecting Liza, though her intrepid friend was certainly more than capable of standing up for herself.

Maybe some of it had to do with the sense of satisfaction she'd felt when she'd played a small role in solving those previous cases.

Maybe it even had to do with her approaching birthday and her vague need to feel that she was finally making something of her life, rather than just surviving.

Hell, maybe she was still trying to prove to Hal DeWitt that the approval he'd always withheld didn't matter anymore because she finally approved of her own worth. The first time she'd felt that way about herself had been when Michael O'Hara had really listened to her insights during his investigation of the murder of her condo president. She never wanted to lose that feeling of accomplishment and self-respect again.

Of course, there was also the undeniable curiosity factor, she admitted ruefully as she awaited Brian's response. She liked digging for clues the way some people liked sifting through rubble for artifacts from another era.

"What do I want to look at an old house for?" Brian grumbled finally. "I wanted to go swimming."

Since telling him a visit to Vizcaya would be educational was likely to be regarded as only one step above eating broccoli, Molly hit on the one thing she knew would fascinate him. It was a low tactic, but guaranteed to work.

"Someone died there last night," she said casually. "During the party."

His eyes immediately widened with excitement. "At the party? Wow! Did you see him? What happened? Did he fall into the buffet table or something?"

"Actually, she fell into the bay."

"Did a shark get her?" he asked with ghoulish enthusiasm.

"No, a shark did not get her."

He looked disappointed. "Will we get to see her if we go?"

"No. They took her away last night."

His interest began to flag. "Then why —"

"We might be able to find clues that will help the police figure out what happened."

He regarded her worriedly. "I thought Michael didn't want you doing stuff like that anymore."

Ever since he'd joined Michael's soccer team, the little traitor thought Michael had hung the moon. When it came to choosing sides, she didn't stand a chance. "I'm sure he'd think this was okay. It's not like I'll be questioning suspects or anything. Do you want to come or not?" she asked, losing patience. "You can stay here and do your homework, if you'd rather."

"I'll go," he said hurriedly. "Let me put my stuff away."

Molly paced impatiently as she waited for Brian to drop his pajamas and video games off in his room. Since that normally consisted of heaving the overnight bag into the middle of the floor, where it would rest until she picked it up, she couldn't imagine what was taking him so long.

Halfway to his room to check on him, she heard his voice. It was hushed and filled with anxiety. As she turned the knob on his door, he said a quick goodbye and hung up in an obvious rush. By the time she had the door open, there was no mistaking his guilty expression.

"Who was that on the phone?" she asked suspiciously.

"Just a friend."

"Does this friend have a name?"

He rolled his eyes. "Of course he has a name, Mom."

"Care to share it with me?"

He considered the request, then shook his head. "Nah."

"Brian!"

"Don't I get any privacy around here?" he muttered in disgust.

Since privacy was a big theme with the two of them these days, Molly found herself neatly caught between a rock and a hard place. "Okay," she said finally, "but if I find out that the person on the other end of that line was Michael O'Hara, somebody around here is going to pay big time for tattling."

Brian met her gaze evenly in a look he'd obviously perfected since knowing the detective. It was even more disconcerting delivered by her son. Maybe she should have told him this tour of Vizcaya was educational and hoped for the best. The truth was, though, that she hadn't wanted to risk his saying no. She wanted company as she wandered those grounds again, even in broad daylight. She didn't expect to encounter any danger with police camped out there, but Brian's cheerful presence might counteract the gloom.

Based on that suspicious phone call, Molly was not all that surprised to find Michael waiting for them at the ticket booth at the entrance gate to the estate. He'd managed to time his arrival perfectly. If she'd noticed him there when she'd driven past on her way to the parking lot, she'd have kept right on going. She directed a sour look at her son.

"I had to tell him, Mom. He and I have a deal. He thinks you're too impet . . . impet . . . something."

"Impetuous," Michael said for himself, ruffling Brian's hair affectionately. His gaze was pinned on Molly, though. "Mind telling me what brought you by here this morning?"

"I don't suppose you'd buy a story about Brian needing to tour the place for a school project."

"Oh, I'd buy it," he said agreeably. "But it does differ somewhat from his version."

"You really didn't need to come running all the way over here. How dangerous could it be to take a guided tour?"

"No tours," he said, pointing to a sign on the ticket booth that she hadn't noticed earlier. "It's a crime scene, remember? The police don't want a lot of people trampling on potential evidence."

"Oh."

He slid his hands into the back pockets of his jeans and rocked back on his heels. "Okay, Molly, out with it. Why did you come back? It's usually the murderer who returns to the scene of the crime. Since you weren't out of my sight until after Tessa's body was found, I think we can rule that out."

Molly considered skirting the truth yet again with some song and dance about simply wanting to walk the grounds, but it was pointless. Besides, with the gates closed to the public she couldn't even get on those grounds alone. With Michael as an ally, she had a shot at checking out the theory that had come to her in the middle of the night.

"Have the police found the murder weapon?" she asked.

"If you're talking about the silver candlestick, they hadn't when we left here last night. I haven't bothered Detective Abrams this morning. I'm sure he has enough theories of his own to check out without dealing with advice from me."

Molly ignored the implied reprimand. "I can think of two places it might be. They're so obvious, no one would ever think of looking there."

"You don't give the police much credit for clarity of thought, do you?"

"Do you honestly want me to answer that?"

"I guess not," he told her. "Okay. Where did the murderer dispose of the weapon?"

"You have to promise to let me check it out with you," she bargained.

"Molly!"

"Promise. This is my theory, remember."

"Okay, fine," he muttered with a resigned shrug. "Just spit it out."

"The pantry. I'll bet there are other

candlesticks stored in there. No one would notice if the caterer's was just stuck in the middle, right?"

"It's possible," he agreed thoughtfully. "What's the other alternative?"

"The catering truck. Neville saw the candlestick was missing from the buffet table. We don't know if he ever searched for it later on the truck. It would have been easy for the killer to steal the candlestick, clobber Tessa, then slip into the catering truck and put it back with the other supplies."

"You could be right."

"Does that mean we can go look?"

"It means we can tell the officer on duty here and maybe he'll agree to let us go along on a search."

"Do you ever do anything that isn't entirely by the book?" Molly inquired grumpily.

"Plenty, according to my superiors."

"Then why are you so stiff-necked with me?"

"For one thing you're a —"

"Don't you dare make some sexist comment."

"I intended to point out that you are a civilian."

"Oh," she said, somewhat pacified. Then she was struck by a distressing possibility.

"You don't suppose they let the catering truck leave last night?"

"I doubt it, especially when they heard about the missing candlestick. I'm sure they'd want to take another look through everything in daylight before releasing anything that was on the grounds last night."

Apparently Michael was particularly persuasive with the duty officer. After a minimum of badge flashing and backslapping, he allowed them access to the pantry, sticking close by to assure they didn't disturb any evidence or make off with any of the museum's valuables. His presence hardly mattered since there was no sign of the missing candlestick amid the supplies stored in the room's cabinets.

Molly barely hid her disappointment. "What about the catering truck? Is it still here?"

"Right outside, ma'am," the officer said. "I think it's locked up tight, though."

It was indeed locked, complete with a strip of crime-scene tape across the freight doors on the back.

"Now what?" Molly asked.

"Now we call Detective Abrams of the Miami Police Department and share your guesswork with him," Michael said.

"Couldn't we maybe pick the lock?"

The duty officer looked horrified. Michael merely shook his head. "Not unless you want to spend Sunday afternoon in a cell."

"They wouldn't arrest you, if you did it," she grumbled.

"I wouldn't count on that. Come on, sweetheart. Let's go into the Grove and have brunch. Maybe we can even catch an early movie."

"Yeah!" Brian said enthusiastically, clearly bored by the lack of action here and fearing he might actually have to view the museum, after all. "Can I have the biggest popcorn they've got? With butter?"

"Only if you'll share with me," Michael said. "Molly?"

"Oh, all right. If I can't solve this mystery, maybe I can figure out why men are born with absolutely no curiosity whatsoever. The bookstore at Cocowalk probably has a whole section of books on that topic alone."

"All written by frustrated women, no doubt," Michael countered.

"Exactly," she agreed. "No man would even be curious enough to try to figure it out."

"Are you guys going to stand around arguing all day?" Brian demanded finally. "I'm starved."

"You're always starved," Molly retorted.

Michael rested his hand on Brian's head. "Just another one of those idiosyncrasies we men share, right, kid?"

"Right," Brian said.

Molly wondered, not for the first time, why the Cuban-American cop understood her son so much better than the Harvard-educated lawyer who'd actually fathered him. The easy rapport between Michael and Brian was just one of the things that made him dangerously seductive to her. It would be very easy to fall for a man who was as easy with kids as Michael was, while at the same time exuding enough sex appeal to stir the most jaded female senses. When his hand moved from Brian's head to her hip, she stopped thinking about anything of substance at all.

In fact, Molly decided eventually, it would probably take something of the magnitude of another murder to drag her attention away from the deliciously wicked way that faintly intimate gesture made her feel.

7

Obviously, she'd tempted the fates once too often just by thinking that another murder might be the only adequate distraction, Molly realized on Monday morning. Her contemplation of a tedious new workweek was interrupted first thing by the one other matter guaranteed to drag her thoughts away from Michael O'Hara, whose unexpected hint of jealousy on Saturday and whose attentiveness on Sunday had tantalized her all night long.

"Your ex is on line one," Jeannette said as she punched the hold button on the office phone. She rolled her eyes, indicating that Molly's ex-husband was probably in one of his surlier moods.

Molly suspected an already lousy morning was about to get a thousand times worse. She groaned at the prospect of dealing with Hal DeWitt, who was no doubt in the mood to pick a fight after reading the morning paper and its enthusiastic reporting of one more body. Seeing his ex-wife's name in print was the only reason he ever called her at work.

"I could tell him you are out, yes?" the Haitian clerk offered, her soft, lilting voice laced with sympathy.

Molly considered the offer, then shook her head. "No. I'll just have to deal with him sooner or later anyway. I might as well get it over with." Reluctantly, she picked up the receiver and injected a note of cheerfulness into her voice, hoping to catch him off guard. "Hi. What's up?"

"As if you didn't know," Hal grumbled. "You were there when Tessa was killed on Saturday, weren't you? Right in the middle of things . . . again."

"It was in the paper that I discovered her body," she said with exaggerated patience, regretting deeply that Ted Ryan had somehow discovered that, after all. "Did you expect me to deny it?"

"I don't know what to expect from you anymore."

His exasperated, aggrieved tone had her twisting the phone cord into a knot. It took everything in her to keep from snapping back with some sharp retort that would only add to his self-righteous annoyance. How had their once-happy relationship deteriorated to this ongoing stream of petty arguments?

"What's your point?" she said finally.

He drew in a deep breath. "Things cannot continue like this," he said flatly. "I won't allow it."

Hal's unusually calm tone sent shivers down Molly's back. She'd learned how to deal with his sarcasm. She could even defuse his anger, but this quiet finality was something else.

"What exactly is that supposed to mean?" she asked equally calmly, refusing to acknowledge exactly how shaken she was by the unspoken threat in his voice.

"You're always telling me how bright you are. Figure it out," he snapped in a tone that was more in character, but no less chilling.

Before Molly could reply, he'd slammed the phone down in her ear.

"Trouble?" Jeannette asked, regarding her worriedly.

"Hal DeWitt is always trouble," Molly replied wearily. "Sometimes I am simply amazed that I was once head over heels in love with that man."

"Perhaps you still have some ambivalence in your feelings," Jeannette suggested, studying her intently.

Molly shook her head. That definitely wasn't what worried her. All she felt most times was irritation that she continued to allow the man to get to her at all. His vague threat had probably meant nothing, she told herself finally. It was just his way of tormenting her.

And yet she couldn't get it out of her mind, not until Liza called in midafternoon. It was the first time they'd talked since late Saturday night. Molly had called her apartment several times on Sunday, but either Liza had had the phone turned off or she'd been out. It wouldn't be the first time she'd holed up, trying to get herself centered, as she explained it, whenever Molly inquired about her sudden reclusiveness. Lord knew, after the murder, getting centered was probably a very good idea. Molly wished she knew how.

"What's up?" she asked Liza now, determined not to plague her with questions it was obvious her friend didn't want to answer.

"Can you get free later this afternoon?"

"Probably. Vince is out of the office and things are slow. September's not the best time to be shooting films or commercials in Miami. There's still too much heat and rain, to say nothing of the threat of hurricanes. What do you need?"

"I want to go see Roger and I really don't want to go over there alone."

"Lafferty?" Molly said with some surprise. "Are you sure you want to pay a condolence call?"

"You remember what Caroline advised. We need to get him to agree to set up a memorial fund. It has to be done today. The services are scheduled for the end of the week, so there's still time to get some sort of announcement of the memorial in the paper. Please, Molly. I need to take care of this and I'd really like the company."

There was no mistaking the odd note of nervousness in Liza's tone. That wasn't the clincher, though. Molly couldn't resist the opportunity to see firsthand how Roger was taking Tessa's death. "You want to meet me here or should I drive to the Lafferty house and meet you there?"

"You're on my way. I'll come by the office," Liza said hurriedly, then added as if she felt a further explanation were needed, "There's no point in taking two cars."

"I'll see you when you get here, then," Molly said, more puzzled than before by Liza's hesitancy to go to the Laffertys' alone. Why would a woman who'd stood in front of a bulldozer to stop destruction in the rain forest be afraid to pay a perfectly normal call on Roger Lafferty? Did Liza fear that Roger would publicly accuse her of the murder, for heaven's sake? If not that, what?

Coming up with no logical answers, Molly swiveled her chair around in time to catch a worried frown on Jeannette's usually impassive face. "This is not a good idea," she said, her tone ominous.

"Oh, come on. It's just a duty call on the bereaved."

The clerk regarded her skeptically. "I read the papers, my friend. This is no ordinary situation. For all you know, this man could have killed his wife."

"We won't be alone with him, Jeannette. He'll be surrounded by friends. Besides, I can't imagine Roger Lafferty killing Tessa, much less Liza and me."

"Who knows what measures a desperate man might be driven to take."

A vague chill stole over Molly for the second time that day. "You aren't having one of those visions of yours, are you?"

"I do not have visions," Jeannette said huffily. "I am just sensitive to certain auras."

"I don't believe in all that stuff. You shouldn't either. You're an educated woman."

"It is because I am educated that I have learned to trust what I feel in my heart," she retorted, her expression quietly serene.

With her mahogany skin and regal bearing, Jeannette came across as a high priestess of some sort, one whose words of wisdom should not be taken lightly. She scared the daylights out of Vince, who was convinced she had the power to cast spells. Molly was less easily frightened, especially when one of Jeannette's feelings butted headlong into her curiosity.

"I'm going," she said firmly.

Jeannette shook her head, but said nothing more. Her visible disapproval did take some of the spirit out of the anticipated meeting, however. Molly could hardly wait to leave the film office with Liza.

Unfortunately, Liza appeared to be as unenthusiastic about going to the Lafferty house as Jeannette. She had dressed in what was, for her, a sedate outfit — black stirrup pants, a black silk tank top, and a loose-fitting jacket in black-and-white silk that floated around her. Chunky onyx and silver jewelry acquired on some Mexican adventure accented the ensemble. Her pixie face, normally animated, seemed pinched. Not even the dash of her clothes could stave off the overall impression of gloom.

As they drove to Roger's, it didn't help that dark, heavy clouds were gathering in the west, promising a typical afternoon thunderstorm. A 'gator pounder, as one local weatherman sometimes referred to the brief but violent storms. With the skies rapidly turning a gunmetal shade of gray, the winding, heavily shaded streets of old Coral Gables took on a threatening ambience. The twisted trunks of the spreading banyan trees along Coral Way added to the eerie atmosphere. If they'd been approaching a dreary castle on the coast of Cornwall, Molly couldn't have felt any more as if she'd stumbled into some gothic novel. She shivered. Obviously, Jeannette's dire warnings had thoroughly spooked her.

"Have you been to Tessa's before?" she asked Liza, hoping that conversation would dispel the odd sense of impending disaster she hadn't been able to shake all day.

"A couple of times for meetings. It's quite a place, built in the thirties and filled with tile and odd-shaped rooms. When Roger and Tessa bought it, ten years ago I think it was, they redid the interior and upgraded the kitchen to something that half the chefs in Dade County would kill to have in their restaurants. They had a major hassle when they painted the outside, though."

"Why?"

Liza grinned. "One of those typical Gables things. The painter didn't check his color chips against those the city of Coral Gables permits. He had to do the whole damned paint job over again, because the shade of paint was slightly darker than the law allows. Roger was fit to be tied, tried pulling strings at City Hall, but to no avail. Coral Gables may not be able to keep out the drug dealers, but they sure as hell can control what color paint people use."

"Wouldn't you love to meet the person in charge of enforcing the color palette?" Molly said, envisioning some poor soul creeping around at dawn matching approved colors to the newly painted exteriors of houses.

As much as they tended to ridicule the restrictions, however, there was no mistaking the effect of the watchdog effort. Even with the storm approaching, there was a quiet serenity to the Gables, a sense of stability and longevity that was lacking in most other hastily developed and haphazardly planned sections of the county.

Or there would have been if it hadn't been for those newly erected walls with their security gates surrounding half a dozen houses within a handful of blocks. The decorative wrought iron gates to the Lafferty house stood open and a circular brick driveway was crowded with cars. An unobtrusive security guard, his uniform clearly distinguishing him from the visitors, stood in the shadows partway between the front gate and the door to the house.

"Quite a crowd," Molly said, smiling at him in the hope of starting a conversation that might reveal exactly what he was doing on the premises.

He nodded, his expression unyielding. Definitely not the friendly sort, she conceded reluctantly. Maybe Liza would have better luck. She nudged her as they walked from the only available parking place at the end of the driveway.

However distracted she might otherwise be, Liza was quick to catch on to Molly's intention. She, too, beamed at the guard. "Lucky for you the rain hasn't started, isn't it?"

The guard was neither so old nor so blind that a woman as stunning and vivacious as Liza couldn't get to him. He sucked in his substantial gut and shrugged indifferently. "When it pours, I just wait it out in my car. I can see most everything from there."

"Is there much to see?" Liza asked. "Seems to me the neighborhood ought to be pretty quiet."

"Seems that way to me, too," he confided, suddenly turning loquacious under Liza's less than subtle encouragement. "Then again, if folks didn't get paranoid, where would I be? Out of a job."

"What on earth did the Laffertys have to be paranoid about?" Liza prodded. "They were one of the nicest, most respectable couples I know. What happened to Tessa was a real tragedy. Do you think it had anything to do with whatever they were worried about?"

Molly waited to see if Liza's fishing expedition would turn up anything, but before the guard could answer, the front door opened and half a dozen people emerged, effectively destroying the moment as they went to their separate cars. The guard's expression turned stoic again, and his eyes focused on some point in the distance. Apparently, he'd seen how the guards at Buckingham Palace did it, Molly thought.

An old black woman, her hair cut short, her uniform so starched it looked downright uncomfortable, admitted Molly and Liza and led them down the long tiled entryway toward the back of the house.

"Mr. Roger's seeing folks in the garden room," she said with old-style formality.

"It's a sad time in this house, a sad time," she added with a shake of her head.

"I'm sure it is," Molly said kindly, sensing the housekeeper truly was distraught. "Have you worked for the Laffertys for a long time?"

"Worked for Miss Tessa since she was a girl. Her family hired me straight out of high school. Good people they were, too. Helped me educate my brothers and sisters. Miss Tessa had her flaws, but she did right by me. Nobody is going to say otherwise," she said in a combative tone.

Molly wondered who she'd heard criticizing her employer and whether the remarks had been made before or after Tessa's death. "Has someone said something unkind about Mrs. Lafferty?"

"Those reporters," she said huffily. "Looking for scandal, so they are. Asking about other men. I wouldn't tell them a thing and I know plenty, believe you me."

Molly decided she didn't want to be lumped in a class with the nosy media in the eyes of this prospective fountain of information. She already had sufficient clues about Tessa's marital infidelities to keep her going for a while. "Will you stay on with Mr. Lafferty?" she asked instead.

"We ain't talked about it yet. If he wants

me here, I'll stay. If not, I've got me a little place to go home to. I'm seventy years old. Might just be time I retired and set a spell. Miss Tessa, she took care of me in her will. She always promised me that. With that and the Social Security, I'll do okay."

She opened the door to the garden room. "You ladies go on in and sit with Mr. Roger now. I'll be bringing a fresh-brewed pitcher of iced tea shortly."

"Thank you," Liza told her. "What's your name?"

"I'm Josiah, ma'am, after my daddy. Miss Tessa called me Josie."

Liza patted her frail hand. "Thank you, Josie."

Molly barely noted the housekeeper's departure. She was too busy staring into the garden room, which had obviously gotten its name from the French doors across the back facing a garden lush with tropical foliage. The theme had been carried over in the white wicker furniture, which was luxuriously padded with chintz-covered cushions splashed with bouquets of pink cabbage roses.

A large, glass-topped wicker table held silver trays laden with tiny sandwiches, painstakingly cut into rounds, along with a punch bowl filled with fresh fruit, and serving plates crowded with freshly baked tarts and petits fours. The spread might have been catered, but Molly suspected Josie had spent all day Sunday lovingly preparing the refreshments for the mourners who might stop by.

As enthralled as she was with the room and the buffet, what really snagged Molly's complete attention and had her scrambling for an explanation was the unlikely trio of men who sat stiffly in a row, like some sort of tribunal waiting to hand down a judgment.

Perhaps it was no more than a fluke of available seating, but lined up side by side were Roger Lafferty, Hernando Viera, and Clark Dupree. Their presence together created something of a quandary, given what Molly knew of their respective relationships with Tessa. What would Miss Manners say under the circumstances? Molly wondered, glancing at the only other people in the room, the Willoughbys, to see how they were handling the awkward situation. There was no outward evidence that they were unnerved. Either they weren't aware of the ties each man had shared with Tessa or they traveled in more sophisticated circles than Molly. Or perhaps, given their stiff, silent demeanor, they'd simply been struck dumb by the audacity of it.

Molly finally settled for offering her condolences without looking any one of the men in the eye. Let them guess who she genuinely felt sorry for, she thought irritably. While they were doing that, she would try to figure out why they were engaged in this oddly polite charade of camaraderie.

8

Roger Lafferty's dazed expression never changed as Liza and Molly recited all the appropriately sympathetic clichés. Molly couldn't help wondering if he was on medication, though she supposed it was possible he was simply in a state of shock. Everyone else seemed to be. Only Hernando Viera actually looked healthy in all that basic black mourning attire, and even he looked stunned.

In fact, the only person in the room to react visibly to their arrival was Mary Ann Willoughby, who determinedly latched on to Liza's arm and dragged her away from Roger. Molly gathered she wasn't pleased to see them. Molly traipsed after Mary Ann and Liza to be there in case tempers flared . . . or on the off chance that Mary Ann might let something interesting slip. Tessa's best friend wasn't known for censoring her tongue, despite her regular efforts to soothe feathers Tessa had ruffled with even less diplomacy.

"How dare you come here?" Mary Ann demanded in an undertone. She practically shook with indignation. Obviously, she took her new role as Roger's protector quite seriously.

"I need to speak with Roger," Liza said, remaining amazingly calm in the face of the older woman's self-righteous outrage.

"Absolutely not. If you had a sensitive bone in your body, you would see that he's in no shape to speak with anyone, least of all one of Tessa's enemies."

Liza drew herself up to her full height. It was an unimpressive five feet two inches, but she managed to create an aura of a much taller woman. "I was not Tessa's enemy," she declared evenly, looking Mary Ann straight in the eye. "Even though we didn't always agree on the best methods for accomplishing our goals, we did agree on the goals."

"You tried to undermine her every chance you got. I watched you do it. Who knows what lengths you might have gone to to grab her power," Mary Ann said so viciously that Molly gasped and prepared to intercede. Liza waved her off.

Mary Ann went on, her venom unchecked.

"Now you think just because Tessa's gone and you have Jason Jeffries eating out of your hand that you'll take over. Well, believe me, it won't happen. Not over my dead body."

"Given what you apparently think I'm capable of, I'm surprised you'd plant that idea in my mind," Liza retorted.

Mary Ann's shocked, faintly dismayed expression indicated she hadn't realized the severity of the charge she'd leveled at Liza. She'd practically accused her of Tessa's murder. Her gasp drew the attention of the men, but Liza paid no attention to the sudden mild commotion. She strode across the room and took the seat next to Roger.

"I really am sorry to bother you, but I'd like to make a request."

Roger blinked several times as if trying to bring her into focus. "Now? Must it be now?"

After a slight hesitation, Liza rested her hand on his. Molly wondered about that infinitesimal delay. Liza was a toucher. Her natural inclination was to pat a cheek or a hand, to give a quick hug of reassurance. Why had she just checked that impulse with Roger? Molly had never seen anyone more in need of comforting. To her astonishment, the normally effusive Liza didn't seem willing to dispense any.

"Yes," she said in a brisk, no-nonsense tone. "It really can't wait."

He sighed heavily, the sound like a child's round plastic inner tube deflating. "Go ahead, then."

"I wondered if you would consider establishing a memorial fund in Tessa's honor, a fund that would take up where she left off in supporting environmental causes. I can't think of anything that would please her more."

Roger stared blankly, but Hernando Viera was already nodding. "That is a very thoughtful idea, Ms. Hastings," he said in English that was precise and barely accented. His mastery of his second language was an accomplishment in which he took great pride. "I could make the arrangements at the bank for you, Roger. What do you say? Tessa would like knowing that her beliefs won't die with her."

With all the attention focused on him, Roger Lafferty finally shrugged. "What does it matter? Do what you like."

"You've made the right decision," Carl Willoughby told him gently. "Tessa really would be pleased."

Even Mary Ann Willoughby gave Liza a look of grudging admiration. "Yes," she agreed. "Tessa would be pleased."

Liza nodded in satisfaction. "Actually, it was Caroline's idea. I know she'll be delighted that you all agree that it's the perfect memorial for Tessa."

The only person who had said nothing through all of the discussion was Clark Dupree. With his mouth set in an angry line, he looked as if he wanted to squash the whole idea, but knew he didn't dare given the enthusiasm of the others in the room.

Molly couldn't resist. "What do you think, Mr. Dupree?"

His furious gaze settled on her, but his tone was temperate, the tone of a man used to masking his emotions in the courtroom. "My opinion doesn't really matter. It's Roger's decision. He must do what he thinks best."

Roger glanced at him, his expression slowly shifting from bemusement into something that might have been pure hatred. "Yes. It is my decision, isn't it?" He sat up just a little straighter. "Thank you for reminding me of that, Clark. You must go ahead with the memorial fund, Ms. Hastings. You and Hernando can work out the details."

Suddenly, the air crackled with tension. It was hardly unexpected given those present, but it was as if all the pent-up emotions of the past forty-eight hours had finally been unleashed. As much as she wanted to know which one of these people was capable of killing Tessa, Molly couldn't wait to leave. Neither, apparently, could Liza.

The instant she had Roger's solid approval for the memorial, she was on her feet. Hernando Viera followed her to the front door. Molly straggled along behind, just in case tempers finally snapped in the garden room. Unfortunately, the only voice she heard was that of Mary Ann Willoughby, who apparently didn't have sense enough to know when to keep her mouth shut. Three male voices all chimed in to tell her.

"I will call you later with an account number," Hernando promised Liza as Molly joined them. "I know you and Tessa didn't always see eye to eye, but it's a wonderful thing you are doing for her memory."

"Hernando, you were very close to Tessa," Molly said in what she considered to be a masterful bit of understatement. "Had she been worried about anything lately?"

He regarded her with a look of puzzlement. "You are thinking she suspected she was about to be murdered?" he said.

"Something like that. They did just recently hire additional security guards here, didn't they?"

His expression hardened. "That had nothing to do with Tessa," he said tersely. "Now I must get back. Ms. Hastings, I will call you."

"Why do you suppose he got all testy when I asked about the security guard?" Molly wondered aloud as they walked to their car. Said security guard was nowhere in sight. Either he'd gone off duty or he was patrolling the grounds.

"Maybe because your timing was off. Perhaps he didn't like being reminded that all the precautions had been wasted."

"Or maybe I hit on the one thing that would help explain how Tessa ended up in Biscayne Bay on Saturday night."

"Did you see that look between Roger Lafferty and Clark Dupree?" Liza said, abruptly changing the subject. "There is definitely no love lost between the two of them."

"What do you expect? They were best friends until Clark started shacking up with Tessa. That would certainly put a strain on the relationship. I'm surprised Clark had the nerve to show up here today."

Liza shook her head. "That's precisely why I think it's something more than that. It's like neither trusts what the other one would do if left to his own devices."

"So, what do you think is behind the distrust?"

"How would I know? Clark's not the only man Tessa ever had an affair with. Hell, she'd had one with Hernando, too, and you didn't see that violent reaction between Roger and him."

"True," Molly conceded thoughtfully. "I wonder what Patrice MacDonald would have to say. She obviously knows about the affair. Do you suppose she was madly in love with Clark?"

"Patrice? I doubt it. Clark was a convenience, someone who knew all the same people and was more than willing to escort her to all the right parties."

"Then why would she cut Tessa dead in that boutique?"

"Well, I suppose there was some element of pride involved, but I still think we're missing a key ingredient."

"Like what?"

"I don't know. It probably has something to do with money. It always does." She grinned at Molly. "I saw that on TV once. *Matlock,* I think."

"I saw the same episode. Some guy kept telling him to look for the money trail or something." Molly shook her head. "I can't imagine that has anything to do with this murder, though. Everyone involved has enough money to paper their walls with it if they wanted to."

"Appearances aren't always fact. Maybe one of them didn't have nearly as much as they wanted everyone to believe. People go broke all the time, especially in this economy. A few bad investments and the whole kit and caboodle can go down the tubes."

"So how do we find out who's in financial trouble?" Molly said, shoving aside the sudden vision of Michael's reaction to his discovery that she was still trying to find out anything having to do with this case.

"I can think of one person who'd know."

"Who?"

"Jason Jeffries. He's got his finger in every financial pie in town."

"How do you suppose he'd feel about us dropping by uninvited?" Molly asked, her curiosity fully aroused. "He thinks we're a couple of tough cookies. He'd probably get a kick out of knowing that we're sleuthing."

"Unless, of course, he's the one who murdered Tessa."

Molly's eyes widened at Liza's matter-of-fact tone. "You don't believe that."

"No," Liza said thoughtfully, "I don't. But who knows what the police think, and at the moment they probably have more evidence than we do. Maybe dropping in isn't such a good idea until after we know more about the status of the investigation."

"And how do you propose we find out any more?"

"You are dating a cop," Liza reminded her.

"I think that's a pretty loose interpretation of what we do," Molly said. "Not only that, Michael is definitely not inclined to feed my insatiable appetite for clues. I say we just go see Jason. We can tell him we're there to talk about the fund-raiser."

"Wouldn't we make an appointment to do that?"

"A couple of tough cookies might not."

Liza nodded finally, glanced at the car clock, and saw that it was barely six, not quite the end of the day for a man like Jeffries. "Let's do it," she said.

Jason Jeffries was still in his office in the penthouse suite of a Brickell Avenue highrise. His secretary confirmed that the minute they walked through the impressive mahogany doors and stepped onto the two-inch-thick pile carpeting. She also confirmed that the odds of their seeing him without an appointment were similar to those for being granted an unscheduled audience with the Pope.

"He has an hour on the twenty-first," she told them, flipping through pages filled with precisely entered notations.

"That's two weeks from now," Molly protested.

The secretary beamed at her quick calculation. "Exactly. Shall I put you down?"

"Perhaps we could wait until after his last appointment this evening," Molly suggested, suddenly determined to see Jason Jeffries today, if she had to wait for him all night. Officious secretaries always firmed up her resolve.

"I don't believe that would be a good idea. When this appointment ends, he must rush to a benefit dinner."

"The appointment could end early."

"It's already run over by ten minutes," the secretary said, her expression disapproving. Clearly, whoever was overstaying his or her welcome would not be granted an appointment so readily the next time if Miss Eloise Parsons had anything at all to say about it.

"Miss Parsons, this really is important," Liza said in the same gently coaxing tone she used to get big bucks for her causes. "If you would just let him know we're here and let him decide."

Miss Parsons looked horrified. "I couldn't

possibly interrupt him."

Molly gathered that they could spend another ten years dreaming up arguments, and the secretary would simply shoot down each and every one. She turned on her heel, walked over to the comfortably appointed reception area, and sat down. Liza followed. The secretary leapt up and came after them.

"This won't do at all," she said, thoroughly flustered by what she obviously considered outrageous audacity. "Must I call security?"

Suddenly, the door to the inner sanctum burst open. "What the devil is all the commotion out here?" Jason Jeffries demanded. His gaze lit on Molly and Liza. A grin spread across his face. "You two. I might have known. Give me a minute and I'll be right with you."

Molly shot a triumphant look at Miss Parsons. The secretary returned to her desk with a sniff, then turned her back on them and began pounding on the keyboard of her computer with a touch that threatened to bounce it off her desk. The last pieces of equipment requiring a touch that firm were the old standard manual typewriters.

"I hope we never need to get past security around here again," Molly observed in a whisper. "She'll have us shot on sight."

"Not if his high holiness in there tells her

otherwise. She is the sort of loyal minion who would never dream of going against her boss's wishes. She'll roll out the red carpet, even fetch us coffee, if he tells her to."

Unfortunately, the next time the door to Jason Jeffries's office opened, the two men who exited with him were all too familiar — Miami's Detective Abrams and Metro's Detective Michael O'Hara. Molly's mouth dropped open in astonishment.

"What are you doing here?" she asked before she could stop herself.

Detective Abrams apparently didn't see the need to explain his presence. He glanced at Michael, his lips quirking with amusement, nodded politely, and kept right on going. To Molly's regret, Michael showed no such inclination.

"I might ask you the same question," he said, studying her intently, then sparing a glance for Liza.

"The fund-raiser," Molly blurted. "We wanted to see Jason about the fund-raiser."

Michael glanced at the philanthropist. "You didn't mention another appointment. I'm sorry if we held you up."

Jason Jeffries smiled benignly. "These gals took me by surprise, but I never turn down the chance to chat with a couple of pretty women."

Clearly offended by the patronizing tone, Liza glared at him. He winked at her. Molly envisioned the entire fund-raiser falling apart without Jason Jeffries's backing, but before she could decide how to mediate, she heard Liza's unexpected chuckle.

"You old fraud," she accused. "You just do that to irritate me, don't you?"

He grinned back at her. "Works every time, too."

Michael took Molly's arm. "Why don't you and I let them have their meeting," he said in a tone that indicated it was an order, not a suggestion.

"Liza needs me there," she protested, then realized that for the moment her friend was perfectly capable of handling Jason Jeffries. That left her free to discover what the devil Michael O'Hara had been doing in Jason Jeffries's office. Unless he and Abrams had been there collecting for the Police Athletic League, which she seriously doubted, then her favorite Metro-Dade homicide cop had been involved in interrogating a witness in a Miami murder case.

"Oh, never mind," she said resignedly. "I'll come with you. Liza, you don't mind, do you?"

"No. You two go on ahead. I'll see you at

home later."

"Stealing one of my girls," Jason Jeffries grumbled at Michael, but he winked when he said it. He turned back to Liza. "Okay, young lady, let's get cracking. I've got things to do. You need a check or something?"

Molly didn't hear Liza's response because Michael was propelling her through the door at a clip that could have earned her first place in the Miami Grand Prix. He didn't say a word as they waited for the elevator. Nor did he open his mouth as the elevator doors slid shut. The silence was beginning to get on Molly's nerves.

"Okay," she snapped finally. "Just say it."

"Say what?"

"Whatever you're going to say."

"I'm much more interested in what you have to say. You don't for a minute think I believe that hogwash about stopping by to do some planning for a fund-raiser that's not even on the calendar yet."

Molly seized the opening like a lifeline. "That's just the point. We needed to set a date. All the best dates at the hotels in town are taken early."

"Nice try, but no dice. Care to take another shot at it?"

"I'd rather hear what you were doing in Jason Jeffries's office with Detective

131

Abrams."

"I'm sure you would," he said blandly.

She surveyed his intractable expression. "But you're not going to tell me, are you?"

"Not until you tell me what you and Liza were up to."

Molly sighed in resignation. When it came to sheer stubbornness, Michael would win out over her every time. "Okay. When we were leaving the Lafferty house . . ."

"Leaving where?" Michael said, his voice climbing ominously.

"We went to pay a condolence call, for heaven's sake. What could be more innocent than that?"

"As I recall, neither you nor Liza were overly fond of Mrs. Lafferty. Doesn't that make such a call hypocritical in the extreme?"

"I didn't ask for a lecture on manners," she snapped. "Besides, Liza needed to talk to Roger about establishing a memorial fund in Tessa's honor."

"And she required your assistance to make this request?"

"Yes." Again, she was reminded of the oddity of that, but she saw no need to mention her reaction to Michael.

It was his turn to sigh. "Go on."

"Anyway, when we were leaving, we

started trying to figure out who in that crowd might be going broke."

"Why on earth would you be wondering about that?"

"Because greed is often a motive for murder, but when everyone is rich, it gets a little trickier. We decided maybe not everyone in that room this afternoon was as rich as they'd want people to believe and we figured Jason Jeffries would know all about their finances."

"An interesting theory," Michael admitted grudgingly. "Too bad you didn't get there in time to hear Jason Jeffries's comments on that very subject."

"That's what you were questioning him about?"

"Exactly."

"Why you, though?"

"Abrams asked me to sit in. He had this crazy idea that since I was at that fundraiser as a paying guest, I knew more about the players than he did. I considered explaining about Liza's strong-arm tactics, but it would have ruined my image, so I just agreed to go along."

"You couldn't resist, could you? Tell the truth, Detective. This case got to you, didn't it?"

"Every case gets to me, Molly. I get paid

to investigate my own."

"I suppose that given the fact that this particular murder involved a charitable cause, you suddenly decided you could do a little poking around for free?"

"Something like that."

She stood on tiptoe and gave him a peck on the cheek that brought an immediate flush to his olive complexion.

"What was that for?" he demanded.

"Because you're such a soft touch."

Judging from his horrified expression, he didn't consider her observation as the praise she'd intended it to be. "Don't you dare go spreading that around," he ordered.

"I wouldn't dream of it. It's enough that I know. Now, what did Jason Jeffries tell you? You and Abrams looked pretty smug when you were coming out of that office."

"Rumor has it that Roger Lafferty is up to his eyeballs in debt."

"Roger?" Molly repeated incredulously. "Are you sure? I thought he had oodles of stock handed down through generations of Lafferty investment geniuses."

"Maybe he did, but he's broke now, or so the rumor goes. It's also suspected that Tessa carried a very hefty insurance policy." He grinned at Molly's astonished expression. "*Sí, amiga.* The way it looks, that policy could be just about enough to bail him out."

9

The morning headline reporting that Roger Lafferty was now officially a prime suspect in Tessa's murder wasn't unexpected, but it successfully drove all remaining thoughts of her ex-husband's disturbing call out of Molly's mind. That was her first big mistake. Her second mistake was in underestimating the depth of Hal's outrage over her involvement in three murder cases in a row, or the extremes to which he might go to punish her for it.

She had tossed aside the paper and was debating the merits of corn flakes over sugarcoated cereal with Brian when the doorbell rang on Tuesday.

"I'll get it," he said, bounding away from the table like a child given a reprieve from finishing his spinach, rather than one who'd had a bowl of cereal and bananas placed in front of him.

"Who are you?" he said a moment later.

"I'd like to speak to your mother," a strange male voice responded.

Trying to imagine how the man had talked his way past the condo's security guards, Molly approached the door warily. Her first glance at the bland face, dull gray suit, and shifty, evasive gaze warned her that the unexpected visitor was not here to turn over a sweepstakes check for a million dollars. Equally uneasy, Brian hovered protectively by her side.

"Yes?" she said.

"You're Mrs. DeWitt? Mrs. Hal DeWitt?"

"I am Mrs. Molly DeWitt," she said firmly. The sudden knot forming in the pit of her stomach was a reminder that lately she regretted that she had to admit to that much. "Can I help you?"

Just like in the movies, the man whipped an official-looking envelope out of his pocket and handed it to her. He turned on his heel and fled down the hall before she could even scan the return address.

"What is it, Mom?"

With her heart suddenly thudding, Molly gave Brian a distracted glance. "Go and finish getting ready for school."

"I am ready."

"Get your books."

"I don't see why —"

"Just do it, Brian. Now!"

His expression hurt, he slunk off, leaving her with no more excuses to avoid opening the letter from Hal's attorney, a senior partner in the firm that sprawled over two entire floors of a downtown office building.

The usual salutation was followed by a terse announcement:

Given the unusual circumstances of your involvement in several murder investigations over the past several months, we feel we have no choice but to file a request with the court to review the custody arrangements for Brian Alan DeWitt. Mr. DeWitt will be asking for full custody of his son, though naturally he will be willing to permit supervised visitation.

The letter went on with legal jargon and what looked at first glance like an outline of the timetable for this action. Molly didn't read it. The first sentence had made her blood run cold. The second made it boil. She was shaking as she punched in Hal's office number, knowing he would be there even though it was barely 8:00 A.M.

"How dare you?" she demanded the instant he picked up his private line. "Have you lost your mind?"

"You got the letter."

"You're damn right I got the letter and if you want a war with me over our son, you've

138

got it," she said, her furious words tumbling out uncensored. It was not the way to win an argument with Hal, but she was too angry to care. "I will not allow you to use this sudden, misguided concern for his welfare to snatch him away from me."

"Oh, really?" he said.

Molly ignored the sarcasm. "What exactly do you intend to do once you have him, Hal? Will you occasionally try to get home from the office before midnight to help him with his homework? Will you see to it that the maid takes him to Pizza Hut once a week? Will you hire someone to go to his soccer games in your place? Goddammit, what are you thinking of? Don't you give a damn about his feelings? He's an eight-year-old boy, not some pawn in a goddamn chess game. If you're angry with me, take it out on me, not Brian."

"I will not talk to you when you're out of control like this," he said.

Since he sounded almost satisfied by her loss of temper, she drew in a deep breath, forcing herself — somewhat belatedly — to sound every bit as cool and rational as he did. "If you think this is out of control, pal, you haven't seen anything yet. My lawyer will be in touch. I suggest you start now if you plan to manufacture a few excuses for

139

the way you've ignored Brian for the past two years. Believe you me, it is not something he or I have forgotten."

She slammed the phone down so hard the table shook. It took everything in her to keep from bursting into hot, angry tears of fear and frustration.

"Mom?" Brian said, his voice tentative.

Molly drew in yet another deep breath, then slowly turned to face him, praying he hadn't heard everything. His terrified expression, freckles standing out against too pale skin, told her that he had. It nearly broke her heart.

"Dad's not going to make me go live with him, is he?"

She saw no point in avoiding the truth. He'd have to know sooner or later. "He's going to try," she admitted.

"He's tried before," Brian said. "He came after me last time and tried to talk me into going with him, remember?"

"I remember."

"Is this the same thing?"

Molly knew that this time it was no idle threat. Hal was dead serious. "No, it's not the same," she said gently, recalling Hal's halfhearted attempts at persuading Brian to choose him over her in the past. "But it won't happen, not unless it's what you

140

want. You're old enough now that the judge will listen to you, if it comes to that."

Brian was across the room in a heartbeat. He flung his arms around her neck and clung to her, his whole body shaking. "I won't go with him. I won't. I never want to see him again as long as I live. I hate him. I hate him." His voice trailed off in sobs.

"Oh, baby," Molly whispered, her own tears finally streaming down her face. What in God's name was wrong with Hal that he could inflict this kind of pain on their son? "You won't have to leave here. I promise."

Admittedly, her promises didn't have such a hot track record, but apparently Brian was reassured anyway. His tears finally ebbed. He slowly extricated himself from her embrace and gave her a wobbly grin. He was far calmer than her pat, clichéd words warranted.

"I don't want you to worry about this," she told him.

"I'm not worried, not anymore," he said with admirable bravado.

"Why not?" she inquired suspiciously.

"Because I have an idea that will fix everything."

"What idea?"

"If you married Michael," he said slyly, "Dad wouldn't be able to take me away,

141

would he?"

Molly gaped at him. "Where on earth would you get an idea like that?"

"He likes you. I know he does. And he's not married. It would solve everything, right?"

Marriage to Michael O'Hara might solve one problem, but Molly was smart enough to know that it would only be the start of a whole slew of new ones. She could hardly explain that to an eight-year-old. "Sorry, sport," she said with some regret. "I think this is one problem we'll have to sort out on our own."

She hadn't counted on the fact that Brian was like a terrier with a bone once he'd gotten an idea into his head. When her phone rang that afternoon the minute she walked in the door from work, she was hoping it would be her attorney with news that Hal had backed down. Instead, the voice that greeted her bore a faint Cuban accent and a definite hint of laughter.

"I understand we're getting married," Michael said.

"Oh, dear Lord," Molly murmured, blushing in embarrassment. "Brian called you."

"He did. He was upset, but you should be proud of him. He wasn't letting it get him down. He has a plan, a rather detailed one,

142

in fact."

"So I've heard."

Michael's tone sobered. "I think maybe the three of us ought to have dinner tonight and talk about this."

"Michael, no. I can handle Brian."

"I was thinking less about Brian than I was about you and your ex-husband. What are you going to do about him, Molly?"

She sighed heavily. "I've spoken with the attorney. He's trying to reason with Hal's attorney, who happens to be one of his law partners."

"I wasn't aware that attorneys ever listened to reason."

"I'm hoping for a first, for Brian's sake."

"I think you'll need a tougher strategy than that. I have to interview some witnesses in one of my cases in about an hour, but I should be out of here by seven at the latest. Why don't I pick you up? We'll go for Italian at that place in South Miami that Brian likes."

"Fine," Molly agreed because she couldn't think of one single reason not to go. If Michael wasn't terrified by Brian's marital scheme for the two of them, then it was silly to avoid him. Besides, she always thought more clearly when she talked things out with him. Maybe together they could formulate a sensible plan of action. His methodical, left-brain approach nicely complemented her own more instinctive reactions to things.

No sooner had she hung up than she heard a rap on the door, then Liza's familiar voice, followed almost immediately by the sound of the key turning in her door. She regarded her in astonishment. Liza was rarely home this early from her various fund-raising efforts all over town. She had more meetings to twist arms than half a dozen CEOs combined.

"What brings you back from the fund-raising wars at this hour?" she asked.

"I have news to report."

"Roger Lafferty is suspect number one in the murder of his wife."

Liza's face fell. "The hunk told you."

"He did, but even if he hadn't it was all over the paper this morning and on the TV and radio news all day. If you'd pay attention, you'd have known that."

"I know enough about what's going on in the world without letting the media bias me."

Molly knew it was pointless to hike down that particular conversational trail again. Liza was stalwart in her refusal to subscribe to the papers or turn on a television. Despite that, Molly was always astounded by how well informed Liza was about the things that mattered to her.

"What happened to you last night?" Molly asked instead. "I expected you to report in the minute you got home."

"Actually, I went to that benefit dinner with Jason Jeffries. I was hoping to pry more information out of him."

"Information or money?"

"Both, as a matter of fact."

"Well?"

"He gave me a sizable donation."

"And?"

"He didn't tell me anything more than he apparently told Michael and Abrams. Roger got way over his head when he tried to take over some company in California. Tessa continued to spend money like there was no tomorrow. A few weeks ago he supposedly took out a new life insurance policy on Tessa, though nobody has actually seen said policy. Suspicion is that he intended all along to use the money to put his company back on a sound financial footing before the irritated stockholders ousted him, Jason being one of said stockholders."

"What about Ted Ryan's information that Roger planned to divorce Tessa?"

Liza shrugged. "Beats me. Either he got it

wrong or that was an alternative plan, whereby he'd try to wrangle a chunk of her family money in a settlement."

"Do you suppose Tessa had any family money left after all this time? I thought that was why she kept latching on to all these wealthy men, so she could take 'em for a bundle in alimony. If she had her own money, wouldn't that hurt her position in getting some kind of obscenely huge divorce settlement?"

"I have no idea what the workings of the court are when both parties in a marriage have money. I do know that Jason's generous alimony ended on the day she married again. He told me that last night."

Molly considered that. "I suppose Josie might know for sure what Tessa's financial status was. She was pretty certain that her boss had provided for her in her will."

"Wouldn't it be a kick in the pants to Roger, if all that money from the life insurance was willed to the housekeeper?"

"I doubt Roger would have paid the premium under those conditions."

"Unless he didn't know about the will. Couldn't that supersede the name on the policy?"

Molly shook her head. "I have no idea."

"I know you and your ex aren't the closest of friends, but he is an attorney. Couldn't you call him and ask?"

The morning's events came crashing back. "Absolutely not," she said so vehemently that Liza simply stared.

"What's Hal done now?" she said finally.

"He's threatening to take me back into court to ask for custody of Brian."

Liza jumped up, her expression instantly sympathetic. "Why didn't you say something when I first walked in, instead of letting me go on and on about this ridiculous murder? What can I do to help?"

"There's nothing to be done for the moment. The attorney's handling it. Brian thinks he has a solution. He's asked Michael to marry me."

"Oh, dear Lord," Liza said, then a grin spread across her face. "Did the hunk say yes?"

"We're all having dinner tonight to discuss it."

"My, my."

"Don't give me that speculative look, Liza Hastings. I am not marrying anyone just to keep custody of my son. And I seriously doubt that Michael O'Hara considers it an option either."

"Are you sure? You know how he feels about family, especially mothers and sons."

Molly knew. After he was separated from his mother and sent to the United States to live with relatives, he was practically obsessed with the subject. "He's also a cop who feels very strongly that he's a bad bet when it comes to marriage," she said. "He doesn't even have relationships."

"What about that woman he lived with, Bianca?"

"The way he tells it, she expected more than he ever intended."

"He certainly took his time extricating himself if that was the case. Ergo, they had a *relationship.*"

"I think what they had was mutual lust. Until she got possessive, he probably saw no reason to back away."

Liza grinned. "Then you're in luck. That's what he has with you, too."

"Not so you'd notice," Molly countered, feeling oddly disgruntled. She pushed aside the feeling. "This is ridiculous. Why are we discussing it?"

"Because your son has proposed on your behalf and now you two are going to have to figure out what to do about it."

"Maybe we can just sit around and figure out if Roger really killed Tessa instead."

"If you would rather discuss murder than marriage with the hunk, you are in serious trouble," Liza observed. "I think I'll leave so you can work on your priorities before he gets here."

"Before you go, there's something I still can't get out of my mind."

"What's that?" Liza said.

"When I found Tessa's body the other night, I looked all over the place for you and I couldn't find you anywhere. Where were you?"

Liza's expression immediately shut down. "You asked me that before."

"I know, and you avoided answering me. You're doing it again. Why?"

Liza sighed and sat back down. "Because I didn't want you to get the wrong idea."

"What on earth could be worse than thinking that you might have had something to do with Tessa's murder?" Molly said incredulously. She waited anxiously while Liza apparently considered whether to answer.

Refusing to meet Molly's worried gaze, Liza finally confessed, "I was upstairs in one of the bedrooms — the Cathay, to be precise."

Molly regarded her closely and realized it was embarrassment, rather than guilt, that had kept Liza silent. "I think I'm getting the picture," she said.

"I doubt it," Liza said ruefully. "I can't believe how naive I was. For God's sake, I have traveled around the world and back on my own. I have challenged world leaders on their environmental policies. I've even ducked out on amorous suitors in a dozen languages. And I still fell for one of the oldest lines in the book."

"Meaning?"

"One of the guests said he wanted to speak with me privately. I assumed he wanted to discuss setting up an endowment or at least increasing his already sizable donation. I suggested we take a walk around the grounds, but he insisted it would be quieter upstairs in the mansion. Who knows, maybe he'd always wanted to get it on in an elegant room done by some European artist who'd never gotten over a visit to China."

"It is a seductive room," Molly said cautiously, recalling the soft jade-and-gold decor, the drapes of fabric that provided a suggestion of a canopy for the narrow bed.

"Obviously, he thought so. The minute we were inside, he was all over me. The last guy who tried to grope me with so little finesse was a college student. I was nineteen at the time."

Molly was horrified at the thought that one of the guests at a fancy gala would attack a woman in an upstairs bedroom. "He didn't . . ." She couldn't even bring herself to phrase the entire question.

"Are you kidding? You don't think I took all those martial arts classes for nothing, do you? The second the first shock wore off, I flipped him off the bed, pinned him to the floor, and suggested that the size of his donation be tripled."

"He agreed, naturally?"

Liza allowed herself a faint grin. "He agreed." Suddenly, the grin faded. "Of course, it's possible that his check is no good."

Molly regarded her in shocked disbelief as she realized what Liza was implying. "Roger?"

"Roger," she confirmed. "Not that I blame the poor bastard. Being married to Tessa would be enough to drive any man to extreme measures."

Molly understood now why Liza had been so insistent that she go with her to the Lafferty house the day before. She also realized why there had been such an odd undercurrent between the two of them. "Liza, you have to tell Michael about this."

"No way," Liza said adamantly. "I refuse to embarrass either one of us by spreading this incident around."

"You have to," Molly insisted.

"Why?"

"Don't you see? You're Roger Lafferty's alibi."

10

The realization that she was Roger Lafferty's alibi had obviously never occurred to Liza. It seemed to have put her into a state of shock.

"Surely, you realized if he was your alibi, then you were his?" Molly said.

"I never thought of him as mine. I would have gone to jail before I'd ever tell a soul that I was lured to a bedroom by that man."

"Don't you think you're being a little melodramatic? 'That man' is a wealthy, prominent businessman, not some creep off the streets. Besides, it wasn't as if you actually slept with him. When you realized his intentions, you put him down . . . literally."

"Maybe so, but he apparently thought I would be amenable to his advances. What does that say about the lengths to which people think I'll go in the name of environmental activism?"

Molly shook her head. "I doubt Roger was

planning to buy his way into your bed. I suspect he simply had the hots for you. He certainly wouldn't be the first man to find your combination of brains and beauty to be seductive."

"Maybe," Liza said doubtfully.

"Liza, just because you are oblivious of the way men look at you, I am not. In fact, it is sometimes very difficult being your friend. We walk into a room and all male eyes focus on you. I'm just part of the scenery."

"Obviously, the hunk doesn't see it that way."

Molly allowed herself a tiny smirk of satisfaction. "No, he doesn't. He seems to be immune, for which I am incredibly grateful. But that's beside the point. You have to talk to him when he gets here and tell him what happened with Roger."

"I can't."

"Oh, for heaven's sake, do you want me to tell him? Or maybe you'd rather talk to that Miami detective, the one who probably lifts cars in his spare time to stay in shape. He certainly looks as if he'd take the news that you were withholding evidence well."

Liza shuddered at the thought of sharing her most embarrassing moment with Detective Abrams, just as Molly had known she would.

"Okay, you win," she conceded with obvious reluctance. "I'll tell Michael."

His arrival, as if on cue, prevented her from changing her mind.

"Tell him," Molly prodded, the minute Michael had a beer in his hand and a comfortable spot on the sofa. Liza looked as if she preferred to wait until he'd finished the beer, maybe several beers.

"Tell me what?" he said, regarding them both suspiciously. "Don't tell me one of you is confessing to the crime."

Molly glared at him. "No."

Liza squirmed awkwardly, her expression miserable. "Look, this isn't really easy for me, but I do have a confession to make. Not about the murder exactly, but about Roger Lafferty. He couldn't have done it."

"Oh?"

His bland response got Molly's attention. She regarded him curiously.

"I was with him," Liza blurted. "I'd rather not go into the circumstances, but there is no doubt in my mind that he couldn't possibly have killed Tessa."

Molly waited again for Michael's exclamation of surprise, maybe even a curse at the loss of the number one suspect. Instead, he merely nodded. "I know."

Liza and Molly both gaped at him.

"What do you mean, you know?" Molly demanded.

"Know what?" Liza said.

"I know that he dragged you off to the Cathay Bedroom in the wild hope of seducing you. I also know it didn't work."

"He told you," Liza said dully.

"After a lot of prodding. One of the other guests saw the two of you disappear into that bedroom. She rather gleefully reported that fact to Detective Abrams. He's been waiting to see how long it would take for the two of you to come clean. Roger caved in first. I'm not sure if he was more humiliated that he'd tried or that he'd failed. Anyway, he told all. Less than an hour ago, as a matter of fact. I talked with Abrams right after he left the Lafferty house."

"If somebody blabbed, why the hell didn't Abrams just ask for confirmation?" Liza grumbled.

"Because it doesn't really matter. We don't know exactly how long you were in that room or the exact time of Tessa's death. Sorry. Neither of you is out of the woods yet."

"Wait a minute," Molly protested. "We do

know the time of death or pretty close to it."

Michael's gaze narrowed. "Explain."

"It was just after nine when we arrived. We saw Tessa, with Liza, in fact," she said, trying to reconstruct the sequence of events. "Don't you remember? The photographer from the morning paper was taking pictures. Tessa was there, very much alive, preening for the camera, in fact. Then Liza came over to talk with us. It couldn't have been more than twenty minutes after that when we got to the edge of the bay and I found the body. That makes it nine-thirty, nine forty-five at the latest."

Molly shivered as she realized how little time Tessa had spent tangled in the mangrove before she'd discovered the body. Was it possible they could have saved her, if she hadn't taken time to go back to the car for that flashlight? It was not something to be dwelled upon.

"Liza, where did you go after you spoke with us? Is that when you ran into Roger?"

Liza shook her head, her expression thoughtful. "Not right away. I think there was a crisis of some sort," she said slowly. "Yes, I remember now. Neville was complaining about the champagne."

"The champagne?" Michael repeated.

157

"What was wrong with it? It tasted great to me."

"No, no," Liza said. "The champagne was donated, but we had to pay corkage. Do you know what that is?"

Michael shook his head.

"It means we had to pay him a small fee for every bottle opened, even though he didn't supply it. It's standard with a lot of hotels and caterers when dealing with charity functions that get donated wine or champagne. Obviously, they'd rather supply it themselves at some exorbitant rate, but some will bend their rules if you pay the corkage fee."

"Sounds like a rip-off," Michael observed, "but I get it. So what was the crisis?"

"We were supposed to have someone standing by all evening to assure that the number of bottles he said he served were actually served. Otherwise we could be overcharged in corkage. It's a pain in the neck, but we insisted."

"Trusting group, aren't you?"

"When you have to account for every penny to a coalition board the way we do, you can't afford to be sloppy."

"Okay, so this person was missing. Who was supposed to be there?"

"I'm not sure. We'd rotated the assignment so no one would have to spend all evening in the catering tent. I can't recall who was supposed to be there. I grabbed someone to fill in until the next person showed up."

"Can you find out who was missing?"

"Sure. The subcommittee chair for the catering should have a list. Patrice never lets details like this slip."

Molly was instantly alert. "Patrice Mac-Donald?"

Liza nodded. "Why are you looking like that?"

"Don't you see? If she was in and out of the catering tent all evening, she would have had ample opportunity to snatch that candlestick. And if she'd been assigned to that particular hour herself and disappeared . . ." She allowed her voice to trail off so they could get the implications all on their own. They didn't fail her.

"Molly, you could be right. It fits with everything we know about Clark Dupree and Tessa, the spat Patrice had with Tessa in Bal Harbour, everything," Liza enthused.

"Slow down," Michael said. "We don't have proof of anything here. We don't even know for sure that the candlestick was the murder weapon. It might not even have been stolen in the first place. Maybe it was just misplaced and this caterer got all bent out of shape for nothing. He seemed like the excitable type."

"He is that," Liza conceded.

"Call him," Molly said. "Ask him if the candlestick has turned up. Liza, you have the number, don't you?"

"Absolutely." She reached into her voluminous purse and drew out a bulging date book that contained an entire section for names and addresses, as well as business cards. It was so well organized that she found the number before Michael could even register a halfhearted protest.

Molly shot him a challenging look. "If you don't call, I will."

To her surprise, Michael nodded. "Maybe that would be better. He'd be less likely to be on guard with you or Liza. In fact, Liza ought to be the one to call. As a member of the committee, surely you would be interested in whether the candlestick had been recovered." He studied her intently. "Can you pull it off?"

"I don't see why not," she said confidently, reaching for the phone. After schmoozing with some underling, she got the caterer on the line. "Neville, darling, it's Liza Hastings. How are you?"

Molly couldn't hear his response, but

judging from the way Liza was gazing heavenward, he was giving her an earful about his current travails.

"I'm so sorry," she murmured with a certain lack of sincerity. "Getting decent help is a problem. Listen, darling, the reason I called is that I need to know when you'll get that final bill to us. We want to settle all the accounts before our next board meeting so we'll know how the event did."

She nodded at his answer. "Friday is terrific. By the way, did that candlestick ever turn up? I know how valuable it was." Her expression changed to one of astonishment. "It did? When?" She glanced pointedly at Michael. "You found it in your office. How odd. How do you suppose it got there? Or was it there all along?"

Molly's spirits sank, but Michael was still watching Liza intently. If he could have, he would have grabbed the phone out of her hand and finished the interrogation himself. Instead, he had to rely on Liza's quick wits to get whatever answer he was after.

"Has anyone from the committee stopped by in the past couple of days?" Liza asked, earning a beaming smile of approval from Michael. "Oh, really. Patrice came by first thing Monday morning. Darling, you didn't happen to notice whether that candlestick

161

was there before she came by, did you?"

Liza's eyes lit with excitement. "Thanks, Neville. Everything was spectacular on Saturday. You're a genius. I'll stop by for the bill on Friday."

She put the receiver back on the hook with careful deliberation, then gave them a smug look. "Bingo."

"The candlestick suddenly materialized after Patrice's visit?" Molly said.

"That's what he seems to recall. Hopefully, he won't figure out quite why I wanted to know. If he does, he's likely to call Patrice and warn her. She sends a lot of business his way. He'll warn her out of loyalty or maybe just because it seems like a great tidbit of gossip to pass on."

Michael nodded grimly. "Then I suggest we pay a visit to Mrs. MacDonald first. I'll call Abrams and tell him what's happening. Molly, is Brian around?"

"He's at the pool."

"Then get him while I call Abrams. I haven't forgotten about that talk we intended to have. We'll go on to dinner after we've stopped by Mrs. MacDonald's. Liza, are you coming?"

"I wouldn't miss it," she said, then glanced at Molly. "On second thought, if you all have things to talk about . . ."

"Come," Molly said, latching on to the excuse to avoid a conversation about marriage with a man who was being strong-armed into proposing.

Liza shook her head. "I'll take my car to Patrice's. Then you all can go on to dinner without me."

Molly decided it was pointless to argue once Liza had made up her mind and foolish to give up the opportunity to hear Michael's insights on the custody mess. "Your car or mine?" she asked Michael.

"Mine. I left it in the circle out front. The guard will have it towed if I don't move it soon."

"Nestor wouldn't dream of it," Molly told him. "He's probably out there polishing it for you as we speak. Ever since you solved the murder of our condo president, our security chief has regarded you as his idol. He told Brian that."

Michael looked embarrassed at the thought that a former Nicaraguan freedom fighter would consider him a hero. "I'll meet you down there in five minutes. Liza, we'll see you at Mrs. MacDonald's. Wait for us to go in."

Liza snapped off a salute.

As it turned out, it hardly mattered who arrived first. Patrice MacDonald wasn't home, according to the housekeeper who answered the door. She cast a sly, approving glance at Michael. He smiled the killer-megawatt smile that encouraged confessions and probably seductions, Molly thought grumpily. At any rate it appeared to be working on the housekeeper. She was volunteering information in Spanish at a clip that was totally beyond Molly's comprehension.

"She went where?" Liza suddenly blurted, drawing a warning glance from Michael.

"What?" Molly demanded.

Michael finally thanked the disappointed housekeeper and said good night. He turned around. "It seems that Mrs. MacDonald is in Europe. Paris, possibly. Maybe Rome. Could be London."

"In other words, she's skipped the country."

"Indeed."

"That certainly puts a new wrinkle into things, doesn't it?" Molly muttered.

"It's certainly beginning to make her look guilty as hell, especially if these vague travel plans of hers were made in the past forty-eight hours or so. Any clue who her travel agent might be?"

Liza retrieved her overstuffed notebook and thumbed through it. "Here's the woman most everyone in Coral Gables society circles uses. I can't swear that Patrice did, but it's worth a shot."

"I don't suppose you have her home number," Michael said.

"Of course," Liza said. "What good is a travel agent if you can't get her in the middle of the night?"

"Obviously, Patrice is of the same mind," Molly noted as Michael dialed the number on his cellular phone. She listened intently to his conversation with the travel agent. It wasn't going nearly as well as he might have liked.

"No, ma'am," he said politely, but firmly. "You don't have the same sort of privileged information situation that an attorney would have. You can make this difficult, but I will get a subpoena. Your boss might not like the fact that an employee did not co-operate with the police, especially when that fact is likely to turn up splashed all over tomorrow morning's newspaper."

Molly grinned at the thought of Michael actually divulging information to Ted Ryan intentionally. Fortunately, it appeared it wouldn't come to that. He was murmuring approvingly at whatever the woman was telling him. "Yes, thank you. You've been a tremendous help."

As soon as he'd hung up, he said, "London. It was the first flight the agent could get her on Monday."

"Then it hadn't been planned."

"Nope. In fact, the poor old girl had to fly coach."

11

Molly tried to envision Patrice MacDonald murdering Tessa, then jetting off to hide out in some cottage in the Cotswolds or having afternoon tea at some swank London hotel. It was a difficult image to conjure up. However, if Patrice actually had intentionally left the rest of them to muster up alibis and undergo police interrogations, Molly could think of a few hundred people who might want to buy round-trip tickets to England themselves just so they could tell Patrice what they thought of her before dragging her back for prosecution.

"It doesn't make sense," Liza said, echoing Molly's thoughts. "Patrice doesn't strike me as the sort of woman who'd skip the country to avoid being charged with a crime. She's so arrogant, she'd be convinced she could hire a hotshot defense lawyer and beat the rap."

"There's only one way to find out," Michael said, already punching in what Molly suspected was Detective Abrams's number.

"Will he fly over to question her?" Molly asked when he'd explained the situation to the Miami detective and hung up again.

"If he eventually has enough evidence against her, yes. If it's all circumstantial — and for the moment it is — he figures the brass will want him to wait until he digs up something more solid before going after a woman with her standing in the community."

"Like what? A witness who saw her club Tessa with that candlestick?" Molly said derisively. "We already know no one saw that."

"Do we?" Michael said.

Molly's gaze narrowed. "Is there a witness?"

"Let's just say that no one has come forward at this time. That doesn't mean that someone didn't see the murderer and Tessa together instants before the crime and just hasn't put the two things together yet. Or perhaps he or she is holding out to protect the killer."

"So we just sit around and wait?" Liza said dejectedly.

Molly shared her impatience. "Couldn't we do something in the meantime? Maybe give Patrice a call?" she suggested hopefully.

"Absolutely not," Michael said.

"But we could sound her out, see what her mood is, determine if she's on the run."

Michael grinned despite himself. "You sound like a bad TV script."

Liza scowled at him. "It is entirely possible that she simply decided to go on a shopping spree or that she hadn't had a decent scone in months. Maybe she's merely soothing her ego after the way Clark Dupree betrayed her. That sounds more like Patrice."

"Why are you making excuses for her?" Michael asked. "A few minutes ago you were ready to hang her."

"We weren't ready to hang her," Molly retorted defensively, knowing full well that they had been. They had latched on to Patrice as the killer faster than old Roger had made his unexpected moves on Liza. "We just got caught up in the way all the evidence was pointing. Now that we've had time to think it through, it doesn't make sense. I can't see a woman like Patrice clubbing Tessa over the head and shoving her into the bay to die."

"I hope you won't mind if I don't report your change of heart to Detective Abrams," Michael said.

The remark seemed a little snide to Molly. "Maybe you should. He shouldn't waste all his energy chasing the wrong suspect, while the real murderer gets away."

While all three adults in the car scowled at each other, Brian scrambled from the back of the wagon to the front. "Are we ever gonna eat?" he inquired plaintively. "I'm starved."

"Soon," Molly murmured distractedly. "Liza, did Patrice take off like this all the time?"

"I have no idea."

Michael nodded reluctantly. "You're wondering if this is just the way she deals with any little upset in her life, by taking a European holiday?"

"Exactly. Maybe the travel agent could tell you that."

"I'll try," he said and called the woman back. He apologized for intruding again on her evening. "I just got to wondering if Mrs. MacDonald was in the habit of taking unexpected trips like this."

Apparently, the answer was a terse and emphatic no.

"She's never been this impulsive, then?" he said. "Okay, thanks. By the way, what was the name of the hotel where you said she always stays in London? Got it," he said, scribbling it down. "Thanks."

He met Liza and Molly's disappointed gazes evenly. "She has never taken a vacation without meticulously planning it ahead of time. The travel agent said she was thoroughly flustered when she called Monday morning and insisted only that she be on a flight by that night. She didn't even seem to care where it took her. Nor, by the way, did she book the return flight. The ticket is open-ended."

"Let Liza call her," Molly coaxed, more convinced than ever that Patrice hadn't fled to escape prosecution for Tessa's murder. "Patrice would stare down any judge or jury that tried to convict her. On the other hand, flight might well be the response of a woman whose pride was in tatters. Liza might be able to get her to open up. She could say she was calling about committee business that couldn't wait." Molly glanced at Liza. "Couldn't you even manufacture an emergency meeting of the coalition board? Patrice wouldn't miss that."

"I could," Liza said, regarding Michael intently. "I was going to schedule one for the end of this week or the beginning of next anyway. I could tell her that, ask when would be best for her. That would tell us when she plans to be back. What do you think?"

After several moments of thoughtful deliberation, he held out the slip of paper and the cellular phone. "Give it a try."

Liza took down the name of the London hotel, but shook her head. "Not now. With the time difference it's the middle of the night. With all the traveling I do, she knows I'd know that and wouldn't risk waking her unless something dreadful had happened. We don't want her getting suspicious and running, if she is guilty."

"You're right," Michael agreed. "You'll call her first thing in the morning, then?"

"First thing, her time," Liza said. "I'm never in bed before two or three in the morning anyway. She ought to be sipping her morning tea about then."

"You'll beep me?" he said. "No matter what time it is?"

Liza grinned at him. "You'll be the first to know." She glanced at Molly. "Or at least the second."

"First," he insisted.

"You could hear the news together," she suggested with a sly wink as she slid out of the car. "Bye-bye. Enjoy your dinner."

Molly glanced at Michael to see how he was taking Liza's innuendo. His lips were twitching, as if he was trying very hard to control a grin.

"First your son, now your best friend," he said idly. "A man could begin to wonder if the whole family intends to gang up on him."

"Not mine," Molly said with absolute certainty, imagining her parents' outrage at the mere idea of her being married to a lowly cop. "They're still holding out for me to stop all this independent foolishness and go back to Hal."

Michael regarded her in astonishment. "They took his side in the divorce?"

"They took his side from the day I met him. In fact, that probably had a lot to do with why we got married in the first place. They were ecstatic that a man of his obvious promise and ambition wanted me." Since she couldn't hide her bitterness over that, she glanced pointedly at Brian, who was playing with one of his handheld computer games. "Could we talk about something else, please?"

Michael reached across and squeezed her hand. The sympathetic gesture immediately brought the sting of tears to her eyes. Apparently, he saw them.

"Molly?" he said gently. "You okay?"

She gave him a watery, forced smile. "Just

173

terrific. I'll be even better once I have a plateful of pasta in front of me. Comfort food, right?"

"So they say," he said. "I always thought it was black beans and rice."

She grinned at the cultural variations between them. "In actual fact, I always reach for hot, yeasty bread. I can remember our housekeeper baking every Friday so we'd have homemade bread and rolls for the weekend. She used to let me sit in the kitchen. Later, whenever I felt down or lonely, that's where I'd go and Arnetta would pull out the flour and the yeast and start baking up a storm." It occurred to her that she wouldn't mind sitting in that kitchen right now with Arnetta mothering her.

"I'm surprised you don't bake bread yourself, then."

"I do," she surprised him by saying. Then she chuckled. "Mostly, it's inedible. Just ask Brian."

"Ask Brian what?" he chimed in from the back as they pulled into the crowded restaurant parking lot just off South Dixie Highway.

"If my homemade bread is any good."

"Yuck," he said succinctly. "But it smells pretty good."

"Talk about damning with faint praise," Molly grumbled, but her spirits were slowly improving, as if just thinking about the housekeeper who'd been her surrogate mother had calmed her fears about Hal's threats. Unfortunately, just as they were sitting down to the much-delayed dinner, and just as she was pushing thoughts of her ex-husband out of her mind again, Michael brought everything back.

"Have you considered sitting down and talking with the jerk?" he asked reasonably.

Molly glanced at Brian, worried about his reaction to the start of this particular conversation. He was busy with the garlic roll he'd snatched up first thing to stave off starvation. He seemed far more interested in consuming the entire basket of rolls than in anything they might have to say.

"Wouldn't talking to DeWitt be better than a court fight?" Michael prodded.

"I don't have any idea what I could say to Hal that I haven't said already," Molly responded. "Besides, we never talk anymore. We argue. He attacks and I respond. It escalates from there. You've seen us in action yourself."

"I've also seen you be pretty persuasive when you set your mind to it."

"I wasn't able to persuade you to help me

find Tessa Lafferty's killer," she reminded him. "It took Detective Abrams to do that."

"That's different." He leaned closer and touched her cheek. "Talk to the man, Molly. You connected once. Surely, neither of you has changed so much that you can't manage to see eye to eye on something as important as Brian."

Molly wondered about that. She had changed tremendously since the days when she was a naive college girl who'd tumbled head over heels in love with handsome, self-confident Hal DeWitt. He had possessed all the strength and certainty that she hadn't. It was only after she'd grown up, pretty much against his will, and discovered that she had a mind of her own that they'd begun to have problems.

"If you want her to see my dad, does that mean you and Mom aren't gonna get married?" Brian demanded indignantly once he'd polished off the entire basket of rolls, a salad, and two slices of pizza.

Molly winced at the blunt question.

"We'll talk about that another time," Michael told him, apparently unflustered by Brian's enthusiasm for that particular solution. "Let's see how things go."

"You won't forget?" Brian prodded, apparently well aware of how any conversation

Molly might have with his father was likely to go.

Michael met his gaze evenly, man to man. "Have you ever known me to forget a promise?"

Satisfied, Brian nodded. "Okay."

It seemed that the evening was destined to end with a lot of promises on the line. Reluctantly taking Michael's advice to heart after he'd left her to do some more soul-searching, she dialed Hal's home number.

"We need to talk," she announced without preamble. "Can you meet me in the Grove?"

To her amazement, he didn't argue. "When?"

"A half hour at Cocowalk."

"What about Brian?"

Molly resented the accusing tone of the question, but under the circumstances she supposed it was a fair one. "Liza will watch him. I'll meet you in front and we'll see which place has a quiet table."

Only when they were seated across from each other did she note the worry lines creasing his brow, the shadows beneath his clear blue eyes. He'd given up trying to disguise his receding hairline, which actually seemed sort of sexy on him.

"You look lousy," she told him.

A faint smile tugged at his lips. "Is that

177

supposed to win me over?"

"Actually, it was an expression of concern. You look exhausted."

"I am."

"You're still working too hard."

"This isn't about work," he said. He ordered a shot of Scotch, waited for her to choose a wine, then met her gaze directly. "I don't want to be at odds with you all the time, Molly. It takes a toll."

There was a genuine weariness and regret in his tone, but she didn't trust it as anything more than a ploy to win sympathy. "Then why the hell did you start this?" she demanded, unable to keep the sudden surge of anger out of her voice.

"Because I'm genuinely worried about Brian."

She shook her head. "I don't think so. I think you're still trying to get even because I left you."

A flash of anger sparked in his eyes, then died. He sighed. "Maybe so." He sipped his drink, as if he was buying time to gather his thoughts, then leveled a look at her. "Maybe I never understood why you left. Your parents can't figure it out either. Your decision has really upset them terribly. They're still not over the divorce."

He didn't have to rub it in. She was well

aware of their opinion of her actions. Unable to hide the pain she felt at discovering that he continued to have a better rapport with her parents than she did, she met his gaze. To her astonishment, she saw honest bemusement and hurt there as well. Maybe they both had suffered.

Responding to that and unable to deal with the whole sorry state of her strained relationship with her parents, she said more softly, "Let's leave my parents out of this for the moment. I never understood why you married me in the first place. Why did you, Hal, especially when it was so clear I could never live up to your expectations?"

He regarded her with evident surprise. "Is that the way it seemed to you?"

"That's the way it was," she said emphatically.

Hal looked even more startled by her adamance. "You really have changed. When we got married, I thought we shared the same goals. I thought you wanted a traditional marriage as much as I did, the kind of marriage our families had."

"Traditional how? With me sitting docilely at home, while you worked until all hours of the night? That's the kind of marriage my parents had. Yours, too, as I recall. I think if I'd heard your father refer to your mother as 'the little woman' one more time, I would have screamed. Do you have any idea how talented your mother was?"

"This isn't about my mother," he said defensively. "You'd never expressed any interest in a career."

"Maybe because I was too young when we married to have given it much thought. Later, when I tried to talk to you about how frustrated and incomplete I felt, you refused to listen. I had a degree, Hal. I didn't go to college just to meet a man."

"You had a degree in liberal arts. What kind of job were you planning to get with that?"

"The kind of job I have now," she said, rising to his derogatory tone. "A very responsible, creative job."

He closed his eyes, stung by her attack. "Okay," he said finally. "Then you thought I was trying to smother you?"

"Maybe not intentionally, but yes."

He shook his head wearily. "All I wanted was for things to turn out the way we'd meant them to."

"And I changed the rules," she guessed, finally understanding the anger and bitterness that had eaten away at their relationship and was still at work long after the divorce.

"Yes," he admitted. "You changed the rules and I resented the hell out of you for doing that."

"Okay, that's fair enough. We both made mistakes. I can understand how angry and betrayed you must have felt, but that was between us, Hal. We can't let it affect Brian. He doesn't deserve it."

"You can't expect me not to worry about him, dammit. He's my son."

"He's my son, too," she reminded him. "I will never, *never* allow anything to happen to him. I would die trying to protect him."

"And that's supposed to be good enough for me?" he said, his frustration evident. "Dammit, Molly, he wouldn't need protection if you'd stop getting mixed up in all these murder investigations."

"Hal, I have to stand up for what I believe in. I have to help my friends when they need me."

"That's all very noble, but at what cost? Your son's life?" he said furiously.

Up until now, Molly had kept a reasonably tight rein on her own temper, had honestly tried to understand Hal's point of view, but now she lost it. "Dammit, stop overreacting! Brian is not in any danger."

"You can't swear to that and I don't like the odds."

"Hal, please," she pleaded, seeing the tentative, newfound rapport slipping away. "Be reasonable. Drop this custody battle before it gets ugly and Brian gets hurt."

Hal shoved the rest of his drink away, then stood up and tossed several bills on the table. "I'll think about it," he said. "That's all I can promise."

He left Molly staring after him in confusion. To her surprise, she was also filled with unexpected regrets.

12

Troubled by her meeting with Hal and knowing that she'd be unable to sleep, Molly decided to wait up with Liza until she could put through the call to Patrice MacDonald in London. At least it would give her something to look forward to.

As soon as Liza started for the door, Molly stopped her. "Don't go. I can use the company. It's already one-thirty. You can call Patrice from here in an hour or so."

Liza regarded her worriedly. "I thought you'd be exhausted from all that confrontational stuff. Do you want to talk about what happened with Hal?"

Molly sighed heavily. "He's thinking."

"About what?"

"Whether my promises to protect Brian with my life are sufficient to overcome his concerns."

Liza's gaze narrowed. "What's this really all about, Molly? He's not just ticked off

183

about these murder investigations, is he?"

"No, not entirely. He's still grappling with the way I've changed. He doesn't like it and he likes even less that he's unable to do anything about it. Hal was always into power and control. He has none anymore where I'm concerned, except through Brian."

"He's still in love with you," Liza said.

"No," Molly said flatly, but she had to admit she'd wondered the same thing herself. Her relations with Hal immediately following the divorce had certainly been uneasy, but he had been increasingly difficult ever since the Sunday afternoon he'd had a run-in with her in Michael's presence. When Michael had stepped in, Hal had realized that the other man was playing some sort of role in her life, as well as in Brian's. Brian had reported that his father had asked several questions about Michael after that. He had even discouraged him from playing soccer on Michael's team. He'd suggested Little League as an alternative, but hadn't offered to coach or even to attend the games.

"Yes," Liza contradicted her. "He's still in love with you. It's as plain as the nose on your face. How does that make you feel?"

Molly sighed. "Besieged," she admitted. "I

don't want Hal to love me."

"Why? Because then you'd have to deal with your feelings for him?"

"I don't have any feelings for him."

"Of course you do. You loved him once. He's the father of your son. As I recall, you didn't divorce him because you hated his guts or even because he was a terrible husband. You divorced him so you could discover who you really are. Now you know. You're a competent, bright, attractive woman. You've taken care of that piece of business. Maybe it's time to reassess your feelings for your ex."

"Liza, please don't start playing amateur psychologist with me," Molly snapped impatiently.

"You're just irritated because you know I'm right."

"Just a few short hours ago, you were encouraging me to consider marrying Michael. I wish you'd make up your mind."

Liza was shaking her head before the statement was out of Molly's mouth. "No. You're the one who needs to make up her mind. Don't hide from your feelings, Molly. If Hal still means something to you, then for goodness' sake, explore it. Don't let foolish pride stand in your way. Just because you made a decision to leave him doesn't mean you can't make another one to go back again."

"And what about the feelings I have for Michael? What am I supposed to do about those?"

A grin slowly spread across Liza's face. "Now, that's more like it. Do you realize that's the first time you've ever admitted you feel something for him?"

"Not so. I've admitted to lusting after him for months. I just don't know if it's ever likely to be anything more than that. I'm not sure he'd ever allow it to be anything more than that." Tired of the entire subject, she said, "Forget it. I can't talk about this anymore. Can we call Patrice yet?"

Liza glanced at her watch. "It's about eight-thirty there. We might wake her, but at least it's a respectable hour."

"I want to listen to the whole conversation," Molly reminded her.

"Then go in the kitchen and pick up the extension as soon as I've finished dialing. I'll tell you when."

Molly waited by the kitchen phone for Liza's signal, then lifted the receiver. She was just in time to hear the hotel operator put the call through to Patrice's room. Since she'd chosen one of London's most expensive hotels, it seemed obvious that Patrice

186

wasn't exactly hiding out. It was the first place anyone in her crowd would have looked for her.

"Yes, hello," Patrice said in an abrupt tone. At least she hadn't been sound asleep.

"Patrice, it's Liza Hastings."

There was a faint hesitation, then a more saccharine response. "Liza, how delightful to hear from you."

To Molly's ear, Patrice sounded surprised, but sincere.

"How on earth did you find me?" she asked.

"I stopped by to see you. Your housekeeper said you were on vacation," Liza said, only slightly skirting the truth. "After that, all it took was some lucky guesswork. I had no idea you were planning to go to London."

"The trip came up unexpectedly. I just felt the need to get away for a bit, have a change of scenery. You know how that is, I'm sure. London is lovely this time of year."

The last Molly had heard they were having a record-setting heat wave. Londoners were fleeing to the shore in droves.

"I'm sure all the publicity surrounding Tessa's death was hard on you," Liza said, alluding to the dead woman's alleged link with Clark Dupree, which had come out in Monday morning's paper.

"If you're referring to her affair with Clark, you needn't mince words. Clark Dupree is a weasel in more ways than one. I'm just sorry I didn't discover it sooner," she said sourly. "Have they locked him up yet?"

It was Liza's turn to hesitate. Molly suspected she, too, was wondering when sexual liaisons had become illegal.

"For what?" Liza said cautiously.

"Tessa's murder, of course. Surely they've figured out by now that he did it."

"Are you certain?" Liza asked.

"Well, of course I am," she said indignantly. "Why else would I have felt the need to get away? I didn't want to sit around and have all my friends pitying me for being duped by that horrible man. I should have known that any man who is unscrupulous enough to take the side of those unconscionable developers should be avoided at all costs. All that pious talk about every defendant deserving equal protection under the law was so much hogwash to justify what he was doing."

"But you've known Clark for years."

"Obviously not as well as I thought I did," she said drily. "Do you honestly think I would consort with a man I thought capable of murder?"

"Patrice, why do you think he did it? Do you have any proof?"

"Who else could it have been? They were having this torrid little affair, right under my nose I might add, and I was too blind to see it."

"There are some who might feel that would give you more cause to murder Tessa than it would Clark," Liza suggested mildly.

"Me?" she said indignantly. "Why on earth would anyone think I'd done it?"

"You did have that altercation with her up in Bal Harbour just a few days before."

"Oh, for heaven's sake, I refused to speak to the little tramp. I didn't pull out a gun and wave it in her face."

"What about the candlestick?"

"What candlestick? What on earth are you talking about?" Patrice said blankly.

Molly would have given anything to jump in and warn Liza that she'd already said far too much, but it was too late. Liza was going to plod through every piece of circumstantial evidence just to see how Patrice would react. If the woman was guilty, she'd be on the next plane out of London and this time she wouldn't be nearly so easy to trace. They'd be lucky if she turned up again for her own funeral.

"One of the candlesticks was missing from

the buffet table," Liza was explaining despite all the warning vibes Molly was trying to send her. "There was some speculation that it might have been used as the murder weapon. It turned up in Neville's office on Monday morning. He noticed it right after you were in there."

Molly could hear Patrice's sharply drawn breath as she put all the hints together and realized what Liza was suggesting. "Dear Lord in heaven, you can't be serious. Are you saying the police think I killed that little twit?"

"It has crossed their minds," Liza conceded.

"You tell that Detective Whatever-his-name-is that I will be on the next plane back to Miami. If one word of his suspicions leaks to the media in the meantime, I will have his sorry little hide hung out to dry. You might also mention to him that he ought to keep close tabs on Clark Dupree's travel plans. He's been salting money away in the Caymans for years."

With that taunt dangling before them, Molly and Liza were left holding a dead line. Molly walked back into the living room, where Liza was looking very pleased with herself.

"I told you she didn't do it," she said smugly.

"Either that or she's one hell of an actress," Molly countered. "Has it occurred to you whose hide is going to be hung out to dry if Patrice MacDonald vanishes without a trace?"

Liza looked slightly taken aback. "Molly, you heard her. She's coming back to defend herself."

"So she says. As Michael likes to point out to me with regularity, someone who's just engaged in murder is hardly likely to be above a little lying." It felt a little odd to suddenly find herself in the role of devil's advocate, Molly decided. Perhaps she ought to leave that, along with all the snide remarks, to Michael.

"Never mind," she said, noting Liza's distraught expression. "I agree with you. I think she'll be here by the end of the day if she has to charter a jet."

"Let us pray," Liza murmured fervently. "Otherwise, I'd just as soon not be around when Michael and Detective Abrams find out she's skipped again. I may be the next one to head for far-off places."

"There are other suspects," Molly pointed out. "If we turn our attention to them and hand over the killer's name, they won't have anything to complain about."

"Good thinking," Liza said, reaching for the legal pad on which she'd been writing coalition press releases while Molly was gone. "Let's get to work."

Molly groaned. "I didn't mean right now. It's the middle of the night and — unlike you — I have a job to get to first thing in the morning."

"It's almost morning now," Liza pointed out. "If you go to sleep for a couple of hours, you'll only feel worse. You might as well stay up."

"All night?" Molly said plaintively.

"Oh, don't be such a wimp. We have a murderer to catch. Who's at the top of the list?"

"Clark Dupree," Molly said resignedly. "Don't forget someone has to look into that Cayman bank account Patrice mentioned."

Liza wrote it down. "And I might as well put down Roger, Patrice, and myself since I know the police haven't given up on us yet."

"Don't forget Hernando Viera. He'd been having an affair with Tessa, too. And I guess we can't leave off Jason Jeffries, though I'm certain he didn't do it."

Those notations made, Liza regarded her speculatively. "Who else?"

"It could have been anyone at the party."

"True, but realistically it must have been someone who knew Tessa well, unless some thief whacked her over the head just to take her jewels."

"Couldn't have been," Molly said. "She was still wearing that diamond ring that is worth a mint."

"So we're back to friends and acquaintances. How about the Willoughbys? And who's that other couple they're with all the time? He's a banker, too."

Molly recalled talking to them after the murder, though she hadn't known them before. "Newton?"

"No, Newcombe," Liza said.

"Right. Harley and Jane. He disliked everyone there," Molly recalled. "I'm not sure he disliked Tessa any more or less than anyone else."

"Maybe he plans to take them all out one by one."

"Liza!"

"Sorry. I'm getting punchy."

"What about Helen Whorton? She and Tessa had apparently been feuding for years. What's that rivalry all about?"

"I doubt they even recalled themselves. Tessa probably snatched all the glory after some event that Helen slaved over. In this crowd, that would certainly do it."

193

"Anyone else?"

Liza shook her head. "Not that I can think of. I'll go over the entire guest list later to see if anything rings a bell. Meantime, shouldn't we divide up these prospects and try to see what we can find out?"

"You know them," Molly reminded her. "I don't. Won't they think it downright peculiar if I come snooping around?"

"When was the last time that stopped you?"

"Okay, let's put it this way. If the opportunity presents itself, I will ask some questions."

Liza grinned in satisfaction. "Molly, dearest, haven't you learned that in life we make our own opportunities?"

Before Molly could respond to that barb, the phone rang. She glanced outside and saw that the sun was already sneaking over the horizon. "Michael, no doubt," she muttered as the phone continued to ring. "What on earth am I supposed to tell him?"

"The truth," Liza suggested.

Molly scowled at her as she grabbed the phone. "Good morning," she said with forced cheer.

"What happened?" Michael asked without preamble.

"I spoke with Hal last night," Molly said,

hoping to divert him. "Thanks for the advice. I think it helped."

"I'm glad, but that's not what I'm talking about and you know it. Since Liza is not at home, I assume she is with you. I also deduce that you were together when she called Patrice MacDonald and have been plotting and scheming ever since."

"Why don't you come over and join us for breakfast?"

"Because I have exactly five minutes before I have to go and testify in a murder case. I would like to go with my mind at rest on other matters. Do you catch my drift here?"

"I do," Molly conceded. "We talked to her."

"And?"

"She's coming home today."

"Was that a decision she made before or after your call?" he inquired suspiciously.

"What does it matter? The point is she's coming home."

"You told her everything, didn't you?" he said, his tone somewhere between resigned and furious.

"I did not," Molly said flatly.

"Okay, Liza did. Don't play games. How much does Mrs. MacDonald know about the current focus of this investigation?"

"Everything," Molly admitted reluctantly, then hurriedly added, "She says Clark Dupree did it."

He groaned. "Terrific. Does she have proof or do we have another amateur detective on our hands?"

"You don't have to be so cranky."

"Yes. I do," he said succinctly. "You two better spend today praying that our prime suspect shows her face."

"I would like to point out that you're the one who said we could call her," Molly retorted.

"I trusted you to use some discretion."

"We did the best we could."

"I'm sure," he muttered along with a few phrases of Spanish, which Molly felt sure were better left untranslated.

"He's furious," Liza guessed when Molly had hung up.

"I'd say that's an understatement. In fact, if you and I know what's good for us, we'll have this case solved before the end of the day or we'll be behind bars ourselves."

Liza looked startled. "He's that mad?"

"Mad enough to charge us with obstruction of justice, I'd say."

Liza ripped the yellow legal paper across the middle and handed half to Molly. "Then let's get busy."

"Has it occurred to you that if we start running around questioning suspects, it will only add fuel to the fire?"

Liza shrugged. "Not if we catch the killer. That ought to take the wind right out of his sails."

13

Since none of Molly's admittedly half-hearted protests had swayed Liza's new-found determination, it was fortunate that her boss at the film office chose to spend the day on the golf course again — doing business, according to him. Whatever, it left Molly free to indulge her best sleuthing techniques. Jeannette, however, scowled disapprovingly every time she started to make a phone call related to the case. Molly finally sent her to the location of a commercial shoot just so she wouldn't have to operate under her coworker's worried scrutiny.

Unfortunately, none of the calls she made turned up one single piece of evidence, much less a solid hint on motive. Hell, they didn't even turn up any of the suspects. Not even Ted Ryan, whom she'd planned to pump for information, was in his office. She decided against trying to track the reporter down at police headquarters, where Detective Abrams might get wind of her nosing around. He might take it well, but it wasn't his reaction she was worried about. Michael would blow sky-high.

Thoroughly frustrated, she opted finally for going to lunch. She would spend the hour trying to clear her head and consuming enough caffeine to keep her awake through the rest of the day. Tonight, if she had any energy left at all, she would kill Liza for getting her into this sorry state of exhaustion.

The players continued to taunt her as she drove from the Vizcaya gatehouse that contained the film office into the Grove. With Roger and Liza both more or less accounted for at the approximate time of Tessa's murder and Patrice MacDonald swearing she was innocent, Molly couldn't get Hernando Viera's affair with Tessa out of her mind. It had all the elements needed for a crime of passion.

What if Hernando had discovered that his mistress was already casting her eye about for another conquest? If Jason Jeffries was to be believed, the chase was far more important to Tessa than any lasting relationship, marital or illicit. That would explain her alleged affair with Clark Dupree.

Or, what if Caroline Viera knew all about her husband's fling and had tired of it? She might have challenged Tessa that night, argued heatedly with her, then cracked her over the skull with that silver candlestick. And then dragged her body all the way to the bay? Molly thought. Not likely. Still, she couldn't rule out anything.

By now the police must have retrieved the weapon from Neville's office. If Patrice hadn't taken it there, could Caroline Viera have been cool and composed enough to sneak it back into the caterer's domain? From what Molly had seen of her, yes. But her guesswork was no substitute for having a cozy little chat with the woman, who just happened to be sitting down for lunch — alone — across the crowded outdoor terrace of one of Cocowalk's liveliest restaurants in the heart of the Grove.

Molly squeezed between tables and gave Caroline one of her friendliest smiles. "How are you? Do you mind if I join you?"

Molly thought she caught a tiny flicker of fear in Caroline's eyes before she gestured resignedly.

"Of course not. I hate eating alone."

"So do I, especially in a place like this. Everyone always seems paired off. Do you come here often?"

"Whenever I have an appointment in this part of town. Several of my accounts are in Coconut Grove."

Caroline pushed her unopened menu aside as if to confirm that she knew every one of its appetizer-portion items by heart. Molly trumped the move with her own menu and a wave to get the attention of the waiter.

When their orders had been placed, Caroline surprised Molly by asking, "Have you heard anything about Tessa's murder?"

"Only that the list of suspects is no shorter than it was on the night it happened. What about you? Surely with Hernando's connections, he must have heard rumors." If the phrase *Hernando's connections* carried a double meaning for Caroline, she managed to hide her reaction. The woman was definitely a master of the polite mask.

"He hasn't mentioned anything to me," she said. "Of course, sometimes we're like two ships that pass in the night. We both have incredible business and social demands. Often we don't get home until midnight and Hernando is always out of the house at the crack of dawn."

Caroline's classic, angular face showed signs of the same weariness and resignation evident in her voice. Of course, guilt could be taxing, Molly thought just as Caroline added, "I don't know how Hernando does it."

"But I'm sure his dedication is one of the things that attracted you," Molly ventured, noting that Caroline seemed to diminish her own not inconsequential accomplishments and hectic schedule when comparing them to her husband's.

"That and the fact that he was terrific in bed," Caroline said with astonishing bluntness. It was the kind of remark deliberately meant to catch the listener off guard.

Dutifully startled, Molly met her gaze and saw that her lovely aquamarine eyes were filled with amusement.

"You're really no good at this," Caroline said. "If you want to know whether I know about Hernando's affair with Tessa, why don't you just ask me?"

Molly tried to hide her chagrin. "Obviously you do know," she said, then matched bluntness with candor. "Did you before the night of the murder?"

Caroline laughed, a full-bodied sound, rather than the nervous titter of someone guilty of a crime. "So you can be direct. Good. Perhaps we can be friends, after all. Yes, I knew all about the affair before that night. I also knew about the dozen or more before Tessa and the half dozen waiting in the wings. I knew when I married Hernando fifteen years ago that he was no saint and that I wasn't going to be the one to change him. Our marriage, however, has its compensations."

"Which are?"

"I thought I'd mentioned the primary one."

"The sex. I suppose it comes from all that practice," Molly said before she could stop herself.

"Indeed," Caroline agreed drily. "Though these days I must admit I worry far more about the consequences of that than I did before."

"AIDS," Molly surmised.

"Yes."

"Still, I guess I can rule out your flying into a jealous rage that night and killing Tessa."

"Why on earth would I? Hernando had dismissed her and moved on. Frankly, if your friend Liza weren't so quick on her feet, I suspect she'd be next in line. She's gorgeous and intelligent. I believe Hernando describes her as a real hellion, something he definitely admires in a woman."

Molly decided it wasn't up to her to defend Liza's moral standards. She regarded

Caroline with a certain amount of admiration. "Why am I beginning to suspect that a hellion is exactly what he got with you?"

Caroline nodded with evident satisfaction. "I may have to change my assessment, Molly. You might be quite good at this, after all."

She glanced at the delicate, expensive gold watch on her wrist. The gesture also showed off an impressive diamond adorning a wide gold band on her ring finger. Either Caroline's business was extremely successful or Hernando paid for his transgressions with jewelry.

"My goodness, look at the time," she said. "I have to run." She took a twenty out of her purse and put it on the table. "Lunch is on me this time. Let's do it again soon."

She picked up her Gucci briefcase and hurried off before Molly could protest her paying the bill or even say goodbye.

When she'd gone, Molly drew out the list she and Liza had compiled and scratched Caroline Viera's name off. Just as she did, a hand reached over her shoulder and plucked the paper off the table.

"What have we here?" Michael inquired, slipping into the chair just vacated by Caroline Viera. He'd dressed formally for his day in court. The dark pin-striped suit and pristine white shirt spoke more of Wall Street than it did Metro-Dade police headquarters. He looked drop-dead gorgeous, just as he had on the day they'd met.

Molly ignored the traitorous quickening of her pulse and regarded him warily. "What are you doing here?"

"Just hunting down suspects. How about you?"

"Am I a suspect now?"

"Nope, but who says I came here looking for you?"

Chagrined, Molly stared at him silently. He winked.

"Actually, I was told I'd find Caroline Viera here, but she was just taking off as I got to the front door. Then I caught a glimpse of you out here and figured you'd done all the advance work for me."

"Oh?"

He glanced at the menu, ordered the pizza with sun-dried tomatoes, then regarded Molly with evident curiosity. "Is she guilty?"

"I don't appreciate your making fun of me," she said stiffly. "I'm trying to help."

He held up his hands in a placating gesture. "I know that. And, actually, my question was a serious one. What's your take on Mrs. Viera?"

"Not guilty," she said succinctly and with

complete conviction.

"No reasonable doubt?"

Molly's defensiveness fell away under his prodding. "I thought that applied to guilt, but no. I'm absolutely convinced she had no motive."

"Not even her husband's affair with Tessa."

"That's nothing out of the ordinary to hear her tell it."

"She doesn't object to his affairs?"

"Apparently not."

Michael looked doubtful. "Do you buy that understanding-woman crap?"

"Surprisingly enough, in this case, yes. And if she had finally gotten fed up, wouldn't she have killed Hernando rather than Tessa?"

"You have a point there. So who's next on this list of yours?" he asked.

"Hernando."

"What about Clark Dupree? I thought he was Mrs. MacDonald's first choice."

"He's on Liza's list."

"Lord, help me, now I've got two of you to keep tabs on?" he said with a moan. "Couldn't you work in tandem, so I can keep track of you?"

"We figured we didn't have much time. If the killer's not in custody by the end of the day, we had a hunch you'd drag us in for obstructing justice."

"The thought had crossed my mind," he admitted. "But I decided to leave that in the hands of the cop officially in charge of this case. Lucky for you, so far he hasn't heard about what the two of you did when you alerted Patrice MacDonald to the police interest in her whereabouts."

Molly breathed a sigh of relief. "Thank you."

"Don't thank me yet. Just pray his suspect turns up."

"Or that we come up with a better one," Molly countered.

"That would do," he agreed.

Molly regarded him curiously. "Are you officially on or off this case?"

"Officially, off. But Abrams has said he'd be more than glad of all the unofficial help I can offer."

"Which makes your status only slightly better than mine," Molly said with satisfaction. "Want to go with me to see Hernando?"

"What's your excuse for dropping in?"

"I thought I'd make a donation to Tessa's memorial fund. He's in charge."

Michael nodded, then took a last sip of his iced tea. "Let's go."

They found Hernando Viera in his spartan office atop the downtown skyscraper where his bank was headquartered. The only thing lavish was the view of Biscayne Bay and the whitecapped waves of the Atlantic before them. On the bay at full mast was a tall ship, which took tourists out of Bayside on a tour along the Brickell Avenue skyline, under the Rickenbacker Causeway and past Vizcaya, the scene of the crime.

"Thank you for seeing us without an appointment," Molly said to the bank president, who'd obviously taken the downfall of another banker down the street to heart. The most expensive thing in the office was Hernando's custom-tailored suit in a shade of gunmetal gray that matched the distinguished traces in his hair and mustache. Everything else in the office was tasteful, but barely more than functional. If he had any art objects or gold fixtures around, they were well hidden.

"It's always a pleasure," he said. "What can I do for the two of you?"

"We wanted to see how Tessa's memorial fund is coming. I have a contribution right here," Molly said, taking a check from her purse. She'd drawn it on the trust fund set up by her parents years ago, money she'd sworn she'd never touch except in a dire emergency. In this instance, the cause seemed worthy of breaking that vow. She supposed there was a certain bitter irony in the fact that she knew they'd object to the cause.

"Wonderful," Hernando said, putting the check in a stack on his desk without glancing at the amount. "Actually, the fund is doing quite well. I think Roger and Liza will be pleased. Has Liza given any thought to how the funds would be disbursed?"

Molly shook her head. "I don't believe so, but she is planning an emergency meeting of the coalition board this week. I'm sure that will be on the agenda." She glanced at Michael as she prepared to shift gears in the way they'd discussed on the drive downtown. "Hernando, have you noticed anything unusual about the contributions made thus far?"

His gaze narrowed thoughtfully. "Unusual in what way?"

"Perhaps from someone unexpected? Perhaps in an amount larger than expected?"

"No, but then I haven't been looking for anything like that. I've just been grateful for every dollar that came in for Tessa's sake."

"Could we see the list of donors?"

"I don't see why not. It'll certainly be a

matter of public record once it's turned over to the coalition anyway. Nonprofits are very careful about their record keeping." He pulled a folder from his desk drawer and handed it to Molly. She passed it straight on to Michael.

As he studied the pages in the folder, Molly tried to find an inoffensive way to phrase her next question. There wasn't one. "Hernando, your relationship with Tessa . . ."

He sighed wearily. "Puts me on the list of suspects. I know that. It was over for Tessa and me. Quite some time ago, as a matter of fact. I believe she considered me a daring indulgence."

Molly was startled by the odd description. "Why on earth would she feel that way?"

"Surely, you know that those in Tessa's circle have yet to fully adapt to the new Miami. Many of them resent the Cubans, whom they feel have taken over. I am tolerated in those circles, because I have a certain power, but I am not liked. If Tessa had chosen to have an affair with a declared criminal, it would have been no less risky for her."

To Molly's astonishment there was little bitterness in his voice, just resignation, perhaps even a measure of understanding for those Anglos who'd been unable to adapt readily to the new Miami power structure in which they were no longer in the majority.

"But despite everything, you and Roger seemed almost cordial the other day," she said. "If what you say is true, wouldn't he be outraged by the affair?"

"Perhaps things are not as they seem," he suggested enigmatically.

Michael glanced up at that, indicating that he had not been quite as absorbed in the paperwork as he'd led them to believe. "In what way?"

"Roger Lafferty owes a great deal of money to this bank. That is yet another reason for him to resent me. However, it is also an excellent reason to remain on friendly terms. Despite his business reversals, Roger is no fool. However he feels about me personally, he will not allow those feelings to show in public. In fact, he has found himself of necessity being my champion among his friends."

"Could all that resentment have boiled over the night of the gala?"

"You mean could he have taken it out on Tessa, since he didn't dare take it out on me? Possible, but doubtful. You see, for all of his indignation over her behavior, Roger still loved Tessa."

"There's a rumor that he planned to divorce her," Molly said.

Hernando appeared genuinely startled by that. "I doubt it. I don't think he would ever have willingly let her go."

"And if she pressed for a divorce, insisted on it?" Michael asked.

Hernando looked troubled as he contemplated that. "Then, yes," he said very softly, regretfully. "Under such a circumstance, he might very well have killed her, rather than let her go."

14

There were far too many unanswered questions about Roger Lafferty, in Molly's opinion. In Michael's, too, for that matter. She could see it in his eyes when Hernando admitted that Roger was capable of killing Tessa to keep from losing her.

However, when she broached the possibility of paying another visit to the bereaved widower, Michael balked, digging in his heels with all the machismo he was capable of mustering.

"No way. Absolutely not. Forget it." He peered at her intently. "Have I made myself clear?"

She flinched under that steady gaze, though she was somewhat less intimidated than she would have been a few months earlier. "Perfectly. So, what do we do next?"

"Nothing. You go back to work. I go back to work. And we let Detective Abrams do his job."

"That is getting to be a very old refrain," Molly pointed out.

"But a prudent one," he said, dropping a light kiss on her forehead. This time it didn't have the dizzying effect he'd probably hoped for. Molly was still thinking clearly and resentfully.

"Go back to work," he repeated. He pointed in the general direction of South Miami Avenue to make sure she got the message.

"Back to work," she repeated prudently. "Right."

By the time she reached her car in the bank's parking garage, she'd already figured out whom she could speak to about Roger without violating Michael's direct order. It was certainly convenient, too, that Clark Dupree's luxurious suite of legal offices was on Brickell, right on her way back to the film office.

Molly noted right off that representing big-time developers obviously paid a bundle. Clark's teal carpet was every bit as thick as Jason Jeffries's down the block. The art in the reception area was by Jackson Pollock and other lesser-known, but no less pricey, contemporary American masters. Maybe it was just an aura created by the classic, subdued gallery lighting, but Molly was certain the paintings were the real thing.

"May I help you?"

The voice was low, cultured, and classy enough to do voice-overs on British television productions. Molly decided the accent was a nice touch. She could see how it would appeal to Clark's desire to create a refined image. It probably made the sleazy characters he represented feel cultured as well. Too bad it was deceptive.

"I'd like to see Mr. Dupree," Molly told the woman whose thick waves of honey-colored hair skimmed shoulders clad in tasteful silk. "I'm Molly DeWitt."

"Do you have an appointment?"

She gave a cursory glance at the mammoth, leather-bound appointment book, but she knew as well as Molly did what she'd find there. Or what she wouldn't. She probably memorized his calendar by eight each morning.

"No, actually, I was hoping to catch him between appointments." Molly offered an apologetic smile. "I know how busy he must be, but if you could fit me in for just a few minutes, I swear I won't take up much of his time."

"Is this an emergency of some sort?"

"Life or death," Molly said without batting an eye.

The woman's gaze turned unexpectedly kind and gentle. "I'll do the best I can."

Every boss should have a receptionist like this one, Molly thought. She was better than Muzak at soothing anxious visitors. While she prepared to wait, Molly took a seat on a chair upholstered in an elegant fabric that reminded her of something she'd seen in Vizcaya. If Clark outfitted his office like this, what on earth must his home be like? she wondered.

She tried to listen as the receptionist spoke to someone deep in the suite's interior, but that cultured voice had dropped to a discreet murmur. Occasional glances in Molly's direction suggested she was the primary topic of conversation.

Finally, the receptionist turned to Molly with a pleased expression. "Mrs. Murchison will see you now."

Molly regarded her blankly. "Who is she?"

"Mr. Dupree's executive assistant. I'm sure she'll be able to help you."

The only help Molly needed was getting past this efficient, feminine security system. She took a chance that Mrs. Murchison would be less stalwart than the receptionist. She had her doubts. She had a hunch the security got tighter the closer one got to the inner sanctum.

Sure enough, Mrs. Murchison looked her over as if checking for weapons. "I'm afraid Mr. Dupree's calendar doesn't permit unscheduled appointments," she said, after deciding that Molly was neither dangerous, nor in grave danger of dropping dead on the spot. Other emergencies probably didn't count for much around here.

"Five minutes," Molly said, trying not to beg. "I swear I won't take any longer than that."

"I'm sorry, but Mr. Dupree is out of the office at the moment anyway."

Molly regarded her doubtfully. Why would either one of these women have gone through with this charade if that were true? The first wave of the guard would have sent her packing. Unfortunately, she couldn't see any way to call her on it short of declaring her a liar or plopping into a chair and waiting to see if Clark eventually came into or out of his office. It hardly seemed worth the energy, especially when she had no concrete plan for effectively cross-examining him once she got inside.

She removed one of her business cards from her purse and handed it to Mrs. Murchison. As she did, she glanced at the bank of phone lines. Several were lit. Two were blinking, but another two were clearly engaged. There were no other legal partners, to Molly's knowledge, not even space for a law clerk. Therefore, unless the receptionist had the ability to speak with more than one person at a time, Clark Dupree himself was on that other line. She gestured toward the phone.

"Give him the card when he gets off the phone and ask him to call me when he gets a chance," she said, leaving the woman staring after her in openmouthed astonishment.

Disgruntled by her lack of success and curious about Clark Dupree's apparent reticence to see her, she was halfway back to the office when she remembered Josie, the Laffertys' dedicated housekeeper. Josie clearly had tales to tell. Molly wondered if she'd care to tell them to her.

She made a quick right turn off Brickell and headed over to Coral Way, then drove on through the Gables to the Lafferty house. Though there were no cars in the driveway this time, she intended to take no chances on encountering Roger. If she could get past the guard without being questioned, she'd go around to the side door and look for Josie in the kitchen.

The guard, the same one who'd been on duty on her last visit, waved — either in recognition or as a signal of general apathy, then went back to the magazine he'd been reading. Apparently, it was absorbing enough or he was so unobservant that he didn't notice her odd route straight past the front door and around to the side of the house.

If Josie was surprised to see her at the kitchen door, she hid it well. Maybe she'd just been around so long that nothing much struck her as peculiar. She waved Molly into the kitchen.

"I've been baking a bit," she announced unnecessarily. The huge room with its restaurant-size stove and ovens was fragrant with the sweet aroma of fruit pies and the nutty, cinnamon scent of coffee cakes. The results of her labors were lined up along one tiled counter. If she did many more, she'd have to open a bakery to get rid of them all.

"Can't seem to keep my mind on anything else," she explained with a shrug. "I figure we'll be needing these before things are done. If not, they freeze up right well. You want to try a piece of my strawberry pie? Ain't nothing like it in any of those fancy restaurants around town." She chuckled. "I know that 'cause I've had a couple of big-time caterers beg me to turn over that recipe."

"Neville Foster was one of them, I'll bet," Molly said as she took the first mouth-watering bite of the sweet concoction with a crust so flaky it melted. "Josie, you deserve a place of honor in heaven for your baking. Neville's customers have probably had this pie here and dreamed of serving it in their own homes."

"Wouldn't give it to the likes of him," she said with an indignant huff.

There was so much derision in her tone that Molly regarded her in astonishment. "You don't like him?"

"He's a sneaky little so-and-so. Wouldn't put it past him to snoop through my cupboards trying to steal my recipes. Caught him at it once, in fact. He claimed he was looking for the rest of the champagne glasses, but he couldn't fool me." She winked at Molly. "Lot of good it did him. I got my recipes hidden where no one can get at 'em." She tapped her head. "Every one of 'em is right up here."

Molly nearly moaned at the thought of losing all those old-fashioned recipes if Josie didn't pass them on before she died. Obviously, for the moment though, the tough old bird had no intention of dying or giving away her secrets. Molly ate the last crumb of her pie and drank some of the herbal iced tea Josie had poured for her. The house-keeper was regarding her speculatively.

"I suppose you got a reason for dropping by to see old Josie?"

Molly considered trying to finesse her way around the old woman's sharp intuition, but opted for being straightforward instead.

"I'm trying to figure some things out," she said candidly. "I've got all these questions going around in my head. I thought maybe you could help me fill in some of the blanks."

"About Miss Tessa?" Josie said, losing some of her vim and vigor. She suddenly looked her age.

"That's right."

"It surely doesn't make a bit of sense to me either," she said, sitting down heavily. "Why would someone go killing a lady like her?"

"You said yourself that she had her flaws."

"She did that, but not the sort of things to go getting killed over," she declared indignantly. "She made Mr. Roger madder than a wet hen sometimes, but I never heard him say a mean word to her."

"They didn't argue?"

"No more than most married folks."

"I'd heard he was thinking of divorcing her."

221

Josie looked convincingly shocked. "Never! Not Mr. Roger. He didn't believe in divorce."

"I thought she'd been divorced before."

"That was all in the past. Had nothing to do with the two of them. Besides, he adored that woman, no matter what. He turned a blind eye to her faults. Now, if her own husband could put up with all her craziness, who else would have reason to hurt her?"

"By all her craziness, I assume you mean the other men," Molly said carefully.

Josie hesitated, clearly uncertain over whether an admission could be considered disloyal. Apparently, she decided it was too late to worry about such things. She nodded. "It puzzles me why a high-class woman would behave like that. It just wasn't right and I told her so more than once. She had everything she could ever need or want. Mr. Roger saw to that. She said to me herself that he was a saint." Josie shook her head sorrowfully. "Didn't make no difference. There was always some other man waiting in the wings."

"Any particular man lately?"

"She never told me their names 'cause she knew I disapproved. I could just tell when there was a new one on the horizon." She

222

regarded Molly confidingly. "You know what the problem was? Low self-esteem. I saw that on Oprah or Geraldo, one of them shows. It was all about women who need a new man all the time to prove how desirable they are. If I'd been able to figure out that fancy VCR machine in the other room, I'd have put that on tape and made Miss Tessa watch it a time or two till she saw things right again." She shook her head. "Low self-esteem. Who would have thought it?"

The concept clearly bemused her almost as much as it distressed her that Tessa might have been a victim of the syndrome.

"But why would Tessa have low self-esteem?" Molly asked, trying to reconcile that with the image of arrogance she presented to the world.

"Now that's a question you'd have to be asking one of them fancy head doctors."

"Are you sure about that? Low self-esteem usually begins in childhood. You said you were hired by her family when she was still a girl. What were her parents like?"

"They were fine people," Josie insisted. "Helped me educate my brothers and sisters. Got 'em all through high school. Two of my brothers even went on to college, thanks to her daddy's help. Same college

Miss Tessa's brother went to."

"What about Tessa? Did she go to college?"

Josie looked perplexed by the question. "Now, why would she need to do that? She had her path in life all cut out for her. She had plenty of money to see that she made the right kind of marriage. Wasn't no need for her to get some fancy education that would just be wasted."

"Is that what her father said?" Molly asked, beginning to get the picture.

"Told her that time and again," Josie confirmed.

"So she wanted to go to college?"

"Had some crazy fool notion about becoming a business tycoon. She wanted to run her daddy's company someday, but everybody knew her brother was going to do that, so what was the point? If you ask me, she should have been satisfied with the way things were."

Maybe so, Molly thought as she drove off a short time later. Maybe Tessa should have played by the rules of the day and been satisfied, but obviously that niche envisioned by her shortsighted father hadn't been enough for her. No wonder she'd constantly sought the approval of powerful, successful men. She'd wanted to prove she could hold her own with any one of them.

For the first time since the investigation had begun, Molly began to feel desperately sorry for the pathetic life Tessa had led in her ill-fated quest for proof that she was somebody important. She couldn't help wondering if that same quest wasn't in some obscure way responsible for her murder.

15

Molly was so intent on learning all she could about Tessa's need for approval and yearning for business success, she didn't notice at first that Vince had finally wandered back to the office.

"Where have you been?" her boss demanded, glancing pointedly at the oversize clock on the wall. The look was mostly for effect. The clock hadn't been right for months now.

"You're in a charming mood," she observed. "What happened? Did you double bogey on the eighteenth hole?"

"The game isn't everything," he shot back, scowling ferociously. "I conduct business on the golf course. I was trying to close a deal out there."

"Oh?"

"I might have done it if I'd been able to reach anyone in this office for some information. Instead, all I got was a recording.

Why the hell should I have a staff, if no one's ever here?"

Molly took the attack in stride. Naturally, now that Vince was off the golf course, he wanted everyone to be as miserable and put-upon as he was. It was Vincent Gates's nature to present a long-suffering facade to the world. He thought it would keep his job secure if his superiors thought he was dreadfully overburdened with work.

"What information did you need?" she inquired sweetly. "I'll be happy to get it and follow up with a phone call to the producer."

"Never mind," he grumbled, clearly happy sulking. "I've taken care of it. Where's Jeannette?" He gave a furtive glance around as if to assure himself she wasn't lurking in the vicinity ready to cast some evil spell over him.

"On location. When are you going to admit that she's the best clerk we've ever had in here and put in for a promotion for her?"

"Don't start on me again."

"You're hoping she'll just give up and go away, aren't you? I've told her she ought to do just that. She's overqualified for this job. Any other boss would appreciate her."

"I do appreciate her. She just makes me

nervous. You've seen the way she looks at me."

Molly bit back a grin. Jeannette's cool, superior looks embodied disdain, not malevolence, but Vince would never believe that. It was probably best not to explain either. He was already regarding her suspiciously.

"I suppose you were on location, too?"

"Nope. I had some personal business to take care of."

Vince didn't have to ponder that more than a heartbeat before he caught on. He rolled his eyes in exasperation. "Not again. Tell me you were not out snooping around on that murder investigation."

She remained stoically silent.

He watched her intently. "You were, weren't you? That's exactly what you were doing. When will you ever learn?" He held up his hands in a gesture of resignation. "I give up. The next time I get called on the carpet by some county official because you can't stay out of things that are none of your concern, you are out of here. Adios. Goodbye. Is that clear?"

Molly nodded obediently, which usually made Vince feel powerful again. "Must have been a triple bogey," she muttered under her breath as she returned to her desk.

"I heard that," he shouted after her.

Hopefully, he wouldn't hear her conversation with Jason Jeffries, she thought as she dialed the philanthropist's office. She had to check out this one last thing while it was on her mind. Then she vowed to get busy and actually do some film office business. It would pacify Vince if he ended the day with a stack of folders on prospective productions sitting on his desk. He could complain to his date all evening about how backed up he was at work.

"What sort of information are you after this time, young lady?" the old man said, an affectionate note behind the cranky question.

"I want to talk about Tessa a minute."

"What about her?"

"Josie . . ."

"Her housekeeper? I didn't even know she was still alive. She must be a hundred, if she's a day."

"She says she's seventy. She also told me that Tessa had some crazy notion of becoming a business tycoon and that her father thwarted her because he didn't see any need to educate a woman."

"Never heard it told quite that way, but I suppose it's true enough," he conceded. "Tessa envied that brother of hers. She resented the fact that he was destined to inherit the business, while all she got was some trust fund. She'd been daddy's little darling all her life until the time came to divvy up the estate. Then he put her in her place. Wasn't all that unusual given the way things worked in those days."

"Could she have run the business?"

Jason gave a snort of derision. "I told you about the books on those fund-raisers. Does that sound like the kind of woman who could manage a big corporation? Tessa had grandiose ideas, but not an ounce of sense when it came to carrying them out. If you ask me, her daddy knew exactly what he was doing. Hell, I doled out her alimony payments a little at a time, because I knew damned well she'd throw it all away and come begging for more if I didn't."

"Thanks," Molly said, unwilling to get into a debate over whether Tessa might have learned to handle money if she'd been given a little responsibility and education. It was too late for such a discussion to do the woman a bit of good, and she doubted if Jason was likely to change his sexist ways at this late date either.

Unless Liza could turn him around. The thought of the struggle brought a smile to her lips.

"I don't know why any of that's important,

but you're welcome," he said. His tone sobered. "You watch where you go sniffing around, young lady. Whoever killed Tessa might see a need to get rid of you, too, if you start getting too close to the truth."

Coming from any of the other principal suspects, Molly might have considered that a mild threat. Coming from Jason Jeffries, it seemed no more than a friendly, concerned warning. She took it to heart.

That didn't stop her from trying to add things up one more time. What if Tessa, in her zeal to prove that she was capable of handling business as well as any man, had gotten herself in over her head? They'd assumed all along that Roger was responsible for whatever financial difficulties he was having, but what if it had been Tessa's foolish decisions that had been their downfall?

Perhaps that had been the one thing Roger couldn't forgive, despite Josie's faith that he would tolerate any of Tessa's myriad sins. Not all that long ago there had been stories in Japan about wives who'd lost the family savings in the stock market and were so terrified of their husbands' wrath that they committed suicide or begged their brokers to hide the truth. Maybe Tessa had suffered a similar humiliation and had infuriated Roger in the process.

Molly decided she needed to see all the suspects together if she was ever going to fully understand the dynamics of the group. For that, she needed Liza's help. If Vince's menacing scowl was anything to go by, however, she figured she'd better wait to ask her.

"Liza, why don't you organize that emergency coalition meeting you've been talking about?" Molly suggested later that night after concluding a reasonably productive afternoon at the office under Vince's watchful eye. "I suppose we could wait for the memorial service, but I heard it's been delayed until late next week. I don't want to put this off that long. I think it would be fascinating to see what the primary topic of conversation is about now, don't you?"

Liza regarded her doubtfully. "You don't honestly expect the killer to confess sometime between the reading of the minutes and old business, do you?"

"I'm not even sure I expect him or her to show up."

"Meaning?"

"We're not dealing with a professional killer here. Whoever murdered Tessa probably did it on the spur of the moment. Unless he or she has absolutely no conscience,

232

the person who tossed Tessa into the bay might find it incredibly awkward to be surrounded by all of her dearest friends."

"Friends?"

"You know what I mean. Who's on the coalition board?"

"Patrice, Mary Ann Willoughby, Helen Whorton, Jason Jeffries, Hernando Viera, and Clark Dupree are on the executive board. The overall committee is much larger. Which group do you want?"

"I'd say the executive board covers the key people. Can you meet in closed session?"

"Not really. We take the Sunshine Law to heart. All our meetings are open."

"I suppose it doesn't really matter. What about Roger? Can you lure him there?"

Liza considered the question, her expression thoughtful. "I suppose I could ask him so we can make the official announcement of Tessa's memorial fund."

Molly nodded. "Perfect."

Liza shook her head. "Why do I think that instead of inviting them to a meeting, I should simply announce 'let the games begin'?"

"An interesting alternative," Molly concurred. "But this is no game. Whoever killed Tessa obviously had a lot more than we know at stake and I want to know what that was."

16

Molly wouldn't have believed the viciousness if she hadn't been seeing it with her own eyes. A half dozen of the best-known names in Miami's philanthropic circles — male and female — were engaged in cutthroat politics that made Republican and Democratic rivalries look like kid stuff.

Observers from several organizations had learned of the meeting of the coalition's executive board and had shown up to stick in their two cents. Michael O'Hara and Detective Abrams, after casting pleased looks at their suspect, just back from London, were lurking in the back of the room, trying to look unobtrusive. They weren't succeeding, but their presence definitely wasn't hampering the discussion or Patrice MacDonald's glares in their direction.

In the absence of a chairman, Liza explained that she had called the group together to discuss the future of the consortium of environmental activists. Their common interests should have assured a certain unanimity.

Instead, the supporters of the Everglades were casting venomous glances at the bird people, who in turn were scowling at those in support of the manatees. The representatives of one of the nation's most active environmental preservation organizations were regarding Florida Keys protectionists with visible disdain.

Helen Whorton, Tessa's most outspoken rival, was surveying the scene with satisfaction. From the sidelines where Molly had determinedly planted herself despite Liza's request that she sit around the conference table, Molly guessed Helen was just waiting for the right opportunity to leap graciously into the leadership breach. She was shooting daggers at Liza because she hadn't gotten out of the way.

Jason Jeffries, clearly an independent thinker and a member of every organization represented, winked at Liza. "Go get 'em," he said in what was no doubt meant to be an undertone but which boomed to the back of the room. Startled glances turned in his direction.

"Ladies and gentlemen," Liza said so softly that those present had to quiet down or risk missing something they might find irritating. "If we continue to focus on our divided loyalties, rather than the unified mission we need so desperately to complete, we will have no chance at all."

"Well said," Jeffries commented, waving his cigar approvingly. It was unlit in deference to Molly. "I'll nominate you to chair this group. Who'll second it?"

"Now, wait just one minute, Jason Jeffries!" Helen Whorton glared at him. "You won't go ramrodding your opinion down our throats this time."

"That's right," Mary Ann Willoughby chimed in, then looked startled that she'd found herself on the same side as Tessa's most vociferous enemy.

"There is a motion on the floor," Liza said firmly. "It requires a second before we can have this discussion."

"I'll second," said a timid voice belonging to a woman who looked as if she ought to be traipsing the trails of the Everglades with a pair of binoculars in her hands. To get Liza's attention, she allowed her fingers to flutter in the air for no more than an instant before demurely folding her hands in her lap again.

"Thank you," Liza said, giving her an appreciative smile. "Now, Helen, what were you saying?"

"I was saying that I will not allow that man to push this through."

"Oh, for goodness' sake, Helen, sit down and shut up," said a tall string bean of a man who was gray from head to toe — hair, suit, socks, shoes, even his complexion had an unhealthy gray pallor. Since he'd said the first sensible thing in the past few minutes, Molly hoped he didn't pass out before they could take a vote.

"You know perfectly well that Liza is the only one here who's actually put her money and her time into this," he declared with annoyance. "She's been to the rain forests. She's protested the haphazard forestry in Washington and Oregon. She's been to Capitol Hill to speak out. She's prepared position papers and lobbied Congress. What the dickens have you ever done besides yammer about it?"

Helen's eyes widened with shock. "How dare you, Lincoln Granview? My name alone counts for plenty and I have given generous donations to these causes besides."

"When it suited your purposes," he countered. "You want the social power. I saw you scrambling to get in one of those pictures for the society pages in the morning paper. Plunked yourself right in there

238

next to Tessa, even though everyone knows you hated her guts. You want to appear politically correct. But you obviously don't give a damn about the environment or you wouldn't have allowed your husband to strip that land in the Keys bare before he built on it."

An outraged murmur built in the room until Molly had visions of a lynch mob being formed. Given the passion with which these people regarded their individual causes, it didn't require a giant leap of faith to accept the possibility that one of them might have murdered Tessa if they felt she'd betrayed them. Molly could hardly wait to question Liza about how each of the attendees had interacted with the recently departed chairwoman, about how much faith they'd had in her dedication to the cause.

"That's enough," Liza said, quieting things down again. "The floor is open to additional nominations." She glanced pointedly at her most vocal critic. "Helen?"

"I suppose there's no point in my going against the majority." She scowled first at Liza, then at Lincoln Granview, finally settling her gaze on Jason Jeffries. "You will get yours one of these days. If not here on earth, then I'm certain there's a special hell waiting for you."

That said, she pulled herself to her feet and stalked from the room.

"Good riddance," Jeffries muttered. "Now, let's get on with business. Call for a vote, Liza."

Liza frowned at him. "Jason, if you don't stop giving me orders, people here might begin to wonder if Helen wasn't right to object to my nomination."

He beamed back at her approvingly. "Well said. You'll do just fine, girl."

Just then Ted Ryan slipped into the room and made his way straight to Molly's side. Michael shot her a wry look as he observed the maneuver.

"What did I miss?" the journalist asked, pulling out his pocket tape recorder and a notebook.

"Liza has been nominated to chair the group. They're about to vote."

"Where's the old battle-ax?" he inquired, glancing around.

Molly regarded him with feigned innocence. "Who?"

"Old lady Whorton."

"I believe she had another pressing engagement," Molly said, deciding that the less said in the media about today's squabble, the better for all concerned. If Helen wanted to make a fool of herself in print, let her call Ted herself and fill him in.

With Liza's election approved by the majority in a vote taken by secret ballot at Mary Ann's insistence, Molly sat back and waited for the routine business of the group to be concluded.

Several mundane reports were given regarding the status of various projects. To her disappointment, none struck Molly as being particularly controversial.

Liza called for new business. When no one spoke out, she said, "We do have two things I'd like to mention. First, I would like to formally express the board's condolences to Roger Lafferty."

Sympathetic glances were cast in his direction. He acknowledged them with a nod.

"As many of you know, Roger graciously determined to open a memorial fund in Tessa's honor. Hernando, I understand we have a first check for the coalition from that fund," Liza said.

The banker stood and gave a courtly half bow in Liza's direction. If his gaze lingered appreciatively an instant longer than necessary, Molly figured she was the only one who noticed. Caroline had planted the idea of Hernando's interest in Liza in her head. Liza seemed oblivious.

"We owe Roger a great debt of gratitude for allowing us to establish this memorial fund in honor of his wife," Hernando said. "Today it is my pleasure to present the coalition with a check in the amount of two hundred and fifty thousand dollars, which accounts for the contributions to date. I have no doubt that with the proper administration this fund will continue to grow."

Molly gasped at the amount that had accumulated in such a short time. She wondered if a single guilty donor had been responsible for pushing the fund well into six figures. As she wondered about that, Roger stood up.

His normally strong voice shook with emotion as he said, "I would like to thank many of you in this room for your generosity. Tessa believed deeply that we have a responsibility to preserve what nature has given us. I hope that this fund will provide support to many environmental causes and that it will make the sort of difference she would have made had she lived to see things through."

"Hear, hear!" Jason Jeffries said, showing considerably more enthusiasm for his ex-wife in death than he had in life. "I think we should form a special task force to determine how these funds should be allocated."

Liza glanced at Roger. "Perhaps you would like to chair such a task force."

He regarded her uncertainly. "I'm not sure that I would be the best person . . ." His voice trailed off.

"Enough of that. Of course you would," Patrice said firmly, ready to rally the troops around him now that his wife was gone. "I am willing to serve as well. Lincoln?"

"Of course."

Liza smiled. "Then I think we have our committee." She paused to lead the group in a round of applause for the new task force. Molly observed the others in the room closely. All seemed to be joining in wholeheartedly. It was the first time all day they'd been unified about anything.

"Now, there is one more piece of business," Liza said, her tone suddenly more grave. "Something has come to my attention just today that I think we ought to take a stand on. Yet another proposal is before the Dade County Commission regarding development in the western part of the county."

"The wetlands?" asked one horrified listener. "Surely, not again."

"Yes, again, I'm sorry to say. There have been some changes on the federal level and local developers have taken that as a sign to try one more time to push progress straight into the Everglades."

An outraged murmur spread around the room. "Who's at it this time?" Patrice demanded. She glared at Clark, then looked pointedly at Michael as if willing him to share her suspicions. "I'm sure you could tell us that," she told Clark. "You're probably representing the devils."

"No, I am not," he said, returning her scowl without flinching.

From the sparks flying between the two, Molly figured it was safe to assume that the pair had removed the kid gloves and intended an all-out battle of wills.

"Stop pussyfooting around, Clark," Patrice demanded. "You know perfectly well that if there's a dollar to be made on development in this town, you know the players."

"I do stay on top of things, yes," he said agreeably. "That's not a crime, Patrice. It's a civic responsibility. You should do the same."

"I'd say 'on top' is the wrong phrase. 'In the middle' would be more like it." She sat back with a satisfied smirk.

Liza apparently decided that the squabble wasn't gaining the group a single bit of information and might well deteriorate into something truly ugly.

"Enough, you two," she said quietly. "I just learned about this today and didn't have time to research it myself. The person who called me right before the meeting did mention the name of the company, Danson Properties, Inc. Has anyone ever heard of it?"

No one acknowledged being familiar with the company. Molly kept her gaze pinned on Clark Dupree, but his expression remained stoic. She couldn't help wondering if the look expressed genuine bafflement or had been perfected to keep from revealing too much. It certainly would be handy in a courtroom. Either way it was clear that details would not be forthcoming from him.

"Would anyone like to propose a statement for the media regarding our stance on this?" Liza suggested.

"Perhaps we should consider getting more information before we go off half-cocked," Clark Dupree suggested mildly. He avoided Patrice's gaze when he said it.

"Of course you'd want us to remain silent," she snapped. "The less said by the opposition, the better to get county approval."

"No," Liza said reasonably. "What Clark

suggests makes sense. We don't want to get a reputation for crying wolf, unless the proposed development is truly a threat to the Everglades. Why don't I look into it and then we can schedule another meeting for next week to firm up our position?"

"What if the commission decides to ramrod it through before that?" Lincoln Granview demanded.

"Any resolution would require more than one reading before the commission," Liza reminded him. "We're not even sure if this has zoning or planning approval. I'll check it out as soon as we leave here today. If I find out it's further along in the process than that, I will notify each of you and we can make plans to appear before the commission to outline our objections. In the meantime, if you require inspiration to remind you of what the fight is all about, reread *River of Grass*. Marjorie Stoneman Douglas said it all in her classic book on the Everglades."

"Perhaps we should send copies to the commissioners," Jason suggested drily.

Patrice regarded him approvingly. "Good idea, Jason. I'll do that myself."

With that the meeting adjourned. To Molly's disappointment, the killer had not revealed himself or herself. That had been too much to hope for, she supposed.

When Liza was finally able to join her, she said, "When exactly did you hear about this development deal? You didn't mention it on the way over here."

"I got a call here right before the meeting started. It was all very mysterious. The caller wouldn't even identify himself."

"Did you recognize anything about the voice?" Michael inquired as he joined them.

Liza shook her head. "I was too furious about the message to worry about the messenger. I wish it hadn't been so last-minute. If I'd had time to check it out, we could have taken a formal stand today and Ted Ryan could have gotten it in tomorrow's paper. I want these people on notice that they won't be able to sneak this through."

She glanced at Molly, her expression genuinely distraught. "Every time I think about these random attacks on the fragile ecology of the Everglades, it makes me sick. There's nothing else like it in the United States. We should be protecting it, not destroying it just to put up another strip mall or plunk down another community of tacky, matching houses."

It was a subject on which Molly shared Liza's views and her fervor. "Half the malls we have now are failing because there are too many of them," she chimed in. "The last time I drove into one of these new developments, most of the houses were unoccupied, the developer had run out of funds, and there was a suit from the few existing homeowners to force him to make good on the amenities he'd promised. They'd read about a similar mess in California that made a deal with the producers of *Lethal Weapon* to wipe the whole thing out. The homeowners invited me out because they wondered if we had any films coming into town that might want to destroy their community as part of the plot."

"So why would anyone want to build another one?" Michael asked.

Molly sensed that the question was rhetorical, but Liza jumped right in to answer anyway.

"I'll tell you why," she said furiously. "Greed. Pure and simple."

"Greed," Molly echoed thoughtfully. "Remember when we said the key to solving Tessa's murder was to find the money. Maybe this is it."

Liza looked startled by the suggestion, but then she nodded. "You could be right. How do we find out the principals in this deal?"

"I'll make a few calls to a friend in another county department, and if the lid on this isn't on too tight, we should know in no time." Molly glanced at Michael to get his reaction to the plan.

He shrugged. "It wouldn't hurt to make the call. If you unearth something, though, call me or Detective Abrams. Don't go chasing down any leads yourselves."

After promising to be careful, Liza broke speed limits getting them back to Molly's office so she could make the call. Unfortunately, the only official record of the zoning request listed no more than the name of the company, Danson Properties, Inc.

Discouraged, Molly hung up the phone. "No luck."

Liza, however, was just getting her second wind. "Don't look so glum. If it's incorporated, then there are records on file with the state. I'll call Tallahassee."

"Do you have a contact who'll do the digging for you?"

Liza grinned. "I have contacts everywhere they might come in handy. You should know that by now."

It took one call and a half hour of impatient pacing to get the answer they were after. When the call came in, Molly reluctantly handed the phone over to Liza, then had to watch as a slow grin spread across her face, only to twist into something else entirely. There were furious sparks in her eyes by the time she hung up.

"Well?" Molly demanded.

"The president of Danson Properties, Inc. is none other than our good friend and board member, Clark Dupree."

Molly started to speak, but Liza held up her hand. "Wait. There's more. The vice president was none other than Tessa Lafferty."

Now that was a turn of events that led to all sorts of fascinating possibilities. It even fit quite nicely with Molly's belief that Tessa had been desperate to prove herself in business. The only question now was who, besides Clark Dupree, had known about Tessa's involvement in Danson Properties.

17

Liza was all for driving straight to Clark Dupree's office and stabbing him in the heart. It took Molly and Jeannette combined to restrain her.

"Two murders don't make a right," Molly reminded her. "We don't know that he killed Tessa. Why would he, if she was his partner?"

"I don't give a damn whether he killed Tessa. He's trying to rape the Everglades. He sat right there today and swore he was not representing Danson Properties."

"He's probably not," Molly said. "Only a fool would represent himself. Isn't that the way the saying goes?"

"More or less," Liza agreed. "But that's a technicality. He basically lied to us. When the others hear about this, they'll want to lynch him."

Molly could believe that. "Which may explain why he declined to comment today," she said drily. "Would you admit to this in a hostile crowd?"

Liza sagged back into her chair. "No. Do you think Patrice knew? Could this be the reason she was so furious with him?"

"You mean this on top of the fact that he was screwing Tessa?"

"To a woman of principle like Patrice, this would probably matter more."

"Based on her reaction earlier, I'd say she might have suspected he was involved with Danson, but I don't think she knew even that for certain, much less knew that he actually owned the company."

"What if Tessa hadn't realized exactly what Danson Properties was buying into?" Liza suggested slowly. "What if she found out and confronted him that night? They argued and Tessa ended up in the bay."

Molly had considered the same possibility and dismissed it. "I have a hard time picturing Tessa morally outraged enough to blow a gasket over Clark's development deals, especially when it was her first big shot at proving her worth as a businesswoman. I know she was on record as an environmentalist, but I had the feeling that, like Helen Whorton, she took that position because it was politically correct. Am I wrong?"

"Not entirely," Liza said dully. "Too bad,

though. I liked that scenario."

"I have a better one," Molly soothed. "What if she found out, maybe Clark even revealed it to her in some intimate moment, and she tried to blackmail him. Clark's always had the law on his side when he's gone into these fights. He's always sounded very high and mighty, stating that everyone under our system of justice deserves the best representation he or she can get. He's acted as if it weren't something he personally would ever do, right?"

"The same argument given by those who defend drug dealers and rapists," Liza said in disgust.

"But the point is he's never been involved himself. In fact, he's gone to the extreme of forking over huge donations to politically correct environmental causes."

"As if that would make up for his choice of clients," Liza grumbled.

"True, but that's not what I'm getting at," Molly said. "I seriously doubt he'd want it known that he was trying to develop the Everglades at the same time he's sitting on a board that's committed to protecting it. Tessa and Roger needed money. We know that. This deal might have held out the promise of a solution. Then when she realized what she'd gotten herself into, she might have tried blackmailing Clark. He strikes me as sleazy enough to murder her to keep her quiet. Maybe she simply tried to bail out, but he wouldn't let her."

"You know what I think of him," Liza said. "But we don't have any proof. All we have is an interesting theory."

The door to Molly's office opened just then. Michael stepped in and beamed at the two of them. "Just in time, I see."

"Just in time for what?"

"To keep you two from dashing off to prove whatever theory it is you've dreamed up. Care to share it with me?"

With some reluctance, Molly recited everything they'd been able to piece together since the meeting earlier in the afternoon. To her surprise, Michael nodded approvingly.

"Good work. That could fit with another piece of evidence we picked up today. Abrams got a call from the captain of a yacht that was cruising on Biscayne Bay Saturday night. He'd taken a party to Bimini and didn't read about the murder until he got back."

"And?"

"He says he heard an argument about the time of the murder. He couldn't be sure because of the way voices carry on the water, but it seemed to be coming from the grounds of Vizcaya. It was a man and woman, but he couldn't tell any more than that."

"So it might have been Clark and Tessa," Molly said.

"But why didn't anyone else hear them?"

Michael shook his head. "Could be the way the wind was blowing. Could have been the music drowned them out."

"The only thing that puzzles me is how Clark would get a candlestick down to the water without Tessa noticing."

"He didn't," Michael said. "Or, rather, the killer didn't. There wasn't a trace of anything to link that to the murder. The wound didn't match either, according to the medical examiner. It wasn't made by something with sharp edges."

"Then why was it missing?"

"For all we know it was never even there. Maybe it had never left Neville's office."

"Believe me," Liza said. "Neville knew exactly what was in that truck when he brought it to Vizcaya. He's fanatical about details like that."

"Then my guess would be that one of Neville's employees figured it was valuable and tucked it away to be fenced later. When he heard rumors that the police thought it

255

might have been the murder weapon, he slipped it back into Neville's office. At any rate, whatever the killer did use to hit Tessa is probably at the bottom of the bay. It wouldn't have taken much to knock her unconscious. A good-size rock would have done the trick. The blow didn't kill her."

"What, then?" Molly asked.

"The medical examiner speculates that she might have come to at some point, but in the dark, tangled in those mangroves and disoriented, she drowned before she could free herself. There was evidence that she'd struggled, but the scratches were more consistent with scrapes she would have sustained underwater than with any she might have gotten in a fight."

"Oh, God," Molly murmured, horrified by the image of such a tortured death. Liza looked equally shaken.

"How could Clark have thrown her in there and walked away, knowing she might still be alive?" Liza said. "What kind of man would do that?"

"One who was desperate," Michael said. "And we don't know it was Clark Dupree. Until we do, you'd be wise not to speculate in public. He's the kind that will sue you for slander, if you're wrong."

"I doubt I'm wrong," Liza said. "But I'll

keep my opinion to myself."

The door to the office, already partially open, was flung wide. Expecting Vince or Jeannette, Molly was dismayed to see Hal DeWitt standing there glaring at her. If the judgmental expression on his face was anything to go by, he'd overheard enough of the conversation to guess what it was about.

"You just can't leave it alone, can you?" he said wearily.

Molly cast a look of pure desperation at Liza and Michael, but they were already on their feet. At least Michael looked torn about leaving her alone with her ex-husband. That didn't stop him from going, though. He gave her a supportive thumbs-up sign from the doorway.

When they'd gone, she felt abandoned. She also felt more frightened than she ever had in her life as she met Hal's furious gaze.

"Why are you here?" she asked.

"I thought we should talk again about the custody suit."

Molly's breath caught in her throat. "You've decided something?"

"I thought I had," he admitted, sinking wearily into the chair just vacated by Michael.

He closed his eyes and rubbed his temples,

as if he was fighting a pounding headache. The tension in Molly's neck promised a headache of her own as she waited for his verdict, a decision that could dramatically affect her life and Brian's.

When Hal finally looked at her again, he said, "Until I walked in that door just now, I was ready to let it go. I'd convinced myself after our talk the other night that you wouldn't knowingly put Brian in danger and that I was overreacting. Then I walk in here and find you plotting and scheming to catch a killer."

"We were talking, batting around ideas," she retorted, trying to make him see reason. It was never an easy task with Hal, especially when he was in a self-righteous mood. "That's hardly dangerous. One of the people involved in that discussion is a police officer."

"The same police officer who hasn't had sense enough to keep you from snooping around in those other two cases. Am I right?"

"Don't try to blame my involvement on Michael."

"Oh, I'm sure you jumped into the fray all on your own. But he could have told you to take a hike, instead of sitting around discussing the case with you, keeping you all

churned up about it. What kind of policeman would do that? I ought to have the guy
checked out."

"Leave Michael out of this. He's not
involved in our situation. And, I repeat,
there is nothing dangerous about comparing notes and exchanging ideas," she said,
clinging desperately to her last shred of
patience.

"It is if all that talk reaches the ears of the
wrong person. I may not be a criminal
lawyer, Molly, but I've seen more than my
share of murder cases that hinged on the
testimony of one key witness. In quite a few
of those cases that witness wound up just as
dead as the original victim. Why do you
think they have witness protection pro-
grams?"

He looked her in the eye, his gaze unflinching. "I don't want that to happen to
you. I really don't," he said flatly. "I won't
allow it to happen to Brian." He got slowly
to his feet. "I guess I'll see you in court,
after all."

Stunned by the finality in his voice, she
tried to prevent him from leaving, but to no
avail. He wouldn't even glance back at her
on his way out the door.

"Oh, God," she whispered, burying her
head in her hands as Michael and Liza

edged back into the office.

"What happened?" Liza asked, regarding her sympathetically.

"Molly?" Michael said gently when she didn't respond.

She glanced up, blinking back tears. "He was going to drop the custody suit."

"*Was* going to?" Liza said.

Molly nodded. "He overheard what we were saying and decided I hadn't learned my lesson, after all. He's going to court."

"He won't win," Michael said firmly. He perched on the edge of her desk and cupped her chin in his hand until she was forced to meet his gaze. "No court would take Brian away from you, okay?"

She wanted to believe him, but Hal had a certain amount of power at the courthouse. "I can't be sure of that. You've never heard Hal in court. He's a brilliant litigator. By the time he's finished, I'll come out sounding like the mother from hell."

"You're forgetting one thing," Michael reminded her, brushing away an errant tear with the pad of his thumb.

"What's that?"

"Brian."

"That's right," Liza said. "Brian doesn't want to live with his father. He also has plenty of details to prove that Hal's interest in his welfare is somewhat belated. How many times has Hal canceled his visits? How many birthday presents came a week late? Or not at all?"

"I'm not sure a judge will compare a missing toy with murder investigations and rule in my favor," Molly said bleakly.

"He will if I have anything to say about it," Michael said, his voice filled with cold, hard determination. "If need be, I can pull in half a dozen cops who are also full-time mothers. Nobody's challenging their ability as parents."

"Maybe because they carry guns," Molly retorted, but she was beginning to feel more encouraged.

"If you think I'm standing by and watching you get a gun, you're crazy," Liza declared. "We have too many on the streets as it is."

Michael grinned. "I don't think we have to arm Molly to prove to the court she's a capable mother."

"Thank you, I think," she said drily.

He regarded her intently. "Are you okay with this now?"

"I'm ready to fight, if that's what you mean."

"Good. Then I want to take off and pay a visit to Clark Dupree."

"Not without me," Molly said.

"Don't you think this would be a good time to go home and spend a little time with your son?" he said. "I promise I'll come by right after the meeting and fill you in on every detail."

Reason won out over curiosity. If Hal decided to spring his decision on Brian tonight, her son would need her. Michael, on the other hand, hardly needed her assistance in questioning a suspect. He'd had more practice.

"You'll come by?"

"I said I would."

She nodded. "Then hurry. My curiosity will be killing me. Liza?"

Her friend looked torn. "I'd really like to hear what Clark has to say, if Michael doesn't mind."

"Actually, your presence might make it more likely that he'll slip up. I have no objection to your coming along."

"Molly?" Liza said.

"Oh, go ahead. There's no reason for two of us to be biting our nails."

She followed them to the parking lot, then watched them start toward Michael's car. They were almost there when he hesitated, then turned and walked back toward her.

Hands stuffed in his pockets, he stood

gazing down at her intently. "Give Brian an extra hug for me, okay?"

Tears sprang to Molly's eyes again. "Yeah. I'll do that," she promised.

He nodded in satisfaction, then went back to join Liza. Molly stood staring after them until his car was out of sight, heading north toward Clark Dupree's Brickell Avenue office.

18

Unfortunately, Clark Dupree wasn't in his Brickell Avenue office. He was waiting in the lobby of Molly's Key Biscayne condominium. He looked as if he'd settled in for a long wait.

Nestor, the Nicaraguan head of security for Ocean Manor, had his eyes on the well-dressed interloper who'd made himself at home on the lobby sofa and was sifting through the papers in his fancy briefcase. Nestor's worried expression deepened as he latched on to Molly's arm and dragged her back outside.

"He ask for you, then for Ms. Hastings. When I tell him you are not here, he say he wait. There is something about the man." He shook his head. "I do not like him. Should I call Señor Michael?"

Molly wasn't wild about the idea that Nestor thought she needed rescuing or that he regarded Michael as her savior in all slightly tricky situations. At the same time, it seemed foolish not to let Michael know that his chief suspect was sitting in her lobby.

"Call him," she told Nestor, giving him Michael's phone number. She tried very hard not to make it sound urgent. She didn't want Michael roaring in here with sirens blasting. "Tell him I'll talk with Mr. Dupree right here in the lobby until he arrives."

She plastered a smile on her face, crossed the lobby, and took a chair next to Clark. "I understand you're looking for me or Liza."

Clark rose slowly. At his six-foot-two-inch height, he was an imposing figure. Normally, in social situations anyway, he sought to temper that impression with soft-spoken charm. Today, however, his smile seemed forced.

"Yes," he said, sitting again once she was settled. "I understand you were looking for me earlier in the week. I had business on the Key and thought I'd drop by to see what you wanted. When the guard said you were out, I asked for Liza. After the meeting this afternoon, I'm sure she has questions for me as well."

"About Danson, you mean?"

He nodded. "You both know by now, I assume."

"We checked out the incorporation records, yes."

"Then you know that I am president of Danson Properties and that Tessa was the vice president." He glanced around the lobby with distaste, an expression that would have appalled those who fought so valiantly for this particular flowery decor. "Could we possibly discuss this upstairs? I really don't like discussing business in the middle of a public lobby like this."

Since the lobby was virtually deserted, Molly thought his request a bit unnecessary. Unless, of course, he was getting very nervous about how much she knew and wanted to clobber her over the head in private. Just in case, she didn't think she'd allow him that opportunity.

She managed a smile. "Actually, it's a lot quieter here than it would be upstairs. My son and his friends are in my apartment. You don't join a group of third-graders if you want peace and quiet."

He took the rejection fairly well. "Perhaps we could go for coffee, then?"

Molly refused to acknowledge the twinge of worry that was beginning to nag at her. Clark might have killed Tessa, but she didn't know that for sure. Besides, what could possibly happen with Nestor not twenty yards away? She simply had to keep him here and talking until Michael arrived. Maybe she could even wrangle a confession out of him.

"Mr. Dupree, I really don't see what we have to discuss," she said, hoping to persuade him that she knew absolutely nothing incriminating about him and wasn't the least bit involved in the investigation. "Your business dealings are no affair of mine, and while I happen to agree with the stance the coalition has taken in the past with regard to the Everglades, I have no official capacity with that organization."

"I think we do share one common interest, however."

"Which is?"

"Discovering who murdered Tessa."

Molly blinked at the smooth delivery. Wouldn't the killer have had a hard time making that remark seem convincing? Was it possible that she and Liza were wrong about Clark, after all?

"Did you and Tessa argue the night of the gala?" she asked point-blank, hoping to startle him into a slip.

Again, he smiled faintly. "You see, I was right. You are interested."

"Of course I'm interested," she said a trifle

impatiently, seeing no need to continue her charade. It hadn't worked anyway. "I discovered Tessa's body. It's not something I'm likely to get over in a hurry. It would help to know who was responsible for her death."

"Then please, let's go for coffee. I'll tell you everything I know about what happened that night. You pick the place. We can even take separate cars," he added, giving her a wry look that told her he knew exactly what she was thinking. While he might consider her fears foolish, he obviously intended to humor her, to make it difficult for her to decline the invitation.

In fact, how could she possibly refuse when it seemed unlikely that she would actually have to be alone with him? She could drive to one of the hotels, the Sheraton or the Sonesta, valet park, and meet him in a coffee shop or the bar. He could hardly run her off the road and shoot her on busy Crandon Boulevard without risking immediate capture.

"We'll go to the Sheraton," she said finally. With its lobby doors facing the ocean, the restaurant was so well lit it was impossible to imagine a less ominous setting. "I'll meet you there."

"Thank you."

Just to make sure he knew she was leaving

a trail, she pointedly told Nestor that she would be at the nearby hotel if Brian or anyone else came looking for her.

Nestor gave her a reluctant nod, indicating that he understood the full implications of her request, even if he wasn't wild about her departure. "I will tell them." He glanced at Clark Dupree. "You wish me to tell Ms. Hastings you are there, if she returns?"

"Why not?" Clark said agreeably. "The more, the merrier."

As Molly drove the few blocks to the oceanfront hotel, she tried to figure out exactly what Clark Dupree was up to. Was he merely trying to invoke some sympathy for his own position as the distraught, bereaved lover? Was he genuinely after Tessa's killer? Or was he simply trying to determine exactly how much Molly knew so he could decide if she posed a danger to him?

Her own reaction to the man was unexpected. She despised his values and she was wary, but she wasn't afraid. Hopefully, her gut instincts were fully operational after the round she'd gone with Hal earlier. Hopefully, Michael and Liza would show up before she had to find out.

Inside the hotel, Clark made no objections to entering the seaside restaurant, which was quieter than Molly might have liked. They chose a table by the doors, which were open to admit the sea breeze. Molly ordered coffee and Clark ordered a martini straight up. Apparently, he needed false fortitude for whatever he had to tell her.

"I asked you earlier if you and Tessa had argued the night she was killed," Molly said when he showed no inclination to get started.

"Tessa and I always argued. It was part of her fascination for me that she never backed down from her strong opinions. I value that strength of character in anyone."

"Did her opinions have some validity?"

"Sometimes. In other instances, her pig-headedness almost drove me crazy."

"Was she right about Danson Properties, in your opinion? Or was she merely being pigheaded, as you put it?"

He stared off toward the window that faced the Atlantic, a faraway look in his eyes. He appeared almost as if he might be overcome with emotion, but when he blinked and gazed back at Molly there was every indication that his usual reserve was firmly in place.

"How much do you know about Tessa and Roger's financial difficulties?"

"Very little, except that they were in some

trouble."

"Tessa had been investing in the stock market, junk bonds as it turns out. She was always so sure of herself, so supremely confident of her business acumen. She was ripe for some unscrupulous broker to rob her blind."

"Did Roger know?"

"He learned far too late to prevent disaster from striking. She'd gone through her inheritance and was well into debt for an amount equal to most of his cash reserves when he caught on and called a halt to things. He threatened to have the broker brought up on charges, but it was an idle threat. In such situations, fraud is difficult to prove. Naturally, Tessa was humiliated by the whole affair."

"And I'm sure Roger was furious."

"Perhaps so, but he didn't let her know how he felt. He simply tried to clean up the mess. That's the kind of man Roger is. Honorable to a fault."

"Honorable? I heard he took out an insurance policy on Tessa."

Clark shook his head ruefully. "So you know about that? Actually, the policy was Tessa's idea, a way to make amends."

"Eventually," Molly pointed out.

"Yes, eventually."

"What does all this have to do with Danson Properties?"

"When the federal authorities began making changes in the laws governing the wetlands, I heard talk starting up about the area again and I saw an opportunity. I began buying up land. I knew about Tessa's difficulties and I offered to cut her in on the deal."

"Did she know where this property was?"

His shoulders slumped dejectedly. "Not until the night of the gala."

"How did she find out?"

"She didn't. Roger did. He mentioned it to her in passing, outraged by the notion that a company was poised to destroy a part of the Everglades again. When he mentioned the name of the company, I gather she almost fainted. By the time I saw her Saturday night, she was livid."

Molly could imagine the confrontation. Tessa, thinking that she had taken a step that might make up for her earlier business disasters, had discovered that instead she had made an even more grievous mistake. Realizing that her lover had intentionally deceived her about the nature of their development plans must have cut her to the quick.

"What did she want you to do?"

"She wanted me to sell the property to the coalition and walk away."

"You refused," Molly guessed.

"Actually, I might have considered it. I would have done anything for Tessa," he said with unmistakable sincerity. "I only involved her in this deal to try to save her pride. I didn't think it through. I never realized how deeply she felt about the coalition. Not many people did. They thought she was shallow. The worst thing was, she knew that. I think that's what made her so angry about this deal, because she knew her detractors would see it as proof that she had caved in when it was expedient for her to do so."

Molly was trying to revise her opinions of Tessa and Clark, to put them in perspective in light of what she'd learned and what had happened next. If she bought his story, then it seemed terribly unlikely that he would have killed her. "What happened that night?" she asked. "After you argued, Clark, what happened next?"

His shoulders slumped in defeat. "I don't know," he said wearily. "I wish to God I did, but I don't. When I walked away from Tessa, she was angry, but she was very much alive. I swear it."

Molly gazed directly at him, until he lifted

his eyes to meet hers. She saw agony in the brown depths, agony and sorrow, but not guilt. Her gut instincts were certain of that much at least.

"Tell me again everything that you and Tessa said that night," she suggested as an idea began to take shape in her mind. It was the only thing that made a sad kind of sense. Slowly, Clark recounted the argument from beginning to end, the revelations about the development deal, Tessa's furious accusations, his own desperate attempts to placate her.

"I told her that I loved her, that I would never have intentionally hurt her."

"What did she say then?"

"She said it was too bad, that she had loved me, too, but it was over between us. She said she would never be able to trust me again."

"So it would have been clear to anyone overhearing the fight that you and Tessa had been lovers?"

"I suppose so, yes," he said thoughtfully. Then as awareness of her point dawned, he whispered, "Roger. You think Roger heard it all and killed her for betraying him."

"He worshipped her. You were his best friend. It makes sense that he would be furious, that it might be the one thing he could

274

never forgive."

"But there were others before me," he protested, albeit weakly.

Molly recalled the expression on Roger's face that day at the house as he regarded Clark with total contempt, the look of a man deeply betrayed on all levels. "None of them were Roger's best friend," she reminded him.

An odd transformation came over Clark then. It was as if all of his own pain gave way to a cold, hard anger. Molly had never seen anything like it before in her life and it sent a shiver down her back.

He raised his hand for the check, handed the waiter the money, and nodded at Molly, his expression already a little distant. "Thank you for joining me," he said politely, but with absolutely no feeling in his tone. Even his gaze had gone blank.

As he walked away from the table, Molly knew where he was going.

She also knew what he was planning to do.

19

Where the hell was Michael? Molly thought as she raced across the hotel lobby and out the door. She wondered if it was possible to arrest someone *before* they committed a crime.

Clark hadn't bothered with valet parking and was already heading for his car, his long-legged strides giving him a distinct advantage over her. Unless he chose to let her, she would never catch up with him on foot. Her only hope would be to follow in her car, using her cellular phone to try to reach Michael and Roger to warn them of Clark Dupree's apparent intentions.

Clark's black Lexus sped from the parking lot, hitting the speed bump at full throttle. It was a wonder he didn't knock himself unconscious on the roof, Molly thought, watching him as she waited impatiently for her own car.

Fortunately, there was only one route off

the Key. If he was, in fact, headed to the Gables, she would have ample opportunity to catch up with him. As she turned onto Crandon Boulevard, heading northwest toward the mainland, she was already punching in Michael's number.

"Come on," she muttered when he didn't pick up immediately. "Dammit, Michael, pick up."

While she listened to the distant ring, she fumbled with her address book, trying to locate the Laffertys' number. As soon as she found it, she disconnected the failed call to Michael and tried to reach Roger. Josie answered. She sounded thoroughly worn out.

"Mr. Roger isn't here, miss. He's been coming home late most nights, if he comes home at all."

"Do you know where he might be?"

"His office, maybe. Or the country club. Sometimes he goes by there."

"Thanks, Josie." She hesitated, trying to find a way to warn the housekeeper about Clark without alarming her. "Josie, if Mr. Dupree comes by, don't tell him where you think Mr. Lafferty might be, okay?"

"Why not?" she asked, sounding puzzled. "They been good friends a long time now. Mr. Roger needs his friends around him at a time like this."

"Mr. Dupree is very upset about something right now. I just don't think it would be the best time for them to talk. If Mr. Lafferty comes home, tell him the same thing. Please, Josie."

Fortunately, the housekeeper had spent a lifetime taking orders from a woman even more of a mystery than Molly. She considered it her duty to follow instructions to the letter, no matter what she thought of them. "Yes, ma'am. I'll tell him."

Molly tried Michael again. Still he didn't answer. Where could he be? Whenever he wasn't in the car, he carried his cell phone with him. That wonder of the technological age was on its tenth or twelfth ring, when a tentative, vaguely familiar voice answered. *"Bueno!"*

"Nestor?" Molly said slowly, fighting astonishment and confusion.

"*Sí*. This is Nestor."

"Nestor, it's Mrs. DeWitt. Where is Michael?"

"Here," he said, sounding distressed. "He and Mr. DeWitt, they are fighting."

"Michael and Hal are fighting?" she said, torn between incredulity and dismay. "You mean brawling? A fistfight?" It was beyond her comprehension.

"No fists. They shout. Very loud. They do not hear the phone. I pick it up."

"Would you tell those two macho jerks to shut up? I need Michael now!"

The urgency in her voice got through to him. "*Sí. Sí.* I tell them."

He put the phone down. Molly could hear his voice climb, issuing commands in Spanish. Then she heard Michael's rapid-fire response, counterpointed by Hal's querulous demands to know what was going on. His stubborn refusal to learn Spanish had put him at a distinct disadvantage, and he was clearly making his dissatisfaction known.

"Molly?" Michael said finally. "Where are you? What's going on?"

She summarized her suspicions as succinctly as possible.

"I'll call Abrams," he promised. "I'm on my way. Molly, don't you dare get in the middle of this. Turn around and come home."

"Not on your life. I will not let Clark Dupree waltz in and kill Roger while you rally the troops."

"How do you intend to stop them? By talking them both to death?"

"Very funny. I've already warned Josie not to tell Clark where Roger might be. In case he does come home before Clark gets there, I've told her to warn him."

"Good going, but that's enough. The police will take it from here."

"The police will take it from here if you stop arguing with me and get moving. Otherwise, I figure I'm on my own. I'm almost to the Lafferty house now and Clark was ahead of me."

He sighed deeply, clearly sensing that her formidable resolve had kicked in. "Promise me you'll stay out of the line of fire, *amiga*. If you go getting yourself killed, we'll never know how all this flirting will end up."

Molly knew exactly where all the flirting was headed. She just didn't know the timetable. She intended to be around for the finale, though. "I'll be careful," she promised.

She heard Hal's shouted demand to know what was going on just as the phone clicked off. Her phone rang within minutes.

"Molly," Hal said, sounding breathless.

Either the fight had taken its toll or he'd raced to his own car phone. He was definitely on the road. She could hear the sounds of traffic, the impatient blaring of his horn.

"Where are you and what is happening?" he demanded.

She gave him an abbreviated version of the same story.

"Clark Dupree is going after Roger? I don't believe it."

"Why? Because attorneys never turn into criminals?" she inquired sarcastically. "I could name a few who engage in criminal behavior all the time."

"Not murder," he said piously. "And we're talking about Clark Dupree here. He's a model citizen."

"A model citizen who was intending to rape the Everglades. A model citizen who was having an affair with his best friend's wife. I actually think he was in love with Tessa. He flipped out when he realized Roger might have killed her."

"Then let the police and the shrinks have at him. Go home to your son."

"That's exactly what I intend to do . . . if they get there in time. Hal, I can't talk to you and drive at the same time. We'll talk later."

"Molly! Molly, don't you dare hang up on me!"

She ignored the order.

It was less easy to ignore the panic and desperation she'd heard in his tone. Maybe she was going to have to admit at last that Hal DeWitt still loved her enough to be terrified for her. Her own feelings toward him were less clear and now was certainly not the time to analyze them. The only thing that did occur to her was that while Michael clearly worried about her, he usually trusted her to use her head in a crisis. That pretty much summed up the difference in the two relationships. Hal still thought she had no more judgment than a head of lettuce.

As she rounded the corner onto Roger's street in the Gables, she saw Clark's car turning into the drive, saw the guard wave him in, and realized that she hadn't thought to tell Josie to warn the guard. She took the turn into the driveway on two wheels and squealed to a stop right behind the fancy black car. There was no sign of Roger's car. Hopefully, he still hadn't come home.

"Clark!" Molly shouted as she climbed out of the car.

The guard cast a startled look in her direction. It was a new guard, one she'd never seen before, though Clark obviously had.

"Is something wrong, miss?" he said, coming toward her.

"He's after Mr. Lafferty. I think he's planning to kill him," she said. "The police are on their way."

Just then Clark spun around as if he'd

heard the words she'd spoken in a deliberate undertone. He looked distraught. "Why did you come?"

"I had to try to talk you out of doing something you'd regret for the rest of your life," Molly said, staying behind the door of her car. It offered scant protection, but it was better than nothing, especially since it was clear that he'd traded his briefcase for a gun. He held it steadily in front of him, aimed in her direction. The guard was trying to inch around behind him, so Molly forced herself to keep talking.

"I know how terrible it must be for you, knowing that Roger killed the woman you loved, but the police will catch him and the courts will see that he's punished."

An odd expression passed over his face, an expression that suddenly had Molly doubting everything she'd surmised over the past couple of hours. Stunned by how badly she'd misread things, she simply stared as he began moving toward her.

"I added it up all wrong, didn't I?" she said with dawning understanding. She was conscious of every slow, careful movement behind Clark as the guard got into position. "You're not here to kill Roger because he murdered Tessa, are you? You want him dead because he saw what really happened

283

that night."

"Very good, Mrs. DeWitt," he said as if she'd mastered a very difficult lesson. "I thought I had you fooled. It was only as we talked that I realized you were right, that Roger must have seen everything, including the fact that Tessa and I struggled, that I grabbed up a rock, knocked her unconscious, and dumped her into the bay."

"But he told no one what he'd seen that night," Molly reminded him, trying not to glance in the direction of the guard who was just about ready to pounce and strip Clark of his gun. "He remained your friend, despite everything you'd done to him."

Clark's laughter sent chills down Molly's spine.

"Friend? If he was there that night, he knew what it would do to me to wait for him to reveal everything. He wasn't being noble, Mrs. DeWitt. He was torturing me, making me wait, letting the guilt work on me."

"That's right," said a voice from behind Molly. As Clark's attention shifted, she recognized the cool, controlled voice of Roger Lafferty, sounding more certain than he had at any time since the devastating events of Saturday night. "And now you're going to pay."

Molly whirled around just in time to see the flash of gunfire, smell the acrid scent of gunpowder. Expecting a volley of shots to be fired, she hit the ground, but there was only the one blast and then quiet fell behind the protective gates that had failed in their job to keep this household safe, after all. She dared to peek and saw that Roger Lafferty had laid the gun on the trunk of her car and was slumped over. She glanced around the car door and saw Clark Dupree on the ground, the security guard hovering over him. Clark was writhing, clutching his leg, so the wound probably wasn't fatal.

Molly reached into the car, grabbed her phone and called 911, just as Michael's car turned into the driveway. Hal's was right on its tail, despite the fact that he must have been speeding the whole way to keep up. She was surprised there wasn't an entire fleet of Coral Gables patrol cars in their wake.

Michael took in the scene at a glance, retrieved Roger's gun, then pulled her into his arms the instant he was assured that the key players were disarmed. "I see you have everything under control," he said drily.

"Not quite," she admitted, understanding now why she could never walk away from whatever the future might have in store for the two of them. Michael was strong, but more than that, he gave her strength. "I had it wrong. Clark was guilty, after all. Roger saw him murder Tessa. That's why Clark came over here to kill him."

She glanced at Roger and saw a broken man, a man who had lost everything that ever mattered to him in a period of a few days. "The only thing I don't understand is why you didn't try to save her," she said to him.

Roger regarded her wearily. "Don't you see? I couldn't. I felt so betrayed, so angry. In the end, you see, I am every bit as guilty as Clark."

Hal had gone to Clark's side and Molly heard him ask if he wanted a lawyer. "I'll call someone for you," he offered.

Clark shook his head. "No. It's over for me. There's no point in doing anything other than pleading guilty. I can certainly do that on my own."

Molly figured it would be a new experience since he usually plea-bargained his clients out of paying for their crimes.

Hal turned finally and walked slowly in her direction. Michael looked from Molly to her ex-husband and back again. He gave her shoulders a squeeze and went to explain what had happened to Detective Abrams, who'd just arrived on the scene. Molly was left alone to face her ex-husband.

Pale and clearly shaken, Hal shoved his hands into his pockets. His gaze surveyed her hungrily as if he needed desperately to assure himself that she was really all right. "You're okay?" he asked, as if he feared his eyes might deceive him.

"Fine."

"You deliberately led Clark away from Brian, didn't you?"

"You mean by taking him to the Sheraton?"

He nodded.

"That was part of it. If he had had anything desperate in mind, I didn't want it to happen around Brian. But to be honest, it was more than that. I also could see he wouldn't talk where we were and I had to know what had really happened to Tessa."

"You couldn't wait to read it in the paper like the rest of us?"

She shook her head. "From the minute I found her body, this wasn't some news story to me. It was personal. If it could happen to Tessa in the middle of a fund-raiser, then it could happen to anyone." She drew in a breath and admitted what was at the heart of everything. "It could happen to me."

His gaze narrowed. "Don't you see? That's

what terrifies me."

"I know you worry. I can't blame you for that. But when I look for the answers behind something like Tessa's murder or Greg Kinsey's or Allan Winecroft's, I feel in control again. I feel like I'm getting an edge up on anyone who might ever try to hurt me or Brian."

Hal nodded slowly. "I guess I can understand that. It's a scary world out there these days. We all need to do whatever we can to be in control of our lives. I suppose that's all I was doing by filing this custody suit."

Molly stepped closer and touched his cheek, wishing that it had never come to this sad state of affairs between them, but knowing that there was no way to go back. "Maybe there's a solution for us short of taking this to court. Now that we both understand where we're coming from, next time, if there is a next time, I will bring Brian to stay with you. That way we'll both know that he's out of harm's way."

"You've never been willing to do that before," he said, sounding surprised by the gesture.

"Because I was always afraid you wouldn't bring him back," she admitted. "Do we have a deal, Hal?"

He cupped her face in his hands and for

288

an instant she was certain he intended to kiss her. Instead, he merely leveled an intense gaze directly into her eyes, then smiled faintly.

"We have a deal." He brushed a kiss on her forehead. "I suppose it doesn't hurt that you have a cop standing by, if things get really out of hand." He shot a grudging glance of respect at Michael, who was hovering a discreet distance away. "Take care of her, O'Hara."

Michael slid his arm around her waist. "She doesn't need me to do that, DeWitt. She can take care of herself." He grinned down at her. "Right, *amiga*?"

Darn right.

Nature always has the last word.

■ ■ ■ ■

HOT SCHEMES

■ ■ ■ ■

1

Miami, Florida
1994

The deafening music pulsed to a Latin beat at Sundays by the Bay, a favorite weekend watering hole of Miami boaters and the singles crowd. Molly DeWitt had long since given up any attempts to carry on a conversation with Detective Michael O'Hara, whose attention seemed to be focused more on the horizon than on her, anyway. His beer sat untouched, warming in the sun. As near as she could tell with his eyes shaded by his favorite reflective sunglasses, he hadn't even noticed the five scantily clad women at the next table. That was how she knew he was far more worried than he was letting on.

"Still no sign of your uncle's boat?" she shouted over the music.

He glanced at her briefly, shook his head, then turned his attention back to the water.

His expression was more somber than she'd ever seen it, even in the midst of some particularly gruesome homicide investigations.

Molly understood his concern. It was now after noon. Tío Miguel should have been back by eleven o'clock, noon at the latest, from his regular Sunday fishing trip. On days he took out charters, he might stay out longer, but Sundays were personal. On Sundays he stayed only long enough to catch enough snapper or grouper for the family's dinner, plus extra to share with friends up and down the block in their Little Havana neighborhood.

The rest of the week Tío Miguel worked nights delivering the morning newspaper door-to-door, then took out his occasional small fishing charters, usually wealthy Latin Americans and their Miami business associates. One or two days a week he worked on the boat, fiddling with the engine to assure top performance, polishing the trim, cleaning it from stem to stern. Though the charter boat wasn't new or top-of-the-line, it was his most prized possession and he cared for it with passionate devotion.

A small, olive-complexioned man with a deep tan and dark-as-midnight eyes, Miguel García had an unmistakable wiry strength even though he was about to turn sixty-five. Molly had met him several months earlier at dinner at Tío Pedro's, yet another of Michael's uncles. She had been instantly charmed by his awkward, soft-spoken blending of English and Spanish and the pride in his voice as he talked of Michael's accomplishments in Miami.

Tío Miguel and Tío Pedro and their wives — both sisters of Michael's mother — had preceded Michael to Miami when Fidel Castro succeeded Batista in Cuba. They had left behind homes, family and once-thriving careers in the hope of regaining freedom. It was to them, via one of the famed Pedro Pan airlifts, that Michael's mother had sent him, alone, at the age of five.

Though Molly had known many other exiles, some successful, some barely making it, none had touched her quite the way Tío Miguel had. When he talked of his native land, there had been such sadness in his eyes and something more, an anger perhaps, that his homeland was out of reach to him now. Unlike his brother-in-law Pedro, who owned a flourishing Cuban restaurant and whose children were now involved in careers of their own, Tío Miguel had never fully adapted to his new land.

Like so many other Cuban exiles who had

come to Miami in the 1960s and who had expected to go back at any moment, Tío Miguel had struggled with English. Fortunately, he lived in a community where shopkeepers spoke Spanish, where parish priests and government officials spoke his language. He had settled for taking menial jobs to support his family, always with the fragile hope that he would return home to a free Cuba someday. As time passed, hope had faded, replaced now by sorrow and the faintest traces of anger and bitterness.

Molly glanced at Michael and saw that his attention was still avidly focused on Biscayne Bay and the Atlantic beyond.

"You're worried, aren't you?" she said.

"He's never been this late before, not on Sunday when he knows Tía Pilar will be waiting and the family will be gathering after Mass."

"Does he have a radio on the boat?"

Michael nodded.

"Then he can call the Coast Guard if he's in trouble. I'm sure he's okay. He probably found a hot spot where the fish were really biting and didn't want to come in yet."

"Maybe," he said tersely. He stood up. "I'm going inside to make a call. Keep an eye out for him, will you?"

"Of course."

Though Tío Miguel had invited Michael, Molly, and her son, Brian, to come fishing with him some Sunday, they had never taken him up on it. Brian had brought it up once or twice, but Molly had discouraged him from pressing Michael about it. Now as she watched the endless rows of sailboats, yachts, and fishing boats dotting the water beyond the marina, she realized she had no idea what his boat was named, much less what it looked like. Except for those with billowing sails, they all looked pretty much alike to her, especially from this distance.

When Michael finally returned, he looked more tense than he had before.

"What did you find out?"

"Nothing. Tía Pilar said she was expecting him home by now, that he'd said nothing about being later than usual. There was something else in her voice, though, that convinced me I'm right to be worried. I called the Coast Guard. They haven't had any distress calls, but they're going out to take a look." He didn't have to say that he'd called in a favor to accomplish that. He drummed his fingers nervously on the table and took another sip of beer. "Damn, I can't stand this. Come on."

"Where?"

"I'll run you home, then come back and

rent a boat. I'm going out myself. I've been fishing with him enough. I probably know better than the Coast Guard does where to start looking." He threw some money on the table, then slipped between the tightly packed tables along the edge of the marina.

They were nearly at the car when Molly touched his arm. "Michael, I want to go with you," she said, unable to ignore his anxiety. She'd learned long ago that Michael was incapable of asking for help, but that didn't mean he couldn't use a little support from a friend once in a while. Predictably, though, he was already shaking his stubborn Cuban-Irish head.

"No. If there's trouble, I don't want you involved."

"What sort of trouble?" she said, puzzled by the implication that something other than an engine breakdown might have delayed Tío Miguel.

He just shook his head again, his expression more tight-lipped and obstinate than usual. "You're going home."

Molly made up in determination what she lacked in stature. And when someone she cared about was in trouble, she didn't want to waste time debating her right to help. She planted herself in front of him, eyes blazing.

"Dammit, Michael O'Hara, don't you pull any of this Latin machismo stuff with me. Two pairs of eyes will be better than one out there. If your uncle is hurt, I might be able to help. You won't be able to manage him and the boat at the same time."

Apparently he saw that arguing would simply waste more precious time. That was the only explanation she could think of for his quick, grudging nod. He changed directions so quickly, she almost lost her footing trying to keep up with him.

Halfway down the marina's first dock, a middle-aged fisherman was just unloading his catch. He greeted Michael with a nod. *"Hola."*

Michael began talking to him in Spanish. The only thing Molly understood for certain was Tío Miguel's name, but the man's head bobbed in agreement.

"He'll take us out," Michael told her, already following the man onto the boat. He held out his hand to help Molly aboard. "He and my uncle are friends. Tío's slip is just two down," he said, gesturing toward the empty space. "He says my uncle went out as usual about dawn."

"Does Tío Miguel usually fish in the same place?" Molly asked.

"More or less. We might have to do some

cruising around, though. I assume you don't get seasick. The water looks a little choppy today."

"Let's just say it's probably best if we don't put the idea into my head," she said just as the powerful engine started throbbing beneath them. Her stomach churned, then settled a bit as they eased away from the dock and into open water. Fresh air replaced gas fumes as they chugged out of the harbor. She tried to ignore the thick, dark clouds gathering in the west and the threat they represented.

"You okay?" Michael asked, removing his sunglasses to peer at her more closely. "You looked a little green there for a minute."

"I'm fine now."

"I want to get up front to help Raúl watch for the boat. You'll be okay back here?"

Molly nodded. "What's the name of the boat? I'll watch from here."

"The Niña Pilar."

She reached out and touched his hand. "We'll find him, Michael."

"I hope so," he said, and turned abruptly, but not before she'd noted the tense set of his jaw and the deepening worry in his eyes in that instant before he'd slipped his sunglasses back into place.

Not only was he Tío Miguel's namesake,

but the two also shared a special bond because of Michael's young age when his mother had sent him to America to live with his aunts and uncles. That, combined with the fact that Michael had never known his own Irish-American father, had cemented their relationship. The closeness was not something Michael ever spoke of, but she had learned over the last months to read the emotions in his eyes, even when his words revealed nothing. If something had happened to Tío Miguel, Michael would be devastated, as would the rest of the close-knit family.

Under the blinding glare of the early afternoon summer sun, a fine mist of salty water dried on Molly's skin almost as soon as it landed, leaving her skin gritty. As the boat chugged into deeper seas, the water turned from a glistening silver to a murky green, then purple, darkened from above by the bank of nearly black clouds rolling in, dumping sheets of rain in the distance and hiding the land from sight.

Whether it was due to the violence of the approaching storm or Michael's anxiety, Molly grew increasingly uneasy as the boat rocked over the choppy waves. All the other boats were making for land, while they continued to head out to sea.

No longer able to stand being left alone, she made her way forward on the slippery deck, clinging to the metal railing as she climbed up to join Michael and Raúl. While the middle-aged Cuban man steered against the powerful northerly currents, a huge cigar clamped between his teeth, Michael kept a pair of borrowed binoculars trained on the horizon.

Molly clung to a railing as the wind ripped at her clothes and tangled her hair. "Any sign of him?"

"Nothing. Raúl's heading south."

Molly's uneasiness mounted. "South? Toward Cuba?"

Michael nodded.

Suddenly dozens of stories flashed through her mind, stories about ill-fated missions against Castro by exiles fanatical in their patriotism and their determination to re-claim their homeland. "Michael?"

He slowly lowered the binoculars and turned toward her, his expression grim.

"You don't believe he went fishing today, do you?"

"I hope to God I'm wrong, but no."

"But surely he wouldn't . . ."

"He would," Michael said tersely. "The goddamned fool would. He's been involved with some underground paramilitary group

302

for years. I looked into them once for Tía Pilar. I decided they were harmless enough, not like Alpha Sixty-six or Comandos L."

Molly recognized the names of two of the most active organizations reputed to carry out terrorist bombings and other clandestine operations against Castro and his supporters. She shuddered to think of the implications had he belonged to one of those. Another group she'd heard of, the one Michael hadn't mentioned, was Brigade 2506, made up of men who had survived the ill-fated Bay of Pigs invasion in 1961. Revered by exiles, the Bay of Pigs veterans claimed to be no longer involved in commando raids, though one of its most prominent members continued to operate a training camp in the county.

"Dammit," Michael swore. "I thought that eventually he would see that there are better ways to end Castro's dictatorship, especially with the fall of communism in the rest of the world."

"But why now, after all this time?" Molly said, unable to imagine the sheer folly of what Michael was suggesting. "You must be wrong. I'm sure he just got caught in a squall or something. He wouldn't try to invade Cuba on his own, for heaven's sake."

"You don't understand what it's been like

303

for him. You can't. Not even I fully understand it. Cuba — the Cuba he remembers,
anyway — is in his soul. It's as if some vital
part of him has been carved away. Whenever
new exiles come, he always meets with
them, soaking up their news of Cuba like a
sponge. For days afterward, his melancholy
deepens."

The sadness, Molly thought. That explained the sorrow that perpetually shadowed Tío Miguel's eyes. And Michael was
right. His heartache was something she had
no way of fully comprehending. She had
always lived in her homeland, and even
though she no longer lived in Virginia,
where she'd grown up, she could go back
anytime she wished.

"Would he have gone alone, though?" she
asked. "Wouldn't there have been others?"

"More than likely, though Raúl says he
has heard nothing of such plans. Such men
operate in secret, but there is almost always
gossip."

As the boat churned through the choppy
waters, they emerged beneath bluer skies.
The wind settled into little more than a
breeze that barely stirred the humid tropical
air. But even with the improved weather,
the tension didn't lessen as the afternoon
wore on.

The one question Molly didn't dare to ask was whether Raúl would risk carrying them all the way into Cuban waters. Nor was she sure she wanted to know whether Michael would allow him to do any less. Fortunately, with nothing but open water in all directions, Molly had no real sense of how close she might be to having both questions answered. Cuba was ninety-six miles from Key West, a hundred and fifty miles from Miami. Unused to nautical speed, she couldn't even be sure how long it would take them to cover that distance.

For all she knew there was little purpose to the zigzagging course they seemed to be on as the summer sun slipped below the horizon in a blaze of orange.

"There!" Michael said eventually, gesturing to Raúl as he kept his binoculars pinned on some tiny speck in the dimming light of a July sunset.

To Molly the boat in the distance was indistinguishable from dozens of others they had seen since leaving the marina. Only as they drew closer did she realize that the boat's engine was still, that its movement was propelled by no more than the drifting currents.

"Tío! Tío Miguel!"

Michael's shouts carried across the water

as they pulled alongside the boat. *Niña Pilar* had been painted on the boat's bow in neat, bright blue letters, a jaunty tribute to a woman Molly couldn't imagine Tío Miguel leaving behind.

"Can you get any closer?" Michael asked Raúl.

"*Sí,*" he said, maneuvering until the boats were touching.

Michael threw a rope across, then looped it through the railing of his uncle's boat until the two were pontooned together. Only then did he leap from Raúl's boat to the deck of his uncle's.

Molly's breath caught in her throat as he made his way carefully from bow to stern. She nearly panicked when he disappeared inside the cabin and failed to return. She had one hand on the railing and was preparing to leap herself, when she heard the boat's engine chug to life, then sputter off again. So, then, Molly thought in dismay, it hadn't been a breakdown. Dear heaven, where was he?

Finally Michael reappeared.

"Michael?" she said softly, her heart hammering as she tried to read the expression on his face.

He swallowed hard before he finally lifted his gaze to meet hers.

"He's gone," he said bleakly. "The inflatable raft is missing, too. I can't tell about life vests, because I'm not certain how many he carried."

"You're sure he's gone back to Cuba, though? Maybe the boat ran out of gas and he took the dinghy to get help," she said, searching desperately for another explanation, even one that flew in the face of the sound she'd just heard, of the engine running perfectly smoothly. "Maybe another fisherman picked him up."

"The boat's fine. Besides, he would never have left it behind," Michael replied with certainty. "We are in Cuban waters, or at least what they view as Cuban waters." He looked to Raúl for confirmation. The fisherman nodded.

"What does that mean?" Molly asked.

"It means the Cuban government extends their territorial rights a couple of miles farther into the waters than international law usually dictates." He sighed with obvious frustration. "Dammit, what has he done? Did he think he could get away with slipping into Cuba? The soldiers will shoot him on sight, either mistaking him for a rafter trying to escape or, if he is armed, seeing him for what he is, an enemy of Castro."

307

Raúl greeted Michael's announcement with a barrage of Spanish. He hurriedly sketched a cross over his chest, his gaze flashing toward heaven. Though she could understand only about one word in ten, something in the fisherman's voice told Molly he disagreed with Michael's interpretation.

Michael questioned him in impatient, rapid-fire Spanish.

"What?" Molly said. "Michael, what is he saying?"

"Estás loco," Michael said derisively to the other man. *"No es posible."*

"Sí," Raúl said just as adamantly.

"What, dammit?" Molly said, shouting over the pair of them.

Michael finally looked at her. "Raúl seems to think it is not possible that my uncle went back to Cuba. He says he would have taken his boat all the way to shore if that had been his intention. He would have tried to land on the beach, not taken a chance crossing the strong currents between here and there in a tiny inflatable raft."

Molly found herself agreeing with Raúl's logic. "Then what does he think happened?"

"He thinks he was murdered," he said in a clipped tone.

"Murdered?" Molly repeated, unable to

308

keep the shock from her voice.

Michael waved a hand dismissively. "You see why I say he is crazy. Who would want to murder an old man who has never done anything to hurt anyone in his life?"

To Molly the passionate disagreements of the exiles had always seemed incomprehensible, but she knew that emotions ran high. Murder was not out of the question, given the right circumstances.

"Can you dismiss what he is saying so easily?" she asked gently, though she didn't want to believe Raúl's theory any more than Michael did. "You're a homicide detective, Michael. You of all people know how important it is to look beyond the obvious. You know that people can be driven to kill for reasons that make no sense to anyone else."

He glared at her. "Maybe just this once I don't want to think like a detective," he snapped. "Maybe just this once I don't want to know anything about someone who might be sick enough to hurt an old man."

She understood his desperation, felt something akin to it herself, and yet clinging to an illusion wouldn't help them to find answers. "I know you, Michael. You won't rest until you know the truth. Not about something as important as this."

A sigh shuddered through him then. He

slid his sunglasses back into place, shading his eyes, though it was long past any need for them. Without another word he secured Tío Miguel's boat to be towed back to Miami, then gestured to Raúl.

"Wait," Molly said. "Couldn't we take the boat back?"

He shook his head. "I don't want to chance destroying any evidence that might be on board." He again gestured for Raúl to begin heading home.

The fishing boat turned to the north and began chugging through the swift currents of the Florida straits. Molly could no longer read Michael's expression in the darkness closing in around them, but he stood facing south — toward his homeland. Toward Cuba.

2

Hours later, by the time the silent trio reached the marina again, Metro-Dade evidence technicians were waiting at the dock, summoned by Michael over Raúl's ship-to-shore radio. Once again Michael leapt aboard his uncle's boat, started the engine, and guided it the last hundred yards into its slip. As soon as the fishing boat was secured, the sleepy, out-of-uniform evidence techs — Ken Marshall and Felipe Domínguez — joined Michael on deck. When Molly made a move to join them, Michael waved her back.

"I want them treating this like a crime scene," he said grimly. "There's no point in adding another set of prints or messing up what's already here. If you'll wait at the restaurant, I'll call a cab for you in a minute."

Molly shook her head. "I'm going to make a phone call, but I'm not leaving."

He opened his mouth, clearly intending to argue, then shrugged. "Fine. I'll give you a lift when we're through."

At the pay phone inside the restaurant, she called her ex-husband. He was not going to appreciate the fact that she was calling at what he would consider the middle of the night or that she hadn't called much earlier. She shrugged off his displeasure. Hal never approved of much she did anyway. He could just add this to the list.

"Where the hell are you?" Hal DeWitt demanded. "I thought you were picking Brian up at eight o'clock. It's the goddamned middle of the night."

She almost laughed at the predictable response. Instead, she managed to sound dutifully contrite. "I'm sorry. I couldn't get to a phone before now."

"The woman who keeps a cellular phone attached to her eardrum?" he retorted with derision.

"Hal, is this really necessary?"

"I think it is." When that was met with silence, he added, "Okay, okay. When are you getting here?"

"I'm not. I really need you to keep Brian another day or so."

That was greeted with his most put-upon sigh. "Couldn't you have called earlier? He could have been in bed by now. You haven't gotten yourself mixed up in another goddamn murder, have you?" he inquired sarcastically.

The last three homicide cases in which Molly had inadvertently become entangled had irritated the daylights out of her ex-husband. He'd acted as if she personally had been responsible for the deaths. He also made it seem as if she'd done it only to aggravate him.

"No," she said, refusing to accept the possibility that Tío Miguel might be dead or to be drawn into an argument. "But a friend of mine is in the middle of a family emergency. I'd like to be able to help out. It'll be easier if Brian stays with you."

Since leaving Brian with him more often was exactly what Hal had been pleading with Molly to do, she guessed he wouldn't dare deny the request, though he'd do his best to make her feel guilty in the meantime.

"I suppose it'll be okay," he said grudgingly.

She bit back a sarcastic retort about his enthusiasm. Instead, her tone deliberately mild, she said only, "Thanks. Since he's still up, anyway, let me speak with him, please."

To her amazement, Hal didn't argue. Maybe he didn't want to know what friend she was helping. He wasn't fond of her best friend, Liza Hastings, and he was downright hostile about Michael. A few seconds later, Brian was on the line.

"Hey, Mom, what's up?"

"I've asked your dad if you can stay with him another night or two. He's agreed."

"How come?"

She didn't want to alarm him about Tío Miguel's disappearance until they knew more. "It's already late and Michael's tied up for a while, so I can't get home. You might as well get a decent night's sleep."

"Oh."

She picked up on his unenthusiastic tone of voice. "You okay with that? Is everything all right at your dad's?"

"I suppose."

It was an amazingly reticent answer for a kid who was never at a loss for words. "Brian? What's going on?"

"He's got this lady here," he finally blurted. "She keeps looking at me like she wishes I'd get lost."

Molly was surprised. Hal had always been careful not to have his dates around when Brian visited, perhaps to give the illusion that he was still pining away for Molly. For a time, anyway, he had been, or so he'd claimed. However, they'd resolved all of that

314

months ago. Apparently he'd finally accepted that they had no future and moved on with his life. Brian was normally just fine with that in theory, possibly because he adored Michael and hoped that something would develop between him and Molly. In fact, he'd done everything up to and including personally proposing marriage to Michael on Molly's behalf. Molly had been horrified. Michael had taken it in stride. He'd had a man-to-man talk with Brian, taken his concerns seriously, and promised to keep the suggestion in mind.

Obviously, unlike Michael, this particular woman hadn't done anything to ingratiate herself with Brian. Apparently she didn't understand the value of having a precocious kid in her corner.

"Don't worry about her," Molly advised. "Your dad wants you there, and that's all that matters. I'll talk to you sometime tomorrow."

"What about summer school? I'll probably be really tired anyway, since it's so late. Do I get to stay home?" he inquired hopefully.

"Not a chance. I know you stay awake playing video games until this hour, when you think I'm already asleep. You'll get by."

"But dad's never taken me to school before."

"Your dad knows the way. He'll drop you off."

"But my homework's at home."

Molly had to hold back a chuckle at this one last try. Homework was not something uppermost on Brian's mind most of the time. "Tell your dad to stop off at the condo so you can pick it up," she advised him.

"Okay," he said, accepting defeat gracefully. "See you, Mom. Tell Michael 'hi' for me. Has he asked you to marry him yet?"

"No, Brian, and he never will if you keep on pestering him about it." She thought about the implications of her response and quickly amended, "Not that I want him to, anyway."

"Yeah, right," Brian teased.

" 'Bye, kiddo. Behave yourself."

When she'd hung up, Molly walked back to the dock. She leaned against a piling, hoping that just watching the investigation on the boat might spark a few theories of her own about what might have happened to Tío Miguel.

As she waited, Raúl once again unloaded the cooler filled with his day's catch. When he caught sight of her, he went back aboard and brought her a rusty lawn chair that had been stored in the cabin, apparently for family outings on the nearby beaches.

"Sit," he instructed her.

Even though the chair had clearly been the victim of too much salt air, it was better than continuing to stand indefinitely. "Thank you."

She studied the middle-aged Cuban, wondering how much English he spoke and understood. He and Michael had spoken only Spanish in her presence. "Raúl, do you speak English?"

"*Sí,* I speak some English," he said haltingly.

"Why do you believe someone harmed Miguel?"

Something that might have been fear darkened his eyes. He shook his head, muttering, "*No comprendo,* señorita."

Molly's knowledge of Spanish was too limited for explaining the complexities of her question. Besides, she had a feeling that Raúl understood her perfectly well. Something about Miguel's disappearance, however, frightened him.

She tried again, hoping to take a more innocuous route to the same information. "Was he alone this morning?"

"*No sé.*"

"You don't know?" she said disbelievingly.

"I thought you saw him."

"*Sí.*"

"But you saw no one else?"

He shrugged.

This was getting her nowhere fast. Either he had seen someone and that someone had terrified him into having a convenient memory lapse or he was implying that someone could have been hiding below-decks on Miguel's boat or on another boat that had followed Miguel to sea or . . . Hell, his vague response could have meant almost anything. Molly sighed.

Raúl regarded her worriedly. "The señorita would like something to drink?" he asked, suddenly finding his English vocabulary.

"No, thank you."

"I have very good rum."

"No."

"Beer?"

Molly regarded him evenly. "Nothing."

He backed away then and picked up his cooler and fishing gear. As he started down the dock, he hesitated. "I am sorry, señorita."

"That's okay, Raúl. You'll call Señor O'Hara if you think of anything, right?"

He bobbed his head. "*Sí, sí,* I will call."

Molly figured Michael shouldn't hold his breath expecting evidence from this particular source, whether he was a friend of Miguel's or not.

She glanced back at the *Niña Pilar* and wondered what was going on belowdecks. What could they find? Fingerprints? On a charter fishing boat wouldn't that be like hoping to use prints to ID a killer in the crowd at Joe Robbie Stadium? Even though Tío Miguel was a fanatic about cleaning up his boat, who knew how many sets of prints could have been scattered around the cabin and on deck since the last time he'd polished everything. Maybe Michael was hoping to find some suspicious piece of evidence, a piece of cloth snagged from someone's shirt, a button, traces of blood indicating a struggle.

The thought of the latter sent a shiver down Molly's spine. Just as she'd anticipated, Michael wasn't likely to ignore any possibility, no matter how absurd or terrifying he personally thought it to be. His success as a homicide detective was based on his gut instincts and his cool, meticulous attention to detail. He would bring that same skill to bear on an investigation of his uncle's mysterious disappearance, no matter how difficult it might be for him to remain objective. If anything, he would be more relentless and thorough than usual.

He was still grim-faced when he finally emerged nearly an hour later. He looked dismayed when he saw her, as if he'd completely forgotten her existence. It was an understandable reaction, but hardly flattering.

"Sorry," he said. "We'll be able to leave soon."

"Don't apologize. Have you found anything?"

He shook his head. "Not a damn thing. Oh, there are plenty of prints, but who knows how long they've been around."

"Any signs that he might have struggled with someone?"

"Nothing."

Molly had a sudden thought. "What about a gun?"

"If he owns one, he took it with him."

"A map of Cuba?"

"He knows those waters and that shoreline like the back of his hand. He wouldn't have needed one." He muttered a curse in Spanish. "We couldn't find one damned thing to indicate what he might have been up to out there besides fishing."

"His gear was still aboard, then?"

"All of it, as far as I could tell."

"Had he caught anything today?"

"What the hell difference . . . ?" Michael

320

began, then grinned. He leaned down and planted a kiss on her forehead. "Molly, you're a genius. If he caught anything, then this was just another fishing trip. I'll be back in a minute."

He jumped aboard the *Niña Pilar* and headed for the stern of the boat, which was apparently where Miguel kept ice-filled coolers for the day's catch. When he came back, his expression was even more somber than before.

"Any fish?"

He shook his head. "But there is melting ice in one cooler as if he'd expected to fill it with fish. Another has ice and beer and a couple of sandwiches. I didn't see any empty bottles. Whatever happened must have happened right after he got out there."

"What do you think that means?"

"I think it means that Raúl could have been right," he admitted with obvious reluctance. "Someone could have forced him off that boat. He wouldn't have headed for Cuba in an inflatable raft without any provisions. Even from where we found his boat, he was hours from shore depending on the currents. Hell, from what I know about the water in the straits, he would have been a goddamned fool to abandon his boat there and head for Cuba on a raft. He'd have been fighting the currents all the way. The rafters leaving Cuba count on those currents to take them north to America, not south."

"Will you tell your aunt that?"

For the first time in all the months she had known the extraordinarily confident detective, Molly saw genuine uncertainty in Michael's eyes.

"I don't know," he said quietly. "I don't know what the hell to say to her. I don't want to alarm her, but . . ."

"Michael, she's already alarmed, I'm sure. She'd have to be. I think you have to concentrate on what's being done to find him, rather than on all the things you don't know."

"Like what? I don't even know where to start," he said angrily. "I'm a cop and I don't have the vaguest idea where to begin."

Molly refused to believe that. "Nonsense. At the moment, you're thinking like a grief-stricken nephew. As soon as you begin thinking like a policeman, you'll know exactly what to do next, what you'd do if this were any other suspicious disappearance."

He shot her a wry look. "I gather from that that you have an idea yourself that you're assuming will come to me once I begin to think clearly. Feel free to share it. I'm coming up blank, and right this minute I will do almost anything, no matter how far-fetched, to postpone going to my aunt's house without answers."

"Call *Hermanos al Rescate*," she suggested, referring to a group of pilots whose name in English meant Brothers to the Rescue. The organization had been formed to try to save at least some of the desperate people who tried to flee Cuba on makeshift rafts. In one recent year over 2,500 people had made the attempt in everything from inner tubes to glued-together Styrofoam. *Hermanos al Rescate* found 103 of these foolhardy, courageous people in its first two years. Molly recalled that they had also found 44 empty rafts between the beaches of Varadero and Mariel and the Florida Keys. It was not an especially cheering statistic. She concentrated on emphasizing the positive.

"I know they usually conduct their searches looking for rafters heading from Cuba to Miami," Molly added, "but I'm sure they'd help look for your uncle, and they're used to flying over those waters looking for tiny specks on the sea. Combined with a Coast Guard search, wouldn't that help to reassure your aunt, at least for now, that everything possible is being done to find Miguel?"

Michael sighed heavily, obviously every bit as aware of the statistics as she was. "At least I'll be able to tell her that people will be looking for Tío Miguel in the morning," he agreed finally. "I know one of the pilots. I'll call him."

Molly was determined to keep prodding him with ideas until his own instincts kicked in. "Shouldn't you call the State Department and see if there have been any incidents along the Cuban beaches?"

He shook his head. "We'll know soon enough if there have been. Castro just loves to carry on about these imperialist attacks on his sovereign shores. In the meantime, I don't want to stir things up in Washington and have them breathing down my aunt's neck for information about his illegal plotting to invade Cuba. It's a violation of the Neutrality Act. Washington issues warnings periodically just to prevent the exile groups from acting on their wild ideas."

"And when the commandos do it anyway, half the time Washington winks and looks the other way," Molly pointed out.

"Only if no one raises a fuss about it. No, I'll handle this myself."

"What about work?"

"I'll take leave time. God knows, I have plenty of it built up. I haven't taken a vacation day off in years."

"Have you officially reported your uncle as missing?"

Michael shook his head.

"How'd you get the evidence techs here, then?"

"Called in a favor," he admitted. "Look, I'm going to make that call to try to get those rescue flights in the air in the morning. At least I can pinpoint where we picked up the boat. It'll give them a starting point for the search. If Ken and Felipe get finished inside, ask them to wait for me."

Molly nodded. She wanted to shadow him, but knew he would be infuriated by the overly protective gesture. She was surprised he'd tolerated her staying around as long as he had. Any second now she expected him to insist on her returning home. To which she intended to reply that he'd have to haul her away kicking and screaming. It wouldn't do a lot for his image as a cool, unemotional cop. She figured he'd grasp the improbability of shaking her loose fairly readily, once she'd explained her intentions to him.

In the meantime, since the search of the boat was pretty much complete, maybe she could sneak in a quick peek before Michael returned to forbid it. She actually made it as far as the aft deck before she heard footsteps behind her.

"Going someplace?" Michael inquired.

"Just taking a look around," she admitted. "Your guys are almost through so I won't be disturbing any evidence now, right?"

"And you honestly think you might spot something that two well-trained evidence technicians missed?"

"You never know."

He gazed toward heaven with a familiar pleading expression, then sighed. "Fine. Look to your heart's content. I'll check with the guys, and then we're out of here."

Unfortunately, Michael's smug attitude appeared to be justified. Molly couldn't discover one single clue to explain Miguel's disappearance. She did, however, hear an odd noise coming from beneath the stacks of life preservers in a built-in wooden storage bin. The faint but unmistakable ticking gave her goose bumps.

It was an unusual place to hide a clock, unless said clock was attached to a timing device. She'd seen enough movies to suspect that a crude bomb could be every bit as effective as one made by professional terrorists.

"Michael!" Molly shouted at the top of her lungs, all the while inching away from the sound.

Michael and the two evidence techs responded to the panic in her voice. She pointed toward the sound. "In there. A bomb, I think."

"Don't be ridiculous," Michael said, just as Ken Marshall gently lifted out first one orange life vest, then another.

"Holy shit!" he murmured, his freckled complexion turning even more pale. "Let's get the hell off this tub and get the bomb squad down here."

The four of them clambered onto the dock. While the crisply efficient Marshall called for backup, Michael and Domínguez went up and down the slips to make sure there was no one in the nearby boats.

"I'm taking the boat out," Michael announced.

"No way, man," Domínguez countered, blocking his way. Shorter than Michael and built more squarely, he looked like a bulldog confronting a sleek, angry Doberman. "You'd have to be *loco* to get anywhere near that bomb."

"I'm not endangering other people," Michael insisted stubbornly. "Who knows how powerful the damn thing is or when it's set to go off."

"Exactly my point," the evidence tech said, trying to hold Michael back. "Let those crazies who like to live on the edge deal with this. That's what the county pays them for."

"It's my responsibility," Michael insisted, breaking free of the other policeman's grasp.

When Molly started to follow him, Felipe Domínguez held her back, his determined grip on her arm almost painful. "You won't stop him, and he sure as hell won't want you with him."

She knew it was useless to fight him, knew that he was right. Biting back a sob, she whispered, "But what if . . . ?"

The policeman cursed at the sound of the engine coming to life. "Jesus, O'Hara," he muttered as the boat began to move.

"Michael!" Molly shouted over the steady throbbing of the engine. Bile rose in her throat and tears stung her eyes as the boat inched away from the dock.

Just then Ken Marshall returned, saw the moving boat and stared after it, open-mouthed with shock. "Mother of God, Felipe, why didn't you stop him?"

Felipe turned his anguished dark-eyed gaze on his colleague. "How? You know what O'Hara's like when he gets something into his head. Did you want me to handcuff him?"

"If that's what it took," Ken snapped in exasperation.

"What time is it?" Molly asked with a dawning sense of horror and a sudden understanding of what the whole day's events could have been about. Her hands were shaking so badly she couldn't see the face of her watch.

"Just before midnight."

"Exactly, dammit!"

"Eleven fifty-eight. Why?"

She lifted her hands helplessly. "I don't know. Just a feeling I have."

"That the bomb would be set for midnight," Ken guessed.

She shook her head. "One minute after."

Both men regarded her with puzzlement. "Why?"

"The date," she said with certainty, her voice choked. "It'll be the anniversary of the goddamned Cuban revolution."

They could already hear sirens in the background as Ken kept his gaze riveted on the second hand of his watch. "Eleven fifty-nine," he breathed. Then added, "Midnight."

The next sixty seconds were the longest of Molly's life. Her heart was in her throat.

The boat was a couple of hundred yards into the bay and still chugging toward open water.

"Twelve-oh-one," Ken said.

Molly's eyes burned from tears and from straining to see through the darkness. There was no mistaking the sudden spark of fire at the back of the boat, the puff of smoke.

"Oh, God," she murmured, wanting to turn away, but unable to. Her gaze was fixed on the *Niña Pilar* with a sort of horrified fascination. Waiting. Waiting.

Just when she thought she could bear the terrible suspense not one second longer, flames shot into the air with an explosion of sound that slammed through the stillness and echoed in her head. One of the policemen, she had no idea which one, gathered her close, rocking her back and forth, even as a steady stream of curses spewed from his mouth.

"Michael?" she whispered, weeping. She looked up into Ken Marshall's stricken face. "Where is he? Did he get off?"

"Even if he did . . ." Felipe began, before Ken shushed him.

Molly didn't need to hear the rest of the words. Even if Michael had gotten off the boat, what were the odds that he was far enough away when the billowing flames danced across the water?

3

The music at Sundays by the Bay trailed off, replaced by screams and the pounding of footsteps as people raced from the restaurant toward the dock, awed by the fireball spreading across the water. Molly clung to Ken Marshall, her gaze riveted on the water, haphazard bits of old, familiar prayers whirling through her head.

The Lord is my Shepherd . . .

Our Father who art in heaven . . .

Now I lay me down to sleep . . .

No one prayer was ever finished before the next took its place, as if her brain was trying to find the one prayer that could magically make this come out right.

When she could finally tear her gaze away, she looked up into Ken Marshall's brimming eyes, eyes that had no doubt seen their share of terrible scenes but nothing so horrifying as this. Domínguez was standing beside them, stone-faced. Only his black-as-onyx eyes reflected the same kind of agony that churned inside Molly. She realized that in calling these two particular policemen earlier, Michael had not just called in favors, he had recruited friends. And these friends were every bit as shaken as she was.

"You have to send somebody after him," she pleaded. "He could be out there, hurt."

"It's not safe, not yet," Ken Marshall responded bluntly. "But we'll find him, I promise you that. We've got paramedics and Coast Guard rescuers pouring in here." His expression softened and his voice turned gentle and cajoling, the kind of voice people used on someone whose state of mind was rightly considered as fragile as spun glass. "Why don't we go up to the restaurant and get you something to drink?"

Molly shook her head. "I'm not leaving here, not until Michael is back."

She heard someone in the crowd offer to bring her coffee, and a moment later a warm cup was placed in her trembling hands. She automatically lifted it to her lips and took a sip of the strong black brew, though her eyes never left the water. Several people who'd apparently been drinking in the bar or having a late meal before going home climbed aboard their boats and turned high-beam searchlights onto the water to aid the rescuers.

Molly had understood Ken Marshall's blunt words. She knew it wouldn't be safe until the last of the flames had burned themselves out, but with every second that passed, her terror mounted. Images passed through her mind, each one more horrifying than the one before. Michael could have been killed outright in the explosion. Or thrown clear of the boat, unconscious, only to drown. Or while plunging into the sea, he could have been coated with the boat's fuel, then turned into a human torch.

She moaned softly, tears coursing down her cheeks. There were so many things she'd never told Michael. She'd never admitted how much stronger she was, thanks to him. Nor how much he meant to her. Was it too late? In that one blinding instant had they been robbed of a future that had promised to be something incredibly special?

"Will you be okay?" Marshall asked, hunkering down beside her as she huddled in the chair Raúl had left for her. "I want to join the search."

She glanced around. Domínguez had already gone, easing away without Molly even noticing. "Please, go," she said. "Find him."

As she waited for some word, Molly was

distantly aware of the arrival of sleepy overnight crews from some of the local television stations. Thankfully none of the reporters seemed to be aware of her or her connection to the bombing story. She couldn't have formed a coherent thought for them right now.

"Molly?"

She glanced up into the worried face of Ted Ryan, a reporter from the morning paper. He'd been assigned to cover some of the same homicide cases that Molly had unofficially investigated. She'd been trying to save her own neck or that of a friend. Ted had provided a more objective eye. He was bright and ambitious, which meant he'd be dogging her with questions regardless of her fragile emotional state.

"Not now," she said in the slim hope it would send him on to more forthcoming sources.

He slid his notebook and pen into the back pocket of his rumpled khaki pants, possibly to indicate that his questions were personal, rather than professional. Molly knew better than to trust him or any journalist on the trail of inside information.

"Was this some sort of film stunt?" he asked.

Though it was a natural enough question

given her profession as an assistant in the Metro-Dade film office, Molly felt like laughing hysterically. If only that was all it had been, a crazy, dangerous movie stunt in which everyone lived except the fictional bad guy.

"No," she said finally, shivering at the memory of Tío Miguel's boat splintering into a million burning pieces with Michael most likely still aboard. "This was the real thing."

Ted nodded as if he'd already guessed as much. "I heard a cop was on that boat right before it blew. Since you're here and it wasn't a movie stunt, I'm guessing the cop was O'Hara," he said, his voice surprisingly subdued. His gaze strayed to the water as if he couldn't quite bear to meet her eyes.

Molly saw no point in denying it. "Yes," she whispered.

To her surprise, Ted's expression registered genuine dismay. He squeezed her hand sympathetically. "I'm sorry. I know he and I are usually at odds, but I liked him. He was a great cop."

The past tense infuriated her. "Is a great cop, dammit! He is not dead."

Ted looked miserable. "God, I'm sorry. I didn't mean to make it worse. Look, is there anything I can do for you?"

"Not unless you can get out there and find him for me."

"I'll go see if there's any word yet," he said, then scurried off as if he couldn't wait to get away from her and the deeply personal pain she didn't even try to hide. At least he hadn't plagued her with questions about the explosion or what had led up to it. She supposed she should be grateful for that much consideration. And she knew that Ted would do nothing to betray her role in this story to his rivals. He was too much of a fierce competitor for that. So for the moment she could sit where she was, alone and anonymous, waiting for word.

It seemed like hours, though it was probably no more than a half hour or sixty minutes, before she finally heard a triumphant shout echo across the water. She stood on unsteady legs and made her way down the dock. Pushing her way through the crowd, she finally spotted a Coast Guard boat speeding toward shore. Paramedics, hauling a stretcher and carrying other critical equipment, rushed through the crowd. When they tried to get Molly to move aside, she stubbornly refused.

"It's okay," Felipe Domínguez told the paramedics, edging in beside her. He put a bracing arm around her waist and pulled her forward. "She was here with O'Hara."

She looked into his troubled eyes. "They've found him, haven't they?"

"*Sí*," he said quietly. He moved his hand to her shoulder and gave her a reassuring squeeze. "They say he's alive, but they have said no more than that, not to me, anyway."

She glanced at the paramedics. "Did they radio in anything about his condition?"

At a nod from Felipe, the dark-haired, tanned paramedic who seemed to be in charge told her, "He's got a nasty bump on the side of his head. He was unconscious when they found him, bobbing along in his life vest."

With Felipe's hand continuing to rest gently on her shoulder, Molly finally faced the most agonizing question of all. Trying to contain a shudder, she asked, "Was he burned?"

"No, ma'am. The explosion threw him in the opposite direction from the worst of the fire. Sounds to me like he might have been about to dive off the bow, when that sucker blew. He's one lucky son of a bitch." At a scowl from his partner, he winced. "Sorry, ma'am."

Molly was too intent on the activity at the end of the pier to worry about the paramedic's language. As the Coast Guard cutter docked, she choked back the sobs that threatened. Holding her breath, she watched as they carried Michael off the boat and lowered him onto the stretcher. His clothes were ripped and singed. They had stripped away his life vest and shirt on the Coast Guard boat and already an IV line was in place. There were gashes on his forehead and arms and his complexion was far too pale, but she could detect the steady rise and fall of his chest. The paramedics didn't fight her as she knelt beside him and clung to his icy, lifeless hand.

"Damn you, Michael O'Hara, you'd better not die on me," she whispered furiously.

Either her words or the tears that spilled onto his bare chest apparently got through to him. His eyelids flickered and his lips tried to curve into a smile. "I'm not going to die, *querida*," he murmured. "Too much unfinished business."

"The explosion," she said with an air of resignation. "And Tío Miguel."

He gave an almost imperceptible shake of his head. "You and me."

They tried to admit Michael at county-run Jackson Memorial Hospital so they could watch him overnight and through the following day. Unfortunately, there weren't enough doctors and nurses in the entire University of Miami-affiliated trauma center to hold him down once he'd made up his mind to go.

"Michael, I will go to see your family," Molly promised in what she guessed was probably a vain attempt to get him to listen to reason. "I will tell them everything that's happened. I've already told them most of it on the phone and convinced them they don't need to rush over here in the middle of the night."

She didn't mention that it had taken all of her persuasive skills to accomplish that. Tío Pedro had been ready to pack the entire family into the car, along with a priest, when she finally got through to him that Michael would more than likely be released first thing in the morning anyway. That might be only a couple of hours away, but she figured those hours were best spent in a hospital bed, not chasing down clues in his uncle's disappearance and the bombing of the fishing boat. She tried one more time to make him see reason.

"You'll think much more clearly after a couple of hours of rest. You won't get that at home with everyone hovering over you. Besides, you have no business leaving the hospital. You've just been through a major trauma."

"A couple of scratches," he argued.

"And a knock on the head that's obviously addled your brain," she countered.

He sat up, wincing with the effort. "This is something I have to do, *amiga*. Will you help me or not?"

Molly glanced at the harried resident trauma surgeon, who shrugged. "If he goes, it's against medical advice, but I can't stop him. If he's not staying, I've got two gunshot wounds out there who are in far greater need of my help."

"By all means, treat your other patients," Michael said with a dismissive wave of his hand. He winced in pain, but remained stubbornly determined. "Molly, find my clothes."

"Your clothes are a little the worse for wear," she reminded him. "They're ripped and soaking wet. I could bring clothes from home in the morning."

"I'll walk out of here stark naked if I have to," he warned.

So much for that. "An interesting possibility," she commented. "That ought to guarantee catching the attention of the nurses. Maybe one of them will convince you to stay."

He scowled at her.

"Okay. Okay," Molly muttered, giving up. "I think I saw some jeans and a T-shirt wadded up in the back of your Jeep, along with all the soccer gear. I'll go get 'em. Meantime, sit still, please. This could be the last rest you get for a while, if you can call it that."

"Are Felipe and Ken out there?"

"Half the Metro-Dade police force is out there. The rest of them are on the bay picking up debris, hoping to piece together some decent evidence. You created quite a commotion, Detective."

"Tell Felipe and Ken I need to talk to them."

"Your boss will be disappointed if he's not in on your powwow."

"Okay, fine. Send him in, too."

"Maybe you should just go into the lobby and hold a damned press conference," she said irritably, as the tight band of tension around her head finally snapped. She started to the door of the treatment room.

"Molly?"

She turned.

"You okay?"

"Sure. I'm just dandy," she retorted. "You get yourself practically blown to smithereens and now it's back to business as usual. You'll have to pardon me if I can't switch emotional gears as quickly as you do."

He eased gingerly off the examining table. "Come here."

"What for?"

"Come on, *amiga,* humor me."

She walked slowly over to him. Her insides were still turning somersaults. He cupped her face in both hands and tilted her head until she was forced to meet his gaze.

"It's over now and I'm okay," he said quietly.

A sigh eased through her, but relief was tantalizingly elusive. Molly slid her arms around Michael's waist and rested her head against his chest. He felt warm and solid and very much alive. If she could have held on like this forever, it might have reassured her. Instead, she knew deep down that this respite would be short-lived. If anything, the real danger was just beginning.

4

Outside the doors of the relatively new trauma-center entrance, the media hounds had gathered like a pack of irritable wolves. Before Molly went through those doors, she found a police spokesman. He was clearly a rookie, judging by his age and the fact that he was hiding inside rather than outside, where he could hobnob with the reporters. She pulled him aside and suggested that this might be the perfect time for some sort of statement.

"Who are you?" he asked suspiciously. "Do you work for the hospital?"

"No, but I have to get something from O'Hara's car for him and I really don't want to be the one they start questioning out there. It'd be a lot better if you gave them an update, something official."

"But nobody's issued anything formal yet," the officer argued.

This was definitely not a man inclined to

climb out on a limb. "I can solve that problem. Tell them the doctors are impressed with Detective O'Hara's hard head," she suggested.

"Huh?"

The challenge of getting through to him lost its appeal. "Never mind. I'm sure you'll be able to think of something innocuous. That's what people in your line of work are best at."

The officer regarded her uncertainly, clearly not sure whether to take offense at her sarcasm. Since she really wanted him to distract the media — and since she frequently had to do the same kind of public-relations tap dance — she apologized.

"Sorry. Just pacify them, okay?"

"I'll get the director."

Obviously this was not a man who craved the limelight. She predicted a very short career in the public information office. "You can forget the director. He's in with O'Hara. You're on your own, Officer."

Just to make sure he didn't turn tail and run, she nudged him out the door ahead of her. As she'd expected, the reporters turned into a frenzied pack, lobbing questions faster than tennis balls flew at the annual Lipton Championship over on Key Biscayne.

Since she didn't trust the reticent young man's ability to satisfy their hunger for information for long, as soon as all attention was focused on him, Molly slipped past the crowd. When she reached Michael's Jeep, which she'd left illegally parked and protectively watched over by a willing hospital security guard, she opened the tailgate and collapsed for a moment on the cool metal. All of the tension of the past few hours caught up with her at once.

"Are you okay, ma'am?" the petite female security guard in her snug navy blue uniform asked.

"Just a delayed reaction."

"How's O'Hara?"

"You know him?" she said, regarding the young African-American woman with surprise. In a hospital complex the size of JMH with its eight thousand or so employees and physicians and its huge daily volume of traffic, she was astonished anyone even remembered the names of their coworkers.

"Sure. He turns up here all the time when probable homicides roll in. That's how I knew it was him. I recognized his car and tag number. The man refuses to park where he's supposed to. You must have got that from him."

"Bad habits do tend to get around."

"So, is he okay? Nobody's come out I could ask. We've got a full moon. The whole damn place is filled up with crazies. Nobody takes a break on a night like this."

"Michael's okay. At any rate, he insists on leaving. I'm supposed to be out here scrounging for clothes for him to wear."

"You sit right where you are. I'll get 'em for you." She scrambled into the back of the wagon, sorted through the clutter of soccer balls and knee pads, and emerged triumphantly clutching a pair of grass-stained jeans and an embarrassingly wrinkled T-shirt. "They're not pretty, but they'll do, right?"

Molly laughed for the first time in hours. "They won't exactly enhance his image as the best-dressed cop on the force."

"He is one slick dude, isn't he?" the guard said, grinning at the comedown from Michael's usual spiffy designer suits. "Serves him right for leaving against advice. That is what he's up to, isn't it?"

"You've got it." Molly took the clothes. "Thanks. We'll no doubt see you shortly."

"Tell him I want this car out of here before shift change or the boss will bust my butt."

"I'll tell him," Molly said. "But I don't think he intends to waste a second more

347

than necessary as a guest of the hospital."

Back inside the treatment room, Molly found Michael trying to persuade Metro-Dade Safety Director Lucas Petty to assign him full-time to investigate the bombing and his uncle's disappearance. The burly black man, with his tough, by-the-book philosophy of operating the department, wasn't buying Michael's reasoning for an instant.

"Last I checked you were a homicide detective, O'Hara. We've got no body."

"Dammit, my uncle left on that boat. Now he's missing and the boat's been bombed. In my book that adds up to reasonable cause to suspect foul play."

"It surely does," Petty said with a genial nod of agreement. "And I will even go along with the idea that your uncle was taken against his will. You, however, will not be conducting whatever investigation this department decides to launch. You'll be home with your sorry butt resting in bed, like the doctor ordered."

Marshall and Domínguez turned away to keep the public safety director from spotting their commiserating grins. Obviously they knew, as did Molly, that Lucas Petty didn't have a prayer of keeping Michael out of this particular investigation. They all waited for his anticipated declaration of intent.

Sure enough, his jaw set stubbornly, he fumbled in the pocket of his ruined pants, came out with his wallet, and removed his badge. "As of now, I'm on leave."

Petty looked as if he wanted to strangle him. He rocked back on his heels and glared. "You take sick leave, then you'd damned sight better stay home and act sick."

"I'm taking vacation leave."

"Not without prior authorization."

"Don't push me, Lucas," Michael said quietly, his expression lethal.

Unfortunately, Lucas Petty didn't appear to be in any mood to have his buttons pushed either. He took two steps forward until he was in Michael's face. "O'Hara, you are treading on very thin ice here."

Michael never even flinched. "Is my leave granted or not?"

"If it's not?"

"Then I'll quit, dammit. Right here and right now. You'll have a hell of a time explaining to the press why one of your best homicide detectives was forced into early retirement. And forget about any hogwash about a medical disability stemming from this damned explosion. When I'm finished with this investigation, I will transfer into the Miami PD, which has been begging me to do just that for the past ten years, and I will look for every opportunity to make you regret this whole lousy episode."

Petty backed up and threw his hands in the air. "Jesus, O'Hara, you know it's bad news taking on an investigation in which you're emotionally involved."

"You don't have the time or the manpower to give this case the attention it deserves," Michael countered. "Nobody will care more than I do about seeing that it's solved."

Lucas Petty cast his gaze heavenward. Judging from his sour expression when he finally looked back at Michael, he hadn't received any divine inspiration. "Okay, okay, you win. Take your leave. How much time do you want?"

"As long as it takes."

"Terrific. Your fellow officers in Homicide will be pleased to take over your workload, I'm sure."

Michael glared at him. "Don't you try to lay a guilt trip on me. I've carried more than my share of work for my entire fifteen years in the department."

Lucas Petty heaved a sigh of resignation. "Yeah, you have. Okay, O'Hara, do what you have to do. Be careful, though. This bombing thing tonight wasn't some amateur prank." He held out his hand and shook Michael's. His expression softened. "I'm glad you're okay, son." He looked at Marshall and Domínguez. "You guys coming?"

They glanced at Michael, who shook his head.

"Not just yet, boss," Marshall replied.

The public safety director's eyes narrowed. "You two aren't on leave. Remember that."

"Yes, sir," Marshall replied, his cheeks flushing with a patch of guilty color.

Domínguez just avoided his gaze.

Petty looked as if he wanted to launch into another lecture, but eventually he just shook his head, muttered something under his breath about maverick cops, and left them alone.

"What do you want us to do?" Felipe Domínguez asked as soon as their boss was gone.

"Ask around on the street, Felipe. I know you have contacts. See what's going on with some of these anti-Castro paramilitary groups. Kenny, when they bring in the remains of the boat, I want you to go over every piece of evidence and tell me exactly what you find. I need to know where to start looking for the people who made that bomb."

Ken Marshall shook his head in disgust. "Exactly how many parts of that bomb do you expect to be recovered from the goddamn bay?"

"One would be enough, if it's the right one, one we can trace."

Domínguez shot him a grin. "Man, you watch too many cop shows on TV. Either that or you've got the soul of some romantic Cuban poet living in a dream world."

Michael grinned back. "I just know what fine, dedicated police officers can come up with when they put their minds to it."

"Oh, man, the pressure," Marshall groaned, but he, too, was grinning now, clearly relieved that Michael was back to his usual bossy behavior, acting as if that explosion had never happened. "You know, O'Hara, one of these days you're going to run the whole damned department. You know exactly how to motivate people."

"Right, pizza and beer at my place at the end of your long, productive days. See you tonight about seven thirty?"

"Tonight?" Domínguez said. "You expect answers tonight?"

"Let's face it, some group out there is going to be very proud of what it did. Most likely they won't be quiet about their accomplishment. My guess is there will be some trumped-up story about Miguel's loyalty to the cause. As for the evidence, if it isn't in the lab today, chances are Kenny's right and it's buried in the muck at the bottom of Biscayne Bay."

To Molly's astonishment, Michael didn't wage a struggle for the keys to his car. After being eased protectively through the crowd of reporters by Marshall and Domínguez, he kidded with the security guard for a moment, then hauled himself into the passenger seat, leaned back, and closed his eyes.

Worried by his ashen complexion, Molly hesitated before turning on the ignition. "You all right?"

"Let's just say I'm glad the kids don't have soccer practice today," he said, referring to the team he coached and on which Molly's son played. "I'm not exactly up to running wind sprints."

"It's not too late to check you in here," she said.

"Not a chance. Most of the people I know who check into this place wind up dead."

"You're a homicide detective," she reminded him as she reluctantly turned on the engine. "You don't come here with folks who are hale and hearty."

"Just drive. I'll be fine." As he said it, he flipped on Spanish-language radio, known for the feverish, generally one-sided, anti-Fidel pitch of its political commentary. It was the first place a terrorist might turn to claim credit for a politically motivated bombing. Molly tried valiantly to pick out distinguishable words from the rapid-fire clip of the newscast. Unfortunately she was lost, even though Spanish classes had left her with at least a serviceable vocabulary.

"Anything?" she asked finally in frustration.

Michael shook his head. "There's mention of the boat blowing up, but no more than that. Perhaps I should go to see Luis myself."

The Luis in question was undoubtedly the controversial news director, Luis Díaz-Nuñez. If Michael was thinking of dropping by the studio, it could only mean he intended to go on the air to stir things up a bit. She could just envision the ensuing on-air shouting match.

"Now?" she asked incredulously. "It is five thirty in the morning. You've just left a hospital — you will note that I did not mention that you were not even officially released from said hospital — and you're wearing clothes that should have hit the laundry at least a month ago."

"It's radio, *amiga,* not TV."

Molly prayed for patience. "Michael, has it occurred to you that perhaps after the disappearance of your uncle, the bombing of his boat, and a concussion, you might not be thinking too clearly?"

"No," he replied matter-of-factly. He looked at her and grinned. "Okay, I will not go to the radio station now." He glanced out the window for the first time as she turned from Twelfth Avenue onto Seventh Street and headed west into the heart of Little Havana. "Where are you taking me?"

"Where do you think?" she said dryly. "To Tío Miguel's, where everyone has gathered for an all-night vigil. If I don't put you on view in front of the family immediately, they'll just come chasing down to Kendall after you the minute they discover that you're out of the hospital."

She regarded him hopefully. "Maybe we can just do a drive-by-and-wave sort of thing."

He laughed at that. "And Felipe accused me of being a dreamer. You don't think I have the energy to do a radio broadcast, but you figure I can undergo an inspection by my relatives? Wait and see, *amiga.* An hour with Luis would have been child's play by comparison."

5

"Castro! I live for the day when I can spit on his grave," Tío Pedro said angrily over the weeping of the three Huerta sisters in Tío Miguel's living room several hours later. It was midmorning and the entire family had been gathered there all through the endless night of waiting.

When Michael and Molly had arrived at dawn, his mother had rushed from the house in her too-large, flowered housedress and matching hot pink flats. Standing on tiptoe, she had kissed him soundly on both cheeks, then held him at arm's length while she examined him visually from head to toe, clucking at every scratch. There were plenty to cluck over.

Rosa Conchita Huerta was a lovely, petite woman with curling black hair, whose lined face still showed the strain of the years she had stayed behind in Cuba after sending her son to be reared by her sisters in Miami.

Her nut-brown eyes followed Michael avidly whenever he was in a room, as if even after all this time, she couldn't make up for the years when he had been out of sight.

Rosa at fifty-five was the youngest of the sisters. Elena, Tío Pedro's wife, was the middle sister. Her round, cheerful face bore none of the lines that kept her younger sister from being truly beautiful. She, too, dressed in bright, flattering colors, even though her figure was no longer girlish. She made no excuses for the fact that she dressed to please her adoring husband and that her abundant figure was the result of sampling too many of the excellent dishes they served in their *Calle Ocho* restaurant.

As for Pilar, the oldest of the Huerta sisters, even on happier occasions she tended to be dressed in somber fabrics and wore her luxuriant black hair pulled back into a well-tamed bun. Her thin, aristocratic face, usually so lovely in repose, had a pinched, haunted look this morning that made her look every one of her sixty-two years. She had managed a watery smile at the sight of Michael, but it was clear she was overcome with grief and worry. Her gaze was fixed on the door and each time it opened, a heartbreaking instant of hope flickered in her eyes, then died at the appearance of each new arrival who was not Miguel.

A half dozen or more of Michael's cousins and as many neighbors were crowded into the minuscule living room. After so many hours on a muggy summer night, the air was stale. Even the chugging air conditioner in the window couldn't seem to cool the room.

Worse from Molly's perspective, the cramped space was filled with so many religious paintings and statues she felt as if she'd wandered into a church rectory. A half-dozen candles were lit in front of a cheap plaster statue of the *La Caridad del Cobre,* the patron saint of Cuba. The candles, each emitting a different perfumed scent, added to the oppressive atmosphere.

Even after Michael had spoken quietly with his aunt for some time, Tía Pilar remained inconsolable, though Molly knew that Michael had kept the two worst-case scenarios to himself. He had told his aunt only that they had found the fishing boat and that his uncle had not been aboard. Molly, too, had tried to reassure the woman that Tío Miguel had no doubt joined another fishing party after his own boat broke down. Tía Pilar had accepted her consoling words with murmured gratitude, but the desolate expression in her eyes never wavered. With the arrival of each neighbor, whether from this Little Havana neighborhood just south of *Calle Ocho* or from her native Cuba, her grief erupted into heart-rending sobs.

After a while, feeling like an intruder in the midst of such openly displayed anguish, Molly had asked to use the phone and gratefully left the cluster of women. In her own family, everyone had been taught to suffer in silence. There would have been no outpouring of grief and, as a result, little comfort offered, since no one ever knew how deeply anyone was affected by loss or illness. As uncomfortable as it made her, she envied Michael's family the ability to let their emotions show. Still, she was glad to have a moment to herself.

The old-fashioned black phone sat on a wobbly table in the hallway, affording Molly little privacy. The sobbing of the women and the passionate arguing of the men provided convenient sound effects for her conversation with her boss. Vince Gates was not going to be overjoyed to be hearing from her two hours after she had been due to arrive at the office. Maybe the background hysteria would convince him that the emergency was real.

"Molly?" he said with an exaggerated air of amazement. "Molly DeWitt? Didn't you used to work here?"

"I thought I still did."

"Then why the hell aren't you here?" he demanded irritably.

"Do you want the short version or the two-hour action-adventure version?"

"I'll take the one that includes your estimated arrival time. I've got Jeannette meeting with a producer who showed up thinking he had an appointment with you."

Molly swallowed hard. "Sorry. Jeannette will do just fine," she reassured him, probably in vain. Vince refused to acknowledge that the Haitian-born clerk was thoroughly overqualified for her entry-level job. He was too worried that she was going to cast some voodoo spell over him, a concern that Jeannette herself did nothing to dispel. In fact, she thoroughly enjoyed taunting him in Creole, managing to inject an ominous note into the most innocuous of words.

"Vince, you know perfectly well Jeannette has worked with me on the last half-dozen projects. She probably knows as much as I do about what production companies need and what resources are available."

"I suppose," he conceded with obvious reluctance. "So when can we expect you?"

"Next week," she blurted, figuring it was better to get the bad news over with in a hurry.

"No wonder you're so anxious to tout Jeannette's virtues," he remarked dryly. "So what's the story? Have you had major surgery over the weekend? Did you wrap your car around a tree?"

Molly noted he asked the questions with more sarcasm than concern. "Actually, Michael's uncle's boat blew up with Michael on board," she retorted casually.

"Yeah, right."

"It did. Don't you ever read those papers that stack up on your desk? Try today's front page. I'm sure Ted Ryan has a full account."

She heard the rustle of paper, then Vince's "Holy shit!"

"So, do I get the week off?"

"Is O'Hara okay?"

"Yes, but as you can tell from the commotion in the background, all is not well with the family. His uncle is missing." She held the phone out for Vince's benefit, allowing him to pick up on the upper decibels of hysteria. Satisfied that her point was made, she asked, "Get the picture?"

"Okay. O'Hara's family is noticeably distraught," he conceded. "Has something changed? Are you about to marry into this

362

family?"

Did middle-of-the-night fantasies count? Probably not. "No," she admitted.

"Then what does this have to do with you, besides the obvious, of course, that you can't keep your nose out of trouble?"

"Let me explain the concept," she said very slowly. "Michael has stuck by me during bad times. He has been a good friend."

She ignored Vince's sarcastic *harrumph* and plowed on. "It's my turn to return the favor. Besides, it's about time you gave Jeannette a break. The only way you'll do that is if I take off on an unscheduled vacation and she has to handle my appointments."

"Maybe I'll find out she's even better than you. Then where will you be?"

"Sitting in clover with a workload that's the size it's supposed to be," she retorted. "So what's it going to be? Do I get the time off?"

"If I say no, what will you do?"

"Take off anyway, which means you'd probably have to fire me and then hunt for a replacement. Could take weeks, maybe even months if I appeal the firing." She obviously had picked up some negotiating skills while watching Michael go at it with Public Safety Director Lucas Petty earlier at the hospital. She had an advantage, though.

363

Vince Gates was a pushover compared to Petty. He was also pragmatic. He wanted to be on a golf course, not fighting her in some personnel dispute. Granting an unscheduled week of leave was the pragmatic answer. She waited for him to figure that out. It didn't take long.

"Okay, fine," he said grudgingly. "As long as you'll check in once a day in case there are any emergencies, I'll okay the leave. Don't get any ideas about next week, though."

Molly didn't even want to think about what would happen if they didn't find Tío Miguel long before that. "Thanks, Vince. I owe you one." It was not a balance of power she adored, but just this once there was no way around it.

When she'd hung up, she skirted the gathering of women and went to Michael's side. She found him in the midst of a quieter but no less emotional exchange between him, his uncle, and the other men from the neighborhood.

"I tell Miguel again and again that all of the plotting and scheming is no good," Tío Pedro said. "If the Bay of Pigs failed, what can one old man do?"

Molly knew a mention of the Bay of Pigs would stir the wrath of those who felt the

United States had betrayed them, leaving a brigade of commandos to fight alone in a losing attack on Cuba. As expected there were immediate, passionate comments about the Cuban heroes of that 1961 attempt to reclaim their homeland and the Democratic politicians who had abandoned them. Only recently had she come to understand that more than anything else that moment in history had been responsible for turning the exile community into such passionate Republicans. Likewise, they had turned conservative because the more liberal Democrats frequently advocated a softer line with Castro.

When the reminiscences about the Bay of Pigs had run their course, Michael brought the conversation back to Miguel and the present. "Then he was still involved with that organization of the revolution or whatever it's called?" he asked.

"Two, three nights a week he sat with them over coffee at this place or that, always moving as if Castro's spies were following them," Pedro said with an air of disbelief. "Saturdays he would wear these military fatigues and go to the Everglades. When I ask him for what, he tells me they are training for the revolution."

"Didn't he read the damned newspapers?"

Michael said. "The Cuban soldiers are shooting down even those who go ashore in an attempt to rescue relatives. How could he think of going back?"

His uncle sighed. "He was heartsick," Tío Pedro said. "He could not accept that the Cuba he left behind is no more. He dreamed of *café Cubano* and the white sand of Varadero beach. He saw Havana as it was when the wealthy, even from this country, came for the nightlife. He saw those who plotted these crazy missions as heroes of the next revolution."

"The leader is still Orestes León Paredes?" Michael asked.

"Leader?" Pedro said with derision. "What kind of leader would play on the emotions of a bunch of old men? You do not see men of your generation joining the ranks of his organization, do you? No, it is only men like Miguel, whose souls live in torment for what was."

Michael, usually so stoic and controlled, regarded his uncle with impatience. "He has been in America for more than thirty years. Why is he still clinging to the past?"

"Because he is Cuban," Pedro replied as the old men surrounding him nodded in solemn agreement. "As are you and I and your mother and your aunts. We are exiles,

366

not Americans. We have been blessed by this country, but it is not ours. We left ours not by choice, but from necessity."

"Over thirty years," Michael repeated angrily.

"A lifetime would not change the truth," Pedro said with passion. "I might not believe that it is up to those of us here to force the changes that will make Cuba free again, but in my heart I am always Cuban."

Molly listened to the exchange with the amazement of an Anglo who had wondered time and again at the exiles' refusal to assimilate American ways. "When Castro is gone, will you go back?" she asked.

"On the first flight," Pedro said with feeling. "And yet I know it will not be the same. Perhaps I won't want to stay, but to see my homeland again? Like Miguel, I dream of it. There are cousins there I haven't seen in all these years. My brothers are there, and nieces and nephews." His eyes took on a dreamy, faraway expression. "The breezes were cooler, the plantains sweeter, the *lechón* more tender."

"*Sí, sí,*" the others murmured. "That is so."

Only the nephews did not join in the chorus. They exchanged the jaded looks of children who have heard it all before time

367

and time again.

"But you can no longer find a plantain or a pig to roast," Michael retorted.

"*Sí,*" Pedro said wearily, ignoring the bitterness in his nephew's voice. "It is the memories which are sweet, not the reality."

"You've never been back to visit?" Molly asked.

"Never. It is a choice I made. Not one dollar of my money will go into that man's pocket." He shrugged ruefully. "Not that I would be allowed back. I am regarded as an enemy of the people because I fought Fidel, because I spoke out as a dissident. Had I not escaped, I would have spent the last years jailed as so many others have."

"And Miguel?" Molly asked.

"He attempted to organize a coup. He was jailed, but made a daring escape. He was shot and left for dead. Another of the guerrillas rescued him and smuggled him aboard a boat that crossed the straits that same night. He arrived in Key West one month after my own arrival. I brought Elena with me. It was nearly a year before Pilar was able to join him. And many years after that before Michael's mother came. As the youngest of the sisters, Rosa was reluctant to leave her mother. She came only after Paolina Huerta died."

"But she sent Michael," Molly said. Michael had once told Molly of the terror of his first days in a new country, sent to live with relatives he barely remembered without the mother he adored. He had been five years old, a baby, when he left Cuba aboard one of the famed Pedro Pan freedom flights. His aching sense of being abandoned had remained with him for years. Only after they were reunited did he begin to understand that his mother had sent him away out of love.

As if all of this rhapsodic talk of a land he'd all but forgotten irritated him, Michael stood up abruptly and crossed the room to his aunt's side. Tía Pilar clasped his hand in hers and regarded him with a tear-streaked face. "Find him," she pleaded.

"I will," he promised.

His mother again stood on tiptoe and kissed him on both cheeks. "Do not take chances."

"I cannot do my job without taking chances," he told her, though a smile seemed to tug at his mouth at the start of an apparently familiar argument.

"And I cannot be a mother without warning you not to," she replied.

She walked with him back to Molly. "Thank you for coming," she said, her

English precise and still reflecting her uneasiness with her second language.

"I'll be praying for Tío Miguel's safe return," Molly told her. "Please tell Tía Pilar that."

"She will be grateful. We all will."

Outside the tiny pink stucco house with its neat white trim, the street was quiet. Bright splashes of fuchsia and purple bougainvillea gave the simple homes a needed touch of jaunty color. Only blocks away on *Calle Ocho,* Southwest Eighth Street, the Little Havana restaurants would be opening their doors for midday meals of grilled Cuban sandwiches, chunks of pork, black beans and rice, *arroz con pollo,* and sweet, fried plantains. The sidewalk stands selling *café Cubano* would already be doing a brisk business. Only Tío Pedro's restaurant would remain closed because of the family emergency.

"I'd like to make another stop before I take you home," Michael said. "Do you mind?"

"Absolutely not."

"Will Brian be okay?" he asked as an afterthought. Suddenly his expression turned worried. "Good Lord, Molly, I haven't even thought about him. Where is he?"

"He's okay. He's with his father. I called Hal from Sunday's last night and asked him to keep Brian a few more days."

Michael regarded her with surprise. "You don't usually give your ex-husband that kind of concession."

She returned his gaze evenly. "I wanted to be free to help you and your family, if you'll let me. Brian will be fine with his dad for a few days. And I called Vince from your aunt's," she said. "I'm taking the week off."

She saw the trouble brewing in Michael's expressive eyes and sought to forestall it. "This isn't open for debate."

He hesitated, then finally slid his mirrored sunglasses into place and turned his attention back to the road. "Nobody's arguing, *amiga.*"

Molly was wise enough not to reach for the ever-present calendar in her purse to note the date on which macho detective Michael O'Hara finally behaved in a perfectly reasonable manner.

6

The old men playing dominoes in Máximo Gómez Park on the corner of *Calle Ocho* and Fifteenth Avenue barely glanced up when Michael and Molly approached with the thimble-size paper cups of potent, sweet *café Cubano* they'd bought across the street. Molly watched as the tiles clicked with the precision of years of play. She listened intently to the rapid-fire Spanish to see if she could detect whether the morning's topic of conversation was the bombing of Miguel García's boat or the more general and constant theme of Castro's imminent downfall.

A portable radio blared the latest news from the most vitriolic of the Spanish-language stations. Molly recognized the histrionics of Luis Díaz-Nuñez. She couldn't interpret half of what he said. This wasn't proper, clearly enunciated Castilian Spanish. Rather, it all ran together in a way that only someone with a trained ear could separate into distinct words. Occasionally she was able to distinguish a name or an organization, but in general she caught only the fact that whatever he was reporting made him angry and probably ought to make anyone who wasn't a traitor to the exile cause angry as well. Unfortunately for the newscaster, on this particular morning with this particular group of men, the outcome of their dominoes games took precedence over politics. Aside from an occasional halfhearted murmur of agreement, their attention was focused elsewhere.

The palm trees provided almost no breeze to stir the muggy, midsummer air. The red-tiled roofs over the tables offered minimal shade. Heat radiated from the sidewalk in shimmering waves. The aroma of cigar smoke from thick, handmade Cuban cigars made in nearby factories swirled around them. In moments their clothes were sticking to them. Still, Michael stood patiently watching the play and sipping his coffee, his expression enigmatic.

Eventually, when the game he was observing most closely concluded amid cheers and back-slapping, he nodded to one of the players. "Señor López?"

Eyes the color of walnuts squinted at Mi-

373

chael through thick lenses. The wiry old man, his hands gnarled, his shoulders bent, finally nodded. "*Sí.* I am José López."

Michael explained in Spanish that he was Miguel García's nephew. Several men, dressed in their khaki shorts and *guayaberas,* or jeans and plain white T-shirts, backed away, looking thoroughly uneasy, as if they expected a gunfight to break out, Western-style. Only Señor López seemed pleased by the introduction.

"Sit," he said, gesturing to a place that was immediately vacated by his opponent in the hotly contested game of dominoes. He glanced distrustfully at Molly and waited until Michael explained who she was.

"You are wondering if I know what has happened to your uncle," he said finally, using his halting English for Molly's benefit.

Michael nodded.

"I spoke to your family last night to tell them of my concern."

"Last night? You had heard the news last night?" Michael asked skeptically. "I cannot imagine that my uncle's disappearance was on an evening newscast. One old man lost at sea for a few hours? What is the news?"

"Word travels quickly among friends. I knew of Miguel's disappearance by nightfall.

Only this morning did I learn of the explosion."

"And how did you learn of that? Also from friends?"

"No, from the radio. I have heard nothing except what was on the *noticias,* the news reports. Díaz-Nuñez has talked of little except the explosion this morning."

"And has he offered an explanation?"

"Nothing."

"He is not calling my uncle a hero?"

Señor López began to look faintly uneasy. "No, those were not his words."

"A traitor, then?"

The old man's gaze sharpened. "Why would you say such a thing?"

"It is possible, is it not? If one does not support the cause wholeheartedly, if one perhaps makes a mistake in trusting the wrong people, then there are those who would be quick to label this person a traitor. We have seen this with something as simple as the condemnation of a singer who had dared to perform in Cuba, *sí?*"

"*Es posible,* yes," Señor López admitted. "But you are speaking of your uncle. I ask again, why would you say such things?"

"Tell me about him," Michael suggested. "As you know him."

"*No comprendo.*"

"I know that you were boyhood friends in Havana. I know that he considers José López to be like a brother. I also know that you used to go with him to meetings of the Organization of the Revolution. He told me that."

A stream of Spanish greeted Michael's statement, then in English he said, "He should not have said that. That is Miguel's problem. He does not know how to be discreet."

"You do not take pride in your membership?"

"That is not the point. Obviously you comprehend that no better than Miguel."

If Michael was irritated by the criticism, Molly couldn't tell it. He was displaying far more patience with this irritable old man than he ever displayed in an interrogation or even with Molly. Clearly, he expected to wheedle something important from Señor López, but Molly couldn't help wondering how long his restraint would last.

"Would that problem have caused him difficulty with Paredes?" he asked bluntly.

Molly watched Señor López's eyes at the mention of Paredes. They betrayed nothing.

He shrugged and conceded, "It is necessary to know the value of silence within a group such as ours."

376

"Where can I find Paredes?"

This time there was no mistaking the flicker of unease in his eyes. López avoided Michael's gaze. "I cannot say."

Michael's hands clenched and Molly guessed that his patience was at an end. He looked as if he wanted badly to reach across to shake the old man.

"Someone put a bomb on my uncle's boat yesterday," he said softly, though there was no mistaking his carefully contained fury. "I want to know who and I want to know why. I believe Paredes can provide the information I need."

The old man's expression shut down completely. He struggled up, and Molly realized with a sense of shock that one leg was missing below the knee. His pant leg was folded up and sewn together. She wondered when and under what circumstances his injury had occurred.

As he balanced himself carefully, one of his friends handed him a pair of crutches. "I must be going now," he said. "My daughter will be expecting me."

"You do not care what has happened to your old friend?" Michael snapped at him. "He could be dead and it does not matter to you?"

Tears brimmed in the old man's eyes

377

before he could blink them away, and he sank back down on the concrete bench. *"Por favor,"* he whispered. "Do not do this. Leave me in peace."

"I will go," Michael said, his expression as hard and forbidding as Molly had ever seen it. "When you tell me how to find Paredes."

Señor López's hands trembled as he tried to stack the dominoes in a neat pile.

"Señor?" Michael prodded.

The dominoes tumbled to the table. "Tomorrow night at La Carreta," López said finally, referring to a chain of Cuban family-style restaurants.

"Which one?"

"Here, on *Calle Ocho.*"

"And Paredes will be there?"

"Perhaps. Perhaps not. But someone there will know how to find him."

Michael gave a curt nod of satisfaction, then rested his hand over the old man's. "Thank you."

"De nada." For nothing. No problem.

It wasn't nothing, though, Molly realized as she studied the soul-weary man across from them. José López looked as if the exchange had drained him of every last bit of energy. Worse, when she gazed into his eyes, all she saw was fear.

As she and Michael walked back to his

378

car, she said to him, "He was afraid. Was it because you're a policeman?"

Michael shook his head. "I believe he is afraid that whatever happened to my uncle could happen to him."

Michael fell sound asleep en route to his recently acquired town house in Kendall. Not even the caffeine in several cups of Cuban coffee could combat the exhaustion of the past twenty-four hours or so. The fact that he was not awake to argue was probably the only reason Molly was actually able to get him to go home. Awake he would have been insisting on going to assist in the rescue flights that had been taking off all morning from Tamiami Airport in search of his uncle and any other misguided rafters who might be lost on the treacherous seas.

He groaned when she gently shook him awake to go inside. "Where are we?"

"Your place."

He yawned and climbed out of the car, leading the way inside the neat cream-colored structure with its red-tiled roof. Inside the air-conditioning blasted, creating an almost Arctic chill.

"I'll take a quick shower and then go out to the airport," he said, his voice still groggy with sleep. "Why don't you get some rest?"

Molly lost patience. "Michael, if you keep this up, you're going to collapse. Then what will your family do? Sleep for a couple of hours at least. Then you can go to the airport and wait for the rescue flights to come in."

"I should be on board one of them."

"Taking the place of someone whose eyes are alert?"

He sighed then. "Okay, you have a point."

"Remind me to mark the occasion."

"Careful, *amiga,* or I will find a way to silence that tart tongue of yours."

She grinned at him. "I'd be worried, if you weren't asleep on your feet."

"There are some things a man can always find the energy to do."

Molly wanted very much to suggest he prove it, but concluded reluctantly that this was definitely not the time. "I'll remind you of that one of these days. Go, get some rest. I'll wake you in a couple of hours."

"You need rest, too, *amiga.*"

"I need to make a couple of calls, then I'll lie down right here on the sofa." She thought it was an amazingly noble suggestion considering where she'd rather be.

To her surprise, he shook his head. "I want you beside me," he said, though there was less amorous intent in his words than a

380

sort of lost desolation. "Please."

Deeply touched, her pulse hammering, Molly nodded. "I'll be there as soon as I check on Brian."

The call to Hal to exact his promise to keep Brian until the crisis with Tío Miguel was resolved took far less time than she'd anticipated, mostly because for once Hal didn't argue with her. In a resigned, only faintly aggrieved tone, he simply agreed.

"I hope everything turns out okay," he said. "I saw the story this morning."

"Did Brian see it?" she asked worriedly.

"No, I didn't even open the paper until I got to the office. O'Hara's okay?"

"Exhausted, but okay. I'll talk to you soon."

"Molly?"

"Yes?"

"I know you don't want to hear this from me, but be careful. You've seen the extremes some of these people will go to, to make a point."

Molly thought of the radio newscaster whose leg had been blown off by a car bomb years before. She recalled the bombs detonated to make a point about a collection of artworks that had contained paintings by artists still living in Cuba. She thought of the campaign of death threats and harassment conducted against the city's news-paper. And then she remembered the fiery explosion just after midnight on the bay and shuddered.

"Yes, I've seen it, all too recently. Tell Brian I love him, okay? I'll call him as soon as I can. Please reassure him that Michael is fine."

When she'd finished talking to her ex-husband, she made one more call, this one to Ted Ryan at the morning paper.

"Molly, this is a switch, you calling me."

She knew she was taking a risk involving the reporter. Michael would be furious if he found out. But her own sources in the Cuban community tended to be middle-class exiles, who maintained an allegiance to their homeland but kept themselves far removed from the politics of terrorism — at least officially. The paper, however, had sources in this exile underground that she would never be able to tap without an introduction. Even Michael would be regarded with suspicion. Señor López's distrustful, frightened reaction had proved that, as had the nervousness of those who'd witnessed the exchange in the park.

"I need your help," she told Ted.

"Anything," he said at once. "You know that."

"I want everything you have in the files about Orestes León Paredes and that organization he leads. Can you do that?"

"No problem. I'll get printouts for you this afternoon. What's he have to do with the bombing?"

"That's what I'm trying to find out. Can you ask around over there and find out where he lives or where he has his headquarters?"

"Sure. Is there a number where I can call you back?"

"I'll call you later." She glanced at the clock on the kitchen wall. It was already afternoon. "How about three o'clock?"

"I'll be here."

"Thanks, Ted."

When she'd hung up, she glanced around Michael's kitchen, amazed as always at its pristine cleanliness. Not one single dirty dish sat in the sink. She knew if she looked into the dishwasher, she would find none in there either. Unlike most bachelor refrigerators, his would be well-stocked with healthy foods, all carefully wrapped. Most impressive was the restaurant-quality espresso machine on the counter and the array of blended coffees displayed beside it. Michael did love his coffee. Hers, he claimed, was weak, sissy stuff.

The first time she had come here, only a few weeks earlier after one of Brian's soccer games, Molly had commented on the neatness of his kitchen. Michael had merely shrugged and gone about the business of putting together a snack for Brian and his teammates with astonishing efficiency. It was, she had since concluded, the same way he approached everything in his life. He kept things precisely ordered so there was no distracting clutter to interfere with the constant mulling of clues and evidence that went on in his head.

Surprised by her own reluctance, she finally forced herself toward the steps leading to the town house's second-floor bedrooms. This was new terrain to her in more ways than one. She wondered if, once she had climbed those stairs, things would ever be the same between them again.

Not because of sex, she told herself. She didn't think that was what was on Michael's mind, anyway. No, because of the vulnerability he had allowed her to see for the first time today. That bond of emotional intimacy was something she had craved far more than physical contact, although there was no denying that more and more lately she'd had restless nights from wanting the sexy, elusive Cuban detective to hold her in his arms.

Taking a deep breath at the partially closed door to his room, she pushed the door open, uncertain of what to expect. Disappointment warred with amusement at what she found.

Michael was sprawled facedown across the bed, his upper body bare, a pair of colorful boxer shorts riding low on his hips, his black hair still damp from his shower.

So much for crawling into bed beside him, she thought ruefully, as she examined the odd patches of space here and there on the king-size bed. He'd taken his side of the bed in the middle. She stood for a long time, just drinking in the sight of all that leanly muscled masculinity. The perfection had been seriously marred by the explosion. Stitched gashes and bright bruises were stark testimony to his close call.

Sighing, she finally plucked up the alarm clock from beside the bed, quietly closed the door, and crept back downstairs for her own desperately needed nap.

She set the clock for two thirty. It was barely more than twenty-four hours since she and Michael had begun worrying that something had happened to Tío Miguel. It seemed like a lifetime ago, a lifetime crammed with emotional extremes.

As she curled up on Michael's oversize cream-colored sofa with its plump pillows, she realized there was no way of knowing how long it might be before either of them slept again.

7

Molly was awakened not by the alarm clock, but by the sound of voices. No, not *voices.* One very loud, angry voice. Michael's.

She glanced at the clock and saw that it was just after two o'clock. Groaning, she turned off the alarm before its shrill could join the commotion from upstairs and buried her face in a pillow. She indulged in a moment's regret that it had been the clock, not the phone, that she had removed from his room. She felt dull and headachy, not rested at all. Michael, on the other hand, seemed to have found the energy to yell. His voice carried through the town house.

"What the hell do you mean, they're calling off the search? My uncle could be dying out there."

There was a brief lull, then . . . "Thunderstorms? Who gives a shit? I don't care if a goddamned hurricane is brewing, I want those planes to cover every square inch of water in the straits."

Molly dragged herself off the sofa. Obviously she needed to get upstairs and explain the concept of winning friends and influencing people to Michael before he alienated the only people actually searching for his uncle.

She found him sitting on the side of his bed, clothed only in those brightly patterned boxer shorts, lines of exhaustion still etched on his face. He barely even glanced at her as she sat down next to him.

Acting instinctively, she put her hand on his bare shoulder in a gesture meant to soothe. It might not have soothed, but it definitely got his attention. Obviously, a woman's hand on his naked flesh was to Michael what a red cape was to a bull — the start of something. Heat flared in his eyes.

"Yeah, yeah, I understand," he muttered distractedly.

His gaze locked with Molly's. She burned under the intensity of his scrutiny. She decided that just maybe he'd gotten the wrong idea.

Or the right idea at the wrong time, to be perfectly honest about it.

He hung up, his gaze still so hot it could melt an icier resolve than Molly's.

"What brings you upstairs, *amiga*?"

"The call of the wild," she replied.

He looked absolutely fascinated. A spark of purely provocative devilment lit his eyes. "Oh, really?"

"You were shouting insults at the top of your lungs. I decided drastic measures were called for to mellow you out."

"How drastic?"

She stood up and backed away from temptation. "Well, much as I'd like to stay and demonstrate, isn't it time we got back to our investigation?"

"Our investigation?"

Heady from earlier successful negotiations with the likes of Vince Gates and Hal DeWitt, she decided to test Michael's limits. "Right. We're a team. Partners. Remember?"

His gaze slid over her. "That's not what I remember. What I remember was inviting you to share my bed."

"Michael, has it occurred to you that you have picked a very odd time to decide you want to seduce me?" She actually thought it was a pretty good show of indignation coming from a woman only one heartbeat away from flinging herself into that bed with him.

He shook his head. Amusement flared in his eyes. "This is not a recent decision, *amiga.*"

"Okay, to act on it, then."

"Does that mean you're not interested in crawling back into this nice, warm bed with me?" he inquired doubtfully. "Tell the truth."

Molly couldn't have lied if her life depended on it. It was just as well. Michael was used to detecting when people were lying through their teeth. It would have been no contest. "Yes. As a matter of fact, the idea holds a great deal of appeal," she admitted.

As he reached for her, his expression reeking of smug satisfaction, she added, "But I'm not sure I can fight these nagging images of Tía Pilar weeping for her missing husband."

Michael put his head in his hands and groaned. "You really know how to spoil a moment, don't you?"

"Better to spoil this one than deal with your regrets the rest of the day."

He shot her a rueful grin. "You have a point."

"I always do. You just rarely listen. Hand me the phone."

"What for?"

She scowled at him. "Just hand it over, please."

When she had it, she dialed Ted Ryan's

number. Michael stood up, found a pair of tan slacks and a soft beige designer shirt and pulled them on while she waited for the reporter to pick up. She studied his polished designer look enviously, then glanced down at her own wrinkled walking shorts and short-sleeved blouse, which she'd been wearing since the day before. She wondered if she'd ever get home long enough to change. She also wondered about a man who saw past the rumpled clothes and still found an attractive, desirable woman. He definitely had to be some sort of national treasure.

Ted picked up while she was still mentally enumerating more of Michael's endearing attributes. "Were you able to get that information I asked for?" she asked.

"Sure did. I've got a huge stack of printouts for you. You can pick them up anytime. I'll leave them at the information desk downstairs in case I'm not here when you stop by. As for Paredes, he lives in Westchester in some nondescript little house on a quiet street." He hesitated. "Molly, are you sure you want to get to him yourself? He maintains a pretty low profile. He won't be pleased to have you drop by, if that's what you have in mind. He's liable to greet you with an assault rifle."

"I can hardly wait," Molly muttered as she jotted down the address on the pad Michael had on the nightstand by the bed. "Thanks."

"Tell me you're not going out there alone," he insisted.

"I'm not."

"That's a relief. One last thing."

"What's that?"

"Forget where you got this information, okay?"

"It just appeared to me in a vision," she agreed.

Michael watched her intently as she hung up. "What was all that about visions? Don't tell me it was a call to the Psychic Friends Network."

Scowling at him, she held out the piece of paper. "Here you go," she said, then added with a certain pointed emphasis, "partner."

Michael looked at the address. "What's this?"

"The closely guarded home address of Orestes León Paredes."

Michael didn't waste time on astonishment or applause. His expression grim, he put on his shoulder holster, added a neatly pressed jacket that made Molly feel more rumpled than ever, and gestured toward the bedroom door. "Let's go, *partner.*"

■ ■ ■ ■

Molly was able to persuade her new investigative partner to detour past the paper by promising him more information than he could possibly gather on his own in days of interrogations, even if he could find people who'd talk to him.

When she emerged from the paper's lobby with an armload of computer printouts, he looked downright impressed and maybe just a little worried.

"Exactly what did you have to promise Ryan to get all this?"

"First crack at any major break in the case."

"Given the way he feels about you, I'm surprised he didn't hold out for a more personal commitment."

She frowned at him. "You're the only one who thinks he has a crush on me."

"Only because you are blind to the signs."

"Why are we arguing over Ted Ryan's amorous intentions, when we should be thanking our lucky stars that he dumped all this information into our laps?"

"You have a point. You read while I drive."

Molly had barely made a dent in the material, when they neared Paredes's neighborhood.

Westchester was a community west of Florida's Turnpike, where many Cubans had eventually settled, leaving Little Havana to a more recent influx of exiles from El Salvador, Nicaragua, and Panama.

Along the Tamiami Trail, yet another designation for *Calle Ocho* or Southwest Eighth Street before it continued west to cut through the Everglades toward Naples, there were strip malls and gun shops, a bowling alley, and dozens of neat little restaurants featuring a mix of ethnic fare. One of the most popular Cuban restaurants, Lila's, with its mounds of crisp *papas fritas* — fried potatoes — atop tender *palomilla* steak, beckoned as Michael and Molly headed for their unscheduled meeting with Paredes.

Refusing to waste time for a sit-down meal, Michael conceded only to picking up two grilled sandwiches — *media noches* as they were called by Cubans and Anglos alike. They ate the sandwiches as he made the turn off the trail into a neighborhood of Spanish-style homes with neat lawns and climbing bougainvillea in vivid shades of purple and fuchsia. Ornamental ironwork covered most of the windows, installed not for its intricate beauty, but to protect against crime. In this respect it was not so different from Little Havana. Here, though, the homes were slightly larger and newer.

"How'd you get the address?" he asked as he checked the numbers on the houses against the slip of paper.

Molly was amazed the question hadn't come up before now. Maybe he just hadn't had the energy to look a gift horse in the mouth. Well fed now, his naturally suspicious brain had kicked in.

"Sources," she said enigmatically.

"What sources?"

"What difference does it make?"

"I'm not sure anyone on the metro police force could get this address, yet one lone county employee just snaps her fingers and has it. It doesn't figure."

"Oh, I'm sure some enterprising cop over there has it tucked away in his Rolodex for a rainy day."

Michael shook his head. "Just about the time anyone pins down his location, Paredes shifts to a new spot. I suppose it's habit after years of moving his guerrilla camps around the Cuban countryside to evade Castro's soldiers. So what did you barter with this so-called source of yours to get it? Or was this just more of Ted Ryan's largesse?"

"Michael, not everything in life has a price tag."

"Yes, *amiga,* sooner or later it does. You just haven't been asked to pay up yet."

Molly decided nothing she was likely to say would counteract that level of ingrained cynicism. She kept her mouth clamped firmly shut.

When they finally reached the address she had been given, the house looked exactly like every other house on the block. There was nothing to distinguish it, right down to the clutter of toys on the front lawn and the rusty, aging sedan in the driveway, along with a newer, though still not brand-new, car parked behind it. Molly glanced up and down the block in amazement.

"I didn't know there were this many old cars still in existence in running order," she said.

"You should see the ones on the streets of Havana. I'm told those make these old clunkers look like the latest models. A lot of people have become very adept mechanics." As he cut off the ignition, he glanced at her, his expression suddenly serious. "*Amiga,* don't get all bent out of shape over this . . ."

"Uh-oh. What?"

"I think it might be best for you to wait in the car."

"Why?" she asked, though she was relatively certain she knew what was coming. She doubted it was because he was ashamed of her appearance.

"If Paredes is even here, he may not be willing to talk with you present," Michael explained cautiously.

"Because I'm an Anglo?"

"Worse," he admitted.

"What could be worse?"

"Because you are a woman."

"Of all the idiotic, chauvinistic attitudes," she said without much energy. As much as she hated the macho world of a certain breed of Hispanic men, it was relatively pointless to flail away at its existence. The discovery that Paredes was such a man wasn't exactly a stunning surprise.

"I don't suppose now is the time to try to mend his ways, though, is it?" she said with an air of resignation.

"Not really."

"Okay. I will wait in the car like the dutiful little woman."

"Thanks."

"No problem." As Michael stepped out of the car, she beckoned him back. "Just one thing."

He regarded her warily. "What?"

"Hand over your cellular phone."

397

He gave it to her with trepidation written all over his face. "You don't know anyone on the other side of the world, do you? Liza, for example," he said, referring to Molly's best friend and neighbor. "Isn't she on some trip to the rain forest again?"

"Worried about me running up your bill? As a matter of fact, Liza's in Tibet," she informed him cheerfully. "Hurry back."

With one last worried look over his shoulder, Michael walked determinedly up to Orestes León Paredes's front door and knocked. Heavy draperies slid aside a fraction while someone peered out. Then the door opened a cautious inch. She noticed Michael did not flash his badge. Whatever he said, though, got him admitted.

Molly caught a brief glimpse of a tall, olive-complexioned man, his military fatigues straining over a potbelly, right before the door slammed shut and what sounded like a seriously heavy-duty bolt slid home. It was not a comforting sound. The only thing keeping her from outright panic was the reassuring weight of that cellular phone and the knowledge that help was only three quick digits away.

8

Huge, heavy black clouds began to build up to the west over the Everglades. Molly put the cellular phone on the dash as thunder rumbled through the muggy air. A jagged bolt of lightning split the sky, followed within seconds by the ear-splitting crack of thunder. The first fat drops of rain splashed against the windshield, followed an instant later by a downpour so intense she could barely see the house only fifteen yards or less away. She felt cut off and isolated as she waited for Michael to return. The feelings of foreboding that had begun with the slamming of that door no longer seemed quite so absurd.

To distract herself, she tried to read more printouts. Gradually she began to put together an impression of Orestes León Paredes. He was a man who came from great wealth in Cuba, only to have his property taken over by the government.

Angered by the loss and young enough to take his ideals to the streets, he had publicly opposed Castro, organizing a band of guerrillas known for the daring and violence of their attacks. He had brought the same attitudes and tenacity with him when he escaped to Miami.

He had participated in the CIA-planned Bay of Pigs invasion, meant to spark an uprising of the Cuban people. It had failed dramatically. But once again the remarkable Paredes luck had held. He had neither died nor been taken prisoner. He had just added to his mystique.

He had also realized during that abysmal failure that any overthrow of Castro was in the hands of those who believed as passionately as he did. They could not count on Washington for the help they needed.

Over the years since then, he had surrounded himself with a veritable army of commandos anxious for their chance to provide the spark that would ignite a revolution. Molly wondered if even now Miguel was in Cuba fanning such flames at Paredes's instigation.

Little was written about his personal life, but judging from the toys scattered on his lawn, he had children or grandchildren. She wondered if he was instilling the same anger and fighting spirit in them.

Eventually she glanced up from the pages. There was still no sign of Michael. "Come on, dammit," she whispered, her gaze pinned on the shadowy outline of the house. She checked her watch again. It was nearly four o'clock. Michael had been inside for little more than a half hour. It just seemed like longer. She would give him another fifteen minutes before she gave in to panic and called 911.

She kept her gaze fixed on the house, unwilling to look away even to read more of the articles Ted had provided. The only time her gaze strayed was when she glanced at her watch. The second hand was moving at a snail's pace. *Tick. Tick. Tick.* She drew in deep gulps of breath with every tick. At this rate, she'd hyperventilate and the 911 call would be for paramedics for her. *Tick. Tick.*

Another streak of lightning split the nearby sky, followed almost at once by the sharp crack of thunder. It was so close that it seemed to rock the car like a child's toy in a giant's grip.

Finally the sheets of rain dwindled into occasional fat drops again. The black clouds rolled on toward the east, leaving blue skies and bright sunshine, with steam rising from the pavement. The rumbling of the thunder receded into the distance. It was almost as if the storm had never happened.

Unfortunately, Molly's pulse still wouldn't settle back into an easy rhythm. The fifteen minutes had passed long ago. Michael had been inside for nearly an hour.

Okay, she thought. So it had been an hour. He and Paredes had a lot to talk about. He wouldn't appreciate her calling for backup if everything inside was perfectly fine. The only way to determine that for sure would be to get a glimpse inside that house. How she was going to do that was a problem.

The front windows were covered by those heavy drapes. There was a fence around the side and back yards. There was, however, a gate on the east side of the house, right at the end of the driveway. She wondered if she could get to that gate without being seen, especially with the passenger door of the car in full view of the house.

Oh, well, nothing beats a try but a failure, she recalled her mother telling her on some occasion when her usually intrepid spirit had failed her. She slid to the driver's side and carefully opened the door. Right before she stepped out, she grabbed the phone and tucked it into the waistband of her walking shorts. Okay, it didn't exactly imply the same level of protection as a gun, but it was all she had.

The air was even steamier after the brief storm. It was sort of like breathing through a damp cloth. Her clothes stuck to her skin. Staying low, she moved from beside Michael's car to the far side of the cars parked in the driveway. With her gaze locked on the front windows of the house, she inched her way toward that gate.

She had one hand on the opened latch and one foot inside when all hell broke loose. Two snapping, snarling pit bulls rounded a corner of the house. With her heart slamming against her chest, Molly rammed the gate closed and prayed the latch would hold against the weight of their frantic bodies being thrown against it again and again as they tried to get to her.

The front door of the house opened and Michael and the man she'd seen earlier came tearing outside. At the sight of Molly standing on the far side of his car, bent over and trying to catch her breath, Michael slowed.

"Going for a walk?" he inquired dryly as the other man sharply ordered the dogs to the back of the house. They slunk away.

Molly couldn't seem to stop shaking. Still, she tried to bluster her way out of the incriminating mess. "Yes. It was hot in the car after the storm. I thought I'd get some air."

Michael looked as if he didn't believe that any more than he believed pigs flew. Obviously, though, he didn't intend to call her on it in front of his host. She'd probably pay for that bit of discretion later.

The man gestured toward Molly. "She is with you?" he asked Michael.

"Yes."

"And you allowed her to remain outside in this heat? I am surprised at you," he said, coming forward. He took Molly's hand and bowed over it in a courtly gesture at odds with the military attire and suburban setting. "Señorita, I am Paredes."

Molly gazed into dark, almost black eyes that reflected intelligence and an innate wariness that belied the polite greeting. He looked to be in his late fifties, his face weathered by time and sun, his dark brown hair streaked with gray. Despite the potbelly, he appeared to be in decent shape. The muscles in his forearms were well-defined. Anyone misjudging his strength would no doubt be in for a rude awakening.

"Molly DeWitt," she said, trying not to recoil from his powerful grip or his intense, distrustful scrutiny. "I'm sorry for disturbing your meeting. I hadn't realized you

404

had dogs."

"Their purpose is better served if they take people by surprise," he said dryly.

"I'm sure."

"You would like to join us, perhaps?"

Michael gave an almost imperceptible shake of his head. "Our meeting is concluded, wouldn't you say, Señor Paredes?"

A flash of anger darkened the older man's eyes, but was hurriedly replaced by a jovial expression. He bowed again to Molly. "Perhaps another time, señorita. I will look forward to it."

"Perhaps." There was something in his voice that made Molly feel as if he'd just made an indecent pass at her, though his actual words and expression couldn't have been more innocuous. She gathered Michael had heard that sleazy note as well since he looked as if he wanted to throttle the man.

Molly didn't relax until they were out of the neighborhood. Michael's stony silence didn't help.

"What did he tell you?" she asked finally.

"You mean besides the forty-five-minute recruitment pitch?"

"He wants you to join the organization?"

"He suggested I would be a traitor to my heritage if I did not."

"Did you sign up?"

Michael scowled at her. "No, *amiga,* I did not sign up. His is a fool's mission."

"He obviously does not feel that way. Nor did Tío Miguel."

"More's the pity."

"Did he tell you anything about your uncle?"

"He praised him as a valiant hero. He said he cannot imagine what has become of him, that there was no secret invasion planned for Sunday. He denied that anyone connected with his organization might have wanted to harm Miguel."

"How does he explain the disappearance?"

"A mishap at sea."

Molly regarded him incredulously. "And the bomb?"

"It is beyond his comprehension," Michael said dryly.

"I'll bet. He's a cold, calculating man."

"Except when he looks at you. Obviously, you stir the hot-blooded passion in him."

Molly glanced at his set jaw. "Surely you are not jealous of him?"

"Men like Paredes can have a certain charismatic charm, *amiga.* That is how they command so many followers."

She shrugged. "I don't see it."

"Good."

■ ■ ■

When Molly and Michael arrived at Tamiami Airport after an amazingly quick trip down the turnpike given the rush-hour conditions, they found not just the pilots who had been searching the waters between Cuba and the Florida Keys that day, but a growing crowd of Cubans, US Immigration officials, and reporters.

Huddled in front of a half-dozen microphones inside a hangar were two young teenage boys who seemed stunned by all the attention. In low voices, they told of their ordeal at sea. Their stories were repeated in English by a translator who stood beside them.

"For months we scoured the countryside in search of old inner tubes and scraps of lumber," Ricardo Rodríguez said. He was painfully thin, his skin parched by the sun. The man who'd introduced him had given his age as sixteen. "It was our dream to come to America, where there is food and work."

"How long were you at sea?" a reporter asked.

"Six days we fought the currents. The waves washed our water and food overboard

407

on the fourth day," the same boy said.

"There were sharks," his companion, Tony Suárez, added. He appeared to be shy, or perhaps he was just terribly shaken. His voice was barely above a whisper. "They came to our raft. I thought for sure we were going to die. Our friend Tomás . . ." His voice faltered.

"There was another boy with you?" a reporter asked, his voice unexpectedly thick with emotion.

The two nodded. "He went crazy. The sun. No water. It made him *loco.* He dove into the sea. He said he wished to swim home."

"When was that?"

"An hour, perhaps two, before we heard the plane," the boy said, his own voice quivering. "If only he had waited . . ."

"Where were they when you found them?" a reporter asked the two pilots standing behind the boys.

"Miles from land. Perhaps in another day or two, perhaps longer, they might have drifted ashore who knows where along the coast. By then, without water or food . . ." He shrugged. "Their fate would have been no better than their friend's."

Molly glanced at Michael and saw that the color had drained out of his face.

Because of those damnable sunglasses, she couldn't gauge the turmoil in his expressive eyes. His tightened jaw, however, was telling enough. She wasn't certain whether his reaction of horror had to do with these courageous boys who had survived thanks to some whim of timing and luck that had brought them into the view of the rescuers. or whether he was thinking of his uncle, who might still be drifting on the same treacherous seas.

When the press conference ended a short time later, Michael went to one of the immigration officials and introduced himself.

"How many are there like this?"

"You mean teens arriving alone?"

Michael nodded.

"I'd say one in eight of every new arrival is between fourteen and twenty-one," he said matter-of-factly. Clearly such statistics were commonplace to him, but Molly was stunned.

"Dear heaven," she whispered.

Michael glanced at the two boys. "What will happen to them now? Do they have relatives here who will take them in?"

"They claim to have an uncle here, but we haven't been able to locate him. They will go to a halfway house designed for the teenagers who have come alone from Cuba.

It is already overcrowded, but they'll make room. The boys will be able to stay there until they acclimate and find work."

He regarded Michael soberly. "It won't be easy for them. They come here so filled with hope, and then they discover that even in Miami, where the Cuban culture has been maintained in so many ways, they are homesick. Worse, they're surrounded by so many material goods and foods for the first time in their lives, and they don't have the money to buy what they want. In some ways, for many of them that is worse than not having it available in the first place."

"So they start to steal," Michael guessed, his gaze pinned on the two youngsters, who were being treated as heroes by the gathering of Cubans who'd heard of the rescue. Their presence confirmed what José López had explained earlier — word of mouth in the exile community was swift.

"Or they try to go back to Cuba," the immigration officer told them.

His expression bleak, Michael walked to the front of the hangar. He introduced himself to the teenagers, who were beginning to show signs of exhaustion. Molly stood beside him as he spoke to them quietly in Spanish. He took his business cards from his pocket and gave one to each of them. As he talked, their eyes never left his face, as if they were experiencing the same intangible bond that had drawn Michael to them. They nodded solemnly as they listened.

At last he grinned and shook their hands. Shy smiles broke across their thin faces, lighting their eyes. Then Michael turned abruptly and walked out of the hangar.

When Molly found him, he was standing in the shade of an overhang, the tarmac around them radiating the late-afternoon heat. His expression looked haunted.

"Michael?"

He reached for her hand and pulled her close, resting his chin atop her head. "I can't imagine it," he said. "I can't imagine what it would be like to be so desperate at their age that I would risk crossing the sea on a bunch of goddamned tires and pieces of lumber."

"You told them you'd help them, didn't you?"

"I will do what I can. Tío Pedro is always looking for willing workers at the restaurant. And I can see that they have clothing and a few of the things that boys need to feel as if they belong."

"If what the man from Immigration said is true, there are many more like them. You

411

can't help them all."

He shrugged. "Perhaps not, but I can do something for these two. I can do it in honor of Tío Miguel. It is what he would want."

9

"Aside from the two boys, we saw only an empty raft today," pilot Ricardo Bienes told Michael when they went back inside the hangar, where the jubilant crowd was still celebrating the rescue of the two teenagers. "I am sorry."

"You are certain the raft was not my uncle's?"

Bienes gestured toward the front of the room, where the makeshift contraption was on display. Molly shuddered as she took a really good look at it for the first time. Even though the boys had described their own similar raft, the sight of those inner tubes and scraps of lumber made her heart ache at the desperation involved in assembling such a craft. It looked pitifully inadequate for crossing any water wider or rougher than a pond. Obviously Michael hadn't even glanced at it or he would never have asked the question.

"As you can see for yourself, it was crudely made," Bienes said. "It is definitely not the sort your uncle would have had on board his boat. It would appear that whoever was aboard this flimsy vessel perished at sea, unless they were rescued earlier by a passing boat."

"How often does that happen?" Molly asked as Michael continued to study the raft with obvious dismay.

"Often enough. Even the *Britannia,* the Queen of England's yacht, has picked up a Cuban rafter trying to reach America. Freighters, cruise ships, fishing boats . . ." The pilot shrugged. "Most anyone will rescue those fleeing Cuba, if they see them. Who could leave a human being aboard a raft such as this on the open seas?"

Once assured that there could be no mistaking this particular raft for his uncle's, Michael lost interest in it and the more general statistics. "You will look for my uncle again tomorrow?"

Bienes shook his head. "I understand your situation, but that is not possible. We are volunteers, my friend. Tomorrow we must work. We go out only three days a week, taking turns so that jobs are not jeopardized."

"Please," Michael implored.

The stark emotion on his face and in his

voice was raw and vulnerable. It was a dramatic contrast to his usual stoic silences and unreadable expressions. Molly wanted to reach out to him, but knew he wouldn't thank her for the gesture. He'd view it as an acknowledgment of a weakness.

"I will make a donation for your time, something to pay for fuel for other flights," he added.

Before Bienes could respond, a second pilot, Jorge Martinez, joined them. He gave Michael's shoulder the reassuring squeeze that Molly hadn't dared.

"Do not worry. We will make arrangements to have someone in the air tomorrow," he promised. At Bienes's surprised expression, he added, "Miguel and Pilar were very good to me and my family when we arrived here. I owe this to him."

"I could take one plane up myself," Michael suggested. "I'm licensed."

"That is not necessary," Martinez said. "Others will volunteer, I am sure," he added with a pointed look at his colleague.

Bienes sighed. "I suppose one more day of missed work will not matter."

"Who would fire you, eh?" Martinez asked him. "You are your own boss."

"And when I am not there, nothing gets done," Bienes countered with a rueful expression. "But under these circumstances, I suppose that does not matter."

"God will reward you for your good deeds," Martinez assured him.

"Perhaps some of my clients will pay their bills, then, yes?"

"For that you need a collection agency, not divine intervention."

"What do you do?" Molly asked Bienes.

"I am an attorney."

"A very well-paid attorney," Martinez added. "Do not let him stir your pity, señorita. He will not wind up in the poorhouse because of one extra day off. Besides, he loves any excuse to fly that fancy new plane of his, a plane paid for by the very clients he would have you believe are deadbeats."

"I think what you're doing is wonderful," Molly told both men. "Not many would dedicate themselves to such exhausting searches, especially when the results are so often tragic."

"But there are days like today," Martinez reminded her, "when our efforts are rewarded. It is these moments we cherish. It is what we owe to those who remained behind in Cuba and now can fight no more, to those who desperately seek to escape the suffering."

"When did you come to the United States?" Molly asked him. "During the freedom flights in the sixties?"

"No. Much later. It was Miguel who rescued us." He glanced at Michael. "You did not know that, did you, my friend? Your uncle brought his fishing boat to Mariel in the days of the boat-lift in 1980. He brought us here at the request of my wife's brother. He took nothing for his time and trouble. As I said before, my family owes Miguel García."

From the distance of a college campus, Molly had read hundreds of similar stories at the tumultuous time of the boat-lift. Every available seaworthy vessel, and some, perhaps, that were not, made trip after trip to Mariel to bring back those who wished to flee the island, along with those Castro himself deemed unfit to stay, including prisoners and the mentally ill. One hundred twenty-five thousand in all.

But now, for the first time, looking into Jorge Martinez's eyes and seeing the gratitude reflected there, she understood the powerful ties binding those who had gone through that particular Cuban exile experience. He clasped Michael's hand.

"We will do this search for Miguel," he said. "You will be more valuable here,

417

conducting your investigation." He patted his pocket. "I have your beeper number. You will know the minute we find him."

"And if you don't?"

"Trust me, my friend. If Miguel is on the seas, we will find him. I make that promise to you."

When they left the airstrip in southwest Dade, Molly debated insisting on going home to Key Biscayne to shower and change, but decided that would give Michael a perfect excuse for dumping her there. Instead, she persuaded him to make a quick stop at Dadeland Mall, where she bought two pairs of lightweight slacks, a couple of T-shirts, and a few other necessities. She was back at the car, where Michael was making phone calls, in the promised twenty minutes.

"Any news?" she asked.

"Nothing. I talked to Tío Pedro and he said there was nothing on the national news or the local news about any kind of guerrilla excursion into Cuba. If that's where Miguel was headed, he arrived safely and without being detected or he is still adrift in those damnable straits." He regarded Molly with a bleak expression. "Who knows how long he can survive out there."

"Those boys were at sea for six days, two of those days without water or food," Molly reminded him.

"But as you said, they are boys. Miguel is an old man. And I saw for myself that his provisions remained on his boat. More and more I am convinced he was forced onto that raft. Perhaps he was intentionally cast adrift to die."

"But why?"

"I don't know," he admitted, his voice tight with frustration. "But I would bet my life that Paredes is the key."

"Maybe Felipe and Ken will have some answers," Molly said as they turned into Michael's town-house development.

Sure enough, both policemen were sitting on the front steps of Michael's condominium. For the first time Molly had a chance to study them more closely. In the chaos of the previous night she had gathered only vague impressions.

Ken Marshall looked to be in his late thirties, though there was already a lot of gray in his curly brown hair. His hazel eyes were unflinching. She had seen for herself that it was a quietly intelligent gaze that could be both compassionate and unnerving. Perhaps that intensity was what made him such an outstanding evidence technician. She could believe that absolutely nothing got past him.

Felipe Domínguez was his opposite in many ways. Short, while Ken was tall, and mischievous, while Ken was serious, Felipe had the square build of a boxer and the attitude of a street fighter.

At the moment they were engaged in an obviously intense discussion. Their expressions turned even more sober at the sight of Michael. Inside, over the promised pizza and beer, they offered little new information.

"We have bits and pieces from the boat," Ken said. "But nothing at all of the bomb." He glanced at Molly. "Felipe and I have been trying to remember any details from that quick look we took. We're coming up blank. Can you recall anything at all about what you saw?"

"I heard it. I didn't get a good look at it. It sounded like a standard wind-up clock."

Ken's gaze narrowed. "Why wind-up?"

"The ticking," she said immediately and without a doubt. "When I was a kid, I had an inexpensive clock that made that same sound by my bed. Electric and digital clocks make a quieter sound, if they make any noise at all."

"She's right," Felipe said. "It sounded like the clock I picked up at the drugstore when our electric clock died a few weeks ago." He paused a minute, then added, "Like that clock the crocodile swallowed in *Peter Pan.*"

"Terrific," Michael muttered. "The timing device could have been bought in any one of hundreds of chain drugstores around town. That really narrows things way the hell down."

Ken regarded him sympathetically. "Hey, pal, I know you're frustrated, but what Molly said comes as no surprise. For all the talk of training exercises and stuff, we're not talking a high-tech military operation here. We're probably not even talking about professional international terrorists. I'd guess this was somebody with an ax to grind and one of those primitive but effective how-to-stir-up-insurrection manuals. Back when people were bombing the hell out of the homes and businesses of anyone they thought was soft on Fidel, they weren't using plastique and that fancy garbage. What they came up with was crude, but it did the job."

"Which brings us back to Paredes and people like him," Michael said, glancing at Felipe. "What did you learn on the streets?"

"I got a lot of shock, a lot of outrage, and not one single lead. When I mentioned Paredes and his organization, a few people looked very nervous but denied knowing of any connection."

"Were they lying?" Michael asked.

Felipe shrugged. "My gut tells me yes. Could I prove it? No way."

Michael shoved his hands through his hair and exchanged a look with the two policemen. "So where the hell does that leave us?"

Ken leaned forward. "I do have one idea. I've got some time coming."

"Forget it," Michael said.

Ken continued as if he hadn't spoken, his expression determined. "I could take leave for the next day or two and do a little diving out where the boat blew up. Maybe I'll find something the others missed."

Michael shook his head. "No way." At a scowl from Molly, he modified his harsh response. "Thanks, but you know those guys combed the bottom for whatever was big enough to be recognizable. I don't want you wasting your leave time like that. You've got a wife and kid who'd never forgive me if your vacation time comes up short."

Ken shrugged. "Hell, you know Teri. She loves to dive even more than I do. She'll be thrilled to have an unexpected excuse to take our boat out in the middle of the week."

"Don't you suppose she'd rather be checking out a coral reef?" Michael asked.

Ken grinned. "I'll explain that this is more challenging."

"Are you sure you want to spend your time off this way?" Michael asked again, his voice filled with doubt. For the first time, though, it also held a wavering hint of hope.

"A boat, a sunny day, my wife in a bikini, a couple of beers," Ken replied. "Does life get any better than that?"

"No, I suppose not," Michael agreed. He held out his hand and clasped Ken's. "Thanks. I really appreciate it."

"No problem. I'll give you a call as soon as I work out the details."

"So what can I do?" Felipe asked. "I'd take leave time, too, but you know I use it as fast as I accumulate it."

Ken rolled his eyes. "He means that every time he gets a hot date, he can't drag himself out of bed to leave her. The time sheets tell the story of his love life."

Felipe muttered something in Spanish that definitely didn't sound complimentary, but both Ken and Michael were laughing. Felipe glanced at Molly. "Excuse them. Neither of them understand how demanding it is to be both single and sexy," he said, his eyes glinting with pure mischief.

"I'm single," Michael reminded him.

Felipe shrugged. "But sexy? That is a matter of opinion."

Michael turned toward Molly. She held up her hands. "No comment."

"*Et tu, Brute?*" he said. "You will pay for that, *amiga.*"

"I didn't realize my role here was to stroke your ego," Molly retorted.

"Perhaps we should discuss precisely what your role here is," Michael replied, his eyes flashing dangerously.

"Uh-oh," Ken said, standing up. "Come on, Felipe. Let some other cop get called to deal with this domestic disturbance. I want no part of it."

"No disturbance," Michael said mildly.

"And it's not domestic," Molly chimed in, her cheeks flaming.

The two cops exchanged glances. Felipe held a hand over his stomach. "My very reliable gut thinks we've got two people here who are protesting too much."

Molly suddenly wondered if it might not be a very good idea to ask if she could hitch a ride home. The gleam in Michael's eyes stopped her before the words could form.

When both men had beat a hasty exit, Michael strolled back into the living room. He reached out and clasped Molly's hand, hauling her to her feet. He didn't let go until she was mere inches away. So close, in fact, that she could feel the heat radiating from his body. His gaze clashed with hers.

"So, *amiga,* you think I am not sexy?"

"I didn't say that."

"Oh?"

"Not exactly."

"Then you think I am sexy?"

"I think you are deliberately trying to intimidate a witness."

"You're no witness. You're the perpetrator here."

"Oh, yeah? What's the crime?"

"Lying under oath."

Molly glanced around. "No judge. No jury. No bible. I'd say you have no case, mister."

He gave her a wry look and laced his fingers through the hair at the nape of her neck. Very slowly he drew her toward him. Only when Molly thought she would never catch her breath again did he slant his mouth over hers.

She had to admit, as she tried to prevent herself from swaying straight into his arms, that it was a very expert kiss. One of the best, in fact. She was also determined that Michael would never, not in a million years, badger that admission out of her. It was, of course, okay with her if he wanted to kiss her from now until doomsday in an attempt to torture the words from her.

The shrill sound of the phone finally forced them apart. From her perspective, it was probably a very timely interruption.

"Yes, what?" Michael demanded gruffly, one arm still looped around her waist as he talked to the caller.

Molly couldn't seem to tear her gaze away. That was probably why she was so quick to note the sudden alertness in his eyes and the tightening of his jaw.

"I'm on my way," he said, already reaching for his gun and jacket as he hung up.

Molly grabbed her purse and raced out the door after him. Apparently he'd expected her to follow automatically, because he never said a single thing to encourage or protest it. Not until they were in his car and pulling out of the driveway into the traffic on Kendall did she ask where they were going.

"To the paper."

"Why?"

"That was your pal Ted Ryan. He says there are about fifty protesters in front of the building, trying to prevent the delivery trucks from going out."

"Why did he call you?"

"Because someone down there said these guys are all followers of Paredes."

10

Even at eleven at night there was still plenty of traffic to contend with between Kendall and downtown. Though Michael drove like a cop after a speeding suspect, it took them close to thirty minutes before they squealed around a corner and screeched to a stop a half block away from the paper.

Just as Ted Ryan had told Michael, protesters blocked the streets leading into and away from the loading dock. The paper's trucks, parked in solid rows along the street and in an adjacent lot, were effectively prevented from leaving the area. The signs carried by the relatively small group of protesters were in Spanish and in English. Those Molly could read protested the unfairness of the paper's coverage. It was a fairly general and oft-repeated charge.

As they left the car, Michael glanced at her. "Why don't you see if you can hook up with Ryan and see what this is all about?

I'm going to try to blend in and see what I can learn from the protesters."

Molly didn't think there was much chance that Michael, still wearing his usual designer suit and expensive shirt, could actually blend in with what at first glance looked to be a ragtag band of aging male picketers, many of whom were wearing military fatigues and waving Cuban flags. Still, with his dark complexion, brown eyes, and dark hair, there was no mistaking that Hispanic blood ran in his veins. Maybe that would be enough to loosen tongues.

She wandered closer, finally selecting a car right at the edge of the protest and leaning against the front bumper. From that vantage point, she realized that there was more diversity among those picketing than she had originally thought. She caught sight of at least three younger men, clad in dress pants, shirts, and ties, and several women who also looked like young professionals. The broader cross section of the exile community surprised her. Maybe Ted Ryan would be able to explain it.

She figured it would be only a matter of minutes before he spotted her. The reporter tended to zero in on her like a homing pigeon. Usually, though, he was after information. Tonight Molly intended to turn the

428

tables. She found she was actually looking forward to transforming a member of the aggressive media into a source. In her job at the film office she so rarely had a chance to make that happen. Vince insisted on a lot of bowing and scraping.

As she'd anticipated, she saw Ted Ryan circle the perimeter of the protesters, pause for a minute under a streetlamp to jot down some notes, then gaze up and down the street. The instant he spotted her, he headed in her direction. His boyish grin widened as he reached her. He looked more like an amiable Clark Kent than a determined Mike Wallace, but Molly knew firsthand that in his case looks were deceiving. Ted had the tenacity of a pit bull.

"I saw O'Hara a minute ago," he said. "I figured you wouldn't be far away." He regarded her intently. "Just how close are you two these days?" he asked with an unusual hint of uncertainty in his voice.

"I like to think of it as a partnership," Molly said dryly. "My guess is Michael would call it something else."

The reporter seemed even more disconcerted by the comment. "A partnership as in wedding bells?"

"No, as in investigative colleagues."

There was no mistaking the look of relief

in Ted's eyes, which confirmed what Michael had been telling Molly for some time: Ted Ryan might have the teeniest little crush on her. Until this instant, Molly had dismissed it as hogwash. Apparently, though, this was the one thing territorial males were capable of sensing instinctively about other men. Since she wasn't prepared to deal with whatever personal interest Ted might have in her, she changed the subject quickly.

"Thanks for calling Michael with the tip about the demonstration. Why did you?"

The reporter accepted the shift in topic almost gratefully. "Don't credit me with being too magnanimous. He's always in the middle of the hottest cases in town. I figured one of these days he'll return the favor and give me a break on a story. Besides, something tells me this protest and what happened to his uncle can't be coincidence."

"Meaning?"

"His uncle worked for Circulation, delivering the papers. The last time anyone saw him, as far as we know, was when he met his route supervisor to get the Sunday edition. Now, just two nights later, we've got the makings of a big-time brouhaha on our front lawn involving what appears to be the same group of exiles in which García was involved."

Molly pointed to the picket signs. "What exactly do they think is unfair about the paper's coverage?"

Ted shook his head. "Hell, sometimes it seems to me they object to anything that isn't violently anti-Castro. Who knows what it's about this time."

Molly regarded him doubtfully. She didn't like the way he was evading her gaze. "Come on, Ted. You're a reporter. Even if you didn't work for this particular paper, you'd make it your business to know every last detail of any controversy in which the media was targeted. So what's with the vague generalities?"

He shook his head. "I'm telling you there's nothing specific I can link this to. I even read the damned Spanish-language edition, which took me hours, I might add, to see if I could figure out why they're bent out of shape. We're not supporting some bill on Capitol Hill that's soft on Castro. We haven't attacked any of their sacred cows. The most controversial story I saw, from their perspective, was another one of those statistical things showing how many Cuban rafters have been welcomed by Immigration and how many boatloads of Haitian refugees have been turned back at sea. They don't

431

like being reminded that the difference in policies seems blatantly discriminatory."

Molly didn't buy that as the cause of tonight's incident. She wished she'd read that morning's edition, but in all the confusion she hadn't had time. She tried to recall anything else she had read in the paper in recent days that could have set things off. "Wasn't there a story in the business pages about a couple of companies that have sent people into Cuba to size up economic opportunities?"

"Yes, but so what? The way economic sanctions are, they can't go in and invest until Castro falls, right?"

Molly sighed. "True. Maybe the protesters are objecting to the fact that these guys spent dollars in Cuba while they were over there scouting things out. You know how violent they get about foreign tourists in Cuba. They feel the money the tourists spend helps to shore up Castro's regime."

Ted shook his head. "Then why not protest the companies, rather than the paper that wrote the story?"

Molly didn't have an argument to counter that. She tried out another thought. "Has the paper backed any cultural events lately?"

"Like what?"

"You know how they're always giving

432

money to support the ballet, the opera, and all these ethnic festivals. I was just wondering if they'd made a donation to something like that and the group in turn had invited a performer who'd recently performed in Cuba."

"I doubt it. I think the paper's gotten real sensitive to that sort of thing. The powers that be may not understand why people get so outraged that a singer or dancer has performed in Havana, but they steer clear of them just the same."

They fell silent then, watching the activity of the demonstrators, until Ted spotted someone in the crowd and called out to him. The man, wearing khaki slacks, a blue oxford-cloth shirt, and loafers, looked to be no more than forty, though his dark blond hair was already thinning on top. He jogged over to join them.

"Hey, Ted, what's up?"

Ted regarded the older reporter with something akin to hero worship. "Molly, this is Walt Hazelton. He's working the story. He's been with the paper fifteen years. For the last ten he's been on the foreign desk covering Caribbean affairs, including Cuba, when they'll grant him a visa to go in. Walt, this is Molly DeWitt. She and O'Hara are friends."

Walt nodded. "I thought I saw him nosing around in the crowd." He looked at Molly. "Any word on his uncle?"

Molly shook her head. "How good are your sources inside Cuba?" she asked. She knew from his highly respected reputation for hard-hitting, award-winning coverage that Walt Hazelton wasn't the sort of journalist who'd rely on rumors, but rather would report only carefully gleaned facts. She suspected he'd made good use of those rarely granted trips to the island to cultivate reliable contacts.

Hazelton's eyes widened as he immediately grasped her meaning. "You think García tried to go in, maybe as part of some commando raid?"

"It's one theory. I just wondered if you knew anyone who might know what's happening on the island?"

The reporter looked thoughtful. "No one else has been reported missing here in town."

"Maybe because no one else has a nephew like Michael, who jumped on his uncle's disappearance immediately," she countered, beginning to warm to the theory. "Maybe that boat was meant to blow up at sea, so there'd be no trace after they'd launched their rafts toward shore. And wouldn't any family members here be warned to remain silent?"

"Did you get the feeling O'Hara's aunt was holding back?" Ted asked.

Molly honestly had no answer to that. She didn't know Tía Pilar well enough to judge when she might be withholding information. Their conversations were conducted in such a halting mix of English and Spanish that they were seldom illuminating anyway. She finally shook her head. "I have no idea."

"It could take a while to get through, but I'll do some checking," Hazelton promised. He reached in his pocket and pulled out a card. "Give me a call tomorrow afternoon."

When he'd walked away, Molly stared after him. "Bright guy. I've read about him. He's picked up several awards for his reporting, hasn't he?"

"A Pulitzer and a bunch of others," Ted agreed. "He deserves every one of them. He's got an advanced degree in international studies. Had a fellowship to study Cuba." He gestured toward the crowd, who were now chanting and waving their signs more aggressively. "Hazelton probably knows more about the island today than half of these protesters ever knew about the way it was thirty, thirty-five years ago when they were last there. They hate his guts, though."

435

"Why?"

"Do you even have to ask? He's not one of them. Worse than not being Cuban, he dares to tell it like it is. He's not keeping the dream alive."

As if to confirm what Ted was saying, apparently someone recognized Hazelton just then. Before Molly could blink, they had surrounded him, making demands, shouting curses. One angry man waved his picket sign threateningly. Hazelton shoved his way through the crowd and made his way to the building entrance. A police escort saw that he made it.

"I can hardly wait to see the final edition," Ted said dryly.

"Do you think this demonstration will be broken up in time for anyone to see it?" Molly asked.

"Oh, the paper will be printed and it will go out," Ted said, regarding the scene with blatant disgust. "In another hour or two the publisher will lose patience, the police will cordon off the road, and the trucks will roll. The paper may be late, but believe me, these bullies won't be allowed to stop it. It amazes me how people can flee a country with no freedom of the press, then try to stifle it in the country that takes them in."

"What about freedom of speech and

freedom to assemble?" Molly countered quietly.

Ted looked at her. "Hey, I have no problem with them protesting. They've got a right to voice their opinions like anyone else. What they don't have is the right to violently prevent me from voicing mine or the paper from voicing its views editorially."

Molly figured it wasn't a debate that was going to be won or lost that night, any more than it was won or lost when opposition sides of the abortion debate clashed on the lawns of abortion clinics. She suspected emotions ran equally high in both controversies.

"You told Michael these protesters were followers of Paredes," she said finally.

"Some of them. I recognize them from other rallies. The others could be part of his organization or representatives of some other groups."

"Is Paredes here?"

"Are you kidding? He's out in Westchester watching it all on TV, happy as a clam at the disruption of the paper's delivery schedule. No doubt, if questioned, he will decry the harassment of Hazelton."

"Just as he decried the bombing of Miguel's boat."

"Of course. But just because there's no

dirt under a guy's fingernails doesn't mean he knows nothing about the seeds being sown in this particular garden of protest."

Molly grinned. "Interesting line. Can I expect to read it in tomorrow's paper?"

Ted grinned back at her. "Not in my story. I'm on page one of the Metro section with a fascinating report on two cops whose police car was stolen while they sipped *café Cubano* on *Calle Ocho*. It seems the driver left the keys in the ignition, thinking his partner was going to stay put. Said partner decided he wanted to join his pal at the take-out window. An alert bystander in need of wheels made off with it before either of them could draw their weapons. Needless to say the two were not available for interviews. I suspect they've been checked into the county hospital, where they're dying of embarrassment."

Molly heard only about half of the story Ted was telling. She'd suddenly noticed the delivery truck drivers, who were all gathered around their vehicles in a lot across the street awaiting an end to the protest.

"Ted, thanks again for the tip tonight," she said distractedly, her attention already focused on the drivers.

"Hey, where are you going?"

"To find Miguel's route supervisor."

"I'll come with you," he said at once, hurrying after her.

She glanced back at him. "Okay, but I ask the questions."

He regarded her with clearly feigned indignation. "Hey, who's the reporter here?"

"You're off duty, remember?"

"Dammit, Molly, O'Hara will kill me if you get into a bind asking questions of the wrong person."

"I am not your responsibility," she reminded him. "I'm not Michael's either, for that matter. Last I heard, I had God-given free will."

"Jesus, we've gone from constitutional rights to the big time," Ted said. "How are you going to find this guy? You don't even know his name, do you?"

"No, but I know where Miguel's route was. He delivered to the houses in the Shenandoah section. That's why he kept his boat on Key Biscayne. He could drive straight over the causeway when he finished his deliveries and be on the water by dawn."

Fortunately, all of the route bosses were clustered in one place. It took only one casually asked inquiry to find the man who supervised the Shenandoah area deliveries. He was a cigar-chomping, overweight hulk of a man who identified himself as Jack Miller. He looked at Ted, his gaze narrowed.

"You're that guy we ran the campaign on a few months back, aren't you? Had your picture on the trucks. Ryan, right?"

Ted nodded, his expression pleased. The recognition apparently served to overcome his reservations about Molly's interviewing the guy. He turned downright expansive, in fact, introducing her as if she was his personal protégée.

Miller removed his cigar from his mouth long enough to mutter a greeting. "You looking for me?"

She nodded. "I'm wondering about Miguel García. Are you his supervisor?"

His gaze narrowed suspiciously. "Now why would you want to know something like that? You a TV reporter? I don't see no camera."

"I'm not a reporter. I'm a close friend of his family's, and it occurred to me that you might have been one of the last people to see him before he disappeared."

Some of his suspicion melted away. "Could be," he conceded.

She decided she'd better seize that scant opening and run with it. "He worked Sunday morning?"

"Like clockwork. He's been one of my best employees."

"Always on time?"

"The man has the constitution of a horse. He's never missed a day I can think of, not without sending somebody to cover his route, anyway."

"What did you think when he didn't show up last night?"

He shrugged. "I didn't think nothing. He wasn't supposed to work."

Molly regarded him with surprise. "He wasn't?"

"No, ma'am. Took vacation. Asked for it a month ago at least."

"How long was he supposed to be off?"

"Two weeks is what he told me. No matter what's gone on, I fully expect him to show up. García's the kind of man I'd rely on if my life depended on it."

"So there was nothing on Sunday you thought was suspicious, nothing in his demeanor that was out of character?"

Miller hesitated over the question, as if he was chewing it over in his head. "Now that I think back on it, there was one thing. Pardon me for saying it, but anyone else I'd have said they were getting lucky." He looked at Molly. "You know what I'm talking about?" At her nod, he continued, "I've seen that look with guys who have something going on on the side. Not García, though. He loved that wife of his. Talked about her all the time."

"What was different about him on Sunday?"

"He looked real happy. Never saw him look that way before, you know what I mean?"

"As if he was looking forward to something," Molly suggested.

Miller bobbed his head. "Exactly. Like he couldn't wait for something special that was going to happen. Like a kid on Christmas morning, you know?"

"Or maybe a man who was going home to Cuba," she said softly.

11

As Ted Ryan had predicted, the Miami police moved the demonstration into a contained area shortly after 1:00 a.m. and the newspaper's delivery trucks began to roll. Before long, with their audience dwindling and their effectiveness stymied, the protesters began to pack up and leave themselves. Michael's expression was grim when he joined Molly and the reporter.

"Did you find out anything?" Molly asked him.

"You mean besides the fact that this paper is run by racist Commies?"

"My boss, the devoted Republican, will be thrilled to know that," Ted said dryly. "Obviously, his journalistic evenhandedness is paying off. He's clearly not inflicting his conservative views on the reading public."

Michael shot a look at the reporter that Molly found troubling. "You did find out what this was all about, didn't you? I mean beyond the usual rhetoric."

"You mean Ryan here hasn't told you?"

"Told me what?"

"It was his story today that set them off. Apparently they felt his portrayal of Miguel made him look like part of some lunatic-fringe organization."

Ted paled at that. "I didn't write anything that wasn't absolutely true," he argued.

Molly began to understand why he'd been so evasive earlier. She also recognized just from the comments he'd made to her that he held certain Anglo prejudices that might very well have come through in his reporting. Alone the story might have been viewed as an example of biased reporting. Added to dozens of other articles, it had triggered a protest. She couldn't blame Ted for wanting to downplay his role in the night's events.

"Look, let's just forget about what started the protest," she suggested. "We need to focus on Miguel. Were you able to learn anything about his disappearance from any of Paredes's backers?"

"No. Trying to talk to these guys was an absolute waste of time," Michael said. "I know damn well that they know something about what happened to Tío Miguel, but they'll deny it with their dying breaths."

"Maybe this was the wrong place to confront them," Molly suggested. "Here they're unified. Naturally no one would break ranks and spill the beans. Did you get names, addresses, phone numbers?"

"From the ones who would tell me," he said, his voice filled with frustration. "Since I wasn't here on official business, I couldn't force them even to give me that much."

"So you'll start tomorrow with the ones who did identify themselves," she said. "Where are your notes?"

"What for?"

"So I can give the names to Ted," she explained patiently. "He can check them out in the newspaper's files and with the foreign desk to see if any of them are prime movers and shakers among the exile groups."

"I could do the same thing at the police station," he countered with a stubborn set to his jaw.

Molly wasn't sure if he was behaving like a jerk because she was trying to involve Ted Ryan — his perceived competition for her affections — in the investigation or if he was just plain exhausted. She decided to assume it was the latter. On two hours' sleep, it was a logical enough assumption. And that conclusion was the only thing enabling her to continue her fragile grip on her patience.

"And then we'll have two angles on the situation, won't we?" she replied quietly.

He scowled at her. "I suppose." He handed over his notes and allowed Ted to copy the names.

"I'll get right on it," Ted said. "Where should I call you?"

"My place," Molly and Michael said simultaneously. They were not referring to the same place.

This time she glared at him. "Mine is closer. You're beat and so am I."

"Okay, fine. Whatever," Michael said. He looked at Ted and added grudgingly, "Thanks for calling earlier."

"No problem. I'll speak to you in the morning. Maybe Walt will have some news by then, too."

"Night, Ted," Molly said.

"Who's Walt?" Michael asked as they walked back to his car.

"Hazelton. He's their chief foreign correspondent for the Caribbean. He's making some calls into Cuba to see if there's any word there about armed guerrillas sneaking onto the island."

"Molly, as much as I'd like to believe otherwise, I don't think Miguel went back

446

to Cuba."

"Twenty-four hours ago that was all you were willing to consider," she reminded him.

"That was before the boat blew to smithereens."

"Then you should have been around when I talked with Tío Miguel's supervisor. He says when he saw him on Sunday morning, he looked happier than he'd ever seen him, like a man who might be going home again."

Michael regarded her in disbelief. "You're basing this cock-and-bull theory on the fact that my uncle was in a good mood, for God's sake? The man was always in a good mood."

"This was different," Molly insisted, refusing to be put off by his skepticism. "Jack Miller could see it and, believe me, he doesn't strike me as a man prone to intuitive guesswork. There had to be some real change in your uncle's demeanor for him to notice it. Haven't you ever noticed that for all of his apparent good humor, Tío Miguel's eyes always look kind of sad and faraway?"

"I suppose," Michael conceded wearily.

"I think we need to talk to your aunt again tomorrow."

"I was planning on it, but you obviously have something specific in mind. What?"

"I think we need to see if she suspects that your uncle has gone back to Cuba, but is afraid to admit it because it might jeopardize some grand scheme these guys have."

"Don't you think she would have told me that?"

"Not if she was afraid that telling would put him in greater danger or might even put you in danger. Don't you remember, when you called her on Sunday afternoon, you said yourself she sounded as if she was worried about something. You detected it in her voice. That's why you were so hell-bent on looking for him right away. Isn't it possible she knew what he was up to?"

Michael looked thoughtful. "You could be right. If that's the case, though, we won't pry it out of her. We'll have to talk to Tía Elena."

Now Molly was having trouble following his logic. "Why her?"

"Because Miguel might have confided in Tío Pedro. Pedro won't break a confidence to talk to me, but he keeps nothing from his wife. Pilar would know that, as well, and she might even have confided in her sister. That's two people talking to Elena."

"And you have always been able to wheedle anything you wanted from her, right?"

He grinned. "I am her favorite nephew,

after all."

Molly shook her head. "I can't imagine why."

He reached over, clasped her hand, and lifted it to his lips. "Sure you can, *amiga*. No one is more aware of my charms than you."

With a sudden leap of her pulse, Molly decided tonight might be a good night to find out exactly how *charming* Michael O'Hara could be . . . if either of them could stay awake long enough.

Apparently Michael intended to give it a try, because he took her hand when they left the car and didn't release it until they were in her bedroom.

"So, *amiga*, how do you feel about finishing what you began in my bedroom earlier today?" he said.

Molly met his serious gaze. "I thought you'd never ask."

His hands framed her face. "We have waited a long time for this, *querida*. We could probably have found a better time, a better night."

She felt herself smiling. "Don't start making excuses for yourself, O'Hara."

"I will need no excuses," he assured her with a touch of macho arrogance that made Molly's heart hammer at its promise.

"And here I was so sure you were out of practice."

"There are some things a man never forgets," he said quietly just as his lips met hers.

With his mouth teaching her amazing nuances of the art of the kiss and his hands deftly exploring other parts of her anatomy, Molly was in no position to argue. In fact, she wondered as they scrambled out of their clothes and into the bed, if Michael would be willing to continue burning the basics into her memory from now 'til doomsday.

It didn't come as a great shock to Molly that even on one of his worst nights, when he was fighting bone-deep exhaustion, Michael was hotter and more thoughtful in bed than the wildest fantasy she had ever had. The man had amazing reserves of stamina and the touch of a sinner.

Unfortunately it also came as no surprise that he was all business in the morning.

"Let's go, *amiga*," he said after what had to have been no more than fifteen minutes of uninterrupted sleep.

Molly mumbled something derogatory and tried to hide under the covers. He smacked her on the bottom and repeated his demand.

"Coffee's on and the train leaves in twenty minutes," he announced.

Molly blinked, inched the covers down to her chin, and peered up at him. "What train?"

"It's a figure of speech. Do you want to sleep all day or do you want to help me find my uncle?"

It was a toss-up, she decided. But given the way she'd groused until he included her as a partner in the investigation, she couldn't bail out now just so she could indulge in some sleepy, steamy reminiscences about the night that had just passed.

Twenty minutes later on the dot, Michael was waiting for her at the front door, a cup of coffee in hand.

"Toast?" she suggested hopefully.

"No time. We'll stop later. I want to catch Luis Díaz-Nuñez before he leaves the radio station."

Molly had forgotten all about the controversial commentator. She had plenty of time to recall his vitriolic personality over the next half hour since Michael kept the car radio tuned to his station as they drove across the causeway and along Coral Way until they reached the broadcast studio. She didn't understand most of Díaz-Nuñez's words, but there was no mistaking the tenor.

451

The morning paper was mentioned often enough for her to guess he had taken up the cause of the previous night's demonstrators.

At the station Molly waited for Michael to try to relegate her to another wait in the car. To her astonishment, he didn't say a word. He just walked around and opened her door.

"You want me to go in?" she asked with undisguised astonishment.

"Something tells me your presence will rattle Díaz-Nuñez."

"Why?"

He grinned. "You are not aware of his reputation?"

"As a commentator, yes," she said.

"He also regards himself as quite a ladies' man. I'm hoping he'll be so engrossed in the amusement of trying to seduce you under my very eyes that he'll be less cautious in the answers he gives me."

"And here I thought you wanted to take advantage of my great interrogation skills."

"Oh, feel free to chime in anytime. Just don't expect him to take you seriously. He is not exactly a modern, liberated male when it comes to his views of women."

Molly detected an odd note in his voice. "Just how well do you know this guy?"

"Well enough," Michael replied curtly.

"Obviously you don't have much respect for him. Why would you know him so well?"

"He was involved with my cousin Ileana for a while. I figure another three years of recovery and she'll have her self-esteem back."

"And you want to throw me to this wolf?"

He squeezed her hand reassuringly. "Never, *amiga.* I just wish to dangle the bait, so to speak."

She frowned at him. "What a pleasant prospect."

In his pin-striped suit and designer loafers, Luis Díaz-Nuñez was younger than Molly had anticipated, maybe in his early forties, and definitely more polished. With his prematurely gray hair, olive complexion, soulful brown eyes, and a smile that transformed his face, he was also better looking. Her heart did a dutiful little pit-a-patter, just as he'd no doubt intended. She could see that flirting was as much second nature to him as cross-examining people was to Michael.

He ushered Michael and Molly into a cramped office cluttered with Spanish-language newspapers and magazines. On the wall were framed photographs of the

453

newscaster with President Reagan, President Bush, and the head of the powerful Cuban-American National Foundation. Clearly this was a man with ties to Washington. No doubt his radio show had given these same political creatures access to a huge Cuban audience that they needed to win support in South Florida.

"It is a terrible thing about your uncle's boat," he said to Michael when they were seated. All the while his gaze was on Molly. On her legs, to be precise. He finally blinked and looked back at Michael. "Do you know who is behind it?"

Michael shook his head. "I thought perhaps you might have some ideas."

Molly leaned forward, a movement that gave her the opportunity to tug her skirt over her knees without being too obvious about it. "Yes, Michael's been telling me how influential your radio show is and what terrific sources you have in the exile community. Surely you have heard things." She made it a statement, rather than a question.

"I have many friends, yes," he agreed, picking up a thin cigar from his desk and running his long fingers over it in a gesture that was obscenely sensual. His eyes met hers and he shrugged. "But about this I have heard nothing."

"What is your good friend Paredes up to these days?" Michael inquired bluntly. Too bluntly, judging from the closed expression that suddenly came over Díaz-Nuñez's face.

Molly jumped in again. "He's a fascinating man, isn't he? I've met him only once, but I was struck with the aura of self-confidence about him. It is difficult these days to find men who are so committed to any cause."

The newscaster's gaze locked with hers. "You admire commitment?"

"Of course. It is the true measure of a man, don't you think?"

"Absolutely. And you are correct about Paredes. He has a vision and he will not rest until it becomes a reality."

"The fall of Castro," Molly said.

"That, yes, but more importantly, the restoration of our homeland to its prior glory. He will be at the forefront of such a recovery."

"And for this he has a plan, no doubt?" she continued, grateful that Michael seemed willing to let her try to seduce answers from Díaz-Nuñez.

"But of course," he said.

"Has he begun to implement this plan?"

The newscaster suddenly snapped the cigar in two and tossed the shredded pieces onto his desk. His gaze was no longer nearly as friendly.

"Mrs. DeWitt, whatever plans Paredes has he will reveal when the time is right," he said coldly. "We are waging a war here, not orchestrating some children's playground skirmish."

Molly refused to let his sharp retort or the sudden coldness in his eyes daunt her. "I understand that some of his men are already in place inside Cuba."

Díaz-Nuñez glanced at Michael. "Do you always allow your woman to speak for you?" he inquired with an air of macho derision.

Molly flinched at the deliberate rebuff. Apparently he'd merely been humoring her and had tired of it. She had a few things she wouldn't mind saying to him about his attitude, but fortunately Michael jumped into the fray before she could get started.

"I do when she's asking all the right questions," he said quietly. "You must find such questions troubling or you wouldn't be shifting the subject so readily."

Díaz-Nuñez's jaw tensed at the insult. "Perhaps, then, I should give you a word of advice," he said, regarding Michael intently. "These questions are dangerous ones, my friend. This is a delicate time when the future of our homeland may very well hang in the balance." His gaze shifted to Molly. "Anyone who threatens this will be disposed of like that," he added with a decisive snap of his fingers.

A chill shot down Molly's back. Michael, however, leaned forward and met Díaz-Nuñez's gaze evenly. "If I learn that anyone involved with this so-called delicate operation has harmed one hair on my uncle's head, or if anyone dares to threaten anyone close to me again, then hell will be a pleasant alternative to the fate I will inflict."

Díaz-Nuñez visibly withered under the lethal intensity of Michael's warning.

Michael stood up, his gaze leveled on the man who had remained seated. "I assume we understand each other, my *friend*," he said in a way that could not be interpreted as friendly.

"Most definitely," the newscaster said without meeting his gaze.

Molly figured the proof of that could be found in the way he continued to keep his eyes averted as they left his office. The kind of man to whom studying a woman's tush was second nature, Díaz-Nuñez suddenly seemed totally absorbed in cleaning up the crushed cigar tobacco that littered his desk.

12

When Michael cut across town on Twenty-seventh Avenue toward Little Havana, Molly gathered they were going to see his family. She decided she needed sustenance before that happened. Her brain cells functioned more efficiently with a little protein and caffeine to charge them.

"You promised me breakfast," she reminded him.

"McDonald's?"

"Not on your life."

"Cuban coffee and a cheese-and-guava pastry?"

"Better."

"Good. Those you can get at Tía Pilar's."

"Too cheap to buy me breakfast," she noted. "I'll remember that."

"Not cheap, *amiga*. Just in a hurry. Time is passing too quickly, and with each hour that passes, I grow more concerned for Miguel. The sooner I speak with Elena, the sooner perhaps I will have new leads."

Molly's teasing ended at once. "Of course. I'm sorry. How do you plan on getting your aunt to talk if everyone's all together at Tía Pilar's? She'll never admit to anything with her husband and sister looking on."

"I'll manage. It's possible Pedro may not even be there. He's probably opening the restaurant again today." He glanced at her worriedly. "You haven't said a word about our meeting with Díaz-Nuñez. Usually you can't wait to dissect every word, every nuance, of a conversation."

"What do you expect me to say? That the guy gave me the creeps? Are you waiting for me to demand a device so I can check my car before I turn on the ignition?"

"It wouldn't be a bad idea," he said.

His tone was far more serious than Molly would have preferred. "Surely you don't take his threat seriously?" she asked, hoping for a denial.

"Yes, I do."

The blunt, matter-of-fact reply chilled her. "But I thought it was a standoff. You warned him what would happen if he or anyone else did anything."

"You don't understand, *amiga*. To a man like Díaz-Nuñez, or to Paredes, the cause is more important than any individual's life, even their own."

"But he's a newscaster, for God's sake. A journalist."

Michael shrugged. "That label does not mean the same thing to him that it does to you. He is as much an advocate of revolution as Paredes. He learned his attitudes at his father's knee. When Raúl Díaz was killed during the Bay of Pigs, Luis made the cause his own. He and his friends would not hesitate to silence anyone perceived as a threat to their goals, and they would be prepared to suffer the consequences."

"But that's . . ." Molly fumbled for a suitable word. "Barbaric."

"In their view, it is warfare."

"I thought such extremist views had died out in the seventies and eighties, even among those most violently opposed to Castro."

"Such passion seldom dissipates. If anything, it only grows stronger the longer the ultimate goal remains elusive. How many times have they had their hopes raised, only to see Castro's strength overcome the odds? Too many by their count. If they again decide terrorist tactics are necessary . . ." He shrugged. "And make no mistake, the average Cuban may disapprove of the violence but will understand its cause."

"You don't."

"Perhaps it is my Irish blood," he said with a shrug. "Or perhaps I was too young when I left. Maybe it is just that as a policeman, I deplore violence of any kind and can make no excuses for it."

Molly thought of Brian, who was currently safe with her ex-husband. Obviously this was one time when it would be not only foolish but irresponsible to bring him home as long as the threat of danger continued. Michael was not an alarmist. If he believed so strongly that she was in danger, then she had to take it seriously, even if the threat was beyond her comprehension.

"I'll have to leave Brian with Hal for a while longer, won't I?"

He glanced over at her. "It would probably be best. And you will stay with me. No arguments, okay?"

Molly thought of the hard, cold expression in Díaz-Nuñez's eyes when he had snapped that cigar in two and shivered. "No arguments."

From what Molly could observe, Tía Elena was not nearly as forthcoming as Michael had anticipated her being. If anything, she was downright coy, denying that anyone had mentioned a word to her about what she

461

referred to indifferently as "political matters."

Michael regarded her with evident frustration. "You are not helping Miguel by staying silent."

"If I knew something of consequence, do you not think I would tell you?" she retorted.

"Pedro has said nothing to you?"

"How many times must I tell you this?"

"Your own sister has not confided in you?"

"My sister is inconsolable with grief. She weeps for her husband. She does not waste time on foolish speculation."

Molly watched Tía Elena's round face as she spoke and listened to the rhythm of her words. There was an almost indiscernible hesitation that only someone listening so intently would have heard. Michael clearly was less attuned to the subtle change.

Molly placed her hand over the older woman's. She had grown genuinely fond of Michael's aunt, and she thought the feeling was reciprocated. Perhaps it was time for less bullying tactics and more woman-to-woman compassion. "But Pilar has speculated, hasn't she?" she said softly.

Michael's aunt met her gaze and her lips trembled slightly. She shot a worried glance at her nephew. "They were the words of a woman who is crazy with worry," she finally admitted with obvious reluctance.

Molly persisted. "Perhaps so, but isn't it possible that she knows something in her heart, even if Tío Miguel never confirmed it."

"What did she tell you?" Michael asked, and this time his own tone was more gentle. The man was nothing if not adaptable. "*Por favor,* Elena? Please."

Elena sighed heavily. "She heard things, in the night when Miguel thought she was asleep. There were men here, arguing, planning, whatever. She could not be sure. She had heard such talk before. Pipe dreams, that is all they were. Surely, no one would attempt such foolishness," Elena said with more hope than conviction.

"An attack?" Michael said. "They were planning to invade Cuba?"

Elena sighed again and gazed toward the heavens, as if for guidance. At last she nodded. "That is what she thought."

"Did she see these men? Was Paredes one of them?"

"She did not say, not to me anyway."

Michael's jaw firmed. "She will tell me."

Elena touched his arm. "She will not, not if she believes it could mean endangering Miguel."

"He is already in danger," Michael snapped. He shoved his hand through his hair. "Dammit, I don't understand this. I don't understand him."

It was the cry of a man one generation removed from the heartache of exile.

Tía Pilar regarded her nephew with a stoic expression. Not all of Michael's gentle cajoling or impatient badgering had been able to shake a single word from her. Not by so much as the flicker of an eyelash did she react when he said he knew that she had overheard something the night before Miguel's disappearance.

"Why won't you tell me?" he said yet again.

"No sé," she insisted as she had since the questions had begun. She knew nothing.

Molly touched Michael's arm and shot him an imploring look. With a curt nod he allowed her to take over.

"Tía Pilar, do you have photographs from Cuba?"

The old woman listened carefully, her ability to translate the English words as halting now as it probably had been when she'd arrived more than thirty years before. Molly touched a framed picture of Miguel sitting on the table by her chair. "More pictures from Cuba?"

She nodded emphatically and her expression softened. *"Sí, sí."*

She stood up and went to a breakfront in the tiny dining room. When she returned, she carried an album. Molly moved to her side. Pilar motioned for Michael to join them. He looked as if he wanted to protest that they were wasting precious time, but he finally relented and hunkered down beside the chair.

Then with great ceremony Pilar opened the book to the first page. Molly felt as if she'd been transported back in time by the black-and-white snapshots and more formal portraits pasted so lovingly into the album, each with a description under it in precise handwriting.

"My parents," Pilar said haltingly, pointing to the lovely dark-haired girl, who wore a cameo at the throat of her lace-trimmed, high-necked blouse, and the solemn man standing formally behind her. "At their wedding."

Pilar glanced at Michael for a reaction. Molly caught the suspicious sheen of tears in his eyes. "You remember them, don't you?" she asked.

He nodded. "I never saw them again after I was sent to this country. My grandfather

465

died right after that. And then, two years later, my grandmother," he said in a voice thick with emotion. "My grandmother was always laughing. That's what I remember when I think of Cuba, not the beauty of the countryside or the way of life, but the sound of her laughter."

Pilar carefully turned the page to her own wedding portrait. She had her mother's classic bone structure and the same luxuriant halo of black hair. Back then it had not been tamed as it was now, and it had framed her face in a way that emphasized her incredible dark eyes. Miguel had been matinee-idol handsome, and the sparkle in his eyes as he regarded his new wife was a stark contrast to the melancholy look with which Molly was familiar.

After that there were mostly snapshots. The three sisters on the beach at Varadero. Two couples — Pilar and Miguel, Elena and Pedro — seated in a dazzling night-club in Havana. And to Molly's surprise, there was one of Rosa, Michael's mother, on stage, standing at the microphone, a big band behind her.

Then there were the children — building sand castles on the beach, lined up in their finest clothes on an Easter Sunday, at someone's first communion. And finally there was Rosa with her baby — Michael. Even though Rosa and the American soldier with the Irish name had not married, the family had not rejected her or her illegitimate son.

"No pictures of your father?" Molly asked quietly.

"None. If my mother ever had one, she destroyed it. I've never seen him."

"Have you ever considered looking for him?"

"For what?" He gestured around the room. "This is my family. Miguel and Pedro, they were my fathers."

When Pilar had turned the last page of the album, a handful of photos tumbled loose. Mostly there were more family snapshots, taken when the children were perhaps a year or two older than they had been in the pictures in the album. But among the candid family photos, there was one of a group of men wearing military fatigues. They were standing at the edge of a field of sugarcane under a brilliant sun. Molly immediately recognized Miguel and Pedro. She wasn't absolutely certain, but she thought the youngest man might have been Orestes León Paredes himself, his expression cocky, his stance arrogant. She glanced up at Michael.

467

"Paredes?"

It was Pilar who answered. "*Sí, es* Paredes."

Michael pointed to the fourth man in the snapshot. "That's José López, isn't it?"

Molly studied it more closely, looking for some sign of a resemblance to the shrunken, injured old man she had seen playing dominoes in the park. The man pictured was powerfully built and exuded vitality. Because she couldn't see it, she looked to Pilar for confirmation.

"*Sí,*" she said with an unmistakable trace of bitterness. "*Es José.*"

Molly exchanged a look with Michael. Obviously, he had caught the odd note in his aunt's voice as well. He asked her a question in Spanish. Rather than answering, she shoved the photos back into the album and snapped it shut. But when she started to stand, Michael gently held her in place.

"Tía Pilar," he said firmly and repeated the question.

Molly understood only López's name and *aquí.* Apparently Michael was asking if the old man had been the one Miguel had seen the night before his disappearance. Had José López been *aquí,* here in this house?

Pilar's jaw set stubbornly, but a tear she

468

couldn't control so easily escaped and tracked down her cheek. It was answer enough.

Michael squeezed her hand. "*Te quiero mucho,* Tía," he said. "I love you."

When they left, Pilar was rocking silently back and forth, the album clutched to her bosom.

13

"Are you going to see Señor López about his meeting with Miguel?" Molly asked as they once again turned right on *Calle Ocho* off Twenty-seventh Avenue and headed west.

Michael shook his head. "Not yet. We're going to stop by La Carreta for lunch."

Molly regarded him in astonishment. "Isn't that some sort of betrayal, going to a restaurant other than Pedro's?"

"We're not going for the food. We're going for the conversation. I'm hoping we'll spot some of the same people who turned out for last night's protest. I'm sure that will be the hot topic of conversation over their *café Cubano* and *media noche* sandwiches. Maybe they'll be more forthcoming in the bright light of day."

Molly figured the odds of that were about equal to the odds of her understanding half of the mostly Spanish conversation — slim.

470

She wasn't sure she wanted to witness Michael's mounting frustration.

"That might be a good time for me to check in with Walt Hazelton at the paper and see if his sources in Cuba have anything to say about a stir in activity among the revolutionaries."

"It's probably a good time for you to call your ex-husband as well and make arrangements for Brian." At Molly's expression of distaste, he grinned. "Like taking a bitter medicine, *amiga,* you should get it over with."

"That's easy for you to say. You're not the one who's about to be the object of one of Hal's guilt-inducing tirades."

He regarded her intently. "If it bothers you so much, I could explain things to him."

Molly did rather like the image of Michael trying to talk reasonably with Hal DeWitt. They'd reacted like instinctive enemies on the past occasions when they'd met. It would be a real test of Michael's communication skills to see if he could get past all that predatory animosity, while keeping his own temper in check.

Regrettably, she also knew letting Michael make that call would be taking the coward's way out. "I'll call," she said resignedly.

To her amazement, when she got Hal on

the line, the conversation actually went as smoothly as their earlier exchanges. The instant she explained the seriousness of the situation, he agreed that Brian should remain with him. He seemed especially pleased that she'd lived up to her promise to turn to him in an emergency.

"How are you two getting along?" Molly asked.

"We've hit a couple of rough patches," he admitted with what was for him amazing candor. He rarely wanted anyone to guess his failings. Hal DeWitt, partner in one of the most prestigious law firms in town, preferred that the world maintain its impression of him as a brilliant, successful attorney who was totally self-confident and untouched by the doubts that plagued ordinary men.

"What sort of rough patches? Over your new girlfriend?"

Hal's chuckle surprised her.

"So he told you about that?" he said.

"Is it something serious?"

"Not anymore."

"Meaning?"

"Seeing her treat Brian like an unwelcome intruder in my home woke me up."

"You don't suppose he did anything intentionally to antagonize her?" Molly asked, knowing that their son could be plenty devious when it suited his purposes.

"Not really. I think his presence was sufficient. I made it clear that his presence was welcome, and if she couldn't accept that, then her presence wasn't."

"And?"

"She left."

"You're okay with that?"

"Trust me, in retrospect I can see that it wasn't a great loss. I'm too old to be trying to keep up with some ambitious twenty-three-year-old law clerk anyway. Sooner or later I'd have begun to wonder if her interest in me was personal or professional."

Molly had no comment on that. Well, to be perfectly honest, she had one, but it was best left unspoken if she intended to maintain this aura of amiability.

Hal hesitated, a rare occurrence for a man known in court for his quick-witted silver tongue. "There is something I should probably tell you."

"What?" Molly asked with a sudden sense of impending doom. Broken arms and chicken pox came to mind. Naturally he'd want her off guard before dropping such a bombshell. "What's wrong?"

"Nothing's wrong," he said irritably, then caught himself. "It's just that having a kid around all the time, well, it can be damned difficult. Not that I haven't loved it, you understand," he added hurriedly.

Molly's mouth dropped open. Hearing such an admission from her extraordinarily competent, smug ex-husband was like unexpectedly wringing an honest response from a politician.

Hal chuckled again. "I've stunned you into silence, haven't I?"

"As a matter of fact, yes."

"The last few days have taught me a greater appreciation of what you've been coping with ever since we split. Juggling work and parenthood isn't quite the snap I expected it to be. I thought it was all a matter of organization. Boys don't always stick to the program, do they?"

"Almost never."

"You've done a good job with him, Molly," he said quietly. "I just wanted you to know that."

She couldn't think of a thing to say except "Thank you."

"Be careful, okay?"

"Always. Tell Brian I love him and I'll try to call him tonight."

"Will do."

Michael came up behind her as she hung up. "Everything okay?"

"Amazingly enough, yes. He was actually decent about everything."

"That will make things easier between the two of you, yes?"

Molly nodded. "I feel as if this great weight has been lifted." She glanced up at Michael and said ruefully, "I wonder how long this accommodating mood will last."

"Just savor the moment," he suggested.

"Probably a good idea." She glanced beyond him toward the restaurant's main dining area. "Anyone here you were hoping to see?"

"There's one group of old men huddled in a corner. I've gotten the table closest to them."

"I'll be with you as soon as I've called Walt Hazelton. Order a sandwich for me, okay?"

Michael nodded. He turned to go, then came back. He reached up and cupped her face in his hands, his gaze steady on hers. "Thank you."

"For what?"

"For sticking with me through this."

She turned her head and pressed a kiss against his palm. "I wouldn't be anyplace else."

Walt Hazelton did have news from inside Cuba. Whether it was good or bad probably depended on the viewpoint. Molly couldn't quite decide what to think when he confirmed that in fact there had been reports of a handful of armed men arriving on the beaches along Cuba's north coast between Cojímar and Santa Cruz del Norte.

"One group was spotted and greeted with a hail of gunfire from Cuban soldiers. One man was killed and two others were wounded. A fourth escaped."

Molly's breath caught in her throat. "Any names?"

"Miguel García was not among them."

She released a pent-up sigh of relief. "Thank God. Were they the only ones?"

"There are several wild rumors circulating, including one saying an entire boatload of guns made it through and that even now guerrillas in the hills are arming themselves for a coup."

"Are you sure this is just a rumor?"

"No one I spoke with had seen these guns for themselves. It was always the friend of a cousin or some such who'd reported it. I wouldn't go to press with information that vague, but I heard it enough to suspect there may be some truth to it."

"But the bottom line is that Miguel could have been part of an attempted invasion and he could be inside Cuba now."

"It's possible," the reporter agreed.

He said it without much enthusiasm. Molly wondered about that. "What aren't you saying?"

"One thing doesn't make sense," he admitted.

"What's that?"

"Miguel took his boat out from here on Sunday morning. You went looking for him at midday and found the boat Sunday night, early Monday morning, right?"

"We found it an hour or so before sunset in Cuban waters. It was just before midnight when we got back. The explosion occurred just after midnight," Molly said.

"According to the people I spoke with, those arrested said they had taken off from Key West," Hazelton reported.

"Perhaps Miguel was to meet up with them," Molly suggested, stretching to find a reasonable explanation. "That would explain why we found his boat adrift where we did and why his raft was missing."

"I don't think so."

"Why not?"

"Because this incident didn't take place until just before dawn this morning. I began getting calls as soon as I hit the office, calls from people I had spoken with just yesterday who had no news of this kind to report."

Molly wasn't willing quite yet to accept the implications of what Walt was saying. "Couldn't they have staged this to go in over a period of days? That way if one wave of guerrillas was picked up, others might still have a chance to get past the soldiers."

"It's possible, but everyone reliable I spoke with indicated that all those arriving safely had also arrived just today."

When Molly said nothing, Walt Hazelton said quietly, "I'm sorry. I know this isn't what you hoped to hear."

"At least it's something," she said finally. "We just have to figure out what it means."

When she told Michael what the foreign correspondent had learned, the color drained from his face.

"Miguel could still have gone in with them," Molly insisted, refusing to give up hope.

"And what has he done since Sunday? It is Tuesday now. Has he been floating around on a raft in Cuban waters waiting to rendezvous with his coconspirators?" He shook his head. "I don't like this. Something tells me Miguel was up to his neck in the planning for this, but that something went terribly wrong."

"You don't know that."

"But I know who would," he said with an

478

air of grim determination.

He rose and walked over to the table of men across the aisle. They regarded him warily as he pulled up a chair and joined them.

Ignoring the food that had just been placed in front of her, Molly watched their faces, hoping she could detect something from their expressions since she couldn't understand their rapidly spoken words. All she heard were what sounded like vehement denials, accompanied by angry gestures. Michael's exasperated shouts rose above the uproar of the others, stunning them into furious, stubborn silence. He threw up his hands in a gesture of disgust and left them.

"What on earth did you say to them?" Molly asked when Michael stalked back to the table, picked up their check, and headed for the door. She had to race to catch up with him as he tossed a handful of bills onto the counter by the cash register.

"Michael?" she prodded him.

"I told them they were crazy old men if they believed they were any match for Castro's guns. I asked them if this was a plot by Paredes. Just like last night, they denied any knowledge of such a plot. Then they gave me a bunch of hogwash about the triumph of freedom against a godless regime."

He settled into the driver's seat of the car and rubbed his eyes before sliding his sunglasses into place. "I don't know how to deal with men like that," he said with a rare display of helplessness. "How can I make them trust me?"

"Not by calling them crazy old men," Molly replied.

He scowled at the rebuke. "Okay, it wasn't exactly tactful," he admitted, "but I'm out of patience and I may well be running out of time. If Miguel is still at sea on that damned raft without provisions, he could be dying while they talk ideals and politics."

Molly had one thought, but she knew instinctively that he was likely to resist it. "Michael, I really do think you must go to Señor López and talk to him."

"About what happened the night before Miguel disappeared?"

"About that, but more importantly about what it was like for them in Cuba when they were young. You saw them in that photo with Paredes. Those ties have never weakened. Paredes isn't likely to open up with so much at stake, but José López might. Maybe more than anyone else, he can make you understand what has gone on in your uncle's head and how he feels in his heart. I think this is something you need to hear."

As she'd expected, he dismissed the idea with a wave of his hand. "I've listened to Pedro. I've listened to all of them. What do you think the talk is at Sunday dinner three hours out of every four? Cuba in the old days. Havana in its glory. The faith that soon they will return. In every toast at every holiday, they repeat that next year's toast will be made in Cuba. No matter how long it's been, they say it with the same deep conviction each time."

Molly regarded him skeptically. "Do they really believe it? Or is it a habit they can't overcome because then they wouldn't know how to go on? They've talked for all these years, but have you listened?"

"I tell you it was impossible growing up in my family not to hear these things," he said impatiently.

"But have you really listened?" she repeated. "Perhaps it's time you discover what it means to be a Cuban in exile, especially to a man like Miguel García."

"I am a Cuban in exile."

She shook her head. "No, you're a Cuban who's grown up here, who has acclimated. If anything, you've rebelled against the dreams of Miguel and the others, just as

481

many teenagers rebel against the expectations of their parents. You were educated here. Your friends are Anglos and African-Americans, as well as Cubans. You're a policeman, for goodness' sake, a part of the system. How much more acclimated could you be?"

When he started to argue, she held up a hand. "No, wait. Have you dreamed of going home, as they do? Are there things you lie awake nights remembering, longing for? Have you wanted to return to the Havana you remember, to walk its streets again? How much do you even remember about the first five years of your life, except for the sound of your grandmother's laughter?"

He sighed heavily. "Perhaps not enough," he admitted eventually. "Perhaps not enough."

14

José López agreed to meet Michael and Molly that night at a performance by Cuban salsa queen Celia Cruz.

"I tried to talk him out of it," Michael told Molly when he'd hung up. "A club is no place for a quiet conversation. He said it would be an appropriate backdrop to what I need to hear, whatever that means."

"It probably means that they heard her perform in the old days in Havana. She really is quite something."

"You've heard her?" he asked, clearly amazed.

"At the *Calle Ocho* festival. She usually performs."

"You've been to the street festival?"

"Why are you so surprised? Hundreds of thousands of people are jammed along Eighth Street every year to hear the music and pig out on the food."

"I'm just amazed that you were one of them."

She regarded him closely. "What about you?"

"I haven't been in years," he admitted. "Pedro talked me into helping with his food booth five or six years ago. There were too damned many people for me. I told him I'd pay somebody to help him out the next time."

"Another rebellion, perhaps?" she inquired dryly.

Michael frowned at her.

"Never mind. Speaking of Pedro, though, do you suppose we could stop by his restaurant and grab another sandwich?" she asked wistfully.

"We just ate."

"Maybe you ate. I barely got to the table before you dragged me out of the place."

"Sorry," he said, looking contrite. "I wasn't thinking." He drove the few blocks east and pulled into the parking lot beside Pedro's restaurant. Inside they found his uncle working the cash register, his expression somber. He gave them a distracted glance.

"Sit anywhere. I will join you when I can."

Although it was nearly two o'clock, the restaurant was still jammed. As they worked

484

their way between the crowded tables, Molly spotted the two young rafters who'd been rescued the day before. She pointed them out to Michael. They were surrounded by people, clearly being treated as heroes. At the sight of Michael, though, they stood up and came forward. Molly was relieved to see that the color in their cheeks was more normal, even though their sunburn blisters had broken and still looked painful.

"Gradas, amigo," Ricardo said to Michael, a smile spreading across his face. "You were right. Your uncle has promised us work. We will work hard to repay his generosity."

Tony clasped Michael's hand. "*Sí,* we are very grateful," he said in his low, shy voice. "We will start tonight. That will be the beginning of our new life."

"I'm glad it worked out," Michael told them. "I see you have found some admirers."

"Everyone has been very good to us," Ricardo agreed with his ready grin.

Tony, however, regarded Michael worriedly. "There is so much to learn."

"You'll do fine," Molly told them. "You already speak English amazingly well. Soon you will fit right in with those your own age. By the time school starts in the fall, you'll already have friends."

"I am not so sure about school," Tony said. "Unless we can locate our uncle and he will take us in, we must work to live here."

"I'm sure my uncle will adjust your hours so that you can attend classes," Michael said, dismissing their concerns. "You'll need an education if you are to get ahead in this country."

"Get ahead?" Ricardo repeated. *"No comprendo."*

"To be a success."

The teenager nodded emphatically. "Ah, yes, a success. The American success story, *sí?*" Both boys glanced down at their new jeans, fancy sneakers, and the teal-and-black T-shirts of the Florida Marlins baseball team. "With these gifts we look American already, yes?" Ricardo asked.

Molly nodded, thinking how desperately they wanted to be part of their new land while so many other exiles simply longed to go home again. Perhaps it was because the two teenagers understood better than anyone the harsh reality and desperation of life in Cuba today. Would they be able to find a common understanding with men like Miguel, or would their perceptions of Cuba be so at odds it would be as if they were speaking of different countries? Would the glamor of this new land wear off when they realized how hard they would have to work to attain what others had? Right now it all must seem a fantasy come true.

When Molly and Michael were alone at their table and the boys had left with their new friends, she looked at him. "How much do you recall about your first days here?"

A faraway look came over his face. "I was just thinking about that, trying to identify with what those two boys must be feeling. I can't. I was so young. All I remember was crying when I realized my mother wasn't getting on that plane with me. I remember how alone I felt, even after I was living with Pedro and Elena and my cousins. A child at that age needs a mother more than freedom, I think."

His expression hardened, as if he'd been transported back in time. "That is why I had so much anger," he said quietly. "I threw incredible tantrums. Sometimes I would go to bed so hoarse from crying, there was no sound left in me. I was probably hoping they would send me back. I didn't understand that they couldn't. I was still angry when my mother finally came. I didn't speak to her for days. I refused to allow her close enough to hug me."

"That must have pained her deeply,"

Molly said, barely able to conceive of the heartbreak she would suffer if Brian ever shut her out so cruelly.

"I suppose it did. I was too caught up in my own hurt to think of hers."

"Perhaps you were afraid."

"Of what?"

"That she would leave you again."

A faint, rueful smile tugged at his lips. "Have I ever told you that you are very wise, *querida*?"

She grinned at him. "Not nearly enough. Do you suppose they would have heard any rumors of an impending attack by guerrillas from the US?"

Michael shook his head. "They are boys. Like all teenage boys, I would guess their interest is in girls, not politics."

"Michael, they risked their lives to get to a new country. That doesn't sound like a couple of kids who are unaware of anything except their hormones. This wasn't some lark or an adventure."

"Are you so sure?"

"Sure? No, of course I can't swear to it. We'd have to ask them. But from everything I've seen about life in Cuba or in any other place that has suffered war or oppression of one sort or another, there is no such thing as a childhood or adolescence as we know

488

it. You've seen the pictures of children from places like Bosnia or Ireland or the Middle East, children whose eyes tell you they are wise beyond their years. Based on that, I say Tony and Ricardo may still be in their teens, but they are men, not children."

"Perhaps they just wanted to live someplace where they could get a Big Mac and a milk shake."

"I guess we'll have to ask them directly when we see them again to see which of us is right." Pedro joined them then. He gave Molly a wan, dispirited smile as he sat down with his tiny cup of *café Cubano* and poured in a healthy dollop of sugar.

"*Qué pasa,* Tío?" Michael asked.

"I should be home with the family," Pedro complained. "But no one else can handle the register at this hour, and we could not remain closed forever."

"Elena and Mother are with Pilar. That's all she really needs right now."

"No, she needs Miguel. As I do. He is like my own brother after all these years."

"Did he come in here often?" Molly asked.

"I tried to persuade him to work for me, but he said his English was not good enough. Still, he would stop almost every afternoon for an hour or so. Even today, I keep glancing toward the door expecting him to appear."

"Was he usually alone?"

Pedro nodded. "He came alone, but always there were two or three friends at the counter. He would join them."

Michael nodded approvingly at Molly as he picked up on where she was headed with the questions. "Are any of those friends here now?" he asked, his gaze on the row of men seated at the Formica-topped counter at the front of the restaurant.

There were one or two men dressed in business suits, but most wore the more traditional *guayabera* shirts from the simplest style to those with tiny rows of fancy tucks. The men seemed to range in age from their sixties upward. One wrinkled old man appeared to be at least eighty, but he spoke with youthful passion and vehemence about whatever topic they were discussing.

Pedro scanned the row. "There is the political satirist Juan Cabrera on the end and next to him is Herman Gómez-Ortega. Juan and Miguel have known each other since the first year of school in Cuba. The Cabrera family lived only a little distance from Miguel's family. They both fought against Castro, but in different ways, Miguel with a gun, Juan with his words. The differences didn't matter in the end. Both were jailed."

"And Gómez-Ortega?"

"I know less about him." Pedro's gaze narrowed when he looked at the stoop-shouldered man bent over his cup of coffee. Molly could see that the man's broad, weathered hands appeared unsteady as he lifted the cup to his mouth. "You don't like him, though, do you?" she asked.

"You are very perceptive," he said bitterly. "Herman has these crazy ideas. Perhaps it is because he spent too long in Castro's prisons. He has been here only since the Mariel boat-lift in 1980. I suspect Castro was glad to get rid of him. He was a dissident, but he was also a troublemaker, a violent man."

"Did Miguel know him in Cuba, or did they meet here?" Michael asked.

"Perhaps it was in prison. I cannot say for sure."

"Could you suggest they join us?" Michael asked.

Pedro looked startled. "You wish to question them?"

Michael shrugged. "They are Miguel's friends. Perhaps he has taken them into his confidence or, if as you say Herman is a little *loco,* perhaps he knows of some crazy scheme to invade the island."

Pedro stood. "I will get them."

"Don't tell them I wish to question them. Say only that Miguel's nephew is here and would like to meet friends of his uncle."

Pedro nodded slowly. *"Comprendo."*

A few moments later the two men joined them. Herman walked with a limp, but his handshake was strong and his eyes were alert and cautious. Molly wondered at once if he was quite as crazy as Pedro thought. He struck her as shrewd. Juan Cabrera was the one with the faraway look in his eyes. Perhaps, though, he was merely dreaming of his next political article or satirical short story.

"I understand you both know my uncle well," Michael said.

"Miguel García is a strong man, a man of conscience," Herman said, settling into a chair with another cup of the strong Cuban coffee. "You should be proud of him."

"I am," Michael agreed. "Right now, though, I have to admit that I'm worried about him. When was the last time you spoke with him?"

"We had coffee here as usual on Saturday," Juan said.

"And what was his mood?"

"He talked of the fish he would catch in the morning. He said he would bring some

492

by for my family, as always," Juan said.

Michael looked skeptical, but rather than cross-examining the old man as he might a witness to a crime, he merely turned his attention to Herman.

"And you? When did you last see him?"

"I was here on Saturday as well. It is something of a habit with us. We are three old men with little to occupy our time except talk and memories."

It sounded awfully disingenuous to Molly.

"And he spoke to you only of fishing?" Michael asked.

"As I recall," Herman said vaguely.

Michael attempted a casual disinterest, but Molly could see the tension in the set of his jaw. "Do either of you know Orestes León Paredes?" he asked.

"Everyone knows of Paredes," Herman said quickly. "Why do you ask?"

"Do you think it is possible that he would have information about my uncle's disappearance?"

"He is a powerful man," Juan said thoughtfully. "It is true he would have many contacts."

Herman's gaze had narrowed. "What is it you are really asking, *amigo*?"

Michael regarded him evenly. "I suppose I'm asking exactly how involved Miguel was in Paredes's organization. As his friends, you would know that, *sí*?"

Herman stood up. "This is not something I care to discuss with a stranger."

Juan objected at once. "Michael is not a stranger. He is the nephew of our friend."

Herman shrugged. "He is also a policeman. Is that not what Miguel told us? I have no use for the police, not in my country and not in this one. *Adiós*." He left the restaurant without glancing either to the right or the left.

"Too many cruel years in prison," Juan explained when he had gone. "I am sorry for his rudeness."

"It's okay," Molly said distractedly, her gaze fixed on Michael's expression. She recognized that look.

"Let's go, *amiga*," he said. He was polite enough to his uncle and to Juan Cabrera, but it was clear his attention was focused on the man who had just left them.

"Are we following Herman?" Molly asked as they got into the car.

Michael nodded, his gaze scanning the parking lot and the nearby curbside. "There," he said finally, and made a quick turn across traffic that had Molly clinging to the door and praying that the cars aimed straight at the passenger side had time

494

enough to stop. She closed her eyes. Tires squealed and horns blew.

"You can open your eyes now," Michael said dryly.

"Don't you suppose that the ruckus you caused making that turn might have gotten Herman's attention?" she said, glancing ahead and hoping for a glimpse of the car they were tailing. She guessed it had to be the late-model white midsize Chevrolet.

Michael dismissed her concern. "My bet is he's too busy trying to get to Paredes to tell him about our chat. Where are those articles Ryan gave you?"

"In the backseat."

"Can you get to them?"

"As long as you don't arrest me for not wearing a seat belt."

"I'll close my eyes," he promised.

"Given the way you drive with them open, it probably wouldn't make that much difference," she observed. She snatched the papers from the back and snapped her seat belt into place. "Okay, what am I looking for?"

"Some mention of Herman in the articles about the organization."

Molly started skimming the printouts. Before she'd made it through the first two articles, Michael slammed on the brakes and muttered an expletive under his breath. For once it wasn't in Spanish, so she knew exactly how exasperated he was.

"What's wrong?"

"I don't get it."

She glanced out the window and spotted Herman at a pay phone in front of a convenience store. "So he's calling Paredes, rather than going to see him."

Michael shook his head. "I don't think so."

"Why not?"

"Because it looks to me like he's holding a long-distance calling card in his hand."

"What does that mean? Do you think he's an infiltrator working for the government?"

"Your imagination is working overtime, *amiga*. Besides, a government operative would have memorized the number."

"Maybe he's just making a business call that has absolutely nothing to do with this."

"Maybe," he agreed, but he sounded doubtful.

"I could go into the store and try to catch some of his conversation." She already had her hand on the door.

"Forget it. It would tip him that we're following him."

"The man looked straight through me the whole time we were sitting there. I doubt he'd even recognize me."

"Don't kid yourself. He could probably give you a detailed description of every single person seated near us in that restaurant. I watched him. He missed nothing."

Molly recalled her own first impression of his alertness. Even though he appeared to have ignored her, Michael was probably right about his generally sharp observance of both her and his surroundings. "So what do we do now?"

"When he gets off that phone and into his car, you go over and take down the number. Then call the operator and say you were disconnected on a long-distance call and ask if she can reconnect."

"He made the call. Won't she think it's odd that I can't tell her what number I made that call to?"

"Bluff. Do the best you can. At the very least, we'll have this number and perhaps the long-distance carrier he used. Perhaps later we can trace the call, if it becomes necessary."

"How will we know the carrier?"

"Because I counted the numbers he dialed. He didn't need an extra access number to reach his carrier, so whatever company the phone is linked to is his carrier. It probably says on the information card on the front of the phone."

Molly kept her awe at his observation skills to herself. "Can I assume that while I'm on the phone, you won't be waiting here patiently?"

"That's right. I'll be following him. If I'm not back in fifteen minutes, take a cab back to Pedro's and I'll pick you up there." He glanced toward the pay phone. "Okay, this is it. Be careful. Don't let him see you."

"Would you like me to lie down on the sidewalk until he's passed by?"

Apparently he missed her sarcasm, because he nodded without taking his eyes off his quarry. "Good idea."

Molly climbed out of the car and hunkered down, inching her way to the van parked two spaces up. Standing behind that, she was sufficiently out of view from the street, but could see the exit from the convenience store lot. She watched as Herman pulled out of the lot and headed west, just as Michael had anticipated. Michael waited until there were several cars in between, then pulled away from the curb and into traffic a few cars behind him.

When they were out of sight, Molly strolled across the street to the pay phone. Unfortunately, all that caution had left the phone unattended. Someone else had taken advantage of the opportunity to grab it. Molly paced impatiently behind the woman, who seemed in no hurry to conclude her astonishingly graphic tête-à-tête. Must have been a lover, Molly decided. Women almost never sneaked out to a pay phone to make calls like that to their husbands, not after the first year of marriage anyway. When the woman finally did hang up, she didn't even spare Molly a glance. Apparently she wasn't the least bit concerned about having the details of her love life overheard.

Molly jotted down the number on the phone, saw that it was an AT&T hookup, then punched the "0" to get the operator. "Hi, I don't know if this is possible, but I'm at a pay phone and I placed a call to someone a few minutes ago. I've managed to lose the piece of paper the number was written on. It's probably in my purse, but I sure can't find it. Isn't it amazing how things can get swallowed up in a woman's handbag? Anyway, we were cut off in the middle of our conversation and I have no idea how to reach him."

She took a hint from the conversation she'd just overheard and threw herself on the operator's mercy. "It's really important. It's this guy. I'm really crazy about him, but I'm beginning to think he's married. I think he had me call him at a pay phone. Can you check for me or maybe get him back on the line? If it was a pay phone or something, I'll know he's cheating on a wife or girl-friend."

She was rather proud of the barrage of words. She waited to see if they'd been effective.

"Hon, I sympathize, but I can't do that."

"You mean because it's illegal?"

"You'd have to have a real emergency and even then I don't have the equipment to do it. Somebody'd have to authorize the check on the outgoing calls from your pay phone."

Molly sighed dramatically. "Oh, well, it was worth a shot." She was ready to hang up, but the operator wasn't through.

"Next time you talk to this guy, hon, you tell him you want to know how to reach him and if he won't tell you, you dump him. Don't waste your time, okay?"

Molly decided the operator had read too many pop psychology books or maybe she'd just seen too many weird episodes of *Geraldo* and hated to think of anyone getting caught up in some bizarre romantic triangle. "Thanks, I'll do that," Molly promised.

Just as she hung up, she spotted Michael's car turning into the lot.

"What did you get?" he asked.

"Advice," she said with disgust. "How about you?"

"Lost. He drove into Coral Gables and the next thing I knew, he'd taken a couple of fast turns and disappeared. The way those streets twist around in there, I was lucky to get back out again. I don't know where the hell I was. I wish they'd put their street signs up on poles where you can read them like any other civilized place."

"They think they're more civilized right where they are, discreetly placed at curb height." She couldn't resist taking a poke at his tailing skills. "So the bottom line is you lost Herman, huh?"

He shrugged. "Probably doesn't matter, since he clearly wasn't heading to see Paredes after all."

"You'll never know that for sure, unless we drive out there and check. Could be Herman just knows his way around the Gables."

Michael looked doubtful, but he turned the car west. It was a good thing he did, too. They arrived in front of Paredes's house in Westchester along with three squad cars and an ambulance.

"What's going on?" Michael demanded of the first cop he saw.

"Somebody tried to murder the guy who

lives here, blasted the hell out of the house with some kind of automatic weapon."

"Is he okay?"

"The lucky son of a bitch wasn't even home. From what the neighbors say, he moved out yesterday."

15

With police everywhere, the neighbors —
mostly women with small children — began
slowly emerging from their houses. While
Michael continued to talk to the investigating officers, Molly wandered over to a
cluster of housewives, all dressed in shorts
and tank tops regardless of their size.

Several of the young women were clutching babies in their arms. She observed them
for several minutes, trying to pick out the
one who was most talkative. The unofficial
spokesperson appeared to be in her late
twenties, slightly older than the others. Her
two children were toddlers, one of whom
was clinging to Mommy's leg and whining.
The women appeared oblivious to the noise.

Molly nodded at several of the women,
hoping she appeared to be a new neighbor,
rather than someone there on official business. Actually, given her lack of official
status, she supposed it wasn't exactly a

stretch to be considered just another nosy passerby. "What happened? I saw all the police and walked over."

As she'd expected, it was the oldest of the women who replied. "I was in the back with the kids and all of a sudden I heard these shots. I looked around, didn't see anyone, so I dragged the kids inside. That's when I finally peeked out the window and saw this car sitting in front of the house over there. Some guy was just blasting away. Scared the hell out of me. I dialed nine-one-one and kept the kids on the floor in the back of the house."

"Has anything like this ever happened around here before?" Molly asked.

"Good God, no. I'd have made my husband move, if it had," she said.

Several other heads nodded in agreement.

"I'm Molly DeWitt, by the way. I don't know a soul around here yet. Who lives there?" she asked.

The women were either cautious enough or distracted enough not to bother offering their own names. Molly's chatty source, however, didn't hesitate over her reply. Like a lot of people who've just gone through a crisis, she was anxious to share the experience. Fortunately she didn't seem suspicious at all of Molly's interest.

"The people only moved in a few months ago," she told Molly. "They stayed to themselves. I hardly ever saw the wife. We went by once to ask her if she wanted to take her kids to the park with us, but she refused. We didn't try again. She was a real pretty woman, way too young for him. I got the feeling that husband of hers kept her on a pretty tight leash. And those dogs of his . . ." She shuddered. "I used to wonder what would happen if they ever got loose. We all told our kids to stay as far away from there as possible."

Having had a close encounter with the dogs herself, Molly understood their concern. "Did they have a lot of visitors? Had you ever seen the guy who shot at the place today before?"

"I suppose it's possible he's been around. The guy seemed to have friends here at all hours. We thought maybe he was into drugs or something. I mean, that's what I told my husband the very first week they lived there, what with all the coming and going. In fact, when I first heard all the gunfire, I thought maybe it was the start of one of those cocaine lab explosions I've seen on the news."

"And you'd never reported your suspicions to the police?"

"Hey, around here we try to mind our own business. It's safer that way. Besides, none of us ever really saw anything. It wasn't like he was collecting money in the street."

Molly nodded. "I see what you mean. Just think how you'd feel if you turned someone in and the only thing he was guilty of was keeping late hours. So," she added nonchalantly, "what kind of car was this guy driving today?"

The woman shrugged. "Are you kidding me? I can't tell a Jeep from a Jaguar. Made my husband put a bright yellow sunflower on our antenna so I could find our car in the parking lot at the mall."

"I think it might have been a Chevy," a young Hispanic woman offered hesitantly. "My brother has a car that looks exactly like it, only his is that pretty bright blue color and this one was white."

A white Chevrolet, Molly thought triumphantly. Exactly like the one Herman Gómez-Ortega had been driving when they followed him from Pedro's restaurant.

She shook her head sorrowfully. "Jeez, it's getting so no place is safe anymore, isn't it? I think I'll go talk to the cops and see if they think this was some random thing or a hit."

One of the younger mothers shivered and held her baby a little tighter. "You think it could have been random, like somebody who might come back to the neighborhood?"

Molly immediately felt guilty. "No. I mean it almost has to be someone who was after the people who lived in that house, don't you think?"

"I wonder if that was why they moved out?" another of the women speculated. "Because they knew someone was after them?"

"All I can say is it's lucky for them they did," Molly's primary source observed. "This time of day, the kids were usually inside taking a nap in the front bedroom and the woman was watching some soap opera on TV right by that window that got blasted out."

This time Molly shuddered right along with them. She glanced toward Michael and wondered if he'd found out about the car. She doubted it. All the witnesses were women and all of them were over here. Obviously the police were too busy inside to worry about chatting with the neighbors yet. She decided it was time to take her piece of information and go.

"I'll let you know if I find out anything

from the police," she said, and walked back across the street.

When she finally got Michael's attention, he joined her beside her car. "I think it's time to run a Department of Motor Vehicles check on Herman," she suggested.

He grinned. "Oh, you do, do you? Who died and left you in charge of a police investigation?"

She frowned at the sarcasm. "It just occurred to me that you might want to see where he lives and what kind of car he drives."

"I know what kind of car he drives. I was following him, remember?"

"Oh, I'd be willing to bet that the car he was in today was not his," she said, advancing a theory that had struck her as she crossed the street.

His gaze narrowed. "Why the hell would you say that?"

"Would you drive your own car if you intended to try to murder someone in broad daylight?"

He regarded her in stunned amazement. "What the hell did those women tell you?"

"Not much," she said modestly. "They did describe the car of the assailant as being a white Chevrolet. Isn't that the kind of car we were tailing?"

Michael's approving expression lasted for half a heartbeat, before he looked more puzzled than ever. "But why would Gómez-Ortega want to kill Paredes? I thought they were coconspirators."

"Guess not," Molly said smugly.

"Unless he knew that Paredes had moved out, knew it was safe to blast away, and just wanted to create a diversion from whatever is really going on," Michael said thoughtfully.

Molly sighed. "Damn, you've done it again."

"Done what?"

"Turned all devious on me, just when I had things figured out all logically."

"It's not my deviousness you need to worry about, *amiga.* We're trying to think like the bad guys."

"That's what worries me," she said. "You do it so well. It's bound to rub off."

Michael called police headquarters and had Felipe run the DMV check on Gómez-Ortega. When Felipe called back as they were driving away from the scene, he confirmed Molly's guess. Gómez-Ortega didn't own a white Chevy or anything that might have been mistaken for one. He had, however, leased one from a small rental car agency on South Dixie Highway, an inde-

509

pendent company that was less likely to ask questions or keep records. Unfortunately for Herman, the trail was still hot when Felipe called.

"Are we going to question him?" Molly asked hopefully.

"Nope. Felipe's offered to have a chat with him. You and I are going to get all dressed up and meet José López."

"But we're not meeting him until nine o'clock," Molly protested.

"With the distractions I have in mind, *amiga,* it will take you that long to get ready."

The salsa beat was seductive. Celia Cruz might be an aging songstress, but she knew exactly how to capture her audience with the passion and soul of her music. People around Molly, Michael, and José López were on their feet, swaying to the provocative rhythm. Molly would have been totally caught up in it herself if it hadn't been for Michael sitting there impatiently tapping a silver spoon on the table. She knew it was impatience, because he wasn't even close to the music's beat.

Señor López, in contrast, couldn't have been happier. In fact, he hadn't looked this pleased when he'd won the dominoes game the day before. His expression was dreamy, as if Celia Cruz's music had reached his soul and transported him back to late-night Havana.

When the set finally ended, the old man dragged his attention from the stage down front in the crowded supper club to Michael. "Your mother was even better," he said. "She sang like a lark. Everyone who heard her fell a little in love with her."

Michael appeared startled. "I don't recall ever hearing her sing."

"Perhaps not. After she fell in love and your father left her, I think the romance went out of her soul."

Molly sensed Michael tensing beside her. She caught a fleeting glimpse of guilt, as if Rosa Huerta's loss of romance was his responsibility. How often, she wondered, had he blamed himself just for being born?

"It is Miguel I want to talk about," Michael said stiffly. "Tell me what you recall of my uncle."

"Miguel García was a dreamer. When Fidel began to talk of a better future for the masses, Miguel was one of the first we knew to embrace his words. He had seen firsthand the struggles of so many of our people to rise above poverty. He dreamed that a classless society was possible."

"What happened to change his mind?"

"Like so many of us, he quickly grew disenchanted when he saw the military force that would be used to make change. It grew worse when he saw that Fidel sought power almost as greedily as he sought change, and worse yet when he saw land and businesses seized indiscriminately. Then, when he saw brothers fighting against brothers, much as they did in this country's Civil War, he rebelled. As he had been among the first to join Fidel's cause, he was also among the first to seek his overthrow. It was only by the grace of Almighty God that he escaped with his life. He brought that passionate hatred for Fidel to this country. He holds himself partly accountable for all that went wrong in Cuba. All these years he has seethed with the need to make things right."

Michael seemed to be struggling to understand such powerful emotions. "He would do anything, then?"

"Anything," the old man agreed.

"Including taking part in a foolhardy invasion even less likely to be successful than the Bay of Pigs?"

"Ideals are not something you give up in the face of hardship. The odds would not have deterred him, not if there were even the slimmest margin of hope."

"Has Paredes staged such an attack?" Michael asked, though he looked no more hopeful of a straightforward response now than before.

"This is not for me to say. You have asked him this, yes? What did he say?"

"He denied knowledge of it." Michael pinned the old man with a piercing gaze. "But he would deny it, even if it were true, wouldn't he? He would deny it because he knows it is a violation of the Neutrality Act to stage a paramilitary attack on Cuba from American soil."

As she listened, Molly had a sudden terrifying thought. "Señor, how would Paredes and the others feel about one of their people working for the newspaper they regard with such hatred?"

For the first time since they'd sat down at the table, José López looked as uneasy as he had on the first day they'd questioned him. Michael clearly recognized that uneasiness.

"Well, señor?" he prodded.

"There are some who might view it as traitorous. But," he added quickly, "they are extremists, and there are few of them."

"It only takes one," Michael said quietly. He leveled another look at López. "I want names of those who might have considered my uncle such a traitor. Would Paredes himself have felt that way?"

Señor López looked pale, even in the restaurant's dim light. "I have heard him say such things, yes."

"But he would not personally have acted on his opinion, would he?" Molly asked.

The old man shook his head. "No, but there are always those who will do anything to please a leader such as Paredes. These men are anxious for violence. They see spies and traitors everywhere."

Michael covered the old man's hand. "Names, señor. For the sake of your good friend, I want you to give me names."

López seemed to struggle with his conscience. "I cannot," he said sorrowfully. "I am making my own inquiries, but I cannot help you with yours."

Michael regarded him shrewdly. "Perhaps your own name should be on that list," he suggested.

A tear spilled down José López's cheek. "Miguel was my friend," he said softly. "Again and again I told him he was embracing the enemy with that damnable job of his, but he would not hear it. He said putting food on his family's table did not constitute a betrayal of the cause."

He lifted his watery gaze to meet Michael's. "But I did not harm him," he said emphatically. "I could no more have harmed Miguel than taken a gun to my own head. No, my friend, if you think I am capable of that, you are a fool and you are wasting precious time."

"It is not I who waste it, but you," Michael said accusingly.

"I am doing what I can." He reached for his crutches then and hobbled away from the table, his shoulders stiff with pride and anger.

Molly exchanged a glance with Michael. "Do you think he was telling the truth?"

"About not being involved in my uncle's disappearance? Probably. About not knowing who was involved? No. I believe he knows or suspects."

"Why wouldn't he tell you, then?"

"And betray the goddamned cause?" Michael said angrily. "Can't you see that he would go to his death first?"

"It is a code of honor among them," Molly reminded him.

"And under other circumstances, perhaps I could admire it. With my uncle's life at stake, *amiga,* I cannot afford to."

16

When they got back to Michael's town house, Molly was the one who spotted the blinking light on his answering machine. Five messages.

"Michael, it's Jorge Martinez," began the first disembodied voice. "I just wanted to let you know we didn't pick up anyone in the straits today, just a couple of empty rafts, the makeshift kind, not anything Miguel would have been on. Sorry, *amigo.* I will go up again myself tomorrow. Call if you've had any word."

"Damn," Michael muttered. "I should have been out there when they came in."

"For what? The bad news? You're doing your part to break the case, while they do theirs. They understand that."

"I suppose," he said as the second message began.

"O'Hara, it's Felipe. Call me at headquarters when you get in. I've had a chat with

Herman. He claims to have no idea where you got the information that he had anything to do with the attack on Paredes's home. He swears he left your uncle's restaurant, stopped to make a call, then cut through Coral Gables to take the car back to the rental agency on Dixie Highway. I can't prove otherwise, because there's no exact time listed for his check-in. Ken said he'd go down and do a search of the car for some trace of gunpowder or shell casings if you want him to. Let me know how you want me to follow up. Should I turn this over to the investigating officers on the Paredes incident?"

Michael sank into a chair and held his head. "Damn, we're drawing blanks everywhere."

The next message began. "Michael, this is Pedro. Call Pilar's when you get in. I am worried about her. She has gone to her bed and won't speak to anyone."

"Terrific," he muttered, hitting the off button on the machine before it could play the remaining messages. "That's just great. Now Pilar is going to have a breakdown."

Molly stood behind him and massaged his shoulders. "Bed is probably the best place for her. She hasn't rested since this all began."

517

"She's not resting, dammit. She's sinking into a depression."

"Then we'll just have to come up with good news to snap her out of it."

Michael reached up and put a hand over hers. "I appreciate your optimism, *amiga,* but I think it is misguided."

Molly turned the answering machine back on. "There are two more messages. Either one of them could be the break we need."

The first, however, was a call from Bianca. Molly bristled when she heard the name. Bianca was the woman with whom Michael had been living when Molly had first met him.

"I am so worried about you," she said in a low, seductive voice that set Molly's teeth on edge. It didn't seem to matter that she was here and the other woman was not.

"Please call me and tell me what I can do to help," the message continued. "I spoke with your mother today and she said you are exhausted. *Por favor, mi amor,* let me do something."

Molly stopped the tape, her gaze pinned on Michael's face. It betrayed no emotion at the sound of his old lover's voice. "Do you want to call her?"

He seemed startled by the question. "For what? It is over between us."

518

"This is a crisis. Obviously she would like to help."

"And my calling would send her the wrong message. It is best to leave things as they are." He touched Molly's cheek. "Do not looked so worried, *amiga,* you have nothing to fear from Bianca."

"I wasn't worried."

His lips curved slightly. "If you say so."

Because it was not a statement she cared to examine any more closely, Molly punched the button to listen to the last message. It was from Walt Hazelton for her.

"I'll be at the paper until midnight or one. Call me." There was a sense of urgency in his voice.

"See, I told you that a break was just around the corner," she said triumphantly. "I'll bet he's learned something."

"Or he's trying to pick your brain."

"For what?"

"To discover what we've learned today."

"Then he'll be disappointed, won't he?"

When she got the correspondent on the line, he said, "I just wanted to be sure you'd heard about what happened out at Paredes's place this afternoon."

Offer of information or sneaky ploy? She supposed the reporter's statement might indicate there was some truth to Michael's cynical suggestion. Molly was willing to play along for the moment. "I was out there right after it happened."

"Then you know he'd moved out," he said.

"Yes. Any idea where he is?"

"I've been making calls all afternoon. He's disappeared without a trace. My sources have clammed up completely. My sense is that something big is about to break."

"Like what? An attempted overthrow of Castro?"

"Could be that or could be another Mariel situation, when the floodgates open. Washington's been working on an emergency plan to cope with another influx of exiles from Cuba or Haiti for months now. If O'Hara picks up anything on Paredes's whereabouts, will you let me know?"

"I'll do my best," Molly said, resigned to the fact that Hazelton knew no more than she did at this point. She was ready to hang up when it occurred to her that the correspondent could save her a lot of time digging into Herman Gómez-Ortega's background. She mentioned his name.

"Why do you ask?"

At a warning look from Michael, she hedged her answer. "Turns out he and Miguel were friends. He didn't particularly strike me as the friendly type."

"He's a mean son of a bitch, actually. He and Paredes are like two peas in a pod, though Herman has more of a reputation for violence. He's been head of military operations for the Paredes organization, though he would deny that. There was talk for a while that he was also the mastermind behind some bombing incidents targeting Cuban diplomats. People in Washington keep a very close eye on him. To hear him tell it, though, he is nothing more than a simple businessman, trying to live out his remaining years in peace."

"Thanks, Walt." When she'd hung up, Molly relayed what he'd said to Michael.

"A simple businessman? Sure doesn't sound like the man who took an assault weapon to Paredes's house today, does it?" he said. "I'll give Felipe a call and fill him in."

Molly paced while Michael was on the phone. His expression turned more and more grim as the mostly one-sided conversation went on. Since she had no idea what Felipe was saying, she had to assume it was more bad news.

"Well?" she asked when he'd hung up.

"Ken went by on his way home and took a look at the rental car. He couldn't find so much as a trace of evidence that it had been used in that shooting incident. He thinks we should turn it over to the investigating officers and let them do a more thorough check, but he doubts they'll come up with any more than he did. He said it looked to him like the damn thing had been gone over by a detail crew. The carpet had been shampooed, the seats cleaned, the whole nine yards."

"Which seems like a lot of trouble to go to before returning a rental car, unless a kid threw up all over the upholstery," Molly commented.

"Or unless someone is trying to cover up something," he added. "Unfortunately, I can't think of a court anywhere who'd take clean carpet and upholstery as evidence of a crime."

Molly awoke in the morning to the sound of glass breaking and a string of expletives in English and Spanish that would have made a sailor blush. She grabbed one of Michael's shirts and buttoned it as she ran down the stairs.

"What on earth?" she said as she skidded to a stop at the kitchen door. The radio was on the floor in pieces, along with a shattered coffee cup and bits of a juice glass. Coffee and orange juice were splattered all over the wall and the carpet. Michael was sitting down, staring at the mess, a dazed expression on his face. He looked as if he wasn't quite sure how it had happened.

Molly picked her way through the shards of glass and hunkered down in front of him, her hands on his thighs. "What happened? What did you hear on the radio?"

"What makes you think I heard something on the radio?"

She gestured toward the bits of plastic, batteries, and knobs scattered every which way. "People have a way of taking out their frustrations over the message on the messenger."

He sighed. "True. If Díaz-Nuñez had been in the vicinity, I might very well have treated him the exact same way."

"Ah, I see. And what did our favorite newscaster have to say this morning?"

"To hear him tell it, Paredes's organization is a hot-bed of traitors and spies who have infiltrated at Castro's behest. Death, he says, is not good enough for those who commit these crimes against the Cuban patriots. What happened to Miguel García, he says, was only a warning to the others."

Molly regarded him in shock. "Luis Díaz-Nuñez called your uncle a traitor? Why?"

"Do you think he felt a need to explain?"

he said bitterly. "It also sounds to me as if he believes he is dead." His eyes blazed with fury as he reached for the phone.

"You aren't calling him?" Molly said.

"Why not? I will not have him slander my family in this way."

"Do you honestly think what you say will matter to a man like Díaz-Nuñez?"

"But my uncle should be defended."

"And in due time, he will be. For now, though, shouldn't you be thinking of Pilar? What will she think when she hears on the radio any hint that Miguel might be dead?"

"Dear God, I never thought of that. Let's go. We have to get over there."

When they arrived at the house, already there were a handful of protesters marching on the front lawn, people spurred on by the rhetoric of Díaz-Nuñez. Molly wondered if she would be able to get Michael to pass them by without his responding to the jeers. A brawl would do nothing to help Pilar, though at the moment it might help Michael to release his pent-up outrage. Come to think of it, she wouldn't mind belting a few of them herself. She recognized them from earlier visits. These same people had been by to express their sympathy and concern for a man they had respected. Now Díaz-Nuñez and his unexplained labeling of

Miguel as a traitor had turned them against their friend.

Michael displayed admirable restraint as he passed by. Inside, they found Pilar being comforted by Michael's mother and Tía Elena. Pedro was trying to keep Michael's cousins from going outside to run off the band of protesters.

"They will only come back," he told them.

"But they are telling lies about Miguel. They say he has betrayed Cuba. He would never do that. How can they turn on him this way?" one of the youngest cousins asked.

"It is easy to stir up old fears," Pedro told them. "Logic and truth are no match for the rhetoric of hatred, given in the guise of patriotism. We know how deeply Miguel believed in Cuba. We know that the words spoken on the radio are lies, that Díaz-Nuñez has offered no facts, just allegations, but to say that we know those things will not be enough. Time will prove us right."

The younger men all looked to Michael. "Do you agree that we should do nothing?"

Michael glanced out the window, his jaw tense with anger. Finally he nodded with obvious reluctance. "Tío Pedro is right. We will not change their minds. It is more important that we keep Pilar's spirits high and that I find Miguel. We cannot lose our focus over this."

When Michael went to speak quietly with his aunt, Pedro pulled Molly aside. "I am worried about him. I can see his anger and his pain, but he keeps it inside."

"He is strong," Molly reassured him. "Stronger than any of us. And he is motivated by love for his uncle."

"You will see that he rests, that he does not drive himself too hard?"

"I will try," she promised. "But Michael knows his own limits, or thinks he does. I have little influence."

Pedro smiled wearily. "You have more than you know, Molly. He cares for you a great deal, I believe. And right now he needs you, whether he admits that to you or not."

The concept of Michael O'Hara's needing anyone was something Michael himself would have rejected out of hand, but Molly believed in her heart that Tío Pedro was right. The tough, stubborn cop needed someone he could rely on, and she intended to do everything in her power to be that person, not just now, but in the future as well.

She gave Tío Pedro a hug. "I'll watch out for him. I promise."

"Then perhaps you'd better hurry," he

said dryly. "He appears to be sneaking out the front door without you."

Molly whirled around just in time to see Michael closing the door behind him. "Michael O'Hara," she shouted as she took off after him. "Don't you dare try to leave me behind."

The rare sound of laughter followed her out the door. She caught up with Michael at his car. "Exactly what did you think you were doing?" she demanded.

"Leaving."

"Without me?"

He pressed his hand to her cheek. "*Amiga,* I knew you would not be far behind."

"You counted on me following?"

"Yes."

"Then why not just tell me it was time to go?"

"Because then I would have had to explain to everyone that we are going to see Díaz-Nuñez and I knew that such an announcement would create a furor. Pedro would have wished to come along. My cousins would have insisted on joining us. Soon we would have had a goddamned parade."

"Haven't you ever heard the expression 'there's strength in numbers'?"

"Yes, but just this once I believe I can make my point more effectively alone. I do not want the others around when I tear that man limb from limb."

"You will not do that," Molly said.

He regarded her with obvious skepticism. "Oh? How can you be so certain?"

"Because you are a policeman and, for better or worse, you believe in the judicial system."

"Then what would you suggest I do to deal with the man who slandered my uncle and brought shame upon my family?"

Molly grinned. "Let me tear him limb from limb."

Michael's burst of laughter momentarily silenced the ragtag band of protesters on the lawn. He pulled Molly into his arms and held her tightly. "Ah, *querida,* have I mentioned that I adore you?"

"No, but I'm glad to hear it."

"Oh?"

"It makes it so much nicer, since I adore you."

17

En route to the radio station, Molly tried to keep Michael focused on a plan of attack that did not involve bloodshed.

"It's possible that Díaz-Nuñez is being fed false information about Miguel. With his strong political sentiments, he would be an easy pawn if someone wanted to start a conspiracy of lies. The merest hint that someone is a traitor or a spy would bring him out swinging. He doesn't strike me as someone who requires facts before going on the air."

Michael considered her suggestion thoughtfully. "You could be right. But why would someone do that?"

"To stir up trouble, perhaps. To divert attention from some other scheme. That will become clearer when you find out who his source is, don't you think?"

"I suppose."

"So you'll ask questions about where he

got his information, right? You'll stay calm and listen to the answers?"

"You ask a lot of a man, *amiga.*"

"Yes," she agreed cheerfully. "But I know you can easily live up to my expectations."

"And if I do not, if I suddenly feel the need to put my fist down the man's throat?"

"Then I'll forgive you," she said generously.

He looked at her. The mirrored sunglasses kept her from detecting the emotion in his eyes, but she guessed she would find tolerant amusement there.

"I do not need your permission or your forgiveness," he pointed out.

"Of course not," she responded dutifully.

He sighed at the too-ready agreement. "I'll do my best not to disappoint you."

"I never doubted it."

Molly had not counted on the fact that she would be the one who wanted very badly to put a fist down the newscaster's throat. She took one look into those smug eyes and felt her civilized veneer being stripped away. Michael, however, suddenly seemed icily calm. If anything, it was more frightening than his hotheaded anger.

"In your office," he said to Díaz-Nuñez when they came face-to-face during a commercial break. The newscaster had stepped

530

into the hallway outside the studio from which he'd been broadcasting.

"I have another hour left on the air," Díaz-Nuñez protested.

"Someone will cover for you, I'm sure." Michael regarded him speculatively. "Or we could play our discussion over the airwaves. Would you prefer that?"

"That will not be necessary," he replied stiffly. "I will make arrangements."

Moments later they heard Latin music pouring from the speakers that lined the hallway. Díaz-Nuñez joined them again, then preceded them into his office. He settled himself behind his desk and reached for one of his cigars.

"I have questions," Michael informed him. "Quite a lot of them, as a matter of fact."

"And if I am not inclined to answer?"

"Then perhaps you would prefer to answer them at police headquarters," Michael said indifferently. "It doesn't matter to me."

"This is an official interrogation, then?"

"Official enough, but I am not charging you with my uncle's death just yet," he said with a magnanimous air.

There was a fleeting hint of panic in Díaz-Nuñez's eyes before he banked it. "Why would you think I know anything of Miguel García's death?"

"Because you are the only one to say he is dead," Michael replied. "The police have not said it. The Coast Guard has not said it. The rescuers flying over the Florida straits have not said it. So, then, I have to ask how you would know this with such certainty, if you are not involved."

"I don't know anything," Díaz-Nuñez protested. "He disappeared days ago. There has been no trace. I assume he is dead."

He couldn't have said anything that would infuriate Michael more. Molly watched the color rise in his cheeks, saw his hands clench until the knuckles turned white.

"And you broadcast this assumption on the air as fact?" Michael said in a low, furious voice. "You dare to distress my aunt in this way, based on assumptions, on guesswork? What sort of journalist are you?"

The newscaster took the criticism without batting an eye. "I rely on a combination of facts, sources, and instincts."

Visibly fighting to bring his temper in check, Michael stood up, placed his hands on the desk, and leaned forward until he was only inches from the other man's face. "And which of those told you my uncle was a traitor?"

Díaz-Nuñez nervously twisted the cigar in his hands. He refused to lift his eyes to meet

Michael's gaze. "For that I had a source," he swore. "A most reliable source."

Seconds ticked by in silence. The newscaster finally looked up and regarded Michael warily, as did Molly. She wasn't sure what he would do in the face of such a bold claim of attribution.

"Who?" he demanded finally. "Who told you this?"

"I cannot reveal that. A journalist must protect his sources," Díaz-Nuñez said piously. "Surely you can understand that."

Michael's expression turned lethal. "I understand that if you do not give me a name, then I must assume that you alone are responsible for the slander. And that it will be you I must deal with."

Suddenly Díaz-Nuñez went on the attack, lifting himself from his chair and leaning toward Michael, who then took a step back. "Why do you defend a man who would betray his brothers?" he asked hotly. "Are you a traitor as well, *O'Hara?*"

He said the name as disparagingly as he could, emphasizing the fact that it was not Hispanic. There was no question Michael understood the intended insult.

Michael snagged a handful of the newscaster's perfectly pressed silk-blend shirt and hauled him halfway across the fancy mahogany desk, scattering papers in his wake. "Miguel García is a Cuban patriot. I would stake my life on that. If you have evidence to the contrary, if you have a source who says otherwise, then produce it. Do not be a coward standing behind a false claim of journalistic ethics."

Molly had managed to stay silent and out of the way until now, but Díaz-Nuñez's eyes were bulging and his face was turning red. It was doubtful he could have answered Michael if he'd wanted to. She put her hand on Michael's tensed arm.

"Michael. It's possible he might be ready to talk," she said quietly. "First, though, he has to be able to breathe."

Michael drew in a deep breath and slowly eased his grip. "Well? Is she right? Do you have something to say?"

The newscaster gasped. When he could finally speak, he choked out, "The source was anonymous."

Michael's grip tightened again. "I don't believe you. I don't believe there was a source."

Díaz-Nuñez wrenched himself free and rubbed his throat. "All right, I will tell you." His expression turned smug. "My source was Paredes himself. He is the one who told me that Miguel García betrayed the organization and his people by leaking confidential information to Castro."

Back in the car, his expression grim, Michael pulled an address book from his pocket and handed it to Molly. "While I drive, you call Felipe and Ken. Tell them we're on our way to headquarters. Tell them I want as many men as possible making contact with sources to locate Paredes. If necessary we'll pull in every known member of his organization."

"Can you do that?" Molly asked even as she took the address book and picked up his cellular phone to begin calling.

"My uncle has been missing for forty-eight hours. Based on the broadcast by Díaz-Nuñez, I think we have probable cause to suspect foul play. I'm certain I can make my boss see this my way, if the need arises."

"If the need arises," Molly repeated. "Meaning if Lucas Petty catches you pulling these people in unofficially."

He refused to meet her gaze. "Just make the calls, *por favor.*"

Though he was scheduled for an afternoon shift, Molly found Felipe already at the station.

"I'll be here when you arrive," he promised. "I heard the newscast and anticipated something like this. How is Michael's mood?"

Molly glanced at the man behind the wheel, whose expression was dark and forbidding. "About what you'd expect."

"That bad, huh? Tell him I said we'll solve this. I came in early to speak with a few of those who follow the activities of organizations such as Paredes's. You have tried to reach Ken?"

"He's next on my list."

"You won't get him. He took the day to go on the dive he promised to make. As we speak, he and Teri are probably searching the bottom of Biscayne Bay. I'll call a few others and ask them to come in early to assist with the calls."

"Thanks. We'll see you soon." When she'd hung up, Molly turned to Michael. "Felipe's already checking."

"And Ken?"

"He's on that dive."

"My guess is that it'll be a waste of his time."

"He's trying to help."

"I know that, *amiga,*" he said with exaggerated patience.

Molly bit back an exasperated retort. Obviously anyone's patience would be worn thin after the tension and sleeplessness of the past couple of days. Michael, for all of his other attributes, was no saint. Rather than fuel his irritability, she dialed another number.

"Who are you calling now?"

"Walt Hazelton. Perhaps he's learned something about Paredes's whereabouts."

"I don't like relying on this correspondent for information," he said stubbornly.

"You have your sources. I have mine," Molly said evenly. Unfortunately, hers didn't know a damned thing.

"I've checked out every single place Paredes has been known to go in the past and I don't mean by calling. I spent hours driving to these places to see personally whether he was there. I did find his wife and children, however."

"Where?"

"They're staying with her sister. She claims to have no idea where her husband is. She says she hasn't seen or spoken to him since they left the Westchester house. She reminds me of those Mafia wives who claim not to have a clue about their husbands' activities."

In this instance, Molly could believe it. Combined with the danger of having too many people know his whereabouts, Paredes would also have a very macho attitude toward his wife's need to know anything except what was necessary for his pleasure or the care of his children. All of which gave her an idea.

"Where does this sister live?"

Hazelton gave her the address in southwest Dade. "You going to see her?"

Molly cast a look at Michael and wondered what he'd have to say about it. "I'm going to try," she said grimly.

He glanced at her as she hung up. "Try what?"

"To convince you to make a detour and let me talk with Paredes's wife."

"You know where she is?"

Molly nodded. "Walt says she doesn't know where her husband is."

"Yet you want to see her. Why?"

"Because like Tía Pilar, she may know more than she is willing to say."

"And you think you have ways of persuading her to talk, when her husband's life might be at risk?"

Molly found his derisive tone irritating. "I know this will come as a shock to your ego, Detective, but I do have a way with people. My presence will be far less threatening to her than yours or even Walt's."

"Is this one of those woman-to-woman things?"

538

"Careful, O'Hara, your macho heritage is showing."

He opened his mouth to reply, then snapped it shut again. Finally he said, "What's the address?"

They found the tiny tract house off the turnpike just north of Homestead in an area that had been hard hit by Hurricane Andrew. Evidence of the violent storm was still visible in houses that remained gutted, their roofs sheared off by the powerful winds, their walls collapsed. Molly was shocked at how much remained just as it had been in the days immediately following the hurricane. She stared at it in openmouthed amazement.

"It's been nearly two years," she said.

"Many of these places were owned by people barely making ends meet," Michael reminded her. "Some had no insurance to rebuild. Others took the money and walked away, refusing to come back after the terror of that August night and the days of hardship that followed while they waited for relief efforts."

"I just didn't realize that it would still be like this in some places."

"What's that address again?"

When she'd given it to him, he made a final turn into a street that was like a patchwork scene of before and after. For every two or three houses that had been rebuilt, there was another one that stood as testimony to the storm's destructiveness.

María Consuela Fernández, Paredes's sister-in-law according to Walt, lived on a cul-de-sac at the end of the block in one of the houses that was livable, though it still bore signs of damage. One large picture window in front remained boarded over. The paint was badly chipped and peeling. There was even a terrible gash in the stucco exterior where some piece of flying debris had rammed the house at high speed.

But the grass was neatly cut and flowers bloomed in a bright border along the sidewalk. A new tree, barely five feet tall and skinny, its trunk still held in place by stakes and an elaborate arrangement of wires, was a testament to faith in the future.

Extracting Michael's promise to sit tight, Molly made her way to the front door through a clutter of tricycles and abandoned toys, the same clutter they'd seen outside Paredes's house. Trepidation combined with anticipation as she rang the bell.

From inside she heard shouts of "no, *niña*, no!" just as the door opened. Molly looked down into the face of a chubby toddler whose big brown eyes gazed back solemnly.

A thin, exhausted-looking woman skidded to a halt on the tile floor behind the child and scooped her up, clutching her protectively.

"Señora Paredes?" Molly said, wondering at how much younger the woman was than she'd anticipated. Perhaps a second marriage for Paredes, she mused.

There was an instant's panic in the woman's eyes that was answer enough. She started to push the door closed, but Molly held it open by bracing a shoulder against it.

"Please. I really need to speak with you. My name is Molly DeWitt. I'm not a reporter. I don't work for the police."

The woman's suspicion didn't lessen, but she did seem to relax slightly. Since it didn't seem likely that she was going to be invited in for tea, Molly decided to press on with her plea right where she was.

"May I tell you a story?" She didn't wait for a response before going on. "An old woman of whom I am very fond is very sad. She desperately misses her husband, to whom she has been married for more than forty years. He left home to go on a fishing trip several days ago and he has not returned. No one knows anything about his disappearance. It is the not knowing that

541

breaks her heart. If her husband is dead, it would be better for her to know that. If he is not, then she would be at peace. I know that you can sympathize, because I am sure there have been times of uncertainty in your life."

The child in Señora Paredes's arms whimpered. Distractedly she put her down and the girl ran off into the house. "Why do you tell me this?" she asked Molly.

"Because you could help."

"How? I do not even know this woman."

"But her husband and your husband were very close, both in Cuba and here. Your husband might help us to locate this old man and return him to his family."

"I do not know where my husband is," she said.

The response was emphatic, but it sounded automatic, almost rehearsed. Molly regarded her intently. "Sometimes women know more than they are supposed to know," she suggested quietly.

Señora Paredes's gaze faltered. It was only a flicker, but Molly knew she had been right. "Please," she implored. "I mean your husband no harm. I just need the answers he might have."

"I understand. I sympathize with your friend, but my husband has responsibilities elsewhere," she said, her gaze now locked with Molly's. "I cannot interfere with this."

Molly couldn't be sure, but it seemed as if the woman was willing her to interpret what she was saying, to guess the answers she sought from the enigmatic response actually given. She played the words again in her mind. *Responsibilities elsewhere* triggered a faint, nagging sensation.

Suddenly the information Walt Hazelton had given her the day before came to mind. An invasion of Cuba, whether full-scale or just a tentative raid, was being staged from Key West. And this house where Señora Paredes and her children waited was squarely between the family's house in Westchester and the Florida Keys.

"He has gone to Key West, hasn't he?" Molly said.

"No sé," the woman said as she hurriedly shut the door.

But in that instant before it closed, Molly caught the truth in her eyes.

18

"Key West!" Michael said incredulously, when Molly joined him in the car again. "You want to drive all the way to Key West to check out some idiotic intuition of yours that that's where Paredes is?"

"What happened to all that talk about my wisdom and intelligence?"

"Logic," he said tersely.

"Yours or mine?" she shot back. "My logic tells me that Paredes is down there with his band of commandos, controlling the entire operation."

"It's a long way to go on a wild-goose chase."

Molly wasn't about to be intimidated by his obvious lack of faith. "If you don't want to make the drive, then take me home to get my car and I'll go on my own."

Their gazes clashed. Molly refused to be the first to back down. Michael finally sighed. "You're convinced of this, aren't you?"

"Absolutely."

"Then we'll go to Key West," he said, turning back onto the turnpike heading south toward Homestead and Key Largo. "Call Felipe again and tell him where we're going. Ask him to concentrate his search down there to try and pinpoint where Paredes might be. Let's just pray that he isn't on a boat bound for Cuba."

Between Felipe's sources at the police department and Walt Hazelton's contacts, Molly and Michael were able to come up with a half-dozen addresses in the tiny resort town of Key West of men known to be Cuban activists, who might be harboring Paredes if he was still in Florida. Just ninety miles from Cuba, the southernmost city in the US had long been a haven for Cuban immigrants fleeing oppression, first from Spain and more recently from Castro's brand of communism. The first arrivals on the boat-lifts from Mariel had landed here before being processed by Immigration and released to family members.

Arriving in Key West in early afternoon, Molly and Michael went from place to place, coming up empty each time. Either all were at work, which was certainly a logical assumption, given the time of day, or these activists were gathered together at some sort of central control point for whatever commando operation they were conducting. Molly was betting on the latter scenario.

"Maybe so," Michael agreed. "But I am not driving around the city looking for such a meeting. I'm starving. Let's have lunch and think this through."

At a restaurant on Duval Street, they sat in an outside garden and considered the possibilities.

"A Cuban restaurant, the old Cuban cigar factory, the San Carlos Theater," Molly suggested. "The San Carlos would be the symbolic place, since that's where Cuban independence from Spain was declared almost a hundred years ago."

Michael appeared to weigh the alternatives, then shook his head. "Too obvious and too public."

"Something at the marina?"

"Why there?"

"To be close to the boats being launched as part of the raid," she speculated.

Michael nodded thoughtfully. "Possible, but I would think Paredes would want to maintain some distance from the boats. He would want it to appear that they're leaving as usual for a fishing trip or a pleasure cruise. I doubt he'd want any hint that an armed flotilla is taking off in violation of US law or that he's involved with it."

"Call the local police and see if there are places and people they keep an eye on for illegal immigration activities."

"Good idea," he said. He stopped a waiter, claiming a need to use a restroom. More likely, he wanted a look around.

While he was gone, Molly studied the clientele of the restaurant. Most were Anglos, a mix of locals on a lunch break from work, and tourists with cameras and street maps. The help, however, appeared to be largely Hispanic. Since the typical Cuban residents of Key West weren't eating lunch here, she wondered where they did tend to congregate. It was true that Paredes and his associates might not do their plotting in public, but surely they had to eat out occasionally.

The next time their waitress came by, Molly asked her about it. "Is there someplace in particular you go with your friends for Cuban food?"

The young woman named several restaurants, describing each of them. All sounded as if they were the kinds of casual places frequented by young couples and families. Molly grinned at her. "And your parents? Where would they go?"

"Casa Rolando," she said at once. "For special celebrations. For a simple evening with friends, however, they would go to the same places I mentioned."

"Can you tell me where they are?"

By the time Michael got back to the table, Molly had a new list of addresses. He had a similar list. Naturally the lists weren't compatible, which meant making a decision about which leads to pursue.

"Where to first?" she asked, when she'd explained her theory. "I'd like to at least try one of the restaurants. I can tell the owner I'm writing a travel article on Key West restaurants frequented by well-known people and ask who has dined there."

"And you'll just casually work Paredes's name into the conversation?" Michael said with blatant skepticism.

"Why not?"

"Because it is not . . ."

"If you accuse me of being illogical again, I'll dump the entire bottle of ketchup over your head."

He shrugged. "Okay, then. Let's just say it is not exactly an orthodox investigating technique."

"So what?"

"Indeed. So what? Okay, *amiga,* I'm a desperate man. We'll try it."

Molly discarded the upscale Casa Rolando in favor of the more casual spots on the theory that Paredes might figure he'd be less conspicuous there. Three restaurants later they had come up with nothing, unless her own case of caffeine jitters counted. *Café Cubano* vendors could probably make a fortune on university campuses around final exam time.

"One more," she bargained when Michael wanted to start checking out his own list of suspected hangouts.

"One more," he agreed resignedly.

The one they chose was only a block from the water and a major marina. Though it was late in the afternoon, the restaurant was still jammed, the air inside thick with a haze of cigar smoke despite health warnings and ordinances to protect against the hazards of secondary smoke.

Though he had dutifully waited in the car on the earlier tries, this time Michael insisted on coming along. "You can say I'm your photographer."

"Where's your camera?"

"I'm just on a preliminary scouting expedition with you. I'll return later for a formal

549

photo shoot."

"Sounds like a pretty complicated ruse."

"And yours isn't?"

Molly rolled her eyes. "You have a point."

Unfortunately, after all their planning, the owner was not on the premises. The hostess, however, was a chatty young woman in her midtwenties who clearly appreciated Michael's finer qualities. Molly wondered how he felt about being examined as a sex object. Then she decided he was probably used to it. At any rate, the hostess agreed to join them as soon as the crowd thinned out.

A waiter brought them both coffee. This time Molly insisted on decaf, which drew startled looks from the waiter and Michael. Twenty minutes later the hostess returned. She tugged a chair closer to Michael's before collapsing wearily onto it. She mostly collapsed in his direction. Another inch or two and he'd have to prop her up.

Before Molly could open her mouth to ask a single question, Michael jumped in with the announcement that he was the one doing the freelance travel piece. Molly gaped at the theft of her planned scenario. She had to admit, though, that the hostess — Lara Veciana-Peña — probably wouldn't have taken her eyes off Michael long enough to answer any question Molly asked. By contrast, she'd probably tell the sexy detective secrets she'd kept hidden from the rest of the world for her entire life. She ran red-tipped fingers through luxuriant shoulder-length black hair in a provocative gesture as she listened intently to every word that tripped from his tongue.

"Celia Cruz was in here once. Is that the sort of thing you mean?" she asked in a voice that was totally unaccented. Molly guessed she'd been born and educated right here in Key West, perhaps of immigrant parents, but more influenced by her American friends.

"Exactly," Michael said, beaming as if she'd just given the correct answer to the trickiest question in final *Jeopardy.*

If this kept up, Molly thought she might be sick.

Lara offered up a few more celebrities in an effort to earn more of Michael's praise.

"What about writers? Politicians?" Molly asked, hoping to inch closer to the purpose of this interrogation.

Lara blinked and gazed at Molly as if she'd just noticed her presence. "Sure. Jeb Bush, you know, the ex-president's son? He came in one night with some Cuban friends. And lots of writers live right here in Key West. They're in all the time, mostly during the season, though not this time of year. Hemingway used to live here in Key West, but of course he's dead now." She named several others who were still living. Michael dutifully wrote them down.

"I was told that a Cuban looking for truly authentic food from his homeland would come here," Michael said. "In fact, the person who gave me the name of this restaurant said his friends from Miami often drive all the way down just to have a meal here."

"Yeah, I guess," Lara said vaguely. "I don't know if they're famous or anything. I've never heard of 'em, anyway."

"Are there people like this, though, on a list, so that when they call you always hold a reservation for them?"

"Sure, we have a priority customer list. My boss is real sensitive to that sort of thing."

"Could I see it?" Michael asked. "I think that's exactly the sort of thing I need for the article."

For the first time, Lara looked uneasy. "I'm not so sure he'd want it published."

Michael put his hand reassuringly over hers. Or maybe he just figured he'd give her a thrill, Molly thought in disgust as she saw the girl's eyes turn bright with something that she doubted was intelligence. She recognized lust when she saw it. She was guilty of it enough herself in Michael's presence.

"I promise not to print it as is or to reveal how I got the information," he said, gazing deeply into her eyes. "Just let me have a peek at it."

Apparently the girl read the promise of greater intimacy in Michael's expression or in his touch, because she practically ran to the reservation book.

"That was disgusting," Molly said under her breath.

He grinned at her unrepentantly. "Worked, didn't it?"

"Just don't be surprised when she turns up in Miami looking for love."

He scowled at her as Lara rejoined them and spread a typed list on the table. Molly tried to get a look at it, but it was upside down and she didn't think standing up to peer anxiously over Michael's shoulder was the thing to do. And Michael, damn him, didn't reveal a damn thing in his expression.

He jotted down a couple of notes. "Any of these people in this week?"

Lara shook her head. "But I took a reservation earlier for tonight from Señor

553

Hernández. He said he was bringing some very important people from out of town."

Molly recognized the name at once. It had been on the contact list given to them by both Felipe and Walt Hazelton. "Did he mention who these friends were?"

"Not to me," she said.

Molly's spirits sank.

"But," Lara said, "my boss said we should pay special attention because this man he's bringing could one day be president of a free Cuba."

Molly shot a triumphant look at Michael. If that wasn't Orestes León Paredes, then she didn't know who it could be.

19

Michael used his considerable persuasive skills to convince the cooperative, smitten Lara to give him and Molly a dinner reservation at a table across the restaurant, but with a clear view of the one being held for Señor Hernández and his party.

"You will not disturb them," she asked worriedly.

It was the first indication that she didn't entirely trust the newfound love of her life. Trust was always the first thing to go, Molly noted dryly.

"Absolutely not," Michael promised, his expression all innocence and reassurance.

Molly was astounded at how easily he blatantly lied to the poor woman. It raised some interesting questions about the things he'd whispered in her ear the past few nights. Of course, given her own willingness to bend veracity for the sake of getting a piece of relevant information, maybe she didn't have a lot of room to talk.

When they left the restaurant, Molly insisted on finding a hotel room, taking a shower, and buying a new dress for dinner, not necessarily in that order.

"Why don't I drop you off back on Duval Street to shop?" Michael suggested. "I'll get the hotel room, pick you up in a couple of hours, and we can take that shower together."

"Are you sure you'd prefer sharing a shower with me, rather than your new conquest?" she inquired crankily.

"That was only business, *querida.*"

Molly was beginning to notice he pulled out the more affectionate term when he wanted something. "Just how far were you willing to take this *business* in order to get answers?"

"I suppose you have never flirted with a man to get what you wanted?"

"Never," Molly said piously.

"Liar," he accused. "I myself have been the victim of your wiles."

She turned on him indignantly. "Michael O'Hara, I never flirted with you to get information."

He grinned unrepentantly. "Ah, then it was only because you wished to flirt with me? Perhaps you've been hoping all this time to seduce me?"

Molly glared at him as the car stopped for a group of pedestrians crossing the street. She opened the door, got out, then slammed it shut. She walked around to Michael's side and leaned in the window. "Better make that two rooms, *amigo.*"

It was amazing how little petty annoyances vanished in a puff of steam, during a long, friendly shower, Molly thought as she and Michael were led to their table that night by someone other than Lara. With the hostess absent, Molly found she could hardly recall what her argument with Michael had been about.

They had arrived fifteen minutes earlier than their quarry, so they would already be seated when the others turned up. With any luck, Paredes wouldn't even notice them until they'd managed to eavesdrop on quite a bit of the conversation.

Actually *eavesdrop* was a polite description for it. Michael had managed to plant a tiny transmitter in a wall plug near the other table and had put a pocket-size receiver in Molly's handbag.

"Isn't this illegal?" Molly inquired when he returned from his surreptitious trip to install the fake plug in the wall outlet. "I mean, don't you need a court order or something before you go tapping somebody's dinner conversation?"

"I would if I had any intention of taking this to court. I'm just an innocent citizen trying to locate a missing relative. The ethics are questionable, but right now the only thing I give a damn about is Miguel's safety."

"But what if you hear them plotting something illegal. You won't even be able to turn them in, will you?"

"An anonymous tip," he said with a shrug. "It would then be up to the authorities to follow up in a by-the-book manner." He slanted a curious look at her. "Why so worried about my ethics?"

"Because you seem to be breaking every rule you live by. I'm just wondering how you're going to feel about that when this is over."

"If I learn the truth about Miguel, the price will not be too high."

Molly wondered about that, but she couldn't debate the point with him because a handful of men in the Hernández party arrived and were led to the table across the room. Based on the deference being paid him, Molly picked out the tall, well-dressed man with silver hair as Señor Hernández.

He, like all the others, looked like a successful middle-class businessman. Despite the season and the summer heat, they wore dark business suits, expensive dress shirts with monogrammed cuffs, and silk ties. She suspected all of them had been told to tuck their checkbooks in their pockets for the occasion. Or perhaps they were the types who'd just peel off hundred-dollar bills from a bundle held together by a sterling-silver money clip. Half a dozen phones were placed on the table, yet another indication of their success.

When Orestes Léon Paredes walked in, escorted by two men the size of small tanks, Molly regarded him with astonishment. The military fatigues had been replaced by a suit that transformed him into a handsome, powerful-looking figure. Though he was shorter than many of the other men, his commanding presence immediately overshadowed them. Perhaps it had something to do with that charisma Michael had mentioned. The only person who was his equal in presence was Señor Hernández, who was treating all of his guests with the manner of a benevolent dictator.

Molly tried to listen to the snatches of conversation being picked up by the transmitter. Michael reached over and touched her shoulder gently.

"Do not stare so intently at your purse," he advised mildly. "People may wonder if it is speaking to you."

She shot upright. "Sorry. Can you hear them?"

"Enough."

"What are they talking about?"

"The Florida Marlins' latest victory over the Atlanta Braves, I believe."

"Oh," she said flatly.

"Never fear. They will get to the point of this gathering soon."

Molly prayed he was right. Michael's tone was calm, but there was no mistaking the tension in the set of his jaw and the watchfulness in his eyes. She wondered how long he would wait patiently before physically trying to force Paredes to give him the answers he sought about Miguel.

Forced to make a show of being there for dinner, they ordered a meal of paella, mainly because Michael knew it would take longer to prepare and guarantee them a reason for lingering. When it eventually came, it might as well have been sawdust for all the attention they paid it. Their worried waiter asked repeatedly if there was some problem with their meal. Michael waved him away, assuring him that their appetites were simply overwhelmed by the delicious seafood dish.

"Damn," Michael muttered irritably when the waiter had been temporarily placated.

"What?"

"I'm beginning to wonder if they are ever going to get beyond these pleasantries after all."

"What if it turns out to be just a friendly get-together?"

Michael shook his head. "At the least, I expect Paredes to ask for money from these men to support his efforts. These are not men who would take up arms and raid Cuba themselves, but they would be sympathetic." His expression turned cynical. "After all, in a free Cuba their businesses would stand to make a small fortune, especially with such well-established influence with a new government headed by their close friend, Orestes León Paredes."

Eventually cigars were passed around, and a haze of smoke rose from the table. Michael nodded in satisfaction. "Good. They will get to the bottom line now."

Listening intently, Molly picked out a smattering of familiar words, most of them bitterly spoken, unflattering descriptions of Fidel Castro, along with talk of his failing health and the already failed economy.

Paredes spoke with feeling. As near as Molly could translate it, he said adamantly, "The end is near for Fidel. I will see to it."

Cheers and a toast greeted his statement, along with promises of support. If she hadn't known the context, Molly would have thought it the same as any other political gathering to generate early support for a candidate. She'd been to a few dinners for prospective candidates for local offices that had been no less hard-sell pitches for money.

"Have they said anything at all about the raids?" she asked Michael.

"Nothing. It appears that is something they dare not speak of in public, or else they talk in terms so vague that no one else can accuse them of plotting the overthrow of a foreign government."

Interestingly enough, it also appeared that no money was going to change hands. Perhaps one of Paredes's minions would take up a collection after the leader had discreetly departed. Even now, he was standing up to go, a royal taking leave of his subjects with a slight bow and no looking back.

"What . . . ?" Molly began before she realized that Michael was already on his feet, clearly intending to intersect Paredes's path at the door.

Before she could make a move to follow, she noticed another man slipping through the shadows on the far side of the restaurant. Just as she recognized Herman Gómez-Ortega, she saw that he had something in his hand, though he held it discreetly at his side.

A gun, she realized with a dawning sense of disbelief. In her haste to warn Michael, she knocked over her chair and bumped into several people as she ran toward the door, trailed by a waiter assuming he was about to be stiffed for the check.

In the back of her mind, Molly couldn't help seeing Paredes's house as it had looked after an assault rifle had blown out the front windows. Was he here tonight in his organization role to protect Paredes or did he intend to repeat the assassination attempt that had failed in Miami? Either way, Michael was in danger, she thought as she ran blindly outside after them.

She was afraid to shout a warning, because she wasn't entirely sure who was armed and who was on which side. Before she could figure out how to get past Gómez-Ortega, she saw Paredes grab Michael's arm, spin him around, and yank him behind the cover of a van parked down the block.

Suddenly men appeared from every direction, all armed and all wearing flak jackets with various official designations on the backs. Apparently the neon letters were meant to help distinguish the good guys from the bad. Molly hated to be the one to tell them, but it didn't help. Everyone on the goddamned street looked downright dangerous. A man whose flak jacket identified him in neon orange letters as POLICE strong-armed Molly back inside the restaurant doorway.

"Stay put," he said, and left her there, trembling violently and face-to-face with their stunned waiter, who'd just caught on that this was no ordinary turn of events involving a couple of deadbeats. As rattled as she was, Molly managed to snatch a handful of bills from her purse and shove them into his hand.

Not thirty seconds later there was a hail of gunfire, accompanied by shouts and screams. Then dead silence. Molly couldn't have stayed where she was if her own life had depended on it. She kept visualizing Michael in the grasp of Orestes León Paredes, a man not known for his peaceful intent.

She shrugged off the detaining hand of the waiter and edged out the doorway and peered down the block. Police officials were kneeling on the pavement over what appeared to be a body.

Smothering a scream with her hand, Molly crept toward the macabre scene, which was bathed in the glow of a street-lamp. Not until she was almost on top of the police and before she could identify the fallen victim did she see a movement from the direction of the van where she'd last seen Michael.

First a policeman emerged, followed by Paredes himself. He didn't look to be in custody. Finally, when her breath seemed to have stopped altogether, she saw Michael, his gaze searching the scene as frantically as her own. By the time he spotted her, she was already running.

He held out his arms, then enfolded her in an embrace. "You are okay, *amiga?*"

She swallowed a sob. "Now that you're here, yes," she said, her voice steady. She looked up into Michael's ashen face. "They shot Herman, didn't they?"

"Yes."

"Because of his attack on Paredes's house yesterday?"

"That and his plan to kill him tonight."

"But why would he want to kill Paredes? I still don't understand."

"Neither do I. Perhaps when things have settled down a bit, Paredes will explain it to us."

At that precise moment, the exile commander walked over to them. Michael held out his hand. "I owe you my life, señor."

"De nada." His grin turned rueful. "Had I not dragged you to safety, you would have persisted in questioning me in plain view of Herman and we both would have been shot to death. I was not prepared to die, not at the hands of a traitor."

"You call Herman Gómez-Ortega a traitor," Molly said with evident confusion. "I thought he was your chief military advisor."

"For a time that is how I thought of him, as well," he said with obvious pain. "It was only recently, in the last few days, in fact, that I learned the truth."

"What truth?"

"He was sent here as a spy by Castro. That is how he won his release from prison, by agreeing to infiltrate our organization and feed information to Cuban intelligence. When I was told by American agents of their suspicions, I called them liars. But with so much at stake, I could not afford to ignore the possibilities. With the assistance of my most loyal associates, we devised a means of learning the truth."

566

He grasped Michael's shoulders. "Your uncle, Miguel García, was vital to our plan. It was his heroic offer to act as the bait which enabled us to trap Herman into showing his hand."

Michael went absolutely still. "You used my uncle as bait?" he said in a voice as cold as ice. "How? Just today Díaz-Nuñez said you had called my uncle a traitor."

Paredes waved off the remark. "He misunderstood. I told him we had discovered a traitor and that we were dealing with him. Because of Miguel García's disappearance, he leapt to a wrong conclusion. It was not unexpected. Even with such errors in judgment, I find him useful."

"Useful?" Michael repeated. "Is that all any of these men are to you, just pawns in your games? Explain how my uncle was useful."

"We made it known he was to be the point man in our raid," Paredes said quietly. His burning gaze never left Michael's. "And, as we anticipated, when he took his boat out on Sunday, the Cuban authorities were waiting to take him captive."

Molly gasped softly.

Michael's expression turned absolutely deadly. "You sent my uncle to sea knowing that he would wind up in a Cuban jail?" He jerked away from the other man's grasp. "Look over your shoulder, Paredes. One day I will see that you share the same fate as Miguel García," he vowed.

20

"How will I tell Tía Pilar?" Michael asked over and over as they drove back to Miami. "How can I tell her that Miguel is back in his beloved Havana, but that he is being held in some harsh Cuban prison where he will probably die?"

The question was rhetorical. He never looked to Molly for an answer. He just spoke and then fell into a brooding silence. It was just as well because she had no answers. She was as horrified as he was that sweet, gentle Tío Miguel was imprisoned in Cuba by a government that would treat him as a traitor. It was possible he would be shot, as others had been, to set an example for those thinking of staging future commando raids. A tear slid down her cheek as she considered that possibility.

It was after midnight when they reached Miami, but Michael drove straight to Little Havana. Rather than going to see Pilar, however, he went to Pedro's restaurant.

They found his uncle nursing a cup of *café Cubano,* surrounded by a group of men actively debating the candidacies of two people running for the Dade County Commission. One was a high-profile attorney, originally from Havana, with ties to the powerful Latin Builders Association. The other was a woman, head of her own interior design company, active in the arts. What seemed to be splitting the group about evenly was the fact that the man had once attended a professional seminar in Latin America at which Fidel had been a speaker. For some, that alone was enough to disqualify him from holding a public office representing the Cuban exile community.

Pedro glanced up and caught sight of them. He motioned them over, but Michael shook his head. *"Por favor,"* he said, and indicated a table in an empty section that had already been closed for the night.

Instantly, Pedro's expression sobered. "You have news, is that it?" he said as he joined them. "And from the look on your faces, it is not good."

"No, it's not good," Michael agreed.

"Miguel is dead?"

"Some would say that would be better news," Michael said, urging his uncle to sit.

Pedro clung to Michael's arms, his gaze fixed on Michael's face. "My God, do not tell me he has been taken captive? Is that what you are saying?"

"I'm sorry," Michael whispered, his voice catching as Pedro slowly sank down onto a chair, his complexion gray. Michael's worried gaze sought his uncle's. "Are you okay?"

"I will be fine."

"Fine?" Michael said angrily. "How can that be? How can any of us be fine again?" He slammed his fist on the table. "Damn them all to hell!"

"Tell me," Pedro insisted quietly.

Michael repeated everything that they had learned from Paredes in Key West. When he'd recited the whole complicated story, Pedro made him go through it all once more, as if he couldn't believe what he was hearing.

"I will begin making calls in the morning," Michael promised, his anger now under control. In a way the calm was worse. His voice was cold and emotionless. "I will call our senators and our representatives. I'll call the State Department. Perhaps it is not too late to bring him back home. What use has Castro for one old man?"

Pedro clasped Michael's hands in his own. "I know you will do what you can. Remember something, though. This was Miguel's choice. No matter how badly it has turned out, you cannot lay the blame entirely with Paredes. Allow Miguel the dignity of respecting his decision."

The simple request seemed to take Michael by surprise. Slowly and with obvious effort, he let the last traces of his anger die. Finally, he nodded. "I will do my best," he said wearily. "But something tells me that knowing Miguel did what he felt he had to do will be cold comfort to Tía Pilar."

"Perhaps not," Tío Pedro agreed. "That is why all of us must be strong for her. We are a family, Michael. We stand together, and from that we will draw whatever strength it takes to get through the coming days."

Despite the lateness of the hour, the García house was crowded with family — Pilar, Elena, Rosa, Michael's cousins. Molly wasn't sure she belonged among them on such a tragic occasion, but Michael's grip on her hand convinced her that he needed her there, whatever the others thought of her intrusion.

Surprisingly, though, the mood was oddly euphoric when they arrived. Apparently several bottles of wine had been consumed with a meal sent over from the restaurant by Pedro. Rosa was even singing along with an old Cuban ballad to the applause of her nieces and nephews.

Standing in the doorway observing the light-hearted moment, Michael and Pedro exchanged looks. Molly wondered which of them would spoil it by revealing the news of Miguel's fate. Apparently that time was to be put off. Glasses of wine were pressed into their hands by Elena.

"Sit. Rosa has been singing all of the old songs for us."

"She has not sung in a long time," Pedro noted.

"*Sí,*" Elena agreed quietly. "But it seems to keep Pilar's spirits high. Look, have you seen her looking so happy since all of this began? She has been that way since dinner-time."

"Perhaps it is the wine," Pedro suggested.

"More likely the call she had from an old friend. They talked for some time. It seemed to give her comfort."

"Whatever it was, I'm glad for her," Michael said, giving his uncle a pointed look. Pedro nodded. Molly guessed they intended to postpone telling Pilar anything, at least for the moment.

Molly, however, was puzzled by Tía Pilar's sudden shift in mood. Compared to earlier visits, this time her expression was actually serene. The older woman looked as if she'd found some sort of inner peace, as if she already knew about her husband's fate and had accepted it. It was not what Molly had expected after watching her state of mind deteriorate hour by hour in the early aftermath of Miguel's disappearance.

Trying to make sense of it, Molly crossed the room and took a seat beside Tía Pilar.

"You are feeling better, then?" she said.

"I must be strong," Pilar said with a faraway smile, her gaze on Rosa as the lyrics of yet another song filled the tiny room. "For Miguel."

"I understand you had a phone call earlier this evening, just before dinner. It was from an old friend?" Molly said, wondering if it was remotely possible that what she was beginning to think could be true.

Pilar regarded her sharply. "Who told you this?"

"Elena. She said the call seemed to lift your spirits."

"It was nothing," Pilar said.

"Elena said you spoke for quite some time."

Pilar's expression suddenly and conveniently went blank. *"No comprendo."*

Molly watched her closely. "I think you

do understand, Pilar. It was Miguel, wasn't it? Did he call you from Cuba?"

"You don't know what you are saying," she said, suddenly agitated. "We don't know where Miguel is."

"No, *we* don't," Molly agreed. "Not exactly, anyway. But I think you do. He's safe, isn't he?"

Pilar glanced around worriedly. "Please, you must not say this."

"But the others deserve to know, especially Michael. He has been worried sick. Tonight he learned from a source that his uncle might be in a Havana prison, but that's not true, is it?"

"I cannot say anything. Miguel made me promise. The danger is too great."

Molly took her hand. "No, Tía Pilar, the danger is over," she told her gently. "You can tell the truth now."

Michael joined them just then. He looked from his aunt's distressed face to Molly and back again. "What is it? What truth are you keeping from us, Tía?"

"Tell him," Molly insisted.

Pilar's hands trembled. She linked them together in her lap to keep them still.

"Tía, what's going on?"

"It is Miguel," she said at last. "I spoke to

him earlier tonight." She lifted her gaze to Michael. "He is alive. He is safe."

21

Before any of them could fully absorb what Tía Pilar was telling them, the front door opened and Miguel García walked in. Dressed as always in khaki pants and a freshly starched *guayabera,* he had the unmistakable look of a man who had just completed a successful mission. His eyes, filled with happiness and affection, were pinned on his wife. For this moment, at least, the sadness had been banished and the strength and purpose of a young man were reflected there.

While Pilar waited patiently, he was immediately surrounded by his emotional children. Tears were shed openly. Molly's own tears were silent, but no less heartfelt.

She looked for Michael and found him standing alone on the perimeter of the scene, his eyes suspiciously damp, his expression filled with longing. In that brief instant, Molly thought she caught a glimpse of the young boy who'd never had a father, who had never quite dared to admit how deeply he loved this uncle for fear that he could lose him as easily as he once had his mother. In the past few days that loss had been vividly transformed from nightmare to reality.

Molly moved to Michael's side and slipped her hand in his as Tío Miguel embraced his weeping wife and attempted to soothe her and make her laugh, even as she scolded him for frightening them all so badly.

"How could he have put us all through so much heartache?" Michael said to Molly. He sounded as if the betrayal by someone he loved so dearly had cut right through him.

"Ask him," she urged.

"I don't need to ask. It's the cause," he said bitterly. "It is always the cause."

"Ask him," she repeated.

At first she didn't think he would take her advice. Then, with a sigh, he took a reluctant step toward the uncle he so clearly loved. Catching the belligerent set to his jaw, she called him back. "Michael!"

He turned.

"Don't just ask. Listen to what he has to say."

He gave her a faint grin. "Yes, *querida,* I

will listen."

In the end, they all listened as Miguel spun his tale of intrigue and international spies. To Molly it was something out of a political thriller, a world that until now had never touched her own. She still wasn't sure she entirely understood such passion and loyalty for a country left behind so long ago. Perhaps without the experience of exile, she could never fully understand the actions of men like Miguel García and Orestes León Paredes.

"We had to know," Miguel explained to Michael in Spanish. Pedro sat by Molly's side and translated for her benefit.

"If any of us were ever to trust each other again, we had to know if what the Americans said of Gómez-Ortega was true. He and he alone was told by Paredes that I would be launching the first stage of an assault on Sunday. I took my boat to just inside Cuban waters. Any closer to shore and we knew the soldiers would capture it at once and we would never know for certain if they had been tipped by a traitor inside our organization. It was necessary for them to seek out a boat they had been anticipating."

"How did you escape, Papá?" one of his sons asked.

"I dropped anchor, then launched my raft

and motored to a pickup point a mile outside Cuban territorial waters. There another boat picked me up and carried me to safety in Key West. For the past few days I have been in hiding there to keep Gómez-Ortega from learning the truth. It was necessary to see how far he would go."

He gazed up at Michael, then reached out and clutched his hand. "I am deeply sorry for what happened to you, my son. You were not meant to find the boat, the soldiers were. And when they did, it was meant to blow them up. Instead, you were the one nearly killed. Had anything happened to you, my boy, I could never have forgiven myself."

"Are you so sure you would not have called it a noble sacrifice?" Michael demanded angrily.

"I would have called it a tragedy and the greatest loss of my life," Miguel replied softly.

Michael drew in a deep breath, but trusting in his uncle's love did not come so easily. "Why didn't you call? Why didn't you let us know you were alive? After the plan had been set in motion, couldn't you have let us know you were safe?"

"It was necessary to keep the charade alive, to let Gómez-Ortega think that the attack was soon to be launched. We hoped he would become desperate, as he did. When he tried to kill Paredes in his own home, we knew for certain, then, that it was true. He was a spy for Castro. He was willing to kill for him. We staged the scene in Key West for the benefit of Gómez-Ortega, after alerting American intelligence agents of what we knew." He closed his eyes and sighed, then looked at Michael. "And again, you were nearly caught in the crossfire."

"Another trap," Michael said wearily. "When will it end?"

"When Cuba is free," Miguel said softly, but emphatically. "Only then."

At Miguel's words, Pedro lifted his glass of wine. *"A una Cuba libre!"*

"A una Cuba libre!" the others echoed.

Michael was the last to lift his glass and repeat the phrase. When he did, his gaze met his uncle's, and a tender, patient smile touched Miguel's lips. It was a moment of shared acceptance and of a deep and abiding love, if not of understanding.

Miguel stood slowly then and held his glass high, his expression a mixture of pride and fierce determination. "Next time in Havana!"

ABOUT THE AUTHOR

With her roots firmly planted in the South, **Sherryl Woods** has written many of her more than 100 books in that distinctive setting, whether in her home state of Virginia, her adopted state, Florida, or her much-adored South Carolina. Sherryl is best known for her ability to creating endearing small town communities and families. She is the *New York Times* and *USA Today* bestselling author of over 75 romances for Silhouette Desire and Special Edition.

The employees of Thorndike Press hope you have enjoyed this Large Print book. All our Thorndike, Wheeler, and Kennebec Large Print titles are designed for easy reading, and all our books are made to last. Other Thorndike Press Large Print books are available at your library, through selected bookstores, or directly from us.

For information about titles, please call:

(800) 223-1244

or visit our website at:

gale.com/thorndike

To share your comments, please write:

Publisher
Thorndike Press
10 Water St., Suite 310
Waterville, ME 04901